By the Same Author
Claire of the Moon

Passion's Shadow

a novel by
Nicole Conn

Simon & Schuster
NEW YORK LONDON TORONTO SYDNEY TOKYO SINGAPORE

SIMON & SCHUSTER

Rockefeller Center
1230 Avenue of the Americas
New York, NY 10020

SIMON & SCHUSTER and colophon are registered trademarks of Simon & Schuster Inc.

Designed by Elina D. Nudelman

Manufactured in the United States of America

10 9 8 7 6 5 4 3 2 1

Library of Congress Cataloging-in-Publication Data

Conn, Nicole, date.
    Passion's shadow / Nicole Conn.
       p.   cm.
     1. Lesbians—Fiction.
    PS3553.0495P37   1995
    813'.54—dc20   95-23476
                                       CIP

ISBN 978-1-4767-6689-8

Acknowledgments

I wish to greatly acknowledge my compadres of the soul,
  comrades in arms, doomed romantics. We formed our
  own Romantics Synonymous, our stories all the same,
  our fragile discourse often grist for the mill.
The more we tried to figure it out, the less we knew.
One thing is certain. I could never have done this without
  them:

Jennifer Bergman, whose belief in me and my work
  is only equal to her unconditional love.
Faith McDevitt, Pal o' Pals, who held my hand,
  caught my tears, slayed dragons for me
  with her profound insight, chief among which being:
              "I don't know!"

And Lisa M. Jones,
    my own "in-house" editor, dearest friend, her loving
      support unequaled but most important the sexiest and
      most masterful straight woman I know.

As well as,
Diane Himes, gentle reader, reliable and regal.
Alan Nevins, not only the most handsome agent in town
  but the one who took the leap for me.

And to the sweetest challenger any writer can have,
  gentle, loving editor Chuck Adams.

For Audra,
who gave me the gift of light
of love and flight
wherever she may be

Live in uncluttered moments of unconscious movement.
Be safe. Be safe.—
Live as if nothing will touch you.
Don't bruise your heart,
  scratch your soul,
    tear the tender fabric of walls that keep you from me.

Live in the shadow of all that you feel.
And die each moment you breathe air
        not life,
Or flee passion's shadow
  into the blinding light that makes you see
        Yourself.

Passion's Shadow

Prologue

I t was true what they said. In that instant before death. Like the memory bits of a computer linked to a single circuit, flickering images of an old home movie on fast forward; rapid-fire images streaked with age one moment, crystal-clear exposures in the next. Her senses became achingly alive as if they knew they were being snuffed out in that brilliant glittering moment. Touch. Became every sensation she had ever felt. The sting from a slap on her hand, ears splitting from the wind in her hair. Cold. She'd felt plenty of that. Gritty earth swirling about her swollen three-year-old toes. Sound. Her mother's voice, its silence, shrill admonition. Sight. The glaring light of her life in front of her. Then as purely felt, but less tangible . . . thoughts, memory and feelings; a simultaneous road show that was happening in and outside of her and all around her, flight to obliteration, its own plane of existence. First date. First kiss. Breathy anticipation, disappointing maneuverings on the leather seats of an old Impala. Baby blue, like her cousin's wedding dress. A dress she dreamed of for her own. Angry crow's feet clawing at her mother's eyes. An argument. Tears. Tinkling laughter. A party. That perfect moment when everything was right, that day love trapped her heart then gave it wings. Apparitions of sudden unanticipated beauty, chiaroscuro slant of sun as it hid the darkness down the hall to her bedroom. All those dark nights. Now her mother's room . . . her shadowed figure, as distant and foggy as she was when alive . . . and then, of course, the swan song and the broken ballerina twisted, deformed, whirling grotesquely about the floor as the music box continued to play. Broken. Shattered illusions. Love into hate. Bitterness born of destruction and loathing. She had to erase it. Blot it from her memory. Forever.

And now she would, for she was a powerful bird flying through the silken gray of a cleansing rain. This weightlessness, this nonchalance of flight was what she had been waiting for. This utter sense of calm. It had eluded her all her life . . . this clarity. Clarity that emitted from inside and shot through her like a drug. If she had had this all along . . . but maybe that was the price. The Devil's bargain. *I will gift you knowledge for your soul.*

She had to laugh, even if what slid through tightened lips was a sound she had never heard before. She had to laugh because this end was such a perfect metaphor for her life: the river below her and the bridge now behind her. She never had been able to get to the other side. Then she caught the fear in her eyes, flung back at her from the rearview mirror. And saw clearly for the first time the stranger who had occupied her body, mouth pinched, primly bitter. Prepared resignation.

Her skull split neatly into thirds when it hit the steering wheel.

Book One

When the wrecking crew pulled the car from the river, eager eyes peered into the darkened windows, until the twisted marionette carried from the remains was lifted to the stretcher. Then heads turned, eyes averted. It wasn't that the mangled body was too horrific to take in. It was that it was alive. That this creature had any vital signs seemed impossible. But it did. An air pocket in the twisted wreckage had kept enough oxygen coursing through its veins to maintain life.

But the eyes. Void. Black. Dale Mezzaroni had worked with his father and brother four years now since high school, dragging old cars from riverbanks, off the side of cliffs, and he bragged to his buddies about the grisly scenes of twisted, gnarled bodies entwined like lovers meshed to steel frames. But Dale had never seen an expression like the one on what had probably been quite a looker before she ditched her car off the Morrison Bridge. Suicide attempt. No question about it. The bridge was definitely on its way up.

The tender heard more than saw the car as it sped up the slow-moving slab of concrete, broke through the guard post, taillights peeping over the side making a "helluva splash."

He gulped his beer, shut his eyes trying to forget, thought instead about his girlfriend and her dream-catcher. She had one hanging over the bed, made of spindly wood with a leather spiderweb net attached, goofy feathers and strings of beads and bangles surrounded by candles and a lot of other nonsense. She said it caught the nightmares. Gave you peaceful sleep. Hell, he couldn't remember his dreams one day to the next. But he couldn't shake it as he downed his fourth beer. Dead deer eyes he had seen. Got himself a four-point with his uncle just last November. These weren't dead. It's like the soul hadn't gone out yet. Soul-catcher. Yeah . . . something caught this woman's soul and he reckoned she was going to be stuck in the middle of it for a good long time. He ordered another beer. Maybe that dream-catcher would come in handy tonight, after all.

Warren "Snag" Peterson paced the somber two-tone hospital corridors as he waited for information. Lindsay's car was in the river, but they couldn't identify the victim. He had been told by no less than four of the administrative staff there was no information to be had "unless you can prove you're a family member."

No one answered at Lindsay's home. Megan couldn't be found. He had spent his last quarter trying for Jared. Got his service. No one in bloody hell was by a phone.

He couldn't keep his hands off the pack of cigarettes in his shirt pocket, a habit born of longing. He glanced about. He would sneak one if it weren't for the elderly woman sitting twenty feet from him smugly pinching her lips, *tsk, tsk, naughty boy.*

He smiled graciously back at her, handsome; an English schoolboy demeanor and a turn-of-the-century dandy, soft brown hair scooped back in a single wave that splayed wildly to either side of his smooth-skinned face. He was excessively anal at the exterior, which prompted his nickname, governed by a sole preoccupation that one of the many garments that filled his closets might develop an unseemly snag. His interior possessed a highly creative mind, gentle and spontaneous heart, and tendency toward droll conversation. He smoked like a character out of a bad B movie.

"Goddamn." Under his breath. He wasn't a man of enduring patience, and knowing someone was in there, dead or alive, faceless yet certain to be one of three, was driving him crazy. He needed a cigarette. If he could smoke, it would fend off the clinging antiseptic smells, shove the relentless moments of waiting behind him.

And these people. Where in the hell did they find these people? Nurses, identically clad in chalky tones—even in a crisis he could despair of fashion—their pastel platitudes doled out like pills. He had found salvation in the guise of an old-timer, her polyester calm belying the harsh reality as she tromped through the unmistakable red EMERGENCY doors. She indicated by gesture, more than anything else, that the person behind those swinging doors was still alive. She was trying to help him, as much as she could under the circumstances. Snag knew she was a thousand-year-old dyke. Her stooped shoulders, raised from years of horrifying stress, almost touched her ears. He knew her hands, raw as scrubbed leather and just as gentle, were tied, and that she was doing her best.

Now he watched her march directly to the information desk.

"Find Dr. Santo yet?"

"Huh?" A lone candy striper, pale and inept, tore herself from her cheese puffs, orange speckles powdered about her Sierra Mauve lipstick.

"I *said*, find Dr. Santo yet?"

"Unh-uh." The candy striper rapidly shook her head.

"Well, get off your candy ass and find him. *Stat!* We got a Code 99 on the bridge victim."

"But I intercommed."

"So now you get your finger outta your goddamn nose and pick up the phone and call every extension till you find him directly. *This decade!*" she barked. She nonchalantly cracked her neck, glanced at Snag, her eyes unwavering, and trudged back into emergency. She had seen it all a million times.

The elevator doors opened. Jared. Snag's Jared. Tall, blond, amaz-

ingly handsome by anyone's standards, he breezed through the waiting room with his graceful gait. Even in despair, people turned to stare
at the distinguished, *GQ* demigod as he made his way to Snag, who
willingly crumbled in Jared's strong arms. The onlookers, momentarily taken from their own personal grief, watched as Jared unabashedly held his young lover, smoothed the hair from his forehead.

"Well?" Jared asked.

"I'm so friggin' glad you got my message." Snag finally loosened his
grip. "I'm so glad you're here. Jesus, Jared . . ."

"What's goin' on?"

"That's just it. This is out of the friggin' *Twilight Zone*. They can't
tell me."

"But—Lindsay's car."

"I know. It's definitely her car. But I overheard one of the guys
through the door. It doesn't sound like her. But what the fuck do I
know? They can't tell me anything. Hospital policy and all that
bullshit." Snag stroked his crumpled cigarette pack again. "There's an
old biddy lesbo though, bless her heart, trying to get something to me.
Anything . . ." Snag's hands trembled as he swept them through un-
manageable hair.

The old-timer came from the swinging doors. Her eyes searched
for Snag.

He questioned back with his hands, "Well?"

The nurse's stooped shoulders shrugged softly. She crooked her
crooked neck. She knew she wasn't supposed to, but closed her eyes
in the affirmative. Hospital rules to hell.

One Year Earlier

Lindsay was tired.

But lately it seemed she was always tired. She sat motionless, except for the churning of a worn eraser into the plans before her. The motion calmed her. It was close to nine, she guessed. She had been sitting precisely so for the past hour, creating little mountains of rubber. She could go home. She certainly wasn't getting anything done here.

Home. She smirked in self-deprecation. It was the old shoemaker's joke: an architect, passionately in love with designing home and hearth for others, lived in a three-bedroom Victorian, cozy, but badly in need of repair. From the intricate and complex designs that painted themselves in her head, a unique essence magically sprang from the mechanics of framed walls, plaster and paint called Home. Homes for her clients. Homes she could, to this date, remember with fondness, every line, every angle, every cut-in. Like children, spoiled, pampered and catered to.

In some vague and ambiguous future she had promised to build one for herself. "As soon as the next project is complete" was her standard defense, but the reality was that she was perfectly content commuting between her creakingly comfortable relic and the minimalist alcove she had installed in her office. The double bed, small bathroom and bookshelves were cramped but space-efficient, an earmark of all her designs. There was a certain harmony to it: warm and cozy for her female side; linear and practical for the side that sparred with the world. Mostly it suited her minimalist lifestyle.

The lobe of her ear itched. She tugged at it vacantly then suddenly remembered the party. Joanne's party. She had promised. She looked at her watch again, not that it mattered. Whatever time it was, she was late. If she didn't go, there would be hell to pay.

"Oh no, really, do you think so?"

"Darling, do get me another martini."

"I'm sure Shelli has had a face-lift—"

"—Oh, no, I heard they're merging. Johnson's got him by the balls. Lots of money to be made—"

Snippets of conversation fired by as she hunted for Joanne. Blanks. All this heavy artillery was pointless drivel. Lindsay loathed these parties, but as Joanne always reminded her, it was a necessary evil. "Just think of schmoozing as a sort of tithing. The basket goes round and round, collecting all those graphically enhanced little cards to make the world a better place. And these parties are like the Holy Church of Networking."

And there Joanne was now, clad in a skimpy black lace bodysuit, revealing her state-of-the-art physique on which she spared neither expense nor effort. Lindsay watched her for a moment as Joanne rummaged through her "little people," her martini-laden laughter floating behind her. Her professional life depended on her ability to put people together, but her parties were another matter. She found it the height of amusement to mismatch ever so slightly, then to breeze through and impress everyone as she cajoled and "made it all better." She was the queen bee, matchmaker and homebreaker, and, without fail, the head turner in any room.

Lindsay always thought the most entertaining thing about Joanne's parties was her performances. She had made a condescending pit stop, addressed a group of star-struck nouveau yuppies entering the world of "players," bequeathing them a moment of her time, then caught Lindsay watching her.

"Ahhh, there you are, darling." Joanne glided forward, kissed the air at the side of Lindsay's face.

"What do you think?" She referred to her knee-length scarf. "I threw it on at the last minute . . . but I think it works. A bit Isadora Duncany, but then . . ." She let the words dangle, much as the scarf would the rest of the evening, over someone's shoulder, getting caught through their arms; a well-planned prop.

"Scintillating, as usual." Lindsay was already terminally bored. "Look, Joanne, I've got a mountain—"

"Built from a molehill I presume—"

"Really. I can only stay for a drink."

"Martini?"

"Sure."

"Don't leave. I want you to meet someone."

And she was off. Lindsay gazed stoically over the bobbing heads. Maybe she could slip out before Joanne got back. She hated wasting time and reminded herself, as penance, that some of her best clients had come from Joanne's parties. It was all part of the game. As if business couldn't be brokered by the simple equation of supply and demand. As if competence, value and trust had no room in this three-ring circus.

And then she saw a nervous blonde, in her late forties, Lindsay guessed, shrinking awkwardly into the pattern of the wallpaper in the corner of the room. Lindsay's heart went out to her. A kindred spirit. With very little armor. Lindsay was about to make her way to her when Joanne snagged the poor woman from a tipsy, badly dressed, anecdote-spewing predator.

"It's OK," Joanne pampered. "I've rescued you." And clamped her hand upon the woman's elbow. "George is a bit much, even for us!"

"Yes . . . well—"

"I know. A nuisance. But I have someone you simply have to

meet—more your genre." Joanne stopped abruptly, the blonde almost bumping into her, raised already arched brows and asked of no one in particular, "Now where the hell is that genre? *Oh!*" and then sped up again, dragging the woman bodily behind her as she continued her speech mid-air. "Here she is. The most fascinating creature out of our very own P-town: Lindsay Brennan."

Joanne thrust her victim before Lindsay. "Lindsay, I have someone you simply have to meet. She's a bit 'whelmed,' " Joanne explained with equal parts sweetness and exasperation.

"I can't imagine why," Lindsay remarked flatly.

"Sondra Pinchot." Joanne held out her hand, presenting Sondra as if she were there for inspection. "Sondra is an interior designer . . . and if I'm not mistaken, looking for a brilliant architect with bold new ideas to remodel her quaint little beach home. And Lindsay"—Joanne shot Lindsay a direct wink—"I can personally attest, is not only brilliant, but very strong in the bold ideas department."

Lindsay dismissed the innuendo as she extended her hand. "I think we can take it from here."

"Nice to meet you." Sondra's voice was small.

"Oh shit, there goes George again." Joanne shook her head. "Maybe he's outlived his usefulness. You know it really is a delicate equation . . . sort of like arbitrage of the annoying—is there a direct correlation of asset to asshole?" Joanne frowned, irritated with the calculation, then dismissed it. "Anyway, you two get acquainted and talk design lingo about beams and all those other complicated things that hold up civilization." Joanne touched Lindsay's arm and took off.

The blonde followed Joanne's movements, and then awkwardly turned back to Lindsay.

"Don't let her get to you," Lindsay murmured.

"Oh, it's not her. I'm a bit rusty. I don't go to parties much."

"Well, I don't think one can exactly be prepared for Joanne's. She plans it that way."

Sondra smiled. "She does a good job."

And then Lindsay smiled. "Yes. She's very good at it."

More silence. "So . . . tell me about your beach house."

"Oh." Sondra seemed grateful to have a focus. "It's . . . well, it's

been a dream of mine, ever since I was a little girl, really. A large
monster of a beach house . . . very badly in need of a complete
makeover."

Lindsay's face set into a bored expression.

"Would you . . . um, be interested in something like that?"

"It's not really my line. I could give you some recommendations."

"Oh, I know a lot of architects. I really need someone who is going
to understand this place. It's very special."

"Well . . ." Lindsay didn't know why the words were tumbling
from her mouth. "I could take a look at it."

"Really?"

"Yeah, sure."

"What's your schedule like?"

She was booked. For the rest of her life.

"I'm going down there next Tuesday. Is that a possibility?" Sondra
cleared her throat. "I mean, if you're interested."

"Sure. That sounds great."

◆ ◆ ◆

Lindsay yawned. Slouched into the pillows on the overstuffed couch
in her living room, relaxing for the first time in hours—weeks—
finally home from that incredibly dull party, comfortable in ancient
sweats so faded and worn they seemed a part of her skin.

The beach house. She laughed out loud. It was absurd to even
contemplate. There was no time. There was never enough time.
Especially for a remodel sixty miles from the city. Why had she said
she would even consider it? The distance alone was more headache
than it would be worth. Besides, remodels brought nothing but loathing to mind. Too many variables. Too little compensation. Dickering
was a language of many dialects she had to learn over and over, cost
control was balancing the federal budget and decision-making became
a weighty religion as clients changed the changes they had just finished
changing like an Islamic bowing over the plans at the clang of a bell.
The final product never resembled the original plans, but the owners
expected the budget to remain the same. And they always had visions
of having been an architect in a previous life. Mechanical pencil envy.

Tuesday would be half-wasted by running to Earlscove. Maybe she could get out of it. But Sondra Pinchot seemed so lost that Lindsay felt sorry for her. And that damn voice. The low smoke-laced hesitation. Her apprehension. The curved line of Sondra's shoulder as she melted against the wall, the way Joanne had thrown her helter-skelter through the uncaring, unseeing throng. It brought to mind a Holocaust survivor she had seen on a documentary a few nights back, the tarnished attitude, a constant checking in, a nervous fear that wasn't unattractive in the least, but rather compelled a protective instinct in Lindsay she hadn't felt since Heather.

Her cat, Ayn, a burnished rust calico, jumped onto her chest. She drew up an abused quilt, the one item she had brought from her father's home, and snuggled deep inside it. She propped the Ryan specs next to her side. They were almost ready to bid. She needed to finish tonight, but first she wanted to close her eyes. Just for a few minutes.

She let her mind go, trying to defy the images that bombarded her. Relaxation. That elusive calm. She concentrated on her breathing as she had been taught in therapy, vaguely concerned she hadn't learned it right from the beginning. Wasn't it a built-in mechanism? Wasn't it supposed to come naturally? Did her shrink's floral imagery of inhaling colors as if one could breathe crayons have any scientific merit, or was it simply a crock of shit?

She had relaxed when she understood the etiology. And then she could embrace it with more enthusiasm, even if a bit self-consciously. In. Longer on the out. It soothed her as she let her hands play with the quilt. The softly frayed edges always made her think of that night. The night everything changed. As she caressed a single thread she thought that out of the big life changes one always remembered the little moments. The way her hands had woven themselves into the fabric of the quilt when he came to tuck her in, street light casting a macabre shadow on her clown (she could never play with it after that night), the smell of Old Spice and nervous sweat, and the tears in her father's eyes.

Funny how smells make you safe. Old Spice was her father. The ships on the bottle were safety, her father, adventurer of the high seas.

Nothing could harm her as long as her father came sailing through the door after work, tossing the paper like an anchor over the side of his easy chair, grabbing her up in his arms, his deep sailor stubble brushing against the smooth of her cheek, the laughter in his eyes, a twinkling pirate in port of call, cologne faded by the fierce wind of his day.

But that morning, shortly after Lindsay's seventh birthday, her mother informed Lindsay and her father, as they sat in the midst of their traditional Saturday-morning pancakes, she was leaving them. Her father dropped his fork; she could hear it ring out as he leapt to his feet. Lindsay sat in confusion, numbly twirling a swollen piece of hotcake in too much syrup as her father spent hours trying to change her mother's decision. Wasn't she just going shopping?

"What about her?" Lindsay's father pointed at her. But her mother would not look in her direction, and Lindsay could never remember what her mother's eyes looked like, even though they were her own.

Her father had loved his wife, deeply, utterly. He considered himself the luckiest man on earth, able to leave his job behind each day to return home to his cherished daughter and beautiful wife. How could he know she begrudged his easy contentment as he worked diligently—although not aggressively—at his trade, a general architect in a large firm? How could he know she resented his gratification as a glorified draftsman? That her love grew cold as he plodded along, that she had become hysterical from years of waiting?

Lindsay could only imagine her mother's frustration years later as she tried to unravel a memory obscured by betrayal. Her own drive and ambition came from a mother never content to simply be. A housewife whose desire for more was manifested in newspaper drives, presidency of the neighborhood association, constant political meetings, and finally in strident accusation. But worse was what the expectation had done to her, the belief that the "more" she craved would someday come. The endless wait, destroyed hope. The fierce light in her eyes as she lashed out in accusation. She had given him the best damn years of her life. . . . "And for what?" she had snarled. "For nothing!" And so she was leaving with Fred, the slick-haired Fred, the father of Lindsay's playmate Charlene. He would take her away from this "hellhole." As Lindsay sat, a silent witness with her bloated pancakes, she watched her father crumble. She could almost hear his heart shrivel, see his soul grow cold. And for that, she would never forgive her mother.

Lindsay knew, as children do, that her father still cared. She had been the object of fatherly adoration for too long. But she also knew, on a level she could not articulate, when her mother deserted them, when they saw the last sweep of her hair as she stormed out the back door, suitcase in hand, she had taken the best part of him with her.

He changed. He no longer came home with a smile on his face. No more laughter and grabbing her up in his arms. No rough warmth against her satin cheek. He went away. Spent hours at work. Her world changed. Became dark and cold. Like a cloud that took the sun out of the day as it rested upon her. And when the cloud moved, she would feel right again. But that didn't happen. The cloud came and never went.

Her father's face had become an impenetrable mask. When he slouched through the doorway in the evenings his paper became his shield, fanned before him until dinner. Before long, thick architectural specifications replaced the daily paper, along with heavy silences broken only by a chaste kiss good night, a "tell Mrs. Gardner I'll be late for dinner," a clearing of the throat that heralded nothing. He came home later and later, until many nights she didn't see him at all.

Mrs. Gardner, their housekeeper, nurtured Lindsay. It wasn't until years later, during her first brief months of therapy, that Lindsay realized she would never have survived the following years if it had not been for Mrs. Gardner. Her therapist questioned over and over her feelings about her mother, but she could come up with none. Mrs. Gardner, for all intents and purposes, had become her mother, with her thick Irish body, her softly cooing "There now, what a good girl you are," her tightly corseted bosom, like a starched pillowcase stuffed with down, deeply comforting in its unyielding stability. It was Mrs. Gardner's insistence that Lindsay join her each summer on her annual vacation to her father's Midwest farm that ultimately saved her.

The first summer Lindsay had been terrified of leaving home. But within two days she was running through the hayfields, jumping bales, playing with Star, the aging German shepherd, making mud pies, climbing trees, scraping knees and forgetting the dismal static of her father's glassy-eyed stare and her mother's absence.

She grew strong, her tender heart healing as her young body basked in the sun, as she swam in the lake behind the barn, slept hard and woke early. She met Billy, who became her best friend and "blood" brother within three hours. They explored the caves in the hillside, played army and space wars. Swapped stories, bragged, and later traded their Hardy Boys mystery books.

"Nancy Drew's for girls!"

"But you are a girl."

They laughed at that for a long time, then wrestled, stole old man Bromwell's cherries, flopped their earth-eaten feet in the creek as they snagged crawdads, double-dared secrets, told nasty jokes they didn't yet understand, and whiled away hours of simple pleasure. By the end of summer Lindsay never wanted to leave. It had been the perfect moment of childhood where everything is sharp and real and nothing is impossible.

Its memories kept her strong when she returned home. Her father's exclusive preoccupation with work had become an unspoken oath never to involve his heart in anything so transient as human life. He focused instead on the career he had never paid attention to, and now began to advance rapidly in his firm.

Days of silence turned into years. At first Lindsay pledged childlike loyalty to her father, clinging to the only secure thing left in her world. Eventually, however, the relentless hours of quiet that passed between them eroded the memories of a loving, benevolent father, replacing them with the stony, pulseless man who read throughout dinner, chewing slowly, methodically wiping his mouth after every few bites. She tried to stare him down, but every time he caught her, he would blink twice as if he'd just realized, oh, yes, there's another person at this table, and then he'd return to his paper.

She played with rebellion. Stayed out past curfew. Ran with the neighborhood bully and his pals. She showed Johnny Darren her privates for a nickel and was caught by Mrs. Darren. But when Mrs. Darren marched Lindsay to her own doorstep and dramatically re-counted her deviant sin, her father simply shrugged and said, "Children will be children, after all." "Well, your daughter is a hoodlum!" Lindsay had thrilled at the hope her father might notice she had turned rotten, but he merely put out his hand for her, pulled her gently inside, saying, "No. My daughter is not a hoodlum," and closed the door.

"You have to pay attention to the girl, Mr. Brennan. That's all this is. A play for your affections." She overheard Mrs. Gardner talking to her father that evening before she went to bed.

"I read her a bedtime story every night."

"Empty words don't fill the heart."

"Look, Mrs. Gardner, I pay you to keep house and take care of Lindsay, not for amateur analysis." His words weren't sharp or sarcastic, just to the point.

She heard Mrs. Gardner harrumph and storm off meaningfully. Lindsay sat on the stairwell. She sighed. It was useless. She lay back, then studied the angle where the stairwell had been cut in and thought how much more interesting it would be if the stairs had a circular shape so that they entered into the living room instead of straight out the door.

She thought about the staircase for a long time that night, then finally went to bed. The next day she drew the stairwell the way she thought it should be. It gave her a sense of calm, and she put it in her small desk drawer in her bedroom, right next to her Spiderman Comics.

Spiderman was always scaling tall-spired buildings with his weblike tentacles, so Lindsay nabbed a few extra sheets of tracing paper at school and spent long afternoons copying the structures he climbed. She omitted his form after several renditions and began to embellish the skyscrapers, giving them a unique flair. When she tired of that exercise she began drawing her own designs, outlandish and futuristic, but she had a reason for every line, every corner.

She began to show her drawings to Mrs. Gardner, who encouraged her heartily, marveling at the room she designed for her in their imaginary new home. She had a cupboard and spot for every appliance Mrs. Gardner used. Mrs. Gardner laughed, but looked carefully at the drawing, amazed by Lindsay's meticulous attention to detail.

Several nights later, Lindsay sat smooshing her Green Giant peas through the tines of her fork. She announced quite suddenly, "I've decided to be an architect, like you, Daddy. Only I'm goin' to build homes for when they land in space."

For once her father glanced from his paper, peered at his daughter as if she were someone he had never seen before. "Oh you are, are you?"

"Yes. And I've already got a house for you and me and Mrs. Gardner for when you retire or as soon as she can afford it."

"Oh you have, have you?" And though there was an edge of gentle amusement in his voice, he continued to watch his daughter.

"And they're quite lovely," Mrs. Gardner added. But just as suddenly as Lindsay had captured her father's interest, he seemed to remember he had no interest in anything. He returned to his paper.

"Don't you want to see it?" Lindsay asked, her voice low, tentative. But he merely wiped his lower lip with his napkin.

Lindsay's crystal-blue eyes grew more enormous as the tears began to swell. Mrs. Gardner's heart would break if she had to watch Lindsay endure any more pain. She grabbed the drawings and shoved them in front of her employer's nose.

"See for yourself. I can't wait till I can afford it." Mrs. Gardner poured him more coffee. She waited with Lindsay as he stared.

Finally he frowned. At first Lindsay thought she was in trouble, but then he slowly turned to her. His eyes touched hers for the first time since his wife had left. He smiled. He returned to the drawings, studying them more thoroughly.

He then glanced at Mrs. Gardner, as if seeing an old acquaintance after years, acknowledged her presence with gratitude. "Come here, you," he said to Lindsay. "These are very good."

He motioned for his daughter to stand beside him, began asking her questions in a low soft voice. Lindsay glanced at Mrs. Gardner, a smile of victory upon her milk-mustached lips.

Whether it had been simple transference or merely a wonderful coincidence, neither she, Mrs. Gardner, nor her father ever knew or cared to question. But from that moment on, Lindsay's natural love for creating became a genuine passion for design. She and her father began to sit for long hours in his den and sketch, intoxicating one another with new ideas and concepts, happy in their isolation. Mrs. Gardner would bring them tea, milk and cookies, quite thrilled with the turn of events. From that day forward, all they knew of each other fell within those parameters.

Lindsay had no inclination to step outside of that haven. Her interest in friends, toys and games became silly nonsense next to the grownup stuff that required skill and patience. School was a necessary evil, but she was an excellent student, attacking her studies with the same energy and enthusiasm she did her drawing, disciplined from a young age to persevere until she succeeded.

If the other students found her somewhat odd, she was nonetheless considered popular. She was straightforward, and her disregard of social mores charmed people rather than put them off. She was one of the lucky few who were different and got away with it.

Dreams of her childhood came less frequently now. Some who worked with Lindsay wondered if she had ever had a childhood, had ever known what it was to have fun. Not that she was without humor—Lindsay was, in fact, capable of devastating humor, but it rarely came out unless she was comfortable, relaxed. And it was often at her own expense. This intenseness, this serious outlook took its toll in relationships. Few ever lasted more than months.

◆ ◆ ◆

Lindsay shrugged in her sleep as Joanne tried to swish the cat away with her hand in the air. "Scat, cat. I'll take over now." But Ayn remained curled next to Lindsay's body.

Joanne used her forefinger to ping Ayn's nose lightly. The cat cast an appalled glance, then quickly made her exit. Free to maneuver, Joanne carefully sidled her way atop, and gently laid the length of her body upon Lindsay's.

"Joanne?" Lindsay stirred, her voice groggy and distant. "Must have fallen off . . ."

"Such a lovely view." Joanne surveyed Lindsay's tousled thick dark hair, her deepset eyes, the beautiful clear skin and handsome mouth.

"God, what time is it?" Lindsay tried to sit upright, but Joanne kept her pinned.

"Don't worry, you've got plenty of time." Joanne nuzzled Lindsay's neck and teased her ear.

"Babe, I've got to get up early—"

"Hmmm, imagine that. . . ." Joanne's smile was dangerous as her hand slithered beneath the comforter and underneath Lindsay's sweatshirt. "And I wouldn't dream of getting in your way," she purred.

Lindsay felt Joanne's fingers glide over her skin and gently cover the softness of her breast. Her perfume and the essence of Joanne, a heady intoxicant unto itself, made their way to her senses.

"Jo . . . anne." Her voice was throaty as she felt her limbs awaken.

"Do you have any idea how terribly tired you sound?" Joanne gently pulsed Lindsay's arched nipple.

"Joanne—"

"Lindsay. Kiss me."

Not another word was spoken.

amantha would do anything to trick the cosmos of ever having met Janet Myers. She had just rung off the phone with Janet's personal assistant, Trina, for the third time. Chaos was the theme for the evening. Janet Myers was entering high society in a matter of moments and she wasn't going to let anyone survive it.

Samantha held up pearl earrings. They washed out against her hair. Diamonds? Maybe if she gathered the richly textured shoulder-length hair into a loose chignon. Her hairdresser gushingly referred to it as "the purest hue of gold I've ever had the pleasure to run my hands through." Yes. Now the pearls worked. Simple and tasteful.

Tasteful being an irrelevant fixture in her life these days. She supposed taste was in the aesthetic of the perceiver much as beauty was in the eye of the beholder. But for Janet Myers taste was simply something she did to test her spaghetti sauce.

Samantha remembered the morning she had landed

her infamous account. She had been thrilled. In ecstasy, she had to admit, at the prospect of the never-ending resource she would have to work with.

But now, five months later, life seemed to have played a cruel joke on that fateful day Janet Myers' pudgy fingers danced a minute waltz upon the yellow pages of the greater Seattle area.

Janet Myers' entrance over the threshold of SAMANTHA PINCHOT's Design Concept Northwest had been grand. And memorable. She could barely make it through the door. She was the largest woman Samantha had ever encountered up close. A fat phobia she didn't know she had rushed to the fore. It wasn't her weight. It was how she used it. So aggressively.

Janet had plunged forward that Friday morning and snarled in her best trailer-park drawl, "We need a job done, and we need it now, and we got money to burn," and by Monday morning Samantha belonged to her. This was *the* Janet Myers and her husband Bud, of lottery fame, their sudden wealth detailed in the Calendar Section a couple of Sundays prior, unimaginatively titled "Rags to Riches."

Whoever said money didn't buy happiness had not lived from Janet's grimy food stamps to Bud's crumpled disability check in a cramped Golden West single-wide in Vista Springs Trailer Park. Forty-two million dollars could buy just a tiny slice of ecstasy.

And ecstasy was where Janet Myers lived every time she purchased a new item. Anything and everything that she could get her hands on, no matter how gauche. All the poverty she had ever endured was slapped cleanly back into an economy that had robbed her of the most basic comforts. From useless gewgaws to the five-thousand-square-foot home nestled cozily amid the upper class of Bainbridge Island.

And that was when she retained Samantha, who deciphered within ten easy minutes that Janet didn't so much want a designer to tell her how to arrange her bizarre assemblage as she wanted yet another ornament of wealth.

Samantha had developed a variety of tactics to deal with neurotic society wives whose singular activity in life was devoted to the remodeling of their homes. Her most frequent and successful approach to these women was simple but effective: reverse psychology. She had become skilled at the subtle suggestion. After all, she was the expert. And occasionally she resorted to camouflaged strong-arm tactics. But there was nothing that worked against the inimitable Janet Myers, whose entire scheme of decor revolved around a massive black velvet portrait of Elvis Presley as he appeared in his more portly Vegas days.

And so tonight Janet Myers would put on display her grotesque world of fashion, exposing her capricious and ignorant whims to the cream of Seattle society. And Samantha, in theory at least, would be the responsible party.

The phone rang again. Samantha gritted her teeth. She wouldn't answer it. She tried to finish her makeup, but the incessant ringing jangled her nerves. She picked it up, anticipating the worst. But it wasn't Janet. It was her mother.

She would have preferred to talk to Janet.

◆ ◆ ◆

"Ready, hon?"

Robert came up behind Samantha, grazing her neck with his lips. The soft touch did not inspire a brushfire to spread through her limbs, but it was warm. Comforting.

"The question remains, is the rest of humanity?" Samantha winked at him from the mirror. She watched his eyes as they followed the contours of her off-the-shoulder cocktail dress. They were bright with appreciation, perhaps a glimmer of lust.

He fastened the back of her dress, as he had a hundred times. Then he stood back, admiring her natural beauty. Her allure would not be that of the Elegant Models by Monique who would litter Janet Myers' party, stark exoticism that beckoned sultrily from the newsstands. Samantha's high cheekbones were not the product of anorexia. A strong jawline gave her face its distinctive character. Aquiline nose and full lips, the bottom of which she often nibbled during moments of intense concentration—all those things made for a sort of head-turning beauty, Robert supposed. But the attraction to Samantha, Robert had realized a scant two minutes after meeting her, was her gray and infinitely intelligent eyes. There lay a secret in their depths he still hadn't unearthed after all this time.

"You don't mind going to this thing?" Samantha's words brought him out of his reverie.

"No. Not as long as you protect me from Cruella DeVille."

Samantha turned and smiled at him. "Don't you think I'm the one who needs protecting? My reputation is about to be destroyed." He walked up to her. She smoothed his left eyebrow distractedly, picked a piece of lint from the lapel of his evening jacket. "You look very handsome."

He took her hand and could tell by her sweating palm that she was nervous. "You're safe with me, babe."

Wildfire hype had made the Janet Myers Gala Event the hottest ticket among Seattle's elite and society wannabes. At the front door, heavily armed by security, giving one's name wasn't enough. Even with her special pass, Samantha and Robert were checked through three lists. "Why don't they just fingerprint me?" Robert muttered as they made their way through the crowded front hall.

Once inside Samantha stopped. She was not a short woman at five seven, but she finally knew what it was to be petite amid the flowing Sea of Tall Women (as she later described it to Jerra, her best friend), the contingent of Models à la Monique that crammed every corner and hung onto wealthy male arms cloaked in Armani suits, their angular hips jutting with a flowing aggression as the evening wore on.

"I think I'll try to find something to make this endurable. Wine for you?"

"Yeah. Make it a double." Samantha could barely breathe. "And don't get lost."

"Hey. I played basketball."

She laughed on impulse and then braced herself, but not in time for the Sea of Tall Women to part. And suddenly there appeared before her a life-size painting of a Mohican Indian, purple circles etched about his body, two earrings of dripping red hearts dangling from either side of this proud warrior who held a bouquet of dead daisies in his hand. Where had this come from? Not even Janet's collection of nouveau crass art was this vulgar. There had to have been a force even more vile than Janet's to persuade her to make the purchase, much less hang it in the home Samantha had worked so hard to prepare for this night of Janet's debut into Seattle society.

And it got worse as she saw the other "artistic" additions that had been made. For a moment the tableau spun about her. She was certain she would faint. Her reputation was no longer in danger of being ruined. In a single evening it would be annihilated.

Moments later Janet Myers barreled through the wavering stalks of beauty trailed by a smug-looking greasy-haired bandit, whom she introduced as the "most imahginative little kre-tur I've ever run into." My lord, Samantha thought, she was now talking like the nouveau riche, only with her trailer-park accent.

"This is Tony." Janet beamed proudly as she turned to one of the deplorable paintings. "He's responsible for all this."

Samantha could only nod. She was still numb, trying to figure out what sort of damage this fiasco was going to do to her career.

"This is the best artwork money can buy," boasted Tony.

"Surely not." The words jumped from Samantha's mouth, a reflex.

Janet gnawed at a pudgy finger—a moment of doubt—but Tony leapt in before it could fester, erupt.

"Everything you see here is out of the hippest galleries in N.Y. and L.A.," he said, pronouncing the initials. Janet's head bobbed happily at this good news.

"Hmmm." Samantha.

"Biggest names." Tony's manner was pleading, yet still laced with arrogance. They both knew Janet couldn't tell art from a ceramic saltshaker.

"You know we've got quite a few artists here in the N.W. ourselves." Samantha monogrammed the letters for Tony's benefit. "Especially Seattle."

"Yeah . . . yeah." Tony lit up a cigarette. "Well, this is what's happenin' in the tightest circles."

"I bet they're tight." Samantha's anger threatened her well-bred manners. "Tell me, how'd you two hook up?"

"Oh." Janet swooned a bit. "He found me. I mean, is that too wonderful or what? He just hunted me down."

Samantha's eyes shot from Janet, poor lost new rich person, to Tony, her cigarette-stained leech. "My, how persistence pays off." She turned before she could say anything further. A scene now would benefit no one. She would have her attorney call Janet Monday morning, have her name removed from any print materials and ban Janet from using her or her firm's name with anything remotely connected to this project. She had to find Robert and get the hell out of there.

◆ ◆ ◆

"That was nice." Samantha lay in Robert's arms. He had made love to her when they returned home, sensitive to her Pyrrhic victory, her emptiness. He wanted to take her pain away, but even as he entered her, he could feel the vacuum their union created. He didn't know how to reach her.

"Quite a party," he remarked later.

"Thank God, *Seattle Design* is the only place my name will appear next to that deplorable trash heap. How many copies do you think we can buy?"

"It's going to be OK." Robert curled his body around her, trying to protect her. They lay silently for a long while.

"Your mother called me at the office today," he said.

"Yeah."

"She's been trying to get a hold of you."

"Yeah." She aimlessly played with the hairs on his chest until she felt the slow rhythmic purring of sleep.

ondra sipped her coffee and drew an exhausting amount of smoke into her lungs. Combined with the raw nip in the coastal air, it made her sputter. Her nerves were chalkboard raw. She had done nothing but drink coffee and smoke her damn Export A's, and then for good measure she had finished a Danish left by the cleaning woman. She was running on nothing but fumes. Lindsay Brennan would be there any minute and she was a basket case.

She stood on the deck of Earlsheart, her grand Victorian relic, the one thing in life she probably would have killed for. She lovingly took in the rotting boards, the mossy undergrowth. The house might be in the latter stages of ruin, but Sondra didn't let that deter her. She understood decay. She understood the luxury and indulgence of it. She also knew she could subdue it. She was going to create a beautiful haven from this eroded wreckage, her childhood fantasy, this treasure the realtor had been only too happy to get off his hands.

The smell of the damp air clung to everything, its

bracing sweet pungency carried on the waves that swept to the shore. Briny traces filtered through her clothes; the scent would linger long after she had returned to the city. She took a deep long breath of it, then impetuously threw her cigarette over the railing and watched the butt fizzle and go cold.

Despite the unseasonable chill that cut its way through every possible crevice of her unprotected skin, she didn't want to go inside and pace. Ever since she had signed the escrow papers and made the decision to relocate from the city to this remote strip of beach, it was as if an IV drip of pure adrenaline coursed through her veins. She felt a constant flutter. Excitement. Fear. Not confusion really, because she was determined to make this change, and it was, after all, what she had been waiting to do for years. But making a move had always been as terrifying for her as not making one.

She sighed. So far she had been met only with grimaces of futility and greedy grins from the architects and contractors who walked through her new home. Couldn't they see what Earlsheart could be? Yes . . . and no. No one seemed to understand what was in her head. To them it was just another job.

This place was her refuge, perhaps even a last chance. That's why she was doing all this. To quasi-retire and to paint. She'd worked for years building up her client base, struggling through excruciating hours, saving enough money to return to the landscape of her childhood summers to paint canvases of terrible seascapes that had been mimicked a million times before. It was to be her reward for toeing the line. Well . . . she had, damn it. For nearly twenty-five years. Even if there had been a few detours.

But since she had arrived almost a week ago, she had done nothing. Nothing. She had managed to consume enormous amounts of coffee—piping hot in the mornings, iced in the afternoons, espresso after dinner—her caffeine consumption a close second to her cigarettes. No shopping at the charming little shops, no leisurely strolls at sunset. She couldn't even get through the two novels or the self-help book her clients had been raving about. She could concentrate on nothing. Instead she slept. She was a champion napper, the ocean air knocking her flat for hours, deep and dreamless.

Her life had drifted from the yellow danger zone to the first orange glow of a screaming red. Listlessness followed cozily by inertia, and after that a certain visit to the abyss. Well, she simply could not allow that. Not this time. Not when she was about to launch into the most important project of her life. She could not afford weeks of paralytic depression.

"Damn it, Sondra, get a hold of yourself," she said aloud. She returned to the house, closed the French doors off the living area, and headed for her pack of Export A's. Lighting up, she felt the murky smoke swim deliciously about the contours of her ravaged mind. She took another drag, feeling safer. Calmer.

There was a knock at the door. That meant the "brilliant" architect had arrived. As Sondra walked to the entrance she wished she were more together, more confident and poised like . . . like, well, practically anyone.

Lindsay stood there, dressed in 501's, white turtleneck and large indigo sweater, battered briefcase by her side. Comfortable, more relaxed, she appeared younger than she had at the party.

"Hello." Sondra extended the hand with the cigarette, laughed nervously as she passed it to the other and shook Lindsay's hand, a brief, abrupt contact. She had always found it difficult to touch other women, no matter how slight.

"I think I was envisioning something like cottage when you said beach house," Lindsay said as she entered, taking in the scope of the massive interior. "This place is enormous! Jesus . . ." She strolled the perimeter and then made her way to Sondra. "Built in the late eighteen hundreds?"

"Eighteen seventy-nine. I know it's large. And needs a lot of work."

"Yes . . . this girl's seen some rough weather." Lindsay's eyes darted about, taking in the disintegration.

"Weather, years, abuse." Sondra smiled uncertainly. "Do you always refer to buildings as female?"

"Oh. No. Not at all. Some are female. Others, like the Graves building? Definitely male." Lindsay turned full circle, taking one last look. "But this place feels very female."

"Yes . . . I suppose it is." Sondra wasn't comfortable with the banter. She could never come up with clever replies. "So. What did you have in mind?" Lindsay's tone spoke business, the small talk over.

"Well, I want to make this into my new home, as well as create a studio in the southwest corner upstairs; not only to continue working for my design clients but . . . to paint. Transform all this"—Sondra put her hands in the air—"into something livable."

Lindsay walked to the large ocean rock fireplace that took up half the east wall. "God, I love these old places. Great design."

"The man who built it was an architect himself. I mostly knew his wife. When I was a kid." She paused, unsure of herself. "Want some coffee?"

"Sure."

Sondra led Lindsay into the kitchen. "My family took a small cabin during the summers about a mile north of here. I used to run down the beach to see Mrs. Hunziker every chance I got. She was always baking something. Pies . . . loganberry, huckleberry . . . God, they were the best pies in the world." Sondra began to feel as if she were chattering aimlessly so busied herself with the coffee. "Anything in it?"

"A little milk."

When Sondra handed Lindsay the mug she again saw the woman from the party, her professional facade firmly intact as she dug out a sketch pad from her briefcase. "So, where do you want to start?"

"Well, here in the kitchen I want to break out this entire west wall, get the full effect of the ocean and take advantage of the natural light. I want to modernize the cabinets, but keep the flavor of the built-ins." There was confidence in her voice now. At least here, in this house, she knew what she wanted. She led Lindsay into what had previously been a library. It was to be converted to a den, she told her. The small dining room off its south side she intended to open up into the kitchen, to make it larger. They moved on to the only bathroom in the house. "I'd like to bring the plumbing up to the twentieth century—"

Lindsay grinned and finished for her, "—but maintain the charm."

"Exactly. And put another bathroom upstairs."

"It's only civilized."

Sondra laughed, then felt awkward again.

When they returned to the living room, Sondra stood next to the mammoth stone fireplace, then sat on the built-in ledge of the hearth. It was magical, and the only place she felt genuine calm. Indeed, it was where she had spent the majority of her waking hours last week. As the sun broke through a cloud, they were both captured by its sudden warmth.

"I love this room." Sondra said, almost a whisper.

"Essences of old rooms"—Lindsay spoke reverently—"always amaze me. All the moments of the living past converge. You can feel a room the minute you walk into it." And it was true, the textures, memories and ghosts merged between the hidden and not so hidden particles that hung in the rays of sun slicing through the room with the glare of a klieg light.

"I almost don't want to change it as much as I do."

"Yes. I know. It's hard to disturb what lies beneath. . . ." Lindsay's eyes were soft, kind. "I've got to be honest with you. I wasn't sure about this. . . ."

Sondra turned to her, a pinched frown creasing her forehead.

"Well, you know how remodels go. Of course, if your clients let you do the work they hired you for, it's one thing. But I've rarely found that the case." Lindsay smiled engagingly. "Have you?"

"In a word, no."

Lindsay assessed the space. "I've got to say . . . this place fascinates me. Yes." She walked around, ruminating. "I'd really like to draw up some prelims."

Sondra exhaled for what felt like the first time since Lindsay walked in the door. "Oh, that is so . . . great. You don't know how happy that makes me. The other architects . . . they, well, they just had no feel for the place."

Lindsay turned, surprised. "How could you not fall in love with it?"

"Earlsheart," Sondra intoned, wistfully. "It has an amazing history. The Hunzikers were very special people. Tom used to say that everything Earlscove was about was right here in the history of this house. It was the heart of the town, and that's how it got its name."

Lindsay checked her watch.

"I'm sorry. I've been rattling on."

"No. No problem. I just want to miss the traffic heading back in. Well," Lindsay closed the notepad. "I can probably get something back to you in a week or so."

"Great."

"Thanks, Mrs. Pinchot. Thanks for sharing your lovely home with me." Lindsay extended her hand.

"Sondra. Please."

"Sondra."

◆ ◆ ◆

Genesis. It began in the core of her. She felt it the way other women felt their partner's seed. Earlsheart would be her lover. The kind of project she adored. More than anything, she loved to blend yesterday's lush architecture with the clean, aesthetic lines of modern simplicity. She could envision the finished project, not as one room after another, but as energy. Her mind fragmented into a million glowing points, a light show of creativity spinning wildly through her synapses, fueled by adrenaline, an instant torch igniting the fire she lived for. It was the ultimate power. Birth power. Power to create. She pushed her foot to the accelerator.

◆ ◆ ◆

Snag sat stalled in a traffic bottleneck at the Morrison Bridge. A large naval vessel slugged its way through the turgid brown river at an interminable crawl. He lit his third cigarette in a row. Chain smoking wasn't his style unless he was power partying, or extremely irritated. Which he was. He had had it up to his doelike eyelashes with Merrick, who had made homophobia an art form of the worst kind: Too angry to hear, too intelligent not to be dangerous. Too ignorant not to believe it was a preference, which he obviously assumed Snag had.

Snag stared at his cigarette, watching the smoke curl and rise. He allowed the nicotine to swirl about in his mind, holding the smoke back, then teased it into a French exhale. His eyes still ached from the previous day, balled up on the couch sobbing over *Jean de Florette* followed by *Manon of the Spring.* Touched by Depardieu's brutish yet simple sensuality. Aroused by his menacing physicality and smoldering sexuality. Wanting Jared until he ached, who clacked by in loafers, crisp oxford shirt, ironed jeans, refusing to "waste an entire afternoon on that rubbish."

If only Jared would let go of his refined containment. Let go. Let himself live. Oh, but Snag loved him. Adored him beyond words. Wouldn't trade him for all the Nordstrom's sales in Pioneer Square. But still he often wished Jared could break free of the hidden constraints that kept Jared safe. Always.

Snag, on the other hand, had devoted his life to spontaneity and passion. He woke with each rising sun as if he were a schoolboy in love, basking in the artless moments of the day, displaying a complete lack of restraint on any level.

It was, of course, exactly this extremism, this ability to live in the moment, that Jared had found so captivating, had caused him to lose all control, and at the ripe age of forty-five to fall overwhelmingly in love for the first time in his life. Or at least as overwhelmingly as Jared did anything. But the very thing he had been drawn to in Snag—his utter disregard, joie de vivre, his spontaneity—was also what drove him mad.

Snag constantly pushed the envelope into realms of "new experience." Whether it was trekking through Africa for a summer, enthralled in the ecstasy of peyote during a lush Mexican sunset, or hang gliding off the coast of New South Wales, his reach knew no limits. Although Jared and his friends objected, no one could convince him why he should do otherwise. Snag would simply retort that he had seen too many of his friends die. That he intended to cram every last minute of every last hour with whatever opportunity life presented.

Clothes, CD's, books, and Snag's latest fixation, laser disks, were the particular opportunities that most often presented themselves. "This has gone beyond stretching the paycheck equation," Jared would pronounce as Snag whistled, alphabetically compiling his own personal library of French cinema. It was true. Paychecks had long ago become chump change. They tended to the basics, while credit cards became his link to a brighter, more expansive world. "Live today, pay tomorrow" was his favorite maxim, right next to his favorite seer's "Life is a banquet and most poor fools are starving to death."

"Yes, doll, but you're making sure you're never even the slightest bit hungry," Jared would point out, himself quite content to live between paychecks *and* to save for a rainy day.

"But you grew up in southern California," Snag would goad. "It never rains there. What are you worried about?"

"You, my vagabond. What if . . . ?" But Jared wouldn't say it. He would never say it. What if one of them got sick?

"Exactly my point," Snag would reply.

Snag despaired of ever finding the inroads to Jared's soul. If he could just once make Jared enjoy something merely for its own sake, then he knew he could help Jared understand the forces that motivated him. Snag knew, of course, that he carried it too far. Knew it was a problem. But he was damned if he would compromise until Jared let his hair down. The idea that he might not frightened him, but it was precisely that challenge that kept him going, just as Jared's need to tame Snag balanced the other side of the equation.

Snag stubbed out his dead cigarette. Jesus, would this traffic never move? Then reviewed with tightening irritation the chain of events that had brought him to this damn gridlock. He thought back to the morning when Megan peeked her cherubically divine face around his door before entering with pastries and coffee in hand.

"Double cap for you." She opened his lid and set it before him.

"Ah, Megs. Read my mind."

"Not me. I wouldn't dare," she assured him.

"It's not always in the gutter!" He sipped his cappuccino, shuddered in ecstasy. "So. Where's our fearless leader this morning?"

"Has a meeting with that . . . ohhh, what's her name . . . it slipped my mind, the one with the remodel at the beach. The only time they could schedule it. It's just a prelim."

Snag knew Megan was diligently trying to keep peace. It had become part of her job description.

"I knew it! Surreptitious and mysteriously absent means only one thing: Lindsay's on the prowl for more work." He grimaced at Megan.

"I know. I know," Megan concurred, shaking her head.

"What in the hell does she think she's doing?"

"Snag. It's what Lindsay does." Megan sipped her latte.

"Yeah . . . well, it ain't what I do."

"She called a few minutes ago and asked if you wouldn't mind taking her place at Merrick's walk-through."

"Fuck. She knows how much I hate that asshole."

"Well, she figured it might work in our favor. Be the shortest walk-through in history." They both chuckled halfheartedly.

"Trust Lindsay to come up with that perspective." Snag had put on his coat, downed half his cappuccino, then turned to Megan, noticing for the first time the emerald-green two-piece tailored outfit that took twenty pounds off the ample girth. Snag secretly found her portliness comforting, though he knew it was a never-ending source of pain for his adorable Megan. "Have I told you this morning how friggin' lovely ye are, Miss Megan?"

"Shit." Snag moaned. Now there appeared something was wrong with the drawbridge. Exhaust swirled from the cars that honked like angry animals. He lit another cigarette. "I suppose it's time for some Michael Crawford." He slipped a CD into the player and felt the tears rim up with the first strains of "The Music of the Night."

By the time she had gotten off the elevator at her seventeenth-floor office, Lindsay was pumped. Primed for the exquisite chaos and disarray that she would will into order, the execution of vision into reality.

Megan sat like a marble statue at her desk, indestructible, immovable and loyal. Lindsay couldn't imagine not seeing this image every time she entered her office. It made complete her sense of well-being.

"Any calls?"

"Yeah. About fifteen. But most of the them were from Snag. Merrick wants you and only you to finish the walk-through. Snag finally gave up. He's on his way in, but stuck on the bridge."

"Shit, I guess I knew that was coming." Lindsay glanced at Snag's closed office door.

Lindsay leafed through the other messages, then glanced at Megan.
"I guess he's pissed."

"Oh, I can tell you for a fact. He's pissed."

"Oh boss gal . . ." Snag waltzed in an hour later and parked his slender
body across from hers at the desk. "That was one ge-fucked guten
morgen."

"I'm sorry, Snag. It wasn't intentional. Actually, I thought it might
work in our favor."

"And how did you figure that, pray tell, when Merrick's a not so
distant cousin of Lon Mabon, babe?"

"Snag—" Lindsay felt terrible.

"No. Spare me the effusive apology." Snag melodramatically inhaled his anger. "He was rude. Intolerably rude. Homophobic little
bugger sat there and had the audacity to tell me he didn't think I was
'qualified,' and wasn't I just a 'draft clerk'? I informed him with great
pleasure that it was I who 'drafted' his plans in the first place and that
I was more than acquainted with his friggin' little strip mall, thank you
very much."

Lindsay waited a moment to be sure his diatribe was complete
before she spoke. "I didn't realize he was that—"

"Abhorrent? Irritating fuck? Well, he is." Snag lost his anger, but
Lindsay could tell he was genuinely disturbed. "And it was extremely
humiliating."

"It won't happen again, Snag. And I am sorry." Lindsay waited a
moment, let the air clear a bit more between them. "Well, Snag, now
for the good news—"

"You think I don't know what you're up to?"

She sighed heavily. This was an oft-trodden, deep-rutted terrain,
two dragsters heading toward each other on the strip. Which one
would veer off before they collided?

"Well, actually, I'm planning on doing this one on my own time."

"Yeah, hon, when's that? You figure out something about virtual
reality I don't know about?"

"I . . . I need this, Snag. It's . . ."

"Yeah, yeah I know." He peered at her, relenting a bit. "The rejuvenator."

"Back me on Ryan. Not a lot. Most of it's done, but we're set to start on the seventeenth. You might have to attend a few meetings—"

"—do battle with the contractors, owners—"

"—just familiarize yourself with it." Lindsay was losing her patience and threw a hefty set of specifications on the corner of the desk.

"Oh sure." Snag's voice was laced with sarcasm. "Say by the middle of next week?"

"Snag. I need your support on this." They were still squarely on a collision course. "Come on, what do you think?" The standoff always came to this point, and they both knew Snag would turn his wheel at the last moment, as he did now.

"What I think, darlin', has always been conveniently beside the point. I am, as always, your un-humble servant. I embrace Thee, Specifications." Snag clutched them to his chest. He turned and was about to leave, then stopped. He glanced back at Lindsay, already refocused on the never-ending pile of work at her desk.

"Hey, boss gal. When it's all said and done, you know it's true what they say."

Startled, Lindsay looked up at Snag. His eyes were dead serious—a rare and unusual event. "You can't take it with you."

◆ ◆ ◆

Joanne's eyes glimmered with delight between the two flickering flames of her candlelit dinner. Lindsay would be home soon. She had put all her culinary skills into a complex recipe for a genuine South of the Border extravaganza. She had spent hours on Mexican rice, a task she performed lovingly and well.

Actually, there wasn't much that Joanne didn't do well, but very little she did lovingly. Doing for Lindsay, however, came naturally. Which was the perfect term to describe the only uncontrived coupling she had ever known. It made Lindsay a source of reality for Joanne, whose sexual experience traveled the gamut from the cold, brusque zipperless fuck to the hot, hyperkinetic gymnastics of drug-induced explorations. Love props, theatrical performances had been a way of life. But with Lindsay, everything was different. Especially the sex.

To say Joanne had been a homely adolescent could never touch the damage that agonizing period had done to her self-confidence. Her tomboy years of lanky-limbed gawkiness persisted flat-chestedly until she was sixteen. And when she blossomed it brought truth to the term "overnight." Hormones kicked in, genetics put the pedal to the metal and she transformed into her mother's daughter: tall and slender with Cyd Charisse legs, thick auburn hair with natural golden highlights, and an almost perfectly symmetrical face. She was graced with dark brown eyes, a patrician nose tipped slightly to the left and lips one ached to touch with one's own. But when she looked in the mirror she still saw the skinny, unpopular freak.

It also had been overnight that she discovered the sexual mechanics of her body when she first brought herself to orgasm. She had read about masturbation in one of the magazines hidden in her father's den. There was an air of repugnance about it, but the mysterious infamy of the whispered term got the better of her, and after her first tenuous exploration, she became an ardent fan.

After two years of daily revisits and variations on the theme, both physically and in her newfound and richly textured fantasy world, Joanne decided she would tempt the whistles and "hey babys" increasingly directed her way and discovered this favored activity was far more fun when engaged in by two. Though she had always been aware of an aesthetic attraction to women, the cultural computation of yin and yang led her to the opposite sex.

Unlike the many bleak and tragic stories of the first unflowering, detailed in painful disgust by her friends, Joanne's loss of virginity was absolutely thrilling. She came with joy and gusto, and despite what she described as the tedium of male conversation, was enraptured with the sensation of orgasm during penetration. But more than the physical sensation, she became addicted to the power of seduction and commodity of obsession. She remained a detached observer in the game of sexual politics but became a skilled participant.

Because no one ever dented Joanne's emotional interior, she was able to soar, unscathed, through her education, receive her master's in business and become a consultant to the very wealthy and insecure. When she described her company to Lindsay the first time they had dinner she applied the euphemism Creative Business Management. In other words, a people broker. She brought parties together, but not simply on a professional level. Her true talent lay in wedding the psychic strengths of one with the ego weaknesses of another so that their union was mutually beneficial. She became so good at it that she worked only when a particular situation interested her. And when Lindsay fell into her lap she became obsessed with marrying the dark architect's talents to those who would appreciate her relentless determination and integrity, but, more importantly, would not be deterred by Lindsay's sometimes less than diplomatic honesty.

Joanne had slept with many women before Lindsay. After years of sampling a variety of sizes and shapes of men and penises, she realized there might be another option when she began spending time with one of her old basketball teammates.

Deborah was a tall and rather handsome brunette who had played center during their varsity years, and now she had moved into the neighborhood. They began getting together after work, sharing a bottle of wine, stories, hardships and trials about running their own businesses. Deborah had invited her over for dinner one night to try her new wok. From the minute she entered the door, Joanne had become obsessed with kissing her, and when Deborah went to her bedroom to retrieve a book Joanne followed. Deborah turned, and before the question in her eyes could find words, Joanne glided to her and stated unequivocally, "I would like to kiss you." Their affair lasted five months, and ended badly.

Once Joanne had dipped her fingers into the cookie jar she gorged herself on the new and fascinating world of womanhood, but continued to dally with both sexes. For variety, she told herself, but she knew it had more to do with her twisted Catholic upbringing than anything else. The day her mother died, she gave up men completely and discovered a new zest for the hunt. Belt notches became passé. She wanted more than just quantity.

And then two years ago, while rummaging about at Nordstrom's in search of the perfect outfit for that night's party of players, she met

Lindsay. They were both in the dressing room. Lindsay appeared from behind the wooden-slatted door wearing a black Claude Montana jacket, a crisp white jacquard shirt, glittering gold and onyx earrings dangling from her ears. Breathtaking. Joanne was in a chic full-length cerise silk evening gown, pushing the opportunity of a V-cut, exposing two of her greatest assets.

They openly admired one another via the reflection of a large three-faced mirror.

"Stunning. In a word," Joanne quipped.

"Ravishing is the word, I believe." Lindsay returned the compliment.

"Big do?"

"Awards banquet."

"Oh. Giving or receiving?"

"Receiving," Lindsay replied modestly.

"Well, that's the only way to attend an awards banquet." Joanne returned to her dressing room. And then inquired over the partition, "What's this award for?" And before Lindsay could answer, she popped in her head from around the door. "Are you someone famous? Should I know you?"

"Not unless you follow the Coalition for Northwest Design."

"You're an architect."

Joanne watched Lindsay's shock with satisfaction. "What? All beauty, no brains?" But before Lindsay could redeem her position, "I do read the *Business Journal*."

"For pleasure, I suppose."

"No. I do other things for that." And it was then Joanne caught and held Lindsay's eyes until neither could breathe, and Lindsay finally escaped into her dressing room. But she was safe only for a couple of minutes before there came a light tap on the door.

"Would you mind awfully?" Lindsay cracked the door open. Joanne was trying to get the zipper unstuck.

"It's not the zipper," Joanne assured her. "I'd never be caught by a cliché. It's my hair. It's tangled in my necklace."

She turned her back to Lindsay. Lindsay put her hands up to Joanne's neck and gently began to unravel the tangle of silky hair.

"I know who you are," Joanne said quietly. "You *are* famous. Or infamous, depending on what circles you run in. I run in both." And then a chill ran down her spine from the warmth of Lindsay's fingers. Her voice was husky. "So when do you receive this token of esteem?"

"Next week."

"Good. Leaves you free to bring that handsome suit of yours to brighten up this party of mine at the MAC club tonight." Joanne smiled seductively, the thing she did best, and then added, "There are some people who would love to meet you, and . . . I think you might be interested in meeting them."

Joanne turned and Lindsay smiled with her eyes. "Sure. Why not?"

"Consider it networking." Joanne's implication had nothing to do with networking. The shimmering contact grew stronger. The pull greater. Finally another shopper entered the dressing room and broke the electrical pulse.

"I'll get you my card." Joanne cleared her throat.

"Eightish?"

"Sounds good."

Lindsay showed up at eight on the nose, punctual, for the first and last time. Joanne opened the door and stepped back, enchanted by the graceful strength with which Lindsay moved.

"Can I get you a drink?" Joanne walked to her well-stocked bar. "I make the best martinis on the West Coast."

"Then by all means." Lindsay strolled into the living room, studying the aesthetic and tasteful artifacts that defined the sharp, modernistic apartment.

"Here you go." Joanne handed Lindsay her drink. They clinked their glasses ever so lightly.

"What are we toasting?" Lindsay was teasing her.

"Toasts are for celebration," Joanne's voice challenged.

"And what shall we honor?" Lindsay countered, moving one step closer.

"How about 'Here's to missing the party'?"

"I'll drink to that." Lindsay put her drink down. Her cobalt-blue eyes were so piercing Joanne suddenly felt lost. This was new, this commanding presence, this wanting to capture someone she wanted so badly.

Lindsay walked to Joanne's side, removed her martini glass and, after the first kiss, the rest was simple. Very simple.

It gave Joanne goose bumps to think of it now, two years later. The draw Lindsay had, the lure of her provocative insouciance. It was something she didn't much like to dwell on. It frightened her. That Lindsay could shatter her well-cultivated control by simply taking away what had by now become a guarded possession.

Lindsay was the first and only person who moved her to feel something beyond two bodies meshing. She hadn't known what she had been missing in those earlier heated, soulless exchanges. It was more than Lindsay being the embodiment of what she adored in women—perfect feminine strength. It was the duality of wanting to break through both Lindsay's facade and her own. That Lindsay would be forced to crack by the potency of their exchange. And that was precisely the hook. Lindsay was the only lover she had ever had who didn't want her more than she wanted them. It terrified her. But there was something unusually redeeming in that insecurity, almost exalting, satisfying finally her desire to need.

She thought about that need now, the candle flames taunting her as the smoke twirled blithely from the half-burned stalks. Ruins now. It was ten and Lindsay still hadn't called.

Joanne poured herself another glass of wine.

lat affect was the term for it. For when you felt nothing. No, not even that. Less than nothing. Although when Samantha thought deeply about what that might feel like, every corner she turned got a little darker, the images more vague, caught in the eternal conundrum. How could you feel nothing? All levels of nothing were something. There simply were no words for it.

Error in thinking is what Robert called it. "Stinkin' thinkin'," they called it in the program. She'd heard her father refer to it time and again. She called it meandering and useless. But she had nothing better to do, sitting at the red light on her way home from Jerra's. Her next job wouldn't start for a week.

Three years ago she would have given up half her library, her old book collection, crinkle-paged volumes the size of a cigarette case, aged and deliciously musty, for the Janet Myers account. It wasn't just the money, although it was nice to see the teller's eyes widen momentarily as she deposited the embarrassingly large retainer in her checking account. This was the breakout client. This was wealth so sickening you couldn't turn away from it, no matter how revolting it got. This was where she had the opportunity to reach a whole new level of clientele, their resources the gift to her creative spirit. The sky was the limit. Except she had overlooked one small point. Money did not grant taste. It simply granted the luxury not to have it.

"Maybe I wasn't cut out to be a designer," Samantha told Jerra after their third afternoon in a row of coffee breaks. "I take it too personally."

"Bullshit. You're one of the best in this town." Jerra was her dearest friend and firmly established as the leading furniture designer in Seattle, so she could say those words and make them sound convincing.

"My reputation has been destroyed."

"Look, you yanked all the press . . . the word about town is the only thing that's responsible for that bloody atrocity on Bainbridge is Janet Myers and that bloody art cretin that wriggles around after her." Jerra puffed her cigarillo, looking incredibly handsome and sophisticated while doing it. Very few women could get away with smoking cigars, Samantha thought. Jerra, with her dark Indian complexion, her tall angular stature and still faintly British accent from her Delhi childhood upbringing, was one of them. Jerra continued to concentrate on fabric swatches. "You could always say it was your Madonna excursion."

"Great." Samantha bent over the fabric-wand, fiddled about with it.

"You know, Sam, I love you and all, but if you don't let me get my work done there's going to be two out-of-work depressed designers on our hands. And I think at least one of us should stay on solid ground."

And, of course, she was right. Samantha had spent the last three weeks there grinding away the hours until it was time to get back to the house to cook dinner. She made a menu each morning, elaborate and demanding, so she could waste time running from the health food store to Spinelli's for fresh bread and pasta. Produce, fresh salmon fillets from the Pike Place Market, sometimes as many as seven stops, which roughly brought her up to midday. Then she'd go through the mail. Had picked up on a sort of stream-of-consciousness correspondence again with old friends she hadn't spoken to in years. Would make some tea, browse through magazines and the daily paper. After that it was time to head to Jerra's.

She played wife. A contemporary food gatherer. A fuel-injected version of her foremothers, zipping about in her Saab, a Chopin CD slipped into the player. It was all so civilized. She wondered distractedly how a haggard cavewoman would have felt if she had but experienced one simple luxury while she concentrated on survival.

Today survival had become a state of mind. Progress had made culture so divinely rich with luxury, ease, sweetness of life, that the only thing one had to survive was the living of it. The guilt-ridden blasphemy of whining. The not going insane. Which was nowhere near her vicinity, unlike situational melancholia, ostensibly hidden between other dreadful sounding disorders in the almighty book of DSM-III diagnostic dysfunction. Or so Robert had informed her.

"It's natural," he had said the night before as they lay in bed reading. Only she wasn't reading. She was simply staring, and he noticed. "You had what you thought was an opportunity of a lifetime . . . your big break. Not only did it turn sour on you, but it opened up a shift in your values."

Robert was her very own prognosticator. His minor in college had been psychology and he maintained a very active interest in it still. She wondered what had made him choose business as a major, but as it turned out his understanding of the human psyche had served him well. He was not only one of the most successful entrepreneurs in Seattle, he was also the nicest. Genuine. He really cared about people. And that's what she adored about him.

Robert was that rarest of breeds: a good man. Which only amplified what she considered her most glaring professional and personal failure, the Janet Myers debacle. No matter how much he tried to persuade her otherwise, she relentlessly held to the belief that she should have known from the moment Janet Myers barged through her office door it would spell disaster.

Robert encouraged her to take time off; he was supportive, caring, always willing to lend an ear. So her life, with the exception of this one small professional blunder, was, by all appearances, nothing less than grand. And when she didn't honor it as such, she felt guilty. And shameful. But there was more to it than that. Like a midlife crisis, only she was about twenty years early. At some point—soon would be good—she was going to have to deal with it. So that walking into the office, paperwork and bills stacked a foot high, did not give her the shakes. So that listening to her clients' whiny messages, unattended like abandoned children, did not sicken her.

◆ ◆ ◆

Finished with the prelims for Earlsheart, Lindsay rested her head against the drafting table. She heard her watch ticking faintly, measuring the units of time that controlled the rest of the universe but of which she was rarely aware. She would get up, make it to the bed in her alcove. Soon. Very soon.

Sleep was trench warfare when she got to this point. Every few moments the earth felt as if it were falling from underneath her and she didn't know if she was awake or simply dreaming she was awake. She felt removed from her physical self.

Of course, when she was at work, she was there. Focused. Concrete. At one. But when she removed herself, walked to the other side of the room for a cup of coffee, her motion became that of a moonwalker, precarious, not quite certain when she might float away, where she might land. She roused herself and stood up. Stiff. "God, what a grandma," she remarked to the shadows as she walked in slow motion to the alcove. It appeared very narrow. She had drunk too much coffee. It often gave her this sense of spatial disorientation.

She dumped her body upon the bed and was asleep within seconds. As she dozed, she danced between planes of reality, not quite here. Or there. Then had the dream. The dream of lines. And when she woke, startled, the only face she remembered was Julie Bracken's. What had made her think of her? After all these years.

Miss Bracken, the new art teacher who arrived halfway through her senior year of high school. Miss Bracken, everyone's favorite. Thin, tall, engaging, not quite beautiful but with an enthusiasm that made her brown eyes incite everything they touched. She was too exciting—breathtaking actually—to be a teacher. She had no business being there, encouraging creativity and wild abandon, gesturing zealously with a paintbrush or stick of chalk above her head. Everyone loved her. But for Lindsay it was more.

It did not occur to her that the long hours she spent in class, staring, taking in every movement, no matter how slight, so that she might replay it later while sitting in the dark silence of her father's den, were anything other than keen fascination. It did not occur to her, as she remembered every detail of Miss Bracken's face, that the feelings she harbored were unseemly or unnatural. She simply adored her and there couldn't be anything wrong with something that felt so good.

Miss Bracken took notice of Lindsay, recognizing her extraordinary talent, excited by her potential. She told Lindsay one afternoon, as Lindsay cleaned her paintbrushes, that she had been very like her, and Lindsay could tell by the way Miss Bracken's eyes held hers that she spoke from the heart.

Yes, Miss Bracken spoke from the heart. And Lindsay responded with her own. For Lindsay had fallen in love as only first love can be. No one had ever shown her so much concern, and with such delicate and tender care. She worshipped the air Miss Bracken breathed, thought every word from her mouth was an epiphany, every gesture entrancing and liquid.

For the first time, Lindsay talked about subjects other than design and architecture, and she would listen intently to Miss Bracken as she extolled the virtues of a whole other world waiting outside the confines of Jefferson High; a world, Miss Bracken gravely insisted, for which she must be prepared.

It was Miss Bracken who helped pick out the best architectural universities in the Northwest; Miss Bracken who defined a sense of style to fit her unique image, convinced her that presentation was as important as performance. It was Miss Bracken who foretold ignorance and hypocrisy, and cautioned acceptance of the power structure while holding on to belief in herself and her gifts. And it was Miss Bracken, the day after graduation, who opened her arms and her heart to their desperate hunger for each other. For Lindsay, it was the birth of physical and emotional ecstasy, and for Miss Bracken, the culmination of many hours of desire.

They spent the entire summer making love in Julie's small apartment, long afternoons idling through each other's bodies and thoughts. It was the first time Lindsay had ever been touched, physically and psychically. Her body was in overdrive, her senses without limitation. She found herself listless and lazy when confronted with an evening holed up beside her father.

Her abstract doodles only fooled her father insofar as guessing the object of her affections. He was happy Lindsay had found a young man. More importantly he saw a new element to her work: passion. But he also couldn't help but fear for her; she was so naive, running out the door, whistling the theme from *Picnic*, Julie's favorite movie.

Wrapped in the sweet gauze of bliss, Lindsay had expected, quite naturally, that all the plans that she and Julie had made would change. That she would remain in Spokane as her lover and attend the community college, and they would live out their days in eternal love.

"I would never have presumed to lay claim to anything other than what we've had." It was two weeks before the new school year. Julie's words shot like ice pellets through her heart. "Furthermore I don't want any more."

Lindsay didn't understand. She couldn't grasp simple words. It was as if Julie spoke a foreign language, and Lindsay needed to hear the rejection over and over again. Lindsay said she wouldn't go. She loved her. But Julie was firm, and the more insistent Lindsay became the more detached Julie got until small disagreements caused heartbreaking arguments, tirades grew increasingly bitter, and finally Julie's gentle eyes turned black. Shattering her illusions, she informed Lindsay she was leaving the next day for her annual visit back east. And, she continued indifferently, she expected to find Lindsay gone, settled at the U of O for her freshman year, when she returned.

Lindsay felt the hope diminish and then expire, her heart battered into a mangled machine. It pumped blood, but not life.

She remembered her father the day her mother walked out, and how he seemed to wander about in a dense fog. Now she felt the same. Nothing had shape. She ambled through motions with no definition. After three days the blur that had become her landscape defined itself into clear actions; pack bags, leave town. She said good-bye to her father and Mrs. Gardner and left the only home she had ever known.

Once settled in Eugene she slipped as easily as her father had, years ago, into a landscape filled with lines and angles. It passed the long and isolated hours and nothing could hurt her there. The more she worked and studied, the less her heart ached. Soon it was filled with a vacant emptiness, and the image of Miss Bracken's crooked smile disappeared into the sketches before her, until it was gone altogether.

When she took the time, she found the city and college opened vistas for her she never could have imagined. Miss Bracken had been right. It was an entirely new world. She roamed the streets, studied the natural architecture, spent hours reading in smoky cafés, began to make acquaintances.

Lindsay preferred isolation to the raucous party life of her fellow students. Those who were tenacious finally made a dent, and she created real friendships with only three. Eric and Mark were lovers and fellow design students. The three of them were bound by their minority and their unlimited passion for architecture. They were joined by Sally, a down-to-earth psych major, fifteen years everyone's senior, who had finished raising a child and was now reentering the halls of academia.

Lindsay and Sally shared an apartment and three years of midnight conversations, bottles of wine, heartache and successes; in short, life in a seamless arrangement. Sally adored Lindsay and found her an inspiration to womanhood, and in Sally's warm and soft, plodding nature, Lindsay found the mother she never had.

A new completeness to Lindsay made her dark mystery even more compelling, and in very little time she became well known on campus as the brilliant eccentric with flair.

She was under keen observation from a small, but growing, collective of women, regarded as the feminist contingent. Lindsay was unaware she was under surveillance until she became lovers with the sandy-haired Heather, an art student devoted to Indian jewelry, tarot cards and LSD. They met at an art exhibit, were drawn to the same painting and stood in silent appreciation for close to an hour. They decided on coffee and, soon after, retired to Heather's cramped studio apartment to make love on a dilapidated futon draped with tie-dyed banners and gauzy scarves. It was not the gentle and emotionally drenched lovemaking she experienced with Miss Bracken, but the collision of two ions unable to control their magnetic attraction, exploding on impact and then repelling with opposite energy.

Although their only link was sheer animal attraction, they remained lovers for almost two years. Mark and Eric found Heather entertaining, "so utterly beyond the beyond," they would tease Lindsay good-naturedly. But Sally had no patience for her pre–New Age esoterica, and insisted, on more than one occasion, that there were women out there dying to take Heather's place with whom Lindsay might have at least more than one thing in common.

But that commonality, their wonderfully self-assured, unpretentious sex, allowed Lindsay to remain absorbed in her work while Heather immersed herself in various intense and revealing drug-induced trips. One of those finally dissolved their union when Heather experienced a visitation from the Planet Xzado (Heather's unrelenting belief in the Ouija board at work), directing her to Nui Jersy (again the Ouija board) to wait further instruction as to who her real parents were (theoretically Xzadians).

Lindsay suspected that her parents were the very ancient and conservative couple in New Jersey who had invited her to join them for Thanksgiving last year, but trying to convince Heather of this was beside the point. She put Heather on a dirty Greyhound bus and began her year-end project a little sooner than she had planned.

Tense and restless without their physical contact, she rapidly fell into casual liaisons with a succession of women, though none of these affairs lasted more than six months—and usually less than a few weeks. They always culminated in angry words: she didn't care, she was unfeeling, all that mattered to her was her goddamn studies.

Six months before the architectural boards, Lindsay opted for celibacy, hoping the reduction in drama might outweigh the benefits of release. This corollary proved true, freeing her to work even more and think less about where she was supposed to be, or to have been hours ago. Her initial physical frustration began to go unnoticed as she threw her heart and soul into preparing for the infamous finals.

Only twenty percent passed. The two eight-hour days of intense work and grueling multiples left most depleted, drained and devastated. The building design task was a mini-market with restricted square footage, so it was necessary to show efficiency of space as well as proper design technique. Seven people walked out, one threw up and another passed out.

When Lindsay completed the exam, she moved with an exaggerated calm, a weightlessness she hadn't felt in months. She returned to her room, threw herself on her bed, and masturbated until tears soaked her cheeks. She had never felt so empty in her life. There was no sense of accomplishment. Just a feeling of termination. She curled into a fetal position and slept for twenty hours.

Of those who had completed the exam, her score was the highest, her design the most innovative. She was hired as a junior designer at Sandruski, Peters, Ingers and Talbot in Portland, which she and other colleagues not so fondly referred to as SPIT. When the firm discovered she was a woman, she was quietly transferred to the drafting room, where her unique strengths were not sought after but challenged. Some of the other junior draftsmen were outright rude, but mostly, as they sat with double scotches at Atwater's, they merely grumbled ugly insinuations about who she banged to make promotion after promotion. And the knowing glances and smarmy grins only worsened after she was named to work as one of three captains on a high-profile team starting a large government project.

She endured the wisecracks and gibes graciously enough, but at night she would crouch wearily on the sofa in her small, dark apartment and wonder how she had ever been transported into this world of intolerance. She would phone Sally: "This is worse than school. Where the hell is the women's movement?"

"Obviously nowhere near your chosen field."

"Sal, I can't believe this." And she couldn't, as she sat staring into the dark. Her beloved art form mired by the most chauvinistic assholes she had ever encountered. "They're Neanderthals."

"And?" This was news to Sally?

"They spew lofty bullshit about better dwellings for mankind, when all they're interested in is the corner office on the fifteenth floor. The money. The commission. There isn't one person I have found in this damn company who gives a shit about architecture." Her voice lost its heat. "I thought it would be different."

"It will never be different. What's important is that you are."

But Lindsay refused to believe it. Instead she battled the immovable powers. Disheartened, she quickly dropped her vows of celibacy and again involved herself in a string of nefarious affairs. She led a desultory life until her internship was complete, at which point her father died of a heart attack.

She returned home to bury him, dismissed Dr. Baine's oratory on the results of overwork. She crumpled up the messages from Julie Bracken. She spent one night with Mrs. Gardner, stoically strong, as Mrs. Gardner held her close, her own tear-rimmed eyes trying to reach the child she once knew, now grown and remote.

Lindsay returned to Portland immediately after the funeral and put the house up for sale through her father's attorney. She felt a dryness in her throat for days, wondered if she was coming down with a cold. An unrealness permeated the objects around her. If she thought about her father, the tightness at her throat, the nausea in her stomach and the heaviness in her chest threatened extinction. It brought the same dizzying array of chaos and horror she had experienced with Miss Bracken. So she denied it.

She began a new structure of incredible scope, which would later become her first commissioned piece and put her name on the map as a "bold and innovative designer of the high-rise." She drafted sketch upon sketch, isolated for days, plans strewn about her apartment until her father's death faded into a distant and obscure memory.

egan walked quickly to keep warm, her head bent into her coat. She had a mission. Get to work. Do not look at the angled tinted windows that lined the stores downtown, take care not to catch her passing reflection, but above all, pass the bakery. Her eyes had been trained to follow the pattern of the tile on the floor, the cracks on sidewalks. She could tell you what every carpet looked like in every architectural firm in this city. From thirteen on she had taken great pains to turn away from mirrors, large sheets of glass, windows of cars—any manmade material, in short, that would offer up direct contact with the image that would shatter her mood, her thoughts. Her world.

Megan smelled the bakery before she actually saw it. Wafts of sweet-glazed confection filled the still darkened street. It beckoned her, as it always did. And Monday mornings were the worst. Too close to the weekend that started Saturday mornings at Mount Tabor Café, gazing at the short stack, drenched in syrup, the butter not quite yet melted, tastebuds savoring the slightly salted mixture wed to the cloying sweetness of thick maple syrup. Two eggs over easy and three wedges of Canadian bacon gaped back at her. And she knew, of course, that when the feast was over, she would walk the streets of Hawthorne, out of breath, bloated from fullness. More than that, however, she knew that when she caught her whalish reflection in the mirrors of the quaint antique and specialty stores, all she would see would be the puffy eyes of her own desperation. No image of lovers laughing giddily over a trinket in the window. No vain self-appraisals. Only one reflection would shimmer there, a phantom specter reminding her of her loneliness. At that point she would invariably head for the video store, rent old movies, and phone Snag.

Before Snag had fallen head over heels in love with Jared, Megan at least had the benefit of laughing hysterically over his uncanny imitations of his favorite movie queens in their most outrageous roles, prancing about the apartment staging their most melodramatic scenes. Then Snag would treat her to an incredible feast of pasta drenched in cream-based sauces, make the most divine garlic bread, and whip up a chocolate amaretto mousse for dessert. But he never gained an ounce.

Saturdays Megan almost believed she was having fun. But Sundays took their toll. Castigation, self-flagellation were her penance for the sins of the past week, and she would bolster herself by planning for the start of her Monday morning diet, vacillating between hope that this time it would be different and despair over the sameness of it all.

And this Monday morning she stood, once again, in the very line she vowed to pass. Fragile moments imprinted her forehead as she coped with the delicacy of indecision, the familiar dialogue battling in her head. *Ohhh . . . yes the deliciously sticky cinnamon roll . . .* It's a gooey lump of sugar. *Fresh out of the oven.* No. Two nonfat bran muffins. *Please . . . let's make it at least a banana nut muffin. Carrot cake muffin with that divine cream cheese frosting.* Do you have any idea how many calories are in cream cheese? *Ahhhh, bear claws. Love bear claws.* No! Are you deaf? *Chocolate eclairs*—Don't even consider it. Chocolate eclairs are for sinners and bulimics. Come on, Megan, just get the nonfat muffins. *Donut holes?* I don't care what you do. OK, *maybe a few—three donut holes—before lunch.* Go ahead. Stay fat the rest of your life. *Then maybe a maple bar and cinnamon pull-aparts for after dinner.* Get real. Instead of dinner.

Her conflict rose, the vacillating voices in her head got louder in proportion to the diminishing line. There was no such thing as being "sorta off" in the black-and-white mind of diet resolution. She would just make a clean start the next day. After all, the body can only absorb so many calories in a given day, and if you've absorbed them already, why fight the numbers?

But the nagging never ceased. Her distorted conscience screamed at her from the back of her skull, a skinny spy infiltrating from her mother's camp. Her mother's brilliant eyes would glare out of a gaunt, bony-edged face. How could she? How could she . . . when she had a life most girls would kill for—the new apartment, a great job? Her mother, who had devoted an entire life to hiding food from her, smothering her with dictates and screaming tirades about fat cells as she shimmered ecstatically in her devotion to thin, a woman who was so emaciated and hollow she was brittle to the touch.

And while the battle raged Megan dedicated her adolescence to filling up the stark emptiness left by her mother's screaming charges gobbling popcorn and Sugar Babies in empty matinees, stuffing twelve-packs of Dunkin' Donuts and stockpiling her secret hoard from the cafeteria's vending machine.

So now when the glazed confections stared back at her, they became ammunition for the battle of old, and she would rationalize a jelly donut as a treat for Snag, and the maple bar for Lindsay, knowing full well the pastry would never touch her lips. To this cache Megan would add two almond croissants, an apple tart, and three peanut butter cookies in case anything rocked her world. And if nothing did, she could, with very little effort, manage to create that particular effect. If only by making a call to her mother.

"I don't trust those nonfat muffins, do you?" It came from behind her. She hadn't realized he was addressing her, until she turned and saw the boyish eyes that were encased in a bearded forty-five-year-old baby face smiling directly into her own. He had longer eyelashes than Snag.

"Uh . . . I guess not." Megan wasn't sure what he wanted from her.

His skin was pale, but pleasant, and his lips wore a youthful grin. "I mean, what mysterious ingredient makes them nonfat?"

"What makes them nonfat is they don't have any fat in them!" snapped the counter woman, ever weary of the question.

"I guess we've been informed!" He winked at her. And then he offered his hand. "My name's Ryan Morgan. I've seen you a couple of times." He shuffled back and forth, trying to stay warm. "I don't mean to be pushy or anything, but if you'd ever like to have coffee," and handed her his business card. He was a freelance technician for computer video consultation and installation. "My schedule's my own. Flexible," he added, because her expression said she didn't understand any of this.

She held the card stupidly. She wasn't used to being accosted by strangers, especially men. "Uh, well, I'm pretty busy . . . with work and all."

"I'm sorry. I didn't mean it as a come-on. Really."

Megan smiled nervously, ordered the cinnamon pull-aparts, two eclairs, two bear claws, and five donut holes. "For the office," she said to Ryan, and then felt sickened and humiliated that she would try to explain that which could not be explained to a perfect stranger.

The donut holes were gone by the time she got to the office. She wiped the glazed flakes from her chin as she got off the elevator. Lindsay was there. She could always feel when Lindsay had stayed the night. She sighed as she put the pastries on her desk, walked to Lindsay's office, knowing as well as she knew the patterns of her own sickness what she would find behind the door.

One dim light combated the early-morning sun over the drafting table and, as she tiptoed around the partition to the alcove, there was Lindsay, balled up, still in her clothes, a blanket half-covering her body. Megan sighed. She bent over and unlaced Lindsay's shoes, gently slipped them off. Lindsay mumbled in protest, but then returned to exhausted slumber as Megan pulled the blanket over her.

◆ ◆ ◆

"I wanted to show you the sketches—make sure I'm on the right track." Lindsay handed Sondra the drawings, leaned over her shoulder ready to answer any questions. Megan had woken her up a little over an hour ago. She'd jumped in the shower, mentally prepared herself for the day. When she presented herself to her new client, she was as fresh as someone who had slumbered eight hours under an eiderdown quilt.

The heady blend of European perfume, coconut oil and lingering traces of tobacco woke Lindsay's senses. Potently exotic and enticing scents. At odds with the woman who sat so self-consciously with the cup of untouched coffee in her fine, small-boned hands; nicely shaped calves crossed at the ankle, a delicate femininity encased in fragility.

Sondra could feel the cross-examination of Lindsay's eyes. Her mind went blank. She was experiencing once again that crazy-all-over feeling that would sweep through her, rendering her inchoate. The sweat prickled nastily from underneath her arms, making a sticky trail down her sides. Calm yourself, she thought. *Concentrate. Focus on the drawings.*

And when she did, she saw that Lindsay's sketches were renderings of her very own thought patterns, an animation of lines only imagined, dreams come to life. She was captivated by Lindsay's uncanny precision, the modern elegance melded to the grandeur of the space, infused by the warmth of an era gone by. It was beyond what she had imagined, beyond what she knew she wanted.

"All this and Christmas too," she sighed. It was more to herself than to Lindsay. Then she looked up at her. "They're beautiful."

Lindsay smiled. Warmly.

"I can't believe it." Sondra felt herself stammering, not out of nervousness, but awe. "I can't believe what you've created. You must be psychic or something."

Lindsay's grin touched her eyes now. The professional side relaxed and the artist emerged.

"I love them all." Sondra sighed earnestly. "It's . . . it's like you were seeing right into my mind."

"It's all from your notes."

"And your interpretation." Sondra picked up the sketches and studied them again, lingering on the kitchen. "I suppose it's because I love it so much. I've always known Earlsheart could be something grand . . . magical." Sondra laughed at herself. "I guess I've been relying so much on an emotional concept I didn't think it could be anything like this."

"So . . . when can I get the floor plans?" Lindsay didn't want to waste any time. The process was begun. She was galvanized by Sondra's enthusiasm and knew it was right, and her vision crystallized in that moment. In the next months her subconscious would relay it to physical reality.

"I left them on your secretary's desk," Sondra responded. Lindsay jumped to retrieve them.

When she returned she rolled them out on the table. She gently unfurled the blueprints, her strong hands flat and smooth, almost caressing. Her movements were not hurried, but there was a graceful urgency to them. And as Sondra watched, she saw in a single moment the physical transformation of Lindsay's eyes as they bled from cobalt blue to a dark gray, their glimmer flare to a torch, an almost discomforting brilliance. The lines that defined her face deepened and merged with the intractable set of her jaw, her countenance sculpted like clay. Almost as if she were witnessing rigor mortis setting in. It was singular focus and it went beyond unease. It was frightening.

Lindsay did not flinch until Sondra's movements reminded her that another person was in her presence. And when she shifted her concentration from her work, her face restructured itself to the image of Lindsay that Sondra felt safe with, more at ease, relaxed. "This is great. I can have them done in a week or two."

Sondra laughed. "It's just that you'd think these were for you." She indicated the drawings.

"Well. They are in a way." Sondra did not turn as Lindsay held her gaze.

◆ ◆ ◆

"You're late!"

Joanne had opened the door before Lindsay could finish unlocking it, eyes narrowed, angry, on fire. Lindsay walked in, slowly set down her briefcase.

"God damn it, Lindsay. What is this, the third night in a row? . . . No, fourth. But who's counting?" Joanne was furious. "For Christ's sakes, why the fuck . . . just once, can't you call?"

"Joanne. I'm sorry—"

"Fuck apology. Not accepted." Joanne marched into the kitchen, belted a shot of scotch and turned to face her. "So . . . what is it this time? A new client? An old client? A client that needs you and only you to design their shitter? You wonder how the rest of the world got built before you came along."

"Joanne, please. I was working with Sondra Pinchot."

"Oh, new slant. Sexually confused client."

Lindsay sighed, her jaws set tight.

"So. What's the angle, so to speak, on this one?"

"No 'angle.' "

"You seem to be highly motivated by her piddly-shit little beach house."

"In case it's slipped your memory, Joanne, you were the one that insisted we meet." Lindsay took off her blazer, then stopped, caught short by Joanne's ardent temper, which brought out the worst and the best of her; exciting, wildly arousing. She went into the kitchen, came up from behind Joanne and put her hands on her shoulders. "Why don't we just eat now?"

"Because dinner was over two hours ago." Joanne shrugged out of her embrace. "Because this spinach soufflé looks like a special effect from *Aliens*." She took the shriveled soufflé from the oven. "Because I only have the stomach for scotch." She heaved it into the kitchen sink, the glassware thudding into fragmented chunks. "And I don't give a fuck if you starve to death." The deflated remains lay splattered across the counter. "Presentation is everything." Joanne stormed into the living room.

"OK, Joanne. What's going on?" Lindsay followed her. "This isn't about a ruined soufflé. How many times do I have to tell you I can't be on a schedule. . . . It doesn't work that way for me."

"What does work for you?" Joanne turned, implication heavy in her words. She poured another scotch. "No, don't tell me. Let me guess. The withdrawn-blonde thing really pulls you in. Doesn't it?

The challenge of digging underneath her paisley personality—oooh, what lurks under that vapid demeanor?—"

"You know damn well I'm not—"

"'Not' what, Lindsay? What are you 'not' doing?"

"Shit, Joanne, if I had time for it, don't you think it would be with you?"

"You know, Linds, I wish it were her. God, if only it were someone else I could deal with it. I could rip whoever it was to shreds . . . or manipulate a way back into your affections. But I'm forced to recite the oldest housewife cliché in the book." Joanne returned to supercilious calm. "Your mistress is your work. Mistress, hell, your everything."

"Joanne." They both heard the quiet desperation in Lindsay's voice. Joanne approached her, musky perfume assaulting Lindsay's senses. Lindsay didn't want to fight. "Come on. Let's not do this."

"No? Then what did you have in mind?" Joanne sipped her scotch, grimaced. "We've gone round this every which way from Sunday, and at first, as you know, it was fine. Really. I didn't care that you needed that goddamn office like you were snorting it up your nose. But I have to admit I've become slightly attached to having this relationship be more than the mad scramble of two cats in heat." Joanne paused, about to take another sip, then set her drink down. "It's hell on my ego."

"I've never made excuses about my work, Joanne." Why was she always having the same conversation, over and over? "Oh . . . I know. You've got it all down. Made the speech in the beginning so you're cleared. Well, fuck your speech."

"You know . . ." Lindsay intimated, "we did agree . . . you are free to get your needs met elsewhere."

"I'm only human, after all." Joanne's direct hit stopped Lindsay short. They rarely got to this point in their well-rehearsed lines. She had been aware of Joanne's absences, but they never spoke of them. To hear it verbalized made her feel awkward and strangely nauseous.

Joanne saw Lindsay's discomfort and could only tolerate it for a moment. She rushed to her, took Lindsay's face in both her hands and kissed her fully on the mouth, her soft lips persuasive, caressing her, easing away any pain. "It's only you, Lindsay. Only you," she said between kisses that grew more passionate.

Joanne drew Lindsay triumphantly to the couch, eased her upon it and then herself upon Lindsay. She kissed her, hands upon her face, Lindsay captivated by Joanne's skilled control, her tongue dancing a prison of desire upon her body, slowly tempting, then deeply inside her until Lindsay thought she would split open from the sensation of Joanne's tongue, deft and delicate, seducing her further inside herself to a place she could not reach without Joanne.

They came together with an angry intensity that penetrated their own separate pain, if only for a moment, then lay quietly for a long time, each in an aftermath of passion light-years apart from the other.

Later, Joanne turned to Lindsay and caressed her body with long teasing strokes. She wanted Lindsay at that moment more than she ever had. Lindsay was still hers. She wasn't about to let that insipid creature get anywhere near her. She would do whatever it took. She wouldn't give up without a fight. Not against person or thing. She began to massage Lindsay's shoulders and then her thighs. She leaned over, trailed her tongue lightly over Lindsay's buttocks. Lindsay moaned in invitation. Joanne burrowed her face into Lindsay's swollen flesh and whispered huskily, "I'm stuck on you, you little shit."

he night she met Robert had been one of the most extraordinary in her life. It wasn't so much the falling. Falling is always extraordinary. It had more to do with the events leading up to the dive, and finding herself at the end of them seeing no other alternative but to continue.

It was a rainy night, as the rain can fall only in Seattle, and Samantha thought she might be coming down with the flu, or her period. Take your pick. A blind date had been arranged and she had wished she'd just bagged the invitation. But there coursed through her that small spark of hope—the infinitesimal possibility—that one of these blind dates might actually turn out to be the magnet.

The one she knew was on the other side of the globe, making world peace, or traveling on business in Japan, who on the fifth leg of his journey would be stopping for a merger in Seattle. He'd stay at The Alexis. Saturday morning he'd take in a few sights, wander lazily through the waterfront, wearing a cardigan his mother had knit, from the visit to his tight-knit family last Christmas. Sapphire blue with gray flecks, perhaps. Stylish. And he'd be buying fruit from the fresh fruit vendor as she was carrying the lilacs she'd just bought from the old Greek at the flower cart right next door. They'd bump into one another. Oh, so sorry, how clumsy of me . . . here, let me help you.

She jammed on the brakes. The car swerved and hit the curb in the sidewalk. She jolted to a stop. Shit! She sat numbly, then jumped from the car, made sure there was no damage. She was sopped instantly. No damage, except a dent to her feeble self-confidence.

She was still shaken by the time she got to the party. She asked for the bathroom, and once there saw her dampened hair, her soak-blotched dress, and decided she would tell Janice, the matchmaker, she had to go home.

"Don't be silly. So you're damp. This is Seattle." No problem. Janice could afford to be cavalier. "Come on. You've got to meet Tim. He's heading for Germany tomorrow and he'll probably meet some little dumpling over there who actually knows how to cook. You've only got tonight to impress the hell out of him."

No pressure. That's what Samantha really found enticing. Janice brought her back a double scotch, which Samantha downed straight away not only to warm her shivering body but to fight off the anxiety rising at her throat.

A few minutes later a bedraggled Samantha entered the throng of Seattle sleek. Trying to smooth her frizzy hair, she was confident Mr. Tim would be running off to meet his new hausfrau tomorrow. Not that she cared. She was feeling a mild buzz as she traipsed through the crowd.

"Ahhhhh, there you are, Samantha." Janice grabbed her by the elbow and thrust her in front of Tim's lanky, six-foot-four frame.

"Hi," she said lamely to his Adam's apple.

"Hey there. Uh, Janice's been telling me about your new design firm. That's great." Tim was innocuously handsome, had energy to spare, and was nowhere even vaguely near her type. Samantha nabbed a glass of passing champagne. She knew better, but what the hell. The evening was such a disaster anyway she had no desire to be present for it.

"It's a full moon," Janice implied, glancing from Samantha to Tim. "I love full moons."

"Yeah, well, I don't believe in full moons," Tim responded. And he didn't look as if he did, either. No doubt he would be a pragmatic, energetic lover, expert at condoms but not with the cosmos.

"But you must," came a voice from behind Janice. And that's when she first saw Robert, lean, fit, strong and capable. "They stir everything up, create havoc, inspire romance. It isn't just a silly myth, you know."

"Exactly." Janice felt vindicated.

"Well, you romantics go slay the world tonight. I have to get up early." Tim checked his watch. "Uh, Robert, this is Samantha—I'm sorry, I forgot your last name."

"Pinchot." Samantha was mesmerized by Robert. His eyes were deep green, sparkling. A black turtleneck emphasized his strong jawline. He had a unique handsomeness almost bordering on fragile, brought out by the thinning brown hair. But what captured her fascination was his sweater: sapphire blue with gray flecks.

She returned his intense gaze, then felt the eyes of Angela, Robert's date, who slithered from across the room, zeroing in like a social torpedo. She put her arm through Robert's. "Our reservations. We shouldn't be late. You in, Tim?"

"No. I've got to get an early start." That was fine by Samantha. Since they were theoretically a date for the evening, if he bailed out, she could go home and soak in a hot tub.

"Oh come on. It'll be fun," Janice insisted. "You can catch all the sleep you need on that transatlantic flight."

And before Samantha could gracefully retreat, Robert took her hand and said, "Come on. You two can catch a ride with Angela and me."

And so it was Samantha found herself shoved between Tim and Janice in the back of Angela's BMW, which she drove like a maniac to the restaurant where they were seated boy, girl, boy, odd girl out. Samantha excused herself to freshen up.

Angela joined her on purpose. "If you're wondering what the hell is going on—"

"Well, actually, I'm not sure what I'm doing here."

Angela flipped open her compact, even though a mirror the size of a mural stood right in front of her. "It goes something like this. I'm here with Robert. Yes, I'm married. But if one intends to stay so for fucking eternal eternaldom, then one must be realistic. I can tell he likes you . . . so if you don't mind, maybe you can cut your evening short. If you get my drift."

Samantha didn't even attempt fixing the disarray she had become. This had now officially gone off the scale of blind-dates-from-hell. She was in a time warp, a blatantly transparent mid-fifties teen movie. Being single in this decade couldn't possibly be this painful. But here they were in a convoluted Frankie and Annette plot twist. They simply had better clothes, faster cars and more sophisticated menus.

"Excuse me," Samantha snapped, brushed past Angela and walked right out the door.

Two days later a bouquet of spring flowers arrived with the note: "As Oscar Wilde said, 'Love is mutual misunderstanding.' I think the same can be said of blind dates. May I make it up to you?" Which redeemed Tim momentarily—until she realized the flowers were from Robert.

She called him. His office was five blocks away. They settled on lunch. He was charming, funny and a gentleman, plus he apologized for Angela.

"You seem to be taking on the sins of the universe," Samantha said.

"No. I could just tell how miserable you were. How miserable everyone was. It couldn't have gotten much worse."

After a few bites of chicken salad: "So what's her story?"

"Angela wants to be an actress, but is a more successful model. We used her on some of our marketing campaigns." His voice got soft, as if an afterthought. "We dated."

"So you're involved."

"No." He laughed. "No. We are not involved."

They finished lunch, headed for safer subjects. He helped her with her coat and at the last minute, turned to her. "You need to get back to the office right away?"

"Not really."

"How 'bout a walk down by the pier?"

And she thought again about the sapphire-blue sweater with gray flecks.

Their courtship was brief but elegant. They dated two long months before they slept together. Robert, unlike most of the men Samantha had gone out with, seemed content with good-night kisses that grew gradually in duration and intensity. It was as if they both knew this relationship was going to be bigger, brighter, more complete than the others, and they were in no hurry to seal their physical attraction. They were busy exploring the two C's: compatibility and companionship. They both loved theater and movies, the beach; he was a wonderful cook; they could spend an entire Sunday scrounging estate sales, gallery hopping, window shopping. They dined at unusual restaurants; he probed gently with many questions. He was interested. Interesting. But the icing on the cake, the thing she probably adored more than anything, was his wonderful family—three brothers, a sister, loud and talkative and full of approval for her. His mother was everything she had dreamed about in the fantasy mother: loving, gentle, ruling the household with quiet humor. He got his good looks from his father, whose prime function appeared to be reading the paper and smoking his pipe. It was as though they had been lifted right out of a Norman Rockwell painting, and she loved every second of it.

And finally the night came. He walked her to her apartment, took her hand, the question in his eyes—not so much may he come inside, but had she seen enough to trust this was going to last. Samantha grasped his hand firmly and led him in. She had fallen in love with him, his family, his goodness, his spirit, and her body responded to all of it.

Six months later they found a cheerful three-bedroom bungalow. Samantha wasn't ready for the financial crunch the purchase entailed. Her business was new and in constant crisis. But Robert was well off, lent her money until she built a solid roster of clients, spent hours helping her with her business, found her a better attorney and a whiz accountant, and located the perfect spot for her office without lease payments that would bankrupt her.

She adored Robert for his help. He took charge and made her life simple. Their first year together she managed to bend her gratitude into desire, her appreciation rich and full, as they shared the twists and turns of fate together. She loved him. Deeply. She was certain she loved him. Was *in*—that preposition which made the world spin or stop—love with him.

"So what's the problem?"

"Who said there's a problem?" Samantha felt a familiar defensiveness around Jerra. Not only because her friend was older and wiser, but because Jerra's relationship with her husband, even with its unusual game rules, was by all appearances the most perfect coupledom on the planet. She knew they had their problems, but it was clear to anyone who spent three minutes around them how completely in love with each other they were, even after fifteen years of marriage.

"What makes you two work? I mean you have nothing in common."

"Oh no? We have everything in common," Jerra replied in that sage voice that made Samantha feel like a small child, shielded from the big bad world. It was Jerra she had interned for; Jerra who had become her mentor and then easily filled the place of best friend, confidante and ally. Jerra to whom she told everything, or as close to everything as she dared tell even herself.

"Like what? He's a welder. You're a designer. He's a sports fanatic, you're a ballet freak. He's—"

"Yes. He and I are different. Our exteriors have very little in common. But our souls? They dance to the same song. That . . . is where our commonality lies."

"Well, Robert and I have tons in common."

"Did I ever say you didn't?"

"No. It's just that, I don't know, I always feel like there's judgment around him. You don't like him."

"What's not to like? He's one of the most pleasant men I've ever met. He's extremely easy on the eyes. I like him fine." Jerra lit a cigar. "The question is, do you?"

But when Samantha returned to her work that day, the question repeated itself like a trite melody in her head. Of course she loved Robert. That wasn't even the question. But what was the question? And as time passed she realized that thinking about it got her nowhere, so she focused on her business, her friendship with Jerra, and on making a commitment to the wonderful man with whom she intended to spend the rest of her life.

But another part of her, the part she managed to successfully keep out of touch with, nagged at her. The sweet tension of that first year had been magical. And while nothing had really changed since then, she knew they would never recapture those moments built on story-book dreams. Could she perpetuate a myth they both approached with utter commitment: simply that they were in love and belonged with one another?

Samantha's business flourished. Each of Robert's successes outmeasured the last. Their lives were swaddled in comfort. They became the quintessential yuppies. But yuppies with consciences, Samantha reassured herself. They were politically active, involved in neighborhood functions, socially sought after, as not only one of the most attractive couples to grace Sunday garden parties, but because they were viewed as that truly unattainable ideal: soulmates.

She laughed at this in her quiet moments, bitter laughter. If they were soulmates, why was life so flat? She began to harbor a desire, willing it to come true, a wish that their commonness, their companionability, their respect for one another, their laughter would miraculously flow into an alchemy of passion. Their eyes would catch one another's and she would see him backlit in flames and she'd march bravely into the jaws of frenzied lust. This was on a good day, her days filled with soft contentment.

On a bad day their gentle and uncontroversial bliss would grate on her like a chafing wind. They rarely argued, and when they did, they did it right. They were evolved. They compromised. They owned their shit. They were everything one could hope to ask for in a relationship. Except for the one ingredient Samantha yearned for. Passion.

"But you always said it was the security and solidness you loved about Robert," Jerra reminded her over Sunday brunch, their girl time.

"I did. I do." Samantha poured herself more champagne.

"You can't have it both ways."

"Why? You do."

"Well, don't think we didn't have to work hard to get there," Jerra replied. "But then we started with the required ingredient."

"Which is?"

"For us it was balls-out lust."

"Well, I want both."

"Sam." Jerra smiled gently, but with a sly edge at the corners. "I know you want to rewrite thousands of years of poetry and literature, but what do you think great love is all about? Passion and security are diametrically opposed. They negate one another as fire does water, noise does silence, a thundercloud does a sunny day. The very nature of one eclipses the other."

"Go on." Samantha grinned. She loved Jerra's little speeches.

"Passion is spontaneous. Security is planned. Passion is combustible. Chaos. Pushing the envelope. Security is inert. Organized. About being safe."

The grin slid off Samantha's face. She was already tipsy but downed the remains of her champagne. "Well. I still want both."

"Well, when you find it"—Jerra's eyes were kind as she reached over and clasped Samantha's hand—"let me know. I'll alert the Muses."

ondra walked around the tarp-covered lumber that had been delivered two days ago, mottled with tide pools of shiny black. The rain had been relentless last week, slowing down the progress of Earlsheart's transformation, but now there was a break. Looking at the sun that gleamed through the center of a large cloud, she felt heartened.

She shook off her slicker as she entered the kitchen, poured herself some coffee, then made her way up to the bedroom, now converted into a temporary office. She wandered to the window, sipping quickly to warm herself, and watched two carpenters below. She never could understand how people worked outdoors, especially in this part of the country. She supposed the only way to adapt was to be indifferent.

Yes . . . that's how these rough he-men treated the weather. And her—with that infuriating and polite indifference. Her exchanges with the carpenters and foreman were formal and meaningless, nonsense chatter, the kind that gave women a bad name. But she couldn't think of what else to say to these gruff, beard-stubbled men. They were working for her but she always felt one down. Perhaps it was the conditioning of her generation to feel inadequate, even inferior. So unlike Lindsay.

These same men offered a variety of responses to Lindsay, but none were indifference. Regardless of circumstance, she was the one they went to for questions, suggestions, additions and complaints. She was, after all, the architect, Sondra reminded herself. But Sondra knew the crew viewed her, the owner, as merely a figurehead, not to be taken seriously. And some days that was how she felt.

Lindsay was so unassuming about it all. When someone came to her for color specifications or small questions of taste or preference, Lindsay would preface her answers with "I believe Mrs. Pinchot wanted the Italian tile," or "We discussed that last night and Mrs. Pinchot would like the deck to extend an additional foot." Diplomacy, subtlety—and a strong ruling hand—got Lindsay everything she wanted, and with a minimum of stress.

As much as it annoyed Sondra that she felt like a helpless female, she was delirious that someone had taken charge so completely. It was uplifting, warming. She felt cared for and fussed over. And it was done in such a way that Sondra never felt beholden; it was like having a good husband around, but without any of the sacrifices.

This newfound security allowed Sondra to drop her frenetic shield. Lindsay imposed an order that made her at least feel she was in control of her life. Lindsay, with her own set of rules, solved all the problems that came up with a directness usually found only in men. Nothing got in her way. She made the edification of Sondra's beloved Earlsheart appear simple and seamless. And she was much more than a colleague; she was fast becoming a friend, a kind of relationship Sondra hadn't had in ages. And as long as Sondra could hold on to the illusion of control, she felt safe, secure enough to be herself around Lindsay.

Yes, things were good, Sondra thought as she looked out over the ocean. Earlsheart was daily becoming a reality; a final haven where she could be whoever she wanted, and the hell with everyone else. Freedom. And Lindsay was an unexpected gift.

She thought back to last week, picturing Lindsay scrunched over a revised set of drawings, heavily involved in a discussion with Sondra and John, the foreman, about the skylights for the bedrooms. The room had been warm, and Lindsay shrugged off her sweater. Sondra had stopped listening to their argument, her eyes casually traveling the gentle crevasse of Lindsay's darkened skin against the tight white V-neck T-shirt. A gold herringbone necklace canvassed her collarbones, gracefully playing with the tendons on her neck, moving in concert with her oration, forming a shallow dip that fluttered as she spoke.

Sondra jarred herself back to reality as she burned her tongue on the coffee. She had never really studied women before, but there was something compelling about Lindsay, her stunning strength and darkness, her resolute eyes. Sondra decided finally it must simply be charisma; satisfied, she lit a cigarette, then remembered she ought to open the window before Lindsay arrived.

The ledge was jammed. Painted shut years ago. And who knew how many times over. She panicked. She had to open it, or put out her cigarette, and that was never an option.

"Hey!" Lindsay said from behind her. "You can give up, it's stuck."

"I know." Sondra turned. She walked to the desk, where she butted out the cigarette in her ashtray.

"I checked them all out the first time through."

"Do you think there's some way we could loosen it?" Did her voice sound as desperate outside her head as it did in it? she wondered.

"Sure." Lindsay left the room and returned with a hammer and chisel, walked to the window and began wedging through layers of paint. "Once I get around this corner maybe it'll come loose."

Sondra went to help her. Side by side they heaved on the jamb. Sondra glanced at Lindsay's hands, at the pale bluish-green tributaries that ran a path up her muscular forearms. One more heave and the seal broke loose and the cool air billowed in, but neither of them moved. They were standing so close to one another, Lindsay's hand next to Sondra's, fingers relaxed now; long, slender. She wanted nothing more than to touch them.

The thought jolted her, and she jerked back from the frame, catching a splinter in her movement. She let out a smothered scream.

"Ohhhh," Lindsay commiserated, "ouch. Here." Lindsay took her hand. The dry, soft fingers sent a spasm through her stomach. Sondra flinched.

"Did I hurt you?"

"No." Couldn't Lindsay notice her agitation? But when her dark eyes caught Sondra's they held nothing but gentle concern. Another spasm. She had definitely had too much coffee that morning.

◆ ◆ ◆

"Hi. It's Ryan."

"Ryan?" Her voice sounded thin, as if she had run out of oxygen.

"Yeah . . . from the bakery."

She had run into him again. On her way to work this morning. He'd been coming out of the store as she was going in. "Hi." His sweet eyes smiled.

"I . . . I'm not going in there." He hadn't asked, merely nodded his head. "I'm late."

"OK. Maybe I can call you?" Flustered, she gave him her work number.

"Are you crazy?" Snag had shrieked. "What if this guy likes fava beans and a wee bit of Chianti with his latest coffee mate?"

"Snag," Lindsay interrupted on her way through the office, "I think she should meet him for coffee. In a public place. Near the office." And then Megan saw Lindsay give Snag the eye—don't discourage this, it said. It was this quality of Lindsay's that Megan loved, the ability to be so endearingly human even when she was in the trance of a project.

"Well . . ." Snag pouted, "I think I'll just watch from a neighboring café. I'll be the one in the thick shades and overcoat—"

"—So engagingly subtle," Lindsay added, "in the nearest phone booth."

"I'm sorry, but you can't be too careful."

"I appreciate it, Snag," Megan said. "But I'm not going out with him."

"Why not?" Lindsay walked to her desk. "Just check it out. What's to lose?"

What's to lose? What's not to lose? There was always something to lose in her life. For Megan, everything was a balancing act. She walked on the tightrope, a monstrous mannequin in spangled sequins, teetering upon the fine, strained cable, food on one end, her mother on the other, and below . . . a dark abyss. It was easy for Snag. He was personable, outgoing, flamboyantly thin. She was—not.

"I've got two tickets to the Basia concert."

"Ohhh . . . uh, yeah, she's good."

"Yeah, well, I'm lucky. I'm always getting tickets from my clients. You want to go?"

As if he'd asked did she want to move to Missoula. Did she want to go deep-sea diving? Did she want to fly to the moon?

"Uh, no thanks. But thank you." The blasting in her ears was her own heart. She had to get off the phone. *"I've got to go. Have fun."*

Who was this man? Why was he interested in spending time with her? What did he want? She was fine. Just the way she was. As long as she had Snag, Lindsay, Felix and Critter, her two stray toms, she didn't need anyone else in her life. Or want anyone else. Yes, she was fine.

She was the last one in the office that night. Lindsay had an early meeting, and as soon as she left Snag had sneaked out. He wanted to get home to make a special dinner for Jared: "Maybe I can surprise some sex right out of him."

Megan suddenly felt isolated in her sterile little cubicle; a familiar emptiness seeped up her spine. A chill of fear rushed up the back-of-her-neck hairs as her mother's skeletal image paraded like the Wicked Witch of the West in her quarantined loneliness. And she remembered back to the time when she truly believed there was no cure for the lonely.

That day, five years ago. When she had interviewed for the position she now performed in her sleep. That day she had seriously considered the options to the void that was her life. It wasn't steeped in melodrama or self-pity. It was about logic. She was not happy. She had never been happy. And from behind the girth of her perception it appeared she never would be happy. That day she had wanted to die. Not like other days, when things simply went wrong and she could eat them into a fog.

That day she was as sick of her self-loathing and frustration as her mother had been. In fact her mother's voice haunted her as she vowed when she got off the bus that if she did not get this job, the last of twelve interviews that week, she would kill herself. And the memory of her mother's shrill demeanor affirmed how simple the act would be.

It didn't matter that Megan typed ninety-five words a minute, created perfect business letters, and made dictation look as if she had time to file her nails. Like any minority, the fat have to be better. But she couldn't look like a hundred and twenty pounds of "secretary-loaf" if her life depended on it. And at that moment, she reminded herself, it well might. She had popped the middle button on her polyester blouse ten minutes before she had entered the room already crammed with thirty other applicants.

Megan never knew what prompted her to wait an hour and a half amid the faceless fleshless limbs in that room. Perhaps she couldn't face the thought of her promise. Perhaps she could rationalize eating an entire Sara Lee cheesecake after sitting through that much misery and humiliation. Megan nervously grasped the two ends of her shirt in her pudgy fingers as she finally managed to enter Lindsay Brennan's office, the last applicant to interview. She prayed her inquisitor would fail to notice the flesh aching to burst the rest of the buttons from the strained material.

But the woman with the criminally beautiful hair (Megan could never get over Lindsay's thick blue-black hair) did notice. Megan could see it the moment she looked into her silver-blue eyes. What she saw there surprised Megan as much as the words that came from her mouth, void of disgust or pity, or even embarrassment. They were warm. Kind.

"Megan. Right?" Clear and calming. It would forever remain the effect that Lindsay's voice had on her. "I had your application out all day. I called your references and tried to interview you right away."

"I got stuck on the bus."

"I thought you had found another job." Lindsay smiled as Megan continued to fidget with her blouse. "So. When can you start?"

"That's it?"

"Well, I won't know until we work together whether we can stand being married eight hours a day." Then she stopped abruptly. "Actually it's more like ten to twelve. I overwork, but then I overpay, so it evens out. What do you think?"

"Of course . . . I can start tomorrow." Megan's voice was not her own. She sighed for a long moment as she realized she didn't have to kill herself after all, and this woman made her feel like laughing hysterically and crying and singing "Climb Every Mountain" all at the same time. And now she wouldn't have to eat an entire Sara Lee cheesecake. But maybe, yes, maybe she could have a Ding Dong or a Snickers bar—something small to celebrate. Shit, she would just start her diet tomorrow.

Yes, she thought as she put away her headset, turned off her computer. It was the dieter's pitiful prayer. There was always another tomorrow.

◆ ◆ ◆

Everything came with a risk, and it wasn't like there were some haranguing salesmen offering warranties for each emotional exchange. Wouldn't it be lovely, Samantha thought as she sat in the dark, to be granted a ninety-day warranty on decisions about which dress to wear on the first date? And a hundred and twenty days on the first sexual experience? One year for pain and labor on that first breakup, five years on the marriage thing. Like all the latest car models had.

They had had the discussion again. The where-is-this-going, we've-been-doing-this-for-five-years, time-to-make-a-commitment discussion. It wasn't even a variation on a theme any longer as it had been in the past. It was always the same.

"Is this OK with you?" Robert would ask, and Samantha would usually think he was talking about something other than the *us* subject. Then he would clarify it was the *us* subject and Samantha would sigh.

"I know you haven't been exposed to the best role models," he would say next, smile sadly but encouragingly, then follow with, "but you've seen the other side as well—"

"Yes, I know," she would interrupt, "look at your family. The Cleavers with nary a skeleton in the closet. How do you live with such perfection?" And then she would hate herself for being so sharp.

"You've gotten so cynical," he would say, at which point she would apologize, get up from whatever she was doing, hug him and ask him if they could possibly have this conversation later.

Part two would commence sometime after dinner, or at breakfast, depending, of course, where part one had left off.

Part two invariably began with, "I know you don't want to talk about this right now, but I want you to think about something until you are ready to talk about it."

And she would wait, knowing the next piece of wisdom was about taking risks, believing in their union, the foundation they had built, that they both said they wanted children, that he loved her. And he did, she knew that, which made her feel guilty, because she loved him too, and what he wanted was completely understandable. So she would go to him and tell him, "I love you too. It's just . . . I'm not ready. I'm just not ready."

"But how do you know? How much more ready can you be? We've been in this five years. I think we know everything we both wanted and probably never wanted to know about each other. And we're still here. That's what it is, after all. Still being here."

" 'Being here' is not reason enough to get married."

"Is it the children? Is that really what you're saying you're not ready for?"

"No. Yes. I'm not ready to have kids. It's . . . it's just too much right now." And it was always the easy excuse, which prompted the dark side of Act II: getting nasty.

"Did you ever really want them? Huh, Sam?" And Robert would start pacing.

"Of course I do. Why is it so difficult to understand that where I am today, right now, it just doesn't work for me? I'm up to here with work. I can't just leave my entire business to go off and have a kid. You're not the one that's going to suffer."

"Suffer." At which point he'd shake his head and laugh that laugh, utterly devoid of humor. "You don't want kids. You're too scared.

Too afraid you're going to turn out like your mother. And you keep sitting in the dark all the goddamn time, that's probably what's going to happen." This last bit was the only new dialogue in their scene. Samantha glanced at his pacing body, strong, lithe, almost feral because he had lost his temper. Usually his movements were more civilized. It excited her momentarily and she decided to skip into the next stage of the argument, which was making love, something that usually happened only after hours of polite silence, sometimes stretching into two, three days. But she so needed something to launch her off the plateau of inertia that she charged forward right into Act III.

But this time Robert wasn't willing to concede. He brushed her off, gently. The phone rang. They looked at one another. It kept ringing until finally Samantha went to pick it up.

◆ ◆ ◆

Sondra had tried to reach Samantha all day long. She had sat in the office since noon, still stunned after talking with her bookkeeper, who had informed her that things were a mess, that her expenses were way out of line, that she hadn't been able to find most receipts, that she still hadn't finished paying her taxes from the previous year, and that once she finished getting the books ready for Sondra's accountant this year, she was going to have to quit.

"Are you saying you're afraid I won't pay you?" Sondra asked, quivering somewhere between humiliation and the defensive.

"I didn't say that, Mrs. Pinchot. The fact of the matter is, I'm moving. But I do have to say that I'd seriously think about filing for Chapter Eleven if I were you."

"Well, thanks for your suggestion," Sondra said as blithely as possible.

Now it was hours later. She'd been left with no option but to open her second pack of the day, against all the rules of her new regime. She smoked defiantly, but nothing could stop the tears that came and swallowed her up as she sat alone in the darkening office.

Sam. If she could just talk to her, make her hear. Sam calmed her, even when the words were angry. Sam was the only solid thing in her life. Sondra had tried to reach her for several days, gotten the damn machine, left scads of messages, but still there had been no return call. Now finally, a half hour before she was to meet Lindsay, she had reached her.

"Look, Mom. I'm in the middle of something here." The tone was aloof as only Sam could be.

"I . . . I—" But what could she say? That she was in trouble? That she was always in trouble?

"I'm sorry, but I have to go. Besides"—and Sondra knew what was coming—"I need more time. And you probably do too." She had hung up before Sondra could reply. Sam didn't want to talk to her. Sam never wanted to talk to her, avoided her like the plague. She made no allowances. What in the hell did Sondra have to do to prove her life was on the mend again?

And then Lindsay appeared, casting light on the somber smoke-filled room as she opened the door, entering, the heroine in a badly lit noir film, Sondra thought.

"Sondra?" Voice without pressure. Lindsay walked to her, touched her shoulder, then sat in the chair opposite her. Sondra continued to smoke, not trusting her voice. She cried. Lindsay sat there, allowing her tears to fall, allowing her dignity.

"One of those days," Sondra faltered between the tears.

"They do have a way of showing up, don't they?"

"Sometimes"—Sondra lit another cigarette—"I wonder . . . what this is all about? I never seem to figure out how the world works." It didn't matter that she was revealing this to this woman, this ally. "I don't know how I'm going to keep it all together." And the unspoken thoughts; her business was thriving itself right into the ground. How would it ultimately be able to support this move? This renovation? The changes Lindsay had made were wonderful, but could she really afford them? What had she been thinking of, taking this on in her life right now? And Sam. She couldn't talk about her. So she talked in roundabout circles, circles that led to other circles of pain, of self-loathing, deception and punishment; circles that all bumped into each other until Sondra had no idea what she was talking about. But Lindsay seemed to understand.

Sondra fished for another cigarette, but before she could light it

Lindsay touched her arm. "Why don't we get something to eat?" she asked gently.

They started meeting regularly, after that, whenever Sondra came to town. Earlsheart was always the preface to other subjects, idle small talk that carefully walked over the line into personal matters, although nothing ever too revealing. Lindsay never pressed for details. They'd spend a few minutes getting business out of the way, and then they would chat, not about much. Soon it became a habit. Soon there wasn't a day that went by they weren't mesmerized over a second and third cup of coffee at Patisserie, or at the very least, over the phone.

Now Sondra was waiting for Lindsay at Earlsheart, up in her new bedroom. She caught her own muted reflection in the window and saw the anticipation in her face. She smiled wryly. It's like a schoolgirl crush, she thought. She leaned back to let the feeling warm her, crossing her long legs as she propped them against the sill, sipping her coffee, smoking her allotted cigarette.

"Hmmm . . . cozy." Lindsay's voice shattered Sondra's reverie. "Sorry I'm late. There was an accident and getting over the pass was a bitch."

"Oh!" Sondra brought her feet down immediately, spilling some of her coffee. She got up, smoothed her skirt, flustered, unable to look Lindsay in the eye.

"Sorry. Didn't mean to scare you." Lindsay walked over to the thermos and poured herself a cup. "I saw the tile man downstairs. Did you see the crap he brought in? I told him to ship it back and if he couldn't get it right, I'd call in a new sub."

"Oh . . . sure." Sondra's voice was small.

"You OK?"

"Yeah."

"You seem . . . preoccupied?"

"Oh, nothing really. Just in another world."

"Any place special?"

"Yes. . . . I mean, no. Just daydreaming." She sounded silly and defensive.

"You sure everything is all right?"

"Yes. What about you?" Sondra tried to regain her composure.

"Trying to catch up. I only have an hour here. I've got to get back to town by two." Lindsay seemed to hesitate for a moment. "Do you want to go over these changes—maybe catch a late dinner tonight?"

Sondra felt the familiar spasm. This time it excited her. She felt awkward. Lindsay seemed intent on her company.

"Yes. That would be nice." The unspoken hung between them, but Sondra wasn't entirely certain of what it was.

"Great. See you at eight? At The Waterfront?" Lindsay broke the spell as she returned to the work at hand.

o then what hap-
pened?" Snag gobbled at a fry suffocated in mayonnaise.

"How can you eat that?"

"It's divine! Decadent. And not in the least harmful
to my relationship."

"What's going on, Snag?"

"Nothing, sugar. That's sort of the point. Anyway,
you're completely avoiding this subject. I want every
single detail, lumps in throat, indiscernible twitches of
the eye, flared nostrils . . . but no nose hairs . . . please."

"Snag!" Megan pushed her unfinished chicken salad
aside. "I can't figure it out."

"What's to figure? He likes you, dollface."

"Yes. That's what I'm trying to understand. Why?"
Megan was puzzled. And worried. None of this made
any sense.

After the Basia concert rejection he'd called the next
day, but she didn't return the call. And then she made
a point of going to the bakery, but he wasn't there.

When she was about to give up on seeing him again, he appeared before her, falling in step beside her as she walked to the office. "You don't mind, do you," he'd asked, "if I walk you to work?" "No." Megan turned to him, only glanced a nanosecond into his eyes. They were tear-rimmed from the cold, but the vulnerable appearance put her at ease. "You're a hard woman to get a hold of." He was teasing her. She heard another meaning, the ugly one between the lines. So she didn't respond. "Look, I don't want to bug you, but I just want to know . . . you want to go out sometime?"

"Well . . . um—"

"Say the word and I'll leave you alone."

And it seemed eons passed with each second of silence and she kept ordering herself to answer him damn it, but the answer was so weighted, either way, and she felt herself back on the tightrope, neither direction appealing. And then she realized she was walking alone, and that he was several feet behind her. When she turned, he gently shrugged.

"OK . . . Yes," she answered, shocked at the words that tumbled from her mouth. "Yes. I'd like that."

"Great."

They had coffee the next day, and lunch the day after. She would listen while he talked. It wasn't that he didn't ask questions. It was just that her answers were monosyllabic and she felt safer being a bystander.

"Megs!" Snag reached over, snapping her from her reverie. "So you're all goonie-pied out. Love it." Then he grabbed her plate. "May I?" But didn't wait for an answer.

His appetite was voracious these days. Sublimation was the name of the game. He and Jared hadn't had sex in three weeks. They'd had other dry spells, but nothing like this. One week and Snag was climbing the curtains. Three weeks and he was dangerous. Something was up, and it wasn't him.

"But why, Snag? Why me? I mean, look at all the women walking the streets of Portland. And he wants to date me. I don't trust this."

"Don't you know how friggin' delicious you are?" But Snag didn't count: he was the king of overstatement.

"Do you . . . like him?"

"Like him? I think he's a doll. Love his beard."

"Especially the little gray spots . . ."

"Megan, I do believe you're gushing."

"I am not." But now she was blushing. "And you think he's nice."

"I told you, he seems divine. We won't know if he's Mr. MPD or a biochem war spy until we've investigated him a bit longer. But you leave that up to me. Now, what's for dessert?"

Sondra put out her cigarette and almost immediately lit another. She felt conspicuous as she sat at the small-but-elegant table waiting for Lindsay at The Waterfront. Like a desperate junkie, she hoarded all the nicotine her lungs could handle before Lindsay arrived. She would keep her smoking to a minimum. She wanted Lindsay's approval, and since Lindsay had that racquetball blush of health to her cheeks, she probably detested smoking. But the rebel inside whispered in a silky voice that cigarettes were the least of her problems. With all the stresses of maintaining the Portland office, her clients, plus the escalating costs of Earlsheart, and the reproachful Sam, who lurked in the back of her mind like a bad headache, she damn well deserved what solace she could find. After all, part of all this was for Sam. She took a deep drag and tried to free her mind of it as she watched the glimmering lights on the river.

"Hi."

Sondra leapt in her chair.

"There I go again. Seems I have a habit of coming up behind you these days." Lindsay eased into a chair. "Hey . . . you look terrific."

And she did. Spectacular in a satin midnight-blue dress, softly padded at the shoulders, deeply veed at the neck, everything sensuous and silky. It brought out the blue in her eyes and the gold in her hair. What gold there was left through the gray, Sondra had been reminded earlier, as she stood in front of her mirror, assessing the damage of sun and, of course, the years.

"Thanks." Sondra lit another cigarette. This one would be it. For now. Later maybe a tasteful after-dinner smoke. "You do too. Look terrific, I mean." Lindsay in black slacks and blazer offset by a vermilion silk undervest, and, of course, her jet-black hair, softly swept back off her forehead. Hair that in minutes would fall forward again, and Lindsay would whisk her beautiful hands through it as an afterthought.

"How do you feel about a nice merlot?" Lindsay asked.

"Hmmm. No, not tonight. Coffee will be fine." Sondra smiled nervously.

Their waiter approached and Lindsay ordered a glass of wine for herself and coffee for Sondra. "Sure you don't want anything?"

"No. Trying to stay on my diet."

"Ohhh . . . that's no fun."

"You, of course, don't have to worry about that."

"What are you talking about? You're in great shape."

"Well, maybe a while back, before I took this up"—Sondra held up her cigarette—"for a sport," and then graciously put it out.

Silence loomed over the table. What had happened to their ease? Sondra wondered. This evening out was no different than meeting at Patisserie for coffee. But it was. They had both dressed. It was an occasion. They weren't here to discuss business.

"I'm having Megan send the change orders for the marble tomorrow." But maybe business was what Lindsay had in mind.

"Oh. Great." But Sondra sounded disappointed.

Another silence swam about them. Lindsay's eyes sought out Sondra's. "Is anything wrong?"

"No. I think I'm just a bit tired. You know. All the back-and-forth."

"Yeah. It's got to be rough." Lindsay sipped her wine.

They both spent an inordinate amount of time studying their menus and then staring out at the water. Finally Lindsay leaned forward. "I am *not* going to say 'What about those Blazers?' "

Sondra laughed. It broke the tension. "I wouldn't know anything about them anyway."

"No. I wouldn't peg you for a sports fan."

"Give me an old-fashioned movie any day." Small talk. Inconsequential but it restored their ease. Still, she was dying for a cigarette. "I don't think I've been to a theater in . . . forever."

"Art house films. I adore them."

"You're like my daughter."

"I didn't know you had a daughter."

"Yeah." Her tone was clipped.

"Well, is she here? In town?"

"No."

"You've never mentioned her."

"Well. I don't see her much."

"What does she—"

"I'm sorry, Lindsay. It's just not a great subject right now." Sondra's voice broke.

"Oh . . . that night." Lindsay's voice was soft.

"Yes."

"Sondra." Lindsay's voice was gentle, concerned. "I certainly would never pry . . . but if you want to talk . . . let me know."

"Thanks." Sondra put a cigarette to her mouth. Lindsay took the lighter from her trembling fingers and lit it for her.

"This . . . this would never have been possible without you." Sondra could not hold Lindsay's gaze, but she wanted to tell her how she felt. Really felt. "Sure. Earlsheart would have been remodeled. But no one else would have put the time and effort into it that you have. Or been such a friend. You've been . . . incredible." And then she really did have to look away.

Dinner arrived, and was removed shortly thereafter, plates barely touched. Lindsay had been musing about her days at Sandruski. But Sondra only half listened to the dissertation on the hardships of male dominance, chauvinism, Lindsay's struggles with the political power dynamic. For Sondra, dealing with man-made law in a man-made world was a given and she never let it bother her. She simply had learned how to maneuver around it. She watched Lindsay's eyes as she talked, saw how they burned—joyously alive—when she spoke of her work. And she watched the nuance of her body and hands, always her hands, captivating her.

"What do you do with yourself when you aren't working?" Sondra interrupted, and the question surprised them both.

"What do you mean?"

"Your free time. I mean, God knows you can't have much of it, but you know . . ." Sondra hedged a moment. "Is there . . . some-one?"

"My work pretty much ties up most of my time," Lindsay said, smiling shyly, "but I do see someone. Occasionally."

"Doesn't it bother him at all, how much you work?"

"I think so. But it isn't that kind of arrangement."

Sondra felt an edge of discomfort. She wondered if this someone was like Carl—someone half desired. No great investment. No great risk. There was no agitation to semi-desirous needs. The smaller the rollercoaster the less upset your stomach got. "I see someone . . . it's the strangest thing. We'll go months without a word, then he'll call out of the blue and say, 'Can you get the time off? The fish are biting.' And I'll say, 'What the hell?' I hate fishing. But there I am up some isolated little river, freezing my tail off." Sondra laughed at herself. "Diversions."

"I don't know. Sounds like you're both getting what you want out of it."

"I rarely think about him. Really. Have you ever had anyone in your life like that?"

"I suppose I have."

The waiter passed by with heated cognacs. Sondra closed her eyes. It only took that long.

"You know, I think I'd like one of those."

Lindsay flagged the waiter. He returned a few minutes later with the drinks. Sondra held the heated snifter in her hands for a very long time, staring into the golden liquid, the fumes rising to her nose, the cognac warming her, deliciously burning her throat, making its way to her stomach.—Yes. One sip. Now another. She had waited so long.

"I wasn't going to tell you this." Sondra wondered if her voice sounded thick or if it was just the sudden dullness inside her head. "I wasn't going to tell you why I was so jumpy this morning. I was a little embarrassed, but I guess I was being silly." Sondra felt safe in sharing half-truths now. "I was sitting there, daydreaming, thinking about all the fun we've had working together, and it really has been the most wonderful experience I could have imagined." Sondra paused, glanced at the river. She might be bolder now, but she still found it difficult to hold Lindsay's gaze. "All of a sudden, out of nowhere, I realized you wouldn't be around very much if you were deeply involved with someone. I guess I sort of assumed that you're not, and the idea made me feel, well, uneasy, or . . ." She trailed off. "And then"—Sondra took a deep drag on her fourth after-dinner cigarette—"I realized I was feeling jealousy. I mean, isn't that altogether ridiculous?" Sondra would not take her eyes from the river.

"I don't know." Lindsay tried to smile reassuringly. "I don't think it's uncommon for people to find themselves wary when they begin a new relationship. Who is this person? Are they around to stay? . . . in whatever context. Thinking something might interfere . . . It's not logical. It just is." Lindsay paused as Sondra turned to her. "Anyway, I'm flattered."

They were silent for a moment. "You've barely touched yours." Sondra indicated her cognac.

"I'm not much of a drinker." Lindsay pushed her drink toward Sondra. "Please, you finish it."

"Well . . . why not?" Why not.

That sense of unspoken communication passed between them again and Sondra couldn't bear it any longer. She felt the cognac. Everywhere. She played at putting on her coat.

"Ready?"

"No. Just chilly." And then they both realized the tables surrounding them were vacant, the waiters were listlessly straightening up.

"Guess we should let them close the place." Lindsay stood and paid the bill, even as Sondra protested. "I'll put it on the account," Lindsay winked, then put on her overcoat.

It was a clear night. The blackest of skies filled the air with a crispness that chilled the bone. It cleared Sondra's head, but not enough for her to know how to end the evening. They shuffled around trying to stay warm.

"Well," Lindsay said quietly, "I enjoyed this, Sondra."

"Me too."

Lindsay's eyes were direct. She moved closer, leaned forward to hug her with one arm, barely brushing Sondra's hair with her cheek. Sondra didn't think. She turned to Lindsay and embraced her fully, both arms wrapping about her shoulders.

They froze. They stood holding one another for a full thirty seconds and then swiftly broke away, their timing uncannily in sync. Lindsay whispered good-bye and turned to go. Sondra remained, feeling a deep thaw caress her body, warding off the chill.

"peaking existentially, of course."

Samantha shivered. It was still chilly and damp even if spring was around the corner, although around-the-corner in Seattle could be a wait to certain hypothermia.

"Of course," Jack answered.

"Isn't it all . . . existential?" Jerra lit a cheroot.

"Jesus Christ, Jer, do you have to do that?"

"See what I mean?" Jerra inhaled delightedly. "This very exercise we go through every night after dinner, existential gibberish . . . meaningless roteness of voices which are nothing more than sound waves banging against one another."

"I think it's called communication, Jerra," Robert pointed out.

"Well, thanks for sharing, Robert." Their gibing was good-natured, as always.

Samantha was ready for the espresso. They were dining at La Cucina, the city's latest trendsetter in northern Italian cuisine. It had been sunny in the afternoon, and they had asked to be seated on the terrace. By five it had poured and by eight, when they arrived, clear skies again prevailed. By the end of the meal they sat beneath the heat lamp, huddled in their coats, debating the new age bent on existentialism. Not Samantha's favorite subject.

"I'm simply referring to the idiocy of the term. If I remember correctly, the textbook definition of 'existential' has something to do with relating to or affirming existence," Jerra provided, "which pretty much sums up every activity we participate in. Existentialism has simply been and always will be a moral mind fuck."

"How can such an unfashionable cynic be such an incurable romantic?" Robert laughed.

"Go ahead." Jack nudged Jerra in the rib cage. "Come on, tell them."

The espressos arrived and they greedily sucked in the warmth.

"Come on, tell them what?" Samantha asked.

"Ah, she speaks." Robert glanced sideways at Samantha. He wasn't sure if they were arguing, mad at each other or in resolve.

"Tell them." But before Jerra could say a word, Jack continued: "A new theory she's come up with. But before she lets you in on it, let's take a friendly poll. What's the single most important factor that makes a person fall in love?"

Silence. The kind that made Jerra know this wasn't the greatest topic for the night. "Finish your espresso and let's go. I'm cold."

"Communication," Robert said with utter commitment.

"Smell," Jack retaliated. "We spend our entire relationships trying to explain what it is that made us fall in love with this one and that, waste hours on the couch, moon over it like it was the eighth god-damn wonder of the world, when it all boils down to is the basic animal function of smell."

"In other words, chemistry?" Samantha wasn't sure she was getting this quite right.

"No! Just plain old smell. It's a scent thing. You see everyone getting all embarrassed when their dogs go sniffin' the neighbor's dog, but actually we do the same damn thing. We sniff out our mate."

"How graceful," Jerra snorted. "So it has nothing at all to do with anything fine about being human; minor things like emotions, feelings, love?"

"Nope."

"I'm glad it's so simple for you, Jack, my man," Robert said as he patted him on the shoulder. "But in one way or another it always boils down to how you communicate. Not just verbally. But all the stuff in between the lines, all the things we don't have words for, like the language we speak when we make love, the language of shared dreams, the way we know we're speaking to each other when we're on opposite sides of the world. It all boils down to communication."

"Come on. Tell them," Jack insisted.

Jerra sighed, discarded her apish companion. "I agree with you, Robert, about communication, but that comes after the fact. It's the glue. But then you must consider that I communicate far better with Samantha than I do with this lout here. I've always communicated better with women than men. And the smell thing, well, that's just plain weird, darling. But, no, I think there's a unique and undefinable essence between two mortals, for want of better words, which act as host bodies, if you will. I, in other words, would be a receptacle for this particular essence—what I call Spirit Essence—and the other yin or yang to this essence would be found presently in the wolf-sniffing prig to my right. Now, this is not to say that simply because you are lovers or married that you are with the other part of your spirit essence. It may be that you haven't found that person yet."

"Soul mates," Robert stated.

"Not quite. Soul mates are intransmutable. We assume that if you and Sam, say, are soul mates, that you are soul mates for life. But with a spirit essence it can float into a person waiting to meet its other half, and flow back out again. And when the two meet, bloody hell! Beyond being off one's feet. The biggest of all love drugs. This isn't your common garden-variety torrid love affair, it's all things being met for which we don't even have communication. It's the goddamn queen of orgasms, king of hearts, jack of spades all rolled into one. There is a hitch, however."

They all stared at one another. Then Samantha narrowed her eyes. "And what is that?" she asked.

"Well, if you don't honor the essence, zap . . . it floats out of your body. What we call 'breaking up is hard to do' is often a result of the essence leaving one person, while remaining in the other. You have to take care of it. Tend it. Nurture it. Treat it with the most honored reverence. Otherwise, it will leave. Oh . . . you might still have a few glops of it resting around your insides, just enough to keep you in that relationship you can't quite get out of. And when the reverse happens, say when *you* have taken care of it and the other person hasn't and he or she just walks about—with a glom behind the ear, say—they look at you with eyes of remote detachment as though you've never met. Oh, they know they knew you. Once upon a time. But the feelings? Swept from their memory."

"Like an amnesiac? What are you saying?"

"I'm saying that the relationship for these people is like looking through an old photo album. They see the pictures, remember the events. But it's outside of their experience. The person still blessed—or cursed—with the essence feels every memory. . . . It lives inside them. Every minute. All of it."

They became somber. Robert sipped his coffee, then asked seriously, "So then what happens? Do you get only one dose of this stuff a lifetime?"

"No. I don't think so. And I also don't think you have any control over it. Whatsoever. That's why you end up falling in love with people you would never dream of falling in love with. It isn't because the person reminds you of your goddamn mother, father, or because she's another alcoholic, or any number of dysfunctional match theories all those self-helper program-steppers are always blithering about. It's simply that you've encountered the other part of the essence."

They drove home in silence. Robert took her hand, and she let him. When he turned into the driveway he let the car run but killed the lights.

"Some theory, huh?" he said, laughing.

"Well, you know Jerra."

"You never answered the question."

"What?" She glanced at him.

"The ingredient. What you think the single most important ingredient is in a relationship." Another silence. She looked back at the garage door and said so softly he could barely hear her, "Passion."

◆ ◆ ◆

Joanne had met Guy Nathan five years ago. Since then he had become one of her favorite clients. Whenever he called she knew she was going to make a lot of money. Nathan never did anything small. Or anything that wasn't a gamble. He had called last week, with an urgency in his voice that meant he had a hot one. Would she meet him at The Grill next Wednesday? he had asked. Absolutely, she had replied.

While she waited for him that Wednesday, she ordered two martinis. They always drank the first one over catch-up, the second over business and the third was anyone's guess. Martinis were homage to that night at KiKi's where they first met, so long ago, a hot-spot nightclub, the trendy man's deal-making drinkery and meat market that celebrated its cultural awareness with two condom machines, one each marked His and Hers. She had been there with Christine, a blonde and voluptuous stripper by night, med student by day.

Nathan had walked in with a business associate. Joanne watched as they took one look at the two of them. She could tell by their locked-in strut to the bar, turning back to them as they ordered their drinks, that they would shortly invite themselves to their table.

Christine had been getting on her nerves that evening, with her never-ending complaints about med school, so Joanne had no problem with the boys joining them halfway into their second drink. She even encouraged Christine to the dance floor with Nathan's sidekick, while she and Nathan squared one another off.

"Interesting little gathering, eh?" He picked up his martini.

"Well, it does have sit-com possibilities." She raised her own.

"What's your story?"

"I thought you figured that out."

Nathan appraised Christine slithering about his associate, but watched her eyes as they blazed at Joanne. "Oh, I know the score, and I commend you on your taste. But what I'm asking is, what do you do?"

"I'm a business consultant."

"That covers a lot of territory."

"Yes," she smiled coyly, "it does."

Their repartee continued and as they cut deeper and more inge-niously into one another they discovered they had a lot in common. Nathan began to tell her about his business.

As they exchanged cards, he smiled. "Would it be fitting to say I hope this is the beginning of a beautiful friendship?"

Joanne grinned as she thought of that night. Christine and several others were long gone, while Nathan continued to be a permanent fixture. She spotted him immediately as he approached the maître d', who waved him forward to their favorite table. He stood, clothed in a slimming Armani suit, ever the distinguished gentleman. He kissed the side of her face, stood back and admired her. "Ah, you look more delicious than ever, Joanne."

"Save it for someone you have a chance with." This was always the rejoinder, their common joke and link.

"Than shall we dive right into business?"

"Why not? It's our preferred pool of sharks."

Lindsay knew Joanne's Porsche would be in the driveway before she rounded the last corner to her house. She opened the door quietly; the digital clock on the mantel blinked 1:50. Shit. She hoped Joanne had given up and gone to sleep. And there she lay, curled on the couch. Guileless as a child. No. She corrected herself. Guileless was not exactly a word she'd use to describe Joanne. Her eyes followed the slender contours of her body, this woman of incredible beauty. She was sleeping peacefully. The only peace she probably ever knew, Lindsay thought grimly.

Joanne's life had been anything but the glittering and gay carnival she paraded about for everyone's amusement. Though they rarely spoke intimately anymore, in the beginning, after they had been drenched in the aftermath of lovemaking, they had quiet, tentative talks, and Lindsay had pieced together a history of a young woman whose intellectual prowess had been surpassed by her sexual need.

That Joanne was beautiful was undeniable to all but Joanne. Her insecurities allowed her to see only her innumerable flaws. A hard-edged, cynical approach to life served her well.

At first Lindsay thought she had fallen prey to Joanne's driving quest to become sexually addictive to whoever was her victim. "You've got a vampire complex," Lindsay had whispered to her one night as Joanne's long graceful fingers lightly trailed over her body.

"What the fuck is that supposed to mean?"

"I think you know."

"I can't help it if everyone finds me wildly irresistible," Joanne bantered, but then turned serious. "All that I care about is that you do."

"What do you want, Joanne?" The question, of course, was rhetorical, but Joanne used it for the obvious opening. Lindsay never did get a clear answer. She knew Joanne enjoyed her work—the hunt, the conquest, the art of making the deal. But the rest remained a puzzle, and Lindsay wasn't sure how much of that was by design and how much was simply a barrier beyond which Joanne found the labyrinth as puzzling as herself.

It brought a quickening of breath to Lindsay to remember the first time she had seen Joanne, how her bold aggressiveness, her assuredness, had transmitted itself to Lindsay, who would never have dreamed they would end up in bed together that night.

Making love with Joanne was an exotic and new experience. Aggressive and without censor. It was hot and adult, unique and expressive. The only thing it lacked was any sense of love. But that had been taken care of very early on in their relationship, maturely and adeptly, as they shared coffee one morning; they categorically confessed undying lust, with the caveat that neither of them was remotely interested in falling in love. It didn't matter. What Lindsay got from their union provided a much needed balance to her work.

Each was aware of the other's shortcomings, but since they spent so very little time together other than when making love, the irritations never became insurmountable. Joanne seemed unflappable. The only emotions that defied her cynical nonchalance were anger or passion, and one invariably fed off the other and led to heightened levels of release. But the occasions when Joanne's vulnerability leaked through were precisely the moments Lindsay did not feel sexual.

The first time Joanne failed to bring her to orgasm, Lindsay's stress was coiled so tightly about her insides that there was no hope of release. Joanne had blamed it on her own inadequacy, laboring for close to an hour, at first cajoling, playing, teasing, and then becoming despondent as she caressed unresponding flesh. Finally she rose to her knees, defeated. Lindsay had tried to assuage her fears, whispering softly to her that this defeat wasn't uncommon. That when she got this tense there was no letting go.

She awoke, hours later, to find Joanne sitting naked in the living room. Staring. Lindsay approached, saw the tearstained face of a child distorted in pain. "I'm sorry" was all she would say. Lindsay held her as Joanne lay unyielding in her arms. Lindsay tried, but couldn't make her way in. Joanne refused to talk.

The next morning Joanne remained quiet and sullen. Lindsay came up from behind her, caressed her neck, kissed the lobe of her ear, ran her hands up the length of her arms, but Joanne brushed her aside. She told her she had to go to San Francisco on business. She would call when she got back into town.

Lindsay did not hear from her for several days, but when she returned, so had her brassy confidence. Evidently she had found someone to restore her faith in herself. She took Lindsay impatiently, angrily, and then again slowly, the seducer, taunting, bringing Lindsay to the brink of climax, almost cruelly, retreating before finally carrying her over the edge. Lindsay realized as she caught the restraint in Joanne's eyes that this act wasn't about making love, it was about power. The power to give and control pleasure, which created the value of her being.

Although Lindsay made no noise, Joanne awoke, slowly, as if she had felt Lindsay watching her. She came to terms with consciousness and noticed the strange expression on Lindsay's face, somewhere between arousal and pity.

"So. We've come home in our pumpkin." Joanne got up and put her arms around Lindsay, checking her watch. "Late night."

"Yes." Where was the anger?

"Want to go to bed?"

"That was the general idea."

"Good. Let me tuck you in," Joanne purred as she took Lindsay's hand and led her into the bedroom. They lay side by side, Joanne snuggled softly against her, and Lindsay found sleep immediately. She dreamed. Of the lines, again. Lines she had drawn, and more lines until everything was lines and everyone who entered her dream had to be drawn first; her mother, whom she couldn't remember, her father, Miss Bracken, Heather, Joanne, even Sondra, all had to be sketched. She kept erasing their arms and legs, wanting to get them just right, never accomplishing the final stroke, so everyone walked around limbless and incomplete. And then more tracings and etchings, page after page, each page larger than the last, until she found herself on a page so large, so cluttered and crammed with her exercises and incomplete renderings that she couldn't find her way to turn it. The drawings began to merge and she began to yell in a loud desperate voice, asking how she was to get off the page. But all the faces stared blankly at her. No one could give her an answer. She had forgotten to draw their mouths. She began to run, running for miles and miles through the pages, running . . . to . . .

. . . she could feel the blood rising warmly to her thighs. The liquid soft tongue, conjuring waves of desire, silkily beckoning her forward. The fingers stroking her skin until she realized she was no longer dreaming. Joanne was making love to her. She was barely conscious until the pressure lifted her to an intense and shattering climax. She lay gasping in the pale blue of early dawn, Joanne slithering up into her arms.

"I thought you might want a wake-up call."

"Yes . . . ?" Lindsay wasn't sure she could form words yet, let alone sentences. Why was Joanne being so nice?

"Well . . . you know I've had a client I've wanted you to meet for some time."

"Hmmm." Lindsay began to run her hands through Joanne's hair.

"He's very keen on your work," Joanne continued. "He needs a team to put together the Darlington Arts Pavilion."

"You're kidding!" Lindsay bolted upright. Joanne knew Lindsay had been eyeing the project since word had broken that the endlessly wealthy Darlingtons had purchased the building, and were completely renovating it in honor of their grandfather's name.

"I thought you might be interested."

"How? I mean how are you connected to them?"

"Darlington's dink grandson, Ray, happens to be in business with the aforementioned client, one Guy Nathan. He owes Nathan a favor. Nathan's not interested in the money. He wants his name splattered all over town as the generous philanthropist who made a difference in cleaning up Old Town. I think it has something to do with redeeming his past, which is rumored to be shady, at best."

"Jesus, Joanne, I can't believe how you get around." Lindsay was wide awake now.

"There's a catch." Joanne gently pushed Lindsay back to a reclining position. "It's fast-track, and I mean fast-track. It has to be completed by Super Bowl Sunday. Only the Darlingtons would try to mix football and opera—"

"—That's impossible!"

"Maybe for some twit who can't draw his way out of a bucket, but not for you."

"It's not just about me. They want more than an overhaul. They want a whole new look. . . ." Lindsay's adrenaline pumped full throttle just thinking about it. Joanne saw the familiar glint in her eyes.

"And that's the other catch." Joanne began tracing curlicues on Lindsay's stomach. "He's very taken with a certain designer he wants to use."

"As in . . ."

"Our very own Mrs. Pinchot." Joanne grinned mischievously.

The light in Lindsay's eyes dimmed. "What?"

"I thought you'd be amused."

"Why would he want her?"

"He was very impressed with her work at The Tower. He finds her very . . ." Joanne paused and leaned down, sucking gently on Lindsay's left nipple, "cutting edge."

"I . . . I don't know, Joanne. I don't think this would be her thing."

"And why is that?" Joanne moved to the other nipple.

"Uh . . . I just don't know about putting her under a lot of pressure."

"Pressure's good," Joanne grinned as she exerted some of her own with her thigh against Lindsay's pelvis. "Haven't you heard? It's the primary motivator for results."

Lindsay felt her body reawaken.

"Yes . . . pressure creates incentive." Joanne gently kneaded her fingers down the flat of Lindsay's stomach. "Pressure," she continued as her fingers met the wet of Lindsay's already swollen lips, "can be just the ticket." Joanne eased inside Lindsay as she moaned with pleasure.

◆ ◆ ◆

He came hard. It had been a long time since they had made love. He grasped her body to his, wanting her to feel the whole of him as he came inside her, filling her up, needing her, wanting her to feel the intense impact being inside her had upon him.

He caught the impenetrable gaze in her eyes. Arousal? Indifference? "Sam," he gasped, "stay with me."

"I'm here, Robert . . . I'm here." She was somewhere in her own rite of lovemaking that had nothing to do with him. He needed her with him. A sense of desperation washed over him as he frantically removed himself, limp, useless to her now, and took sweet bites of her skin as he traveled south and took her in his mouth, aching to make her feel him. "Oh yes," she moaned. Her need excited him and he continued to make love to her with his tongue, swiftly, deftly, a wonderful lover, gentle and pleasing. She came, came in his mouth, and he wallowed in it.

She held out her hands and pulled him to her. "Hold me."

Later, she went to the kitchen and made coffee as she did every morning, walked to get the paper from the front porch, returned and poured some cranberry juice.

Robert came in, took her hands, drew her close, mimicking a slow dance from days gone by, crooning softly, " 'When I fall in love, it will be forever.' "

Samantha put her arm about his neck, but didn't want to dance.

"So, what's up for your day?" he asked.

"Not much. Thought I'd catch up on the bills, the house stuff, you know. You and Tim golfing?" Sam removed herself from his grasp, poured them coffee.

"Not in this rain. How about an early matinee?"

"Sure." Samantha really didn't care one way or the other, but figured it might be a nice change.

Joanne put the coffee under Lindsay's nose and watched as her eyes opened in delight. "Ohhhh, coffee in bed. What did I do to deserve that?"

"Simply a woman with good taste." Joanne considered. "Or a woman that tastes good."

Lindsay smiled and sipped her coffee. "Yeesss . . . ecstasy." She took another sip. "God, what time is it?"

"It's early, and besides, what difference does it make? It's Saturday. I'm demanding that you take the day off. Completely."

"And why is that?"

"Because you've been working yourself to death, and because . . ." Joanne whispered victoriously, "you owe me."

"I do, huh?" Lindsay smiled appreciatively, then pinched her lips in decision. "OK. What do you want to do?"

"I want to have a tremendously fattening omelet, go shopping, take a stroll in the rain, see a movie. I don't know. Let's play it by ear."

"I'm supposed to meet Sondra at noon."

The smile slipped from Joanne's face. "Can't it wait?"

"I suppose so, but I'll have to call. She's expecting me."

"So am I, Lindsay."

They stood at the checkout counter at Dania. Robert had wanted to buy a couple of new deck chairs for their patio. She had reminded him summer was almost over, and pointed out that the rain seemed to have started early this year. But the chairs were on sale and they had been putting this off forever. Would she mind awfully? Why not.

"So what movie do you want to see?"

"I don't care." Her apathy had become an ambient shadow. There seemed to be nothing she could get excited over. Jerra and Robert had been right, of course. Her reputation had survived Janet Myers mostly unscathed. But it had been months now and she still couldn't engage her heart in any of her new projects.

"I . . . I think I need a change." They were in the car, on the way to a movie she had finally decided on.

"Don't want to see *Notorious?*" It was playing at a revival house. She adored Hitchcock and this one was her favorite. Cary Grant exceedingly cool, the passion just held at bay, while Ingrid Bergman wore hers on her sleeve like a bad spill.

"I'm not talking about the movie."

"What then?"

"Just . . ." But she didn't know what. Exactly.

"What?"

"Nothing. Everything. I don't know. Just a change. A vacation. A couple of days . . . somewhere. Anywhere."

"That's fine, babe. Do you want me to go with you, or do you want some time to yourself?" Robert's smile was encouraging as he glanced at her and then back at the road.

That was the problem. He was so damn supportive. He was so healthy and stable and solid and so incredibly intact.

She attributed this consistency in his ability to ground himself, no matter what the circumstance. At home, with her, at work, the many negotiations he dealt with at his firm, he simply let it roll off him. She wondered if that was the test of depth or the absolute lack of it. Why was he never tortured over anything? But she gave him his due. Robert was one of the most together persons, regardless of gender, she had ever met. He rarely lost his temper. And the worst part about it was that when he did actually exhibit a human flaw he rarely got defensive. He'd smile, say, "You know, you're right, I did sort of fuck up, didn't I?" And he'd know why, then tell her the psychological etiology of the dispute and calmly resolve it. She longed to have one, just one, screaming, lunging, out-for-blood argument. A single tiff that wasn't processed, remarked upon, compartmentalized and duly recorded. Couldn't they just once embrace inappropriate behavior?

"I . . . I don't know. It's just me, Robert. I'm kind of stuck."

"Want to talk about it?" And that was another thing. He was never invasive, always considered her feelings, her needs, and oftentimes compromised his own desires to make their lives easier.

"Maybe later."

"OK. Still feel up to a movie?"

"Sure."

◆ ◆ ◆

"I'm telling you, it's the prime distinction between a butch and a femme."

"You really think so?" Lindsay asked. She and Joanne were splitting a cinnamon roll steeped in melted butter.

"Absolutely. A butch enters a room and never thinks about herself. Just who she might want to sleep with. Whereas a femme immediately sees every other woman in relationship to herself. How does she stack up? Who's her competition? What assets does she employ for maximum allure? It's all in the approach."

"Jesus, Joanne, you can't be serious. That's what you think every time you walk into a room?"

"Sure. Unless it's full of men. . . ."

"And even then," Lindsay finished for her. They laughed.

"Oh, God, I can't eat another bite."

Lindsay looked at her watch.

"Oh, for Christ's sake, Lindsay, do you have to do that?"

"What?"

"Time. You're on time. For everything today. We're being spontaneous, see? And you can't be late for that." Joanne's irritation mounted.

"I just wanted to call Sondra, tell her I wasn't going to make it."

"She'll figure that out when you don't show up." Joanne pushed the plate away. She had promised herself she wasn't going to get worked up about that woman. But it had started, and now she needed to finish it. "What's with you two, anyway?"

"Come on, let's not ruin it."

"Well, there's something going on between the two of you."

"Jesus, Joanne, the woman's as straight as they come."

"But curious."

"I don't think so." Lindsay's tone wasn't convincing, even to herself.

"Well, I do. I watched her the last time I saw you two together at your office. She's like a schoolgirl with a crush. She looks at you like you're the paragon of virtue, for Christ's sake. And if you can't see the danger signs in that . . ." Joanne's voice was tight.

"I'm not going to sit here and argue about Sondra. Besides, she isn't the problem."

"What in the hell is that supposed to mean?"

"Do we really have to do this? Today?"

"Seems like as good a day as any."

"It's just . . ." Lindsay faltered. "Us."

" 'Us' seemed fine until she entered the picture."

"We don't even seem to know each other anymore." Lindsay put her coffee down. "If we ever have."

"And what is it you'd like to know?" Joanne angrily flicked a crumb from the table. "You're all rolled up in your goddamn plans and precious blueprints and when you decide to come home after a day and a half's work, I make you feel like you can go out and do it all over again. You have your work and I have your cunt, and I think the trade's worked admirably so far."

Lindsay flinched. "Listen to you. What the hell kind of relationship is that?"

"In broad terms, probably shallow. In more definitive language, we have great sex. No—exceptional sex. It's a helluva lot more than most people have." Joanne threw some money on the table, but before they could leave the restaurant, or the argument, she continued. "And what the hell is this newfound awareness about knowing each other, anyway?" Joanne's voice turned bitter. "So what? You want to paint new scenery, put little Miss Massengill douche in the picture? It won't change a thing about who you are, Lindsay." Joanne grinned nastily. "So . . . she's got an itch. But for how long? I'm here now. And I love it. I love doing you so much I'm willing to put up with this shithole of a relationship." She stood and put on her coat. "Just remember, Lindsay, we all know what curiosity did to the little pussy!" And then she left Lindsay, sitting at the table, trying to digest her breakfast along with Joanne's vitriol.

◆ ◆ ◆

They sat in the theater. Robert had found Samantha's hand and held it through the last half of the movie. She had leaned her head against his shoulder and pretended to pay attention to the flickering images on the screen. But her mind kept floating to things in the past, to her life before Robert. With David and before then. Her mother. Dad.

Maybe she would call Dad and go to dinner. He and his wife, Stella, were great for advice, even if at times their Big Book hyperbole and program rhetoric took their toll. Her father had a great enthusiasm for applying the "steps" to every problem they encountered, individually or as a couple, No, maybe it wasn't such a good idea to see them. But maybe she could call him later tonight, find out if he'd heard from her mother. They rarely communicated unless there was trouble, and something was going on. Why was her mother spending all this money on Earlsheart? What was happening to her and was it necessary that she care?

For that matter, was it necessary for her to care about anything? Indifference bloated her insides until she wondered if she could feel her skin. She checked just to make sure. Robert felt her movements, held her closer. She wondered if the movie would ever end.

They walked out hand in hand, stopped for espresso while Robert chattered excitedly about the movie, and then went home. Samantha told him she would cook, but that he had to leave the kitchen. She couldn't tolerate him hovering about, being solicitous of her mood, caring about her feelings. If he were any more sensitive, she might have to take his head off on the chopping block. Besides. She wanted to pour herself a healthy glass of wine, and no matter how much

Robert insisted her drinking patterns appeared entirely social, the combination of her past and her parents' own problems with alcohol made her self-conscious. She knew she was tempting fate every time she took a sip, and his eyes relayed that nonjudgmental fact to her. Robert kissed her forehead and left her in the kitchen to herself. Later, when she heard the phone ring, she knew immediately who it was, as if electronics were simply an extension of the umbilical cord. She waited for Robert to walk in with the portable, his hand over the mouthpiece, pointing with the other as he lipped the words "Guess who." She didn't want to talk with her. Robert nudged the phone in her direction. She silently mouthed the words "I'm busy."

"Yeah . . . she's right here," Robert wasn't being mean. He simply wanted her to deal with it. "Sounds great, Mom. Congratulations. You deserve it." He signed off, handed her the phone and left her in privacy.

"Hi."

"Sam?"

"Yeah. Hi, Mom."

"Oh, Sammy. I've got the greatest news."

"Yeah, what's that?" Samantha looked at the glass of wine on the counter.

"Well, you know this architect, the one who's working on the house? She called today and we may have the Darlington Arts Pavilion."

"No kidding?" This *was* impressive. Samantha's voice got warmer. "That's great, Mom. I mean really."

"I know. I just couldn't wait to tell you." Sondra's voice was a bit thick, but Samantha couldn't tell if she had been drinking. It could be just a slight head cold.

"When will you know?"

"Probably sometime this week. It's got to be done on this horrendous schedule . . . before the end of January . . . so I'm not sure about plans for Christmas—"

"—We don't have to worry about that. It's only August—"

"—but they'll probably decide right away."

"God, Mom, this is great." It wasn't hard to make her tone genuine. This was just what her mother needed. It would keep her on track. "Congratulations."

"Well, don't congratulate me yet. Just keep your fingers crossed."

"I will. Promise." Samantha leaned against the cool of the refrigerator. "Well, Mom, I'm right in the middle of cooking dinner. Can I call you back?"

"Uh . . . sure, sweetie. But don't bother. I just wanted to tell you the good news. It's come at a great time—you know, with all the expenses and everything."

"Yes, it has. Well . . . take care." Samantha hated this part, about figuring out good-bye.

"Yes, you too, Sammy. I miss you."

"Yeah, Mom. Me too."

She hung up the phone, walked over to the wine glass and poured the contents into the sink.

◆ ◆ ◆

Lindsay made her way into Joanne's apartment with several bags of takeout from the Bangkok Kitchen in her arms. There were no signs of life. Lindsay wondered where Joanne had stormed to after their fight. A shopping spree, one of her pals, another lover? Lindsay had sat numbly staring at the remains of their breakfast until the waitress asked if they could possibly use the table. She walked to the office, then called Sondra, apologizing for her absence.

"Oh, no problem. Really," Sondra had answered.

"Have you got a cold?"

"Yes. I think I'm coming down with one." Had she been crying? Lindsay wondered. Her heart immediately went out to this lonely woman and she damned Joanne for making her miss the meeting.

"Hey, I could stop by now. Show you the catalogues I picked up."

"Really?"

"Yeah. And I may have some great news."

"Great. I could use some."

"Say in an hour?"

Lindsay finished her other calls as quickly as possible and found herself zipping through traffic to Sondra's tastefully designed apartment, an homage to her talents.

Sondra offered coffee and they sat on the sofa. Lindsay glanced at Sondra, sensed her slight nervousness, always conspicuous until she regained her confidence; and noticed, really noticed, what a beautiful woman Sondra was at that moment, so fragile and pale. Lindsay's heart ached to make her feel at ease.

They talked about Earlsheart, and Sondra shared her concerns about money. Lindsay told her they could work out an arrangement with her fee. "God knows, this project has been nothing but a godsend for me. It's been so rewarding . . . please don't worry about the money."

"Oh, things aren't that bad," Sondra said, "just a bit tight."

"Well, then I have some good news for you."

"Oh, yes? Please," Sondra laughed, "good news would be nice."

Lindsay told Sondra about her conversation with Joanne, and what she had told her about Guy Nathan. Yes, Sondra had heard of him, and was surprised but flattered by his interest in her work. But Lindsay found it difficult to pay attention to what she said, as she was very conscious of Sondra's eyes, her lips, the way her head tilted to the side when she listened.

They chatted for another hour and Lindsay felt the warmth in Sondra's laughter, saw the eyes shining into her own and heard Joanne's words in the back of her mind. But no. This woman sitting before her was so removed from herself, her sexuality. If anything, she was lonely and found she could rely on Lindsay, felt safe with her. That's all there was to it.

"You know Joanne pretty well?"

"Uh . . . yes." It caught Lindsay off guard and a swift prick of guilt shot through her. Joanne was off somewhere licking her wounds as Lindsay was tiptoeing into unknown waters. "I really should be going. I didn't realize how late it was."

"Oh. But don't leave on my account."

"No. It's just . . . I'm running late." But she wasn't sure for what. Lindsay got up. Sondra walked with her to the door.

"Thanks for the good news."

Lindsay turned. They stood very close. For a moment both women were still. Then Sondra backed away. "I guess I'll see you Monday."

"Yes. Monday."

And now Lindsay set out the cartons of vegetable beef, chicken in peanut sauce, pan-fried noodles and spring rolls, lit two candles, opened a bottle of gewürztraminer and paced until Joanne might, or might not, show up.

◆ ◆ ◆

Samantha walked around the chopping block in the middle of the kitchen. She stopped the third time around, peered out the window. Was it a goddamn full moon or what? And, as a matter of fact, it appeared to be.

She finished sautéing the mushrooms for her special spaghetti sauce. It was Robert's favorite, and she figured it was the least she could do. Feed him well. She had done nothing else that day to make him the least bit happy.

But what about making herself happy? Maybe what she needed was simply to get back into her life. She didn't need time off. She needed time on. She opened a box of noodles, put water on to boil. Yes. She would reimmerse herself into the life that was, by all measures, practically more than one could ask for.

She checked the time on the stove, wiped her hands on the apron she had never donned, and went to find Robert.

He sat in the study. He was hunched over, staring at something in his hands. She came up behind him and saw it was the small framed photo of the two of them, taken on their trip to Hawaii that first year, freshly sunburned, giddy from daiquiris and love. A tenderness welled up in her, gentle affection for her small boy who had scraped his knee, hurt. She put her hands through his hair, one of the things he loved most, stroked him gently. He turned to her. He had been crying.

"Oh, Robert." Samantha grasped him in her arms. "I'm sorry." She held him as he sobbed, quietly, but with great emotion. "I'm sorry."

And they both knew her lamentations were not for the day, but for their future.

◆ ◆ ◆

"Well, if this isn't the foot wearing the other shoe," Joanne said as she strolled in on Lindsay's frigid remains of Thai food, burnt-out candles.

Lindsay woke, glanced at her watch: 2:15. "It was an attempt, anyway."

Joanne stood there. She was a bit tipsy, overwhelmed by the conflicting emotions of anger and forgiveness. Lindsay was trying. Hell, they were both trying. And tired. They needed time. Away together. Romance.

"Lindsay." Joanne sat down on the couch where Lindsay had crashed. "Shall we at least give it the college try?"

Lindsay wasn't quite awake, but in that moment of semiawareness, while pieces of information floated about, she knew, with absolute certainty, that Joanne and she would never make it.

"At least pretend to make an effort?"

"OK." Lindsay returned to a consciousness dedicated to denial. "OK." Besides, she loved Joanne's droll honesty.

t didn't happen overnight. They had now been on seventeen dates, if one counted all the coffees, lunches, dinners, movies and theater. Though a part of her basked in unparalleled bliss, being with Ryan came with its own stresses, brought on by her relentless negative self-vision. But he adored her. Completely. It was a phenomenon that confounded Megan's every waking moment: what in the world did he find so fascinating about her? After all, he was a normal person, and she was not.

She had not made it easy. But Ryan had patiently wooed her and she had finally begun to melt. Trusting words, tender gestures and a reliable constancy had allowed her shields to lower, bit by bit. It helped that Lindsay raved about him, and that Snag, after meeting him, gave an unqualified thumbs-up and teased her mercilessly about Ryan's "obvious state of gagarama." Even then she spent half her time preoccupied with the why of it, as opposed to the acceptance of it.

She thought of his beard, the sweetest slightly graying beard. She knew it would be soft and often wanted nothing more than to touch it, as Ryan kept showing up for dinner, or to take her out to movies or the theater. He was opening up a whole new world for her. "Bit of an Auntie Mame, eh, ol' girl?" Snag observed one morning after she ranted on about Portland's Art Walk. And Megan thought about it a moment and answered shyly, "Yes. I guess he is."

She smiled in the mirror. She had lost five pounds this week, not from dieting, but from worry. He was taking her to see a production of *Camelot*. Snag had gone shopping with her. "Sing to me, baby," he bellowed as she walked from the fitting room, then shook his head, woefully disappointed time and again. Nothing seemed to fit. But in the end, they found the perfect dress, an ivory-colored angora. A bit tight, but Snag assured her it was flattering, and she knew he wouldn't lie on that score. This was too important to her.

All through the joyously romantic performance of *Camelot,* Ryan held her hand. It started with a tentative approach to the backside of her fingers. He simply laid his hand over hers. She felt the heat permeating through her hand, straight to her palm, through the thickness of her dress, panty hose, until her thigh tingled. Somewhere between "How to Handle a Woman" and "If Ever I Would Leave You" their hands clasped, a slight moisture wedding their palms together.

They decided on Rimsky-Korsakoffee's for dessert. Terribly romantic, dimly lit, wonderful classical music—it seemed the coffeehouse for lovers. Ryan reached over his dessert and put his hand across the table, catching Megan's before she could nervously remove it. "What do you see when you look at me?" he asked.

Megan could barely swallow. The renewed contact of his warm fingers for all the world to see, or at least three other couples anyway, jarred her into a physical sensation she was not altogether comfortable with. She cleared her throat, but the tone of her voice was constricted. "What . . . what do you mean?"

"What do you see?" Ryan's pressure upon her fingers did not change, but somehow her hand felt hotter. "Does this make you uncomfortable?" He looked at their hands, and then back up at her. "Out of curiosity?"

But she wasn't sure which question she was answering. The bit about the hands, or what she saw in him.

"I'm not trying to push you, Megan. It's just, well . . . frankly, I've fallen in love with you, and I thought you might want to know."

Megan pulled her hand away, almost choking now. She couldn't bear this kind of pressure. The pressure to feel, respond, even though her body had been doing just that all evening. "Please. Can we go?"

Ryan paid the bill and they drove home in silence. Megan only dared one peek at him, his wonderfully calm face pinched in pain. He pulled the car to the curb, the motor still running. A deathly silence fell between them. They had never not been able to talk. She was ruining it. She was destroying this wonderful friendship.

She never knew what prompted the courage, but she leaned over, and before Ryan could say a word, she kissed him full on the mouth, their lips joined as if it were the most complete feeling in the world. And then it was over, and Megan jumped from the car. She ran to the steps, but then turned back, opened the door.

"Why?"

"What?"

"Why are you in love with me?"

"Because you are the most beautiful and precious creature on the planet, and I don't think that I want to live without you."

"OK." Megan was still breathless. From the kiss. From Ryan's proclamations. From fear. From the truth.

"OK. What?"

"OK. That's a good reason." Megan tried to calm herself.

"So. What do you think?" Ryan's eyes were brimming with tears.

Megan paused for a very long time, her breathing still jagged, but this time from desire. "I think," she exhaled huskily, "I think you should come upstairs."

uy Nathan lost his virginity at the age of thirteen in a rundown tenement building in Old Town. He had been on the streets since he was seven with his old man, a drunkard and a thief. He watched his father vomit and defecate on himself as a daily ritual, and at the tender age of ten cut whatever emotion he may have felt for the rotting creature and struck out on his own.

He learned quickly how to protect himself. He was swift, wiry, muscular; but most important, he was smart. When he discovered a misplaced carton of cigarettes he came to understand the most important concept about survival he would ever learn: the law of supply and demand.

Nathan channeled all his energy into a singular enterprise: hustling the rudimentary elements of street life necessary for survival, and then reselling them, either from the limited currency pried from the filthy pockets of his customers, or in exchange for bartered services. He built a small empire on this principle alone.

Before long his hard work paid off. Instead of laying his head on a stuffed bag of mildewed clothing, he was able to afford a mangy pillow and broken-springed mattress in Old Town's cheapest flophouse. His mind did not encounter the myriad pleasantries and stresses of adolescence before sleep grabbed his soul. It simply slept. The machine woke in the mornings, flexed its muscles against his world view: survival.

He began to sideline as a pimp for some of the younger boys, keeping them safe and primed for a thriving business to white-collar johns, as well as to the insatiable owner of Pal's Liquor, who discounted MD 20-20, Thunderbird and Night Train as payment.

Pal liked Nathan's drive, and hired him to manage the store while he concentrated his time on lower pursuits. Nathan doubled revenues in the first three months. He went uptown, studied the bars, stores and retail displays. He knew Pal's was perfectly located for commuters, but inconveniently placed in their sensibilities. No uptown breeder was going to hop over the drunks in the doorway. Nathan wasn't opposed to classism. He just wanted to be on the healthy side of it.

Nathan spent a weekend tearing down the facade, refurbishing the storefront. For the first time he felt the pride of ownership as he proudly hung the UNDER NEW MANAGEMENT sign. He then spent an afternoon trafficking indigents to the back, where they received free coffee and discounted booze.

Pal's thrived. A convenience store down the street did not. Nathan bought Shop-and-Go with his profits and turned it into another rapid success, targeting the consumer with every need from coffee and donuts in the morning to flowers for the wife in the evening. He catered to the bums from the alley in the back, effectively serving both sides of the track.

Nathan began pursuing distress sales of small properties and rental turnarounds. His life was one voracious takeover machine. His hunger for success and desire to pull himself from the gutter overshadowed any emotion that might be buried inside, until one fateful Sunday afternoon, when he was perusing a condemned business being sold at government auction.

A business broker for a large firm was the only other interested party. She was not beautiful, but there was a raw and primal urgency simmering beneath the stoic facade that made her exceptionally striking. Nathan knew instinctively that she had the same appetite for success, the same drive at all costs, and when he caught her keenly predatory eyes, he felt a new hunger.

He married her two days after the bid was officially awarded to Nathan's Development Corp. For a brief and blissful two years they combined forces, sating their sexual need for one another as they continued to amass properties. A week after their second anniversary she died in a car accident. Nathan was twenty-eight, a millionaire and a widower.

Three weeks after her death he almost tripped over a bum as he walked into Pal's to check on the store. He bent with distaste to the snoring vagabond, shook him by the shoulders. Slowly the gnarly-haired, flea-infested vagrant turned to him. It was his father.

Nathan leaned only slightly closer, whispered in his ear, "Move to the other side of the street, or I'll have the police do it for you," and calmly brushed his soiled hands against his pants.

And now he sat at an inconspicuous table at the Café des Amis, waiting for Miss Brennan and Mrs. Pinchot. The preliminaries were complete. Lindsay and Nathan had met several times with Joanne. The deal was set. All that remained was the signing of the contracts.

Sondra had arrived first, early and nervous. Shortly thereafter she had spotted a distinguished gentleman, replete in the finest Savile Row tailoring money could buy, a handsome man, graceful and immaculate. Despite the silver in his hair, his face was youthful, his physicality lean and agile. Sondra was aware of his notorious reputation with women, and could understand why after he flashed his disarming grin, his steely gray eyes peering deeply into her own. His well-manicured hand grasped hers firmly as he helped her to her seat. Being a widower all these years lent an air of mystique to his persona, a wariness few women could resist.

"Ahhh, I've heard a great deal about your work, Mrs. Pinchot," Nathan remarked gracefully after they had been seated. "Shall we start with a cocktail while we wait?"

"Oh. No, thank you."

"I'll order one if you don't mind." She deferred. Her mind salivated as he ordered a manhattan for himself. Where was Lindsay? she wondered. What was keeping her?

As he studied the visibly nervous woman seated across from him, Nathan was reminded of his initial reluctance to take her on as part of this project:

"I don't know, Joanne." Nathan's jaw had tightened. "I'm really set on a designer from New York."

"Trust me. She's the one for this project."

"Yes, but what's she done?"

Joanne recounted Sondra's best work, citing the interior of the U.S. Bank Tower as a showpiece.

"Really, Joanne, don't you think it's a bit schoolmarm conservative? It's impressive . . . but hardly innovative. We need cutting edge."

"Come on, Guy, consider the assholes who own the place. A bunch of conservative yahoos who wouldn't know cutting edge if it sliced them on the ass."

"You do have a point there." Nathan had smiled, pursed his lips thinking. "She's got style, I'll give her that . . . a sense of color. But—"

"You're forgetting the most important element. Lindsay Brennan. Everything she touches is brilliant."

"Now there I agree a thousand percent."

"Have I ever steered you wrong?"

"No, my dear, you haven't."

And now he wondered if his first impression hadn't been correct. There was something about this woman he found irritating. Ah, yes. Vulnerability. He could smell it a mile away. It surprised him. Joanne very rarely associated with this breed of animal.

At that moment Lindsay appeared and joined the table. Nathan stood and shook her hand. This was his kind of animal. He knew it the moment he had laid eyes on her. A winner; sleek, well trained and begging to jump out of the gate. He saw his own drive in her eyes and knew no matter what happened she would clear the finish line way ahead of the pack.

"Sorry I'm late. Last-minute emergency. Sondra." Lindsay sat.

"Cocktail?" Nathan offered.

"I'll take a Perrier, thanks. Now . . ." Lindsay opened her briefcase. She immediately launched into several variations of what Nathan could expect if they followed Darlington's design concept. "I think it was wise of you to investigate another avenue with Brock out of New York. I've worked with him before and he's a great conceptualist for public works—"

"—That are privately owned—"

"Precisely." Lindsay continued and Nathan listened intently. "You've got to be careful when you're mixing the two."

Sondra sat in silence, feeling completely out of the loop. When the waiter came with Lindsay's Perrier, she ordered a martini.

"Well, Lindsay, every time I meet you I'm more impressed. I knew from your work at the bank and my favorite, the modern art wing at the museum, that you would be perfect for this job."

A heavy silence fell, all keenly aware of Sondra's peripheral existence.

"I think my strengths, combined with Sondra's eye for style, will give you the team you need." Lindsay unobtrusively saved the situation.

"Then I guess we're all jumping into bed together." Nathan raised his manhattan, Sondra her martini, and Lindsay her Perrier. "To the Darlington Pavilion."

They drank. Their salads arrived, followed by their main courses. As Sondra loosened up, she began to add to the conversation.

"I've got a contact in the Mideast," Sondra interjected, "who can deliver the most exquisite velvet for the proscenium curtain. And you've never seen anything quite like this color I'm thinking about . . . it runs between a royal blue and a shimmering teal, depending on the way the light hits it."

"Yes," Nathan considered, "that could work very well." Maybe his prejudgment of this woman had been hasty. Maybe she just needed time to get comfortable. Maybe he intimidated her. The thought warmed him.

He focused his attention on her and reevaluated her. A sweet blush had softened her cheeks and, though she was nearing his age, she was in fine shape. He very rarely found women over forty attractive, but Mrs. Pinchot had some very interesting qualities.

Lunch was cleared. "I think this calls for champagne." A bottle appeared. The waiter poured three glasses. Nathan lifted his glass. "To success." Only two glasses were emptied.

Lindsay raised her Perrier. "To meeting the deadline."

They all laughed.

◆ ◆ ◆

Lindsay drove Sondra back to her apartment. Sondra asked her in for coffee.

"Whew! I haven't had champagne in the middle of the day in ages." She went to the kitchen and put on some coffee. When she returned, Lindsay watched as she walked to the stereo and put on some light jazz, her movements sensual and lazy—probably a result of the drink but very attractive.

"You like jazz?"

"Yeah. Food for the soul."

"Is that what it's called?"

"That's what I call it." Lindsay was about to check the time, but decided what the hell. It was Friday afternoon. "May I use your phone?"

"Sure. It's by the desk." Sondra returned to the kitchen to get the coffee.

Megan rattled off a number of messages that had come in for Lindsay. "Oh. And Joanne wants you to call her as soon as possible. She's very anxious to know how it went."

"Thanks." Lindsay hung up, dialed Joanne, got her machine. "All's well that begins well? We can only keep our fingers crossed. Well . . . looks like we're going forward, thanks to you. I'll touch base later."

"She seems to take an inordinate interest in your career," Sondra said as she came from the kitchen with two mugs.

"Hmmm?" Lindsay took the coffee.

"Joanne Weatherly."

"Well, yes. She's brought me quite a bit of work."

"But it seems more than that."

"We're close friends."

"Hmmm." Sondra sat down. She took a sip and stretched backward against the sofa.

Lindsay's eyes traveled the length of Sondra's body, noting how it basked, languorously, as though it craved a nap, a massage, to be touched. And then she felt it. Out of nowhere. It wasn't the immediate sexual response she experienced with Joanne, basic, familiar, predictable. This was a newly awakened desire to touch, to feel and explore someone different, someone who could break if you touched her. She had never paused to see Sondra in this light, for obvious reasons. She was straight. As straight as they came, seemingly, and even with Joanne's not-so-subtle insinuations, Lindsay had not seriously considered any other possibility.

She reacted sharply. "You know, I really should get back to the office."

"Oh." Disappointment clouded Sondra's face. "That's too bad." Lindsay took another sip of coffee.

"I was actually going to invite you to stay for dinner. Have our own celebration." Sondra's eyes were light and playful. Yes, obviously there were aspects to this woman either Lindsay had never seen or Sondra had never shown.

"Well, I think that might still be arranged," Lindsay found herself saying. "Maybe I could . . . um . . . come back later."

"Really? That would be great. I haven't cooked in a long time, and I know just enough not to be dangerous in the kitchen." Sondra sat up with excitement. "I do a mean pasta."

"I adore pasta."

"Good. Can you make it, say, around eight?"

Lindsay got up. She felt awkward now. "I'll be here."

Joanne paced the floor, holding the phone tightly. "What do you mean you can't make it? I've made reservations."

"I'm sorry you went to all the trouble. Maybe tomorrow night. I've got to work late." Lindsay sat in her office, wading through the mass of paperwork that was stacked on her desk. She had decided the moment she sat down she would cancel with Sondra. What had she been thinking? Even if she worked the entire weekend she wouldn't catch up.

"Please don't, Lindsay. We've been doing so well." Joanne was pleading now and Lindsay couldn't stand it. She felt pulled in too many directions: her work, the Nathan contract, Joanne, and now this inexplicable weave toward Sondra that spelled nothing but disaster. She would retreat into her favorite cocoon, swaddled in paperwork. It was the one thing that offered stability, that would make her feel safe.

"Joanne. I need some time. Can we make it tomorrow?"

"Or will tomorrow just be another today? Too busy, too tired, too this, too that. Fuck you, Lindsay. Fuck you." Lindsay recoiled from the slam of the phone, the dial tone as dead as their relationship.

As though nothing had happened she began to sort through papers, initiating her ritual of withdrawal. She would call Sondra later, once she organized the stack of change orders, contracts, punch lists, invoices, correspondence and new leads that swam about her. She plodded through, but found it difficult to concentrate, and it wasn't long before a dizzying disorientation swept over her, a wave of nausea, her heart skipping a beat.

She was having another of her anxiety attacks. Lindsay inhaled slowly, controlling her breathing with measured rhythm. She walked to the picture window framing the city. It had started to rain.

"Now what?" she asked her reflection.

◆ ◆ ◆

"Where the hell is my lighter?" Sondra danced on a sword's edge as she consumed her quotient of cigarettes before Lindsay was to arrive.

One part of her primped and preened, carefully examining the lines in her face, hoping she didn't appear too old to Lindsay, hoping she might notice her eyes instead, always her best feature. The deep burgundy silk she was wearing highlighted those eyes, brought the blue out of the gray, made her appear younger. Yes. She was very presentable.

"Yes, but for what?" the other part of her interrogated sharply. It tangled with the sweetness of her mood. Mounting irritation joined the nagger's voice in the back of her mind, a voice that second-guessed her every move, a voice that intruded with reminders of despair over her finances. Earlsheart was almost finished and nowhere near being paid off.

The depression that was merely a matter of time, that beckoned to her with increasing familiarity, was being held at bay by only one thing, the bottle. This was where everyone's perception of her drinking was askew. Rather than causing it, the bottle often circumvented her fall into the abyss.

She had been nipping at the Hennessy's all afternoon while preparing the pasta sauce for dinner. It had been so long since she had cooked for anyone other than Carl, and he was a meat-and-potatoes man. She hadn't thought about him in a long time. His quiet unassuming presence simply didn't demand it. She supposed she ought to think of him more often, but he truly was out of sight, out of mind.

Sondra glanced at her watch: 7:50. She dashed from the kitchen to the small dinette, then to her makeup table in the bedroom, attending to everything with precision and care inspired by loose freedom, her body fluid motion. She lit another Export A, spritzed one last mist of Pheromone to waltz through, checked her tomato basil sauce, dimmed the lights, and lit the candles. Then blew them out, turned the lights back up. She shook her head. What was she doing? What would Lindsay think? Then she dimmed the lights, lit the candles again. There was nothing wrong with sharing an intimate dinner between friends, she decided.

The doorbell rang. It was her.

Sondra smoothed her dress, peered into the mirror in the hallway one last time. "Not bad for an old broad," she grumbled, sucked in her tummy, and answered the door.

Lindsay was clad in jeans, boots, a navy linen blazer and a crisp white banded-collar shirt. Sondra's first thought was how dashing she is, then she laughed inwardly. What an odd word, but that's exactly how she appeared. She held flowers and a bottle of champagne in her hands.

"Oh, you shouldn't have," Sondra said. "Actually I don't know why anyone says that. They're wonderful and thank you." Sondra took the bouquet of summer flowers and led Lindsay into the apartment.

Lindsay stood dumbly as Sondra went into the kitchen to get a vase. She had not intended to be here, had planned to cancel, and now here she was. She watched Sondra when she returned, saw the slinky wine-colored dress sway with her movements as she placed the flowers on the table.

"Great dress."

"Oh. Thanks. I haven't worn it in a couple of years." Sondra wondered how that sounded. "But I thought, what the hell. We're celebrating."

"Yes." Lindsay held out the champagne.

"Thank you again." Sondra took the champagne, set it by the flowers.

"Well, this *is* a double celebration. The Nathan project, and . . ."

". . . Earlsheart?" Sondra finished for her, but a frown pinched her forehead.

"It is a celebration, right?"

"Of course." Sondra smiled.

"But?"

"Nothing. Really."

"But there is . . . something."

"No." Sondra touched Lindsay's forearm, then quickly removed her hand. "Sit down." She went to the stereo, put on more jazz, this time slow and sultry.

Sondra walked slowly to the couch where Lindsay sat. "I'll get glasses for the champagne," she said and disappeared again.

Lindsay let out a long sigh. Sondra returned. Lindsay opened the champagne. They were both awkward. Stilted.

"So," Lindsay said as she poured the tulip glasses half full, "which should we drink to first?"

"Partnership," Sondra said and smiled. They toasted and sipped.

"And to Earlsheart." Lindsay's eyes sparkled with genuine pride.

"A thing of beauty that has brought an enormous amount of joy to my life."

"Thank you. Thank you so much for making Earlsheart so perfect," Sondra whispered, her voice wavering.

"Sondra, what's the matter?"

"Nothing. It's . . . well, to be quite honest, I'm a little strapped and I had a major client pull out. But with the Arts Pavilion, things should be OK. You know . . . cash flow stuff."

Lindsay put her glass down. "I hope I don't have to say this again, but if you need time on my fee, take it."

"Thanks, Lindsay. I appreciate it. I'm just hoping it won't come to that."

"Don't even think about it."

The champagne floated through Lindsay's limbs. She seldom drank and felt pleasantly intoxicated, finally beginning to relax, the anxiety subsiding.

"You hungry?" Sondra asked.

"To be honest? Not terribly."

"Neither am I."

They sat in silence, less awkward, enjoying the music. Each was aware of the other's movements. Sondra finished her champagne, refilled their glasses and then curved her body so that she was fully facing Lindsay. Slipping her shoes off, she tucked her legs beneath her on the sofa. "Lindsay. Do you mind if I ask you a personal question?"

Lindsay turned to her.

"You never talk about your past. I mean, I was wondering this afternoon, I don't think I've ever heard you mention any family . . . brothers, sisters . . . anyone, actually, and I realized most of the time we've ever delved into anything personal, it's been about me."

Lindsay noticeably relaxed. "Oh. Well. That's because there's not much to tell. My father passed away years ago and my mother left us both when I was still a kid."

"Tell me."

"What?"

"Tell me . . . something. Anything."

Lindsay groped at first, then found her footing, sparse words to trace a sketchy past. Sondra listened intently and then Lindsay began asking questions and they both reached out somewhere in the middle and each spoke of vague histories, never receding too deeply into the unbidden, offering just enough to stave off silence. They needed conversation because when silence fell between them the air grew thick, and though they both enjoyed the fullness of the tension that filled the room, it grew increasingly apparent that if they didn't talk, they were going to have to do something else.

Sondra got up to retrieve her cigarettes, and when she sat again her knee gently brushed against Lindsay's leg. She put her hand up on the back of the couch, inches from Lindsay's hairline.

Lindsay continued to tell Sondra the story of her debut into the world of business, and Sondra nodded in the appropriate places, although Lindsay's concentration faltered. Sondra didn't seem to notice. Every time Lindsay's eyes caught Sondra's, they were peering back with a new intensity, a new awareness.

". . . I started in a small one-room office in the Southeast, and it wasn't until I finished the hospital wing that I decided I could afford to move up in the world, so to speak, and that's when I found the office on Morrison—"

And then Lindsay felt Sondra's fingers in her hair, at her neckline, and Sondra couldn't believe that she was actually doing what she had thought of since Lindsay walked in the door.

Lindsay stopped talking. She looked Sondra squarely in the eyes.

"You're used to women," Sondra said. It wasn't a question.

"Yes."

Sondra's hand slid from Lindsay's neck and slowly made its way to Lindsay's hand. Lindsay's hands. They were all she had thought about while she shopped, prepared dinner . . . Lindsay's hands upon her lips, her breasts, touching her, inside her. Taking her. Sondra's fingers traced the finely sculpted veins then slid lightly between Lindsay's fingers, the sensation like a high-pitched siren as she grasped Lindsay's hand in her own. She could barely breathe. She took Lindsay's hand, brought it to her flushed face and rested it against her cheek. She leaned forward, reaching for Lindsay, afraid the spell would snap, afraid it wouldn't. Her lips parted. She felt Lindsay's tongue probing softly, gently, almost fearful, but Sondra's hunger overrode fear. She seized Lindsay to her, tight craving commanding her movements, hands caressing Lindsay's face and hair.

The longing in Sondra grew, the sweet pain of it swelling outward, touching every surface of her body. She pushed Lindsay back on the couch, sliding her body in its silky satin against her, their breathing ragged now, Lindsay's hands, as she had dreamed, finding their way through the folds of her dress, tearing at the fabric, demanding it away, while Sondra's hands trembled to release Lindsay from her blazer, unbuttoning the shirt which felt cool against her cheek, and then exposing the dark skin, in utter contrast to the white of the shirt. She heard the zipper, felt Lindsay's hands, yes, those hands, knead into her back, bringing Sondra down on her now, Sondra tearing at the lacy white bra, her mouth on Lindsay's nipples, eagerly biting them, each body in rhythm with the other. Free of the dress now, she felt Lindsay's skin meet her own, felt the full impact of Lindsay's body, needing the firmness of it against every part of her. Mind racing, images flashing she could not capture, her only awareness that she was making love with another woman, her tongue thrusting to meet Lindsay's own gentle motion, Lindsay's steely hard nipples touching her own soft, slower flesh, and then she dug her nails into Lindsay's forearms as she screamed in orgasm, unprepared, engulfed by its unexpected intensity.

Sondra held Lindsay tightly to her, unable to open her eyes, her breathing irregular, her entire body racked by desire. She removed Lindsay's unclasped pants as Lindsay moved on top of her, sliding her hands over the smooth and hardened buttocks, Lindsay moaning lightly as she slithered from their captivity and then straddling Sondra's thigh, wet between her own. Sondra had to touch this wetness, this woman's desire, moved her hand quickly to embrace the hardened pinnacle grinding into her, deeper, deeper into her, until Lindsay gasped, contracting her entire body over and over until they both lay quietly in each other's arms.

◆ ◆ ◆

When she woke the first time, Lindsay couldn't get her bearings. Strange bed. Strange lighting in the room. She glanced toward the outline of the body she had made love with, covered loosely by a sheet, the blond hair just discernible in the darkness. She felt the tug in her chest. Anxiety. She breathed deeply, closed her eyes, hoping sleep would meet them.

The second time she woke she smelled coffee brewing. She found her shirt, walked down the short narrow hallway and saw Sondra staring out the window, a cup of coffee in her hand. She turned. They studied one another, both seeing the other differently, everything changed once past the threshold of intimacy.

Sondra had a question in her eyes. Lindsay walked over to her, stood close. Sondra took a sip of her coffee, offered it to Lindsay. Lindsay coughed at the unexpected taste. "What is it?"

"Cognac." Sondra took another sip, and then, as if to justify, "It's Saturday."

An awkward silence passed between them.

"Well . . ." Lindsay wanted to ask if they had made a huge mistake, but was silenced by Sondra's mouth, kissing her passionately, both surprised by her forwardness.

"You are the most incredible woman I have ever known, Lindsay." Sondra lifted her mug in salute. Lindsay looked down in apparent embarrassment. "I can't wholly believe last night happened, but here you are." She indicated Lindsay's shirt, open to her waist, her breasts barely exposed. Sondra wore only her robe.

"Are you OK?" Lindsay asked.

"I'm very OK," Sondra answered convincingly, took Lindsay's hand, kissed it hungrily and left them both breathless with her aggression. She led her back to the bedroom.

The weekend was filled with lovemaking, a continual motion of entwined limbs, lust and need for more, the eating and drinking of excess, the excess of new discovery. It was illuminated by a brilliant shine, blinded by the worlds of their own desires, differing motives, but with the same result: they existed in a bubble of unreality.

The bubble burst Monday morning. Lindsay could not remember when she had made love more often. Not even with Joanne. She couldn't remember when she had drunk more either. She woke with the second hangover of her life. Groggy and disconcerted, she picked up her clothes, feeling somewhat depressed, but heartened to be returning to work. That was excess she understood.

Sondra stumbled into the kitchen, poured some coffee. She looked at Lindsay, freshly showered and dressed, the lines in her face already transforming to the facade that Sondra had learned well.

"You know, it might be nice for us to visit Earlsheart. Together."

"Yeah." Lindsay smiled noncommittally.

"You should take some time off. Maybe this weekend?" There wasn't much strength to Sondra's invitation.

"I'll think about it." Lindsay got up then, kissed Sondra, but not with the heat that had propelled her throughout the weekend. "I'll call later."

Sondra followed her to the door, closed it behind her. She ran to the window, watched Lindsay walk to her car, admiring the grace of her movements, then remembered this woman naked, beneath her, the lines of her body, the strength as she towered above her, her arms. Her hands. Thinking about her made her want her so much at that moment, she returned to the bedroom and lay on the sheets, swimming in the scent of Lindsay, masturbating, crying softly, low primal utterances until she lay empty, spent.

Suddenly, her head cleared. What was she doing? It was minutes, hours later. She had no frame of time as her mind bolted into panic for the first time since Lindsay had walked in the door Friday night. A moment of glaring reality fought its way to the surface. What had she done? It was the cognac. Of course, it was her drinking that had swept her into the eroticism of the unusual. The forbidden. How else could she explain this frenzied passion? It had to be the drinking. She hadn't been herself.

She rushed from the bedroom, furiously hunted for a pack of cigarettes. After she lit one she ran to the cupboard, poured herself a healthy shot of Hennessy's and sat down to think. Think, damn it. She choked on the intoxicating fumes, chugging it back in one swallow, coughing until it settled. Better. She lit a cigarette, inhaled deeply. Much better. OK. She would write a letter. She would tell Lindsay it was over, that it never should have begun. They would put it behind them and concentrate on the Nathan project. Their friendship was too important. She grabbed some paper and a pen.

She would just have one more shot of cognac and it would all become clearer.

amantha sipped her tepid coffee slowly, more out of habit than anything else. She browsed through the paper, wondering what her Sunday might bring. Not that Sunday was different from any other day these past weeks. As though she needed a day of rest.

She had found a book a few weeks ago, when her malaise first made itself known. It was a book in a new-age crystal shop, a curio she never would have entered had the vague smell of patchouli not wafted out at the very moment she passed, and if a young stringy-haired blonde in a lavender cotton dress adorned in a jumble of scarves, heart and crystal pendants hadn't come out. She kept the door open as if Samantha had intended to enter. Why not? And once inside, among several candle and incense holders, she stumbled upon *After You Have It All*. She picked up the slim book, leafed through it, recognized the symptoms the author listed, but could not identify the cause. Still she bought it—something different. At least she was keeping an open mind.

Robert was always trying to get her to do just that, although she wasn't so sure that what Jerra coined "the ookey pookey of transcendental puberty" was how she was going to achieve that particular goal. Jerra and Robert constantly argued. Jerra conformed to classic philosophy while Robert was firmly steeped in new-age metaphysics. There was nothing, no device of new-age spiritualism that Jerra couldn't pin to a prior philosophical tenet—idea, concept. "They just have to come up with a new jargon because they're too illiterate to understand the great minds of the past," she would declare, and then she and Robert would debate for hours. But it was all in good fun and it was nice to have her best friend and partner spend time with ease and companionability, even though she suspected beneath their good manners they didn't care for each other as much as they pretended. They did have one thing in common, however: they both loved Samantha fiercely, and wanted what was best for her. They had no desire to get in each other's way.

She'd finished a small job Friday and had jobs out to bid, although she had padded twice what she normally would. She didn't want to be competitive. She just wanted to waltz into their homes and tell them what they needed done and if that wasn't good enough for them, well, then she really had no investment whether that young naive waiting-for-the-world-to-lay-bounty-at-their-feet couple lived with hideously outdated pinstriped wallpaper, garish green carpeting. True. She supposed she did feel sorry for the dentist's patients forced to stare at large dancing molars on the ceiling while he poked about in their mouth.

It wasn't as if she didn't need the money, but it wasn't as if she were desperate for it either. Everything was smack in the middle. She needed to work for self-preservation, she reminded herself. It had been months now since the night of Janet Myers' party, but she could not rid herself of the vague ambient neurosis which had manifested itself in her newfound indifference. There was absolutely nothing, without exception, in her life that remotely bordered on extreme. Everything, from her work, her relationship with Robert, her diet, her social activity, hobbies, more pointedly her feelings—everything floated in a vacuum of medium. Mediocrity. Just fine. OK. No verys about it. Even her apathy did not strike her as severe.

Robert recognized her behavior, the signs of a mild depression, and was the first to encourage her to take time off. But that freedom had allowed her mind to float into new and uncharted territories, exploring thoughts she hadn't visited since just after school, before Robert, when her life had hit a similar spot. That time had been about fear. And hunger. Life was still a challenge to her professionally and, of course, she had been waiting for the man in the sapphire-blue cardigan with gray flecks. But now she was all grown up with nowhere to go.

She turned the pages of the *Seattle Post*, skimming disinterestedly. Then she saw it. A photo of her mother. In the society pages yet. Ahhh, yes, the Darlington Arts Pavilion. And a man, very distinguished. Must be Guy Nathan. And next to him a woman's profile obscured by the waving hand of a society matron. Samantha smiled. This would be so good for her mother. This project. Put her back on her feet. And maybe . . . just maybe, this time she'd stay up on them.

◆ ◆ ◆

Snag peered over Megan's shoulder as she read the caption underneath the picture of Lindsay, Nathan and Sondra Pinchot at the hefty one-hundred-dollar-a-plate dinner celebrating the announcement of Nathan's co-acquisition of the Darlington Arts Pavilion and the signing of Lindsay Brennan as the "renowned architect" helming the renovation.

"How droll, our tepid society pages," Snag commented. Having lived in New York and San Francisco, he found them a lame imitation.

"I think it's wonderful," Megan said, and took the creamer away from Snag as if he were a naughty child. "It'll give Lindsay the kind of recognition she deserves."

"I'm not talking about her. It's him." Snag tapped Nathan's face with his finger.

"I think he's handsome and mysterious," Megan countered.

"But not nearly as mysterious as Mr. Ryan here, who seems to have kept you locked in the dungeon of love far beyond the prerequisite seventy-two hours," Snag teased Megan and Ryan who sat next to her, holding her hand. Snag had completely fallen in love with Ryan.

And now the four of them—Snag and Jared, Megan and Ryan—had become the perfect double dates, and were in fact having brunch at the The Heathman that Sunday. Ryan and Jared got up to refill their plates from the restaurant's lavish buffet.

"Anything else, pumpkin?" Ryan used his favorite endearment with Megan before he went back to the line. Slightly embarrassed, she shook her head no. Her commitment to her diet hadn't wavered in two weeks, and she was radiant from pride, not to mention the glorious state of love she kept having to relive and recount to make sure was real.

"So, 'pumpkin'?" Snag queried.

"So what?"

"What? What every inquiring mind wants to know. What's he like in bed?"

She blushed, but happily. "Well, you know I have so much experience in this area . . . but, Snag"—and her eyes became crystal clear, serious—"I never knew . . . never could have imagined a person, a body could feel this way."

"You do have it bad." But Snag's voice was gentle, encouraging.

Ryan and Jared returned with their plates. Jared's was heaped with pastries he would share with Snag, while Ryan's was full of fruit and yogurt. Ryan turned to her, picked up a strawberry, his eyes playful, as he dipped it in whipped cream and presented it to her lips.

"Would you two like to be alone?" Snag asked.

But neither of them was listening. Megan ate the strawberry, paying tribute to a night not too long ago when Ryan had ushered her into the bedroom where she was met with candlelight, champagne and strawberries with whipped cream (nonfat). It was a display she had seen only in bad soap operas. She didn't know real people could be so romantic. But Ryan was the ultimate romantic.

Megan now speared a piece of watermelon from Ryan's plate.

"So, what do you guys think?" Snag asked as he sneaked a chocolate-covered croissant from Jared's plate, then dropped it on the floor. "Just call me the graceful debutante."

"Listen, from the looks of these two, they neither want to barbecue nor go to your Depardieu fest," Jared observed.

"So it's Depardieu or Barbecue, is it?" Snag put the choice to the table.

"I think barbecue at the house is much more enticing than your primal brute." Jared touched Snag's knee.

"I second that motion," Ryan added.

"You know what, Megs?" Snag said, leaning toward her conspiratorially. "I think we married the same guy!"

Megan almost choked at the word, then quickly covered her embarrassment by taking another bite of melon, and let her eyes dart about and rest anywhere but on Ryan.

 *eath.*

It was sudden. Terror, like a shot in the night.

I am going to die. I am dying. . . . I feel myself leaving my body, nothing left to me. Breathing ragged, chills of fear fragmenting through her body as she was seized with the utter conviction that it was true. As true and concrete in that moment as breathing air. *This is my last breath* drilled to the core of her until she could think of nothing else. *Breathe in . . . breathe out . . . it's simple, involuntary I can't make it stop . . . it won't stop, it's stopping. I can't breathe. I can't breathe.* Louder in her mind, taking over her mind. She stood, walked to the window. Dizzying vertigo spun about her, waves of fear getting blacker. She tried to clear her throat. It felt thick. She couldn't swallow.

It's OK. I'm having one. Attack. Anxiety. Panic. The doctor said to breathe colors. If you breathe colors you can't have them. *Colors . . . blue . . .* dark blue like the night she looked into. *I can feel my heart. It's beating so hard, too much pressure. What if I stop feeling it. What if it simply stops.*

After her first attack Lindsay slept on her back. She couldn't stand to hear the beating of that involuntary muscle, over which she had no control, faint thudding in her ears. The reassurance that she lived might cease. *Colors . . . remember breathe in calming peach, peach inside my chest.* But *what if it burst,* like tiny rabbits scurrying for their life, predator closer now, fire pounding through their racing bodies until their overexerted hearts exploded in their chests. Her heart. Bursting, the pumping walls taxed beyond capacity. *Found in the morning, chest a gaping hole, aliens ripping at softened flesh . . . bad design for such vulnerable beings. Get a grip. Colors. Blue. Jesus Christ. Please. Help me.*

Shortness of breath. Dizziness. Tachycardia. Overabundance of serotonin. Depersonalization. Desensitization. All symptoms of panic disorder. Of course. That's all this was. That was the detached clinical diagnosis of her mutated neurochemistry. Part of it was biochemical, the other stress induced. She could control some of it; the other was so beyond her control it made her feel absolutely helpless.

Her doctor had warned her. Repeatedly. But there were times, hell there were times for everyone, when it just got too big.

Stop! But she knew she wouldn't. She never did. At first the very stresses that brought on the attacks seemed to be the diversion that washed them into the background. If she felt one coming while lying in bed, or was woken from a still sleep, she would focus on work and the symptoms would lesson. She willed the ability to push them back.

But one night, long after Megan and Snag had left the office, she had felt a jolt in her chest. She couldn't breathe. She gasped for air, panic-stricken. A series of tremors followed, not painful, but her heart beat so erratically she knew she was having a heart attack. *I'm too young,* she thought as her face went hot, sweat slick and clammy at her brow, upper lip. And the pressure built as if there were a noose about her neck, blocking the ability to think, her hands shaking, not at all sure her legs were still beneath her.

"There's nothing wrong with you physically," Dr. Steinfeld had remarked in her brusque Teutonic accent as she leafed through the results of her tests.

"Don't tell me this is psychosomatic, Hanna." Lindsay's eyes were rimmed with dark circles.

"No. Very real. Classic, in fact. You're having anxiety and panic attacks. A chemical imbalance. But which came first? Are they purely organic—or more than likely induced and enhanced by your severe workload?" Dr. Steinfeld smiled kindly, but her eyes were scolding a naughty child. "It's called overwork, Lindsay."

Hanna got up and walked around to face Lindsay. "There's a very simple cure. Rest. Relaxation."

"Yes, I've heard of it," Lindsay remarked dryly.

"Then you might try to exercise it to a small degree, ja?"

And then Dr. Steinfeld had given her a prescription, a necessity which filled Lindsay with a sick humiliation, hating her physicality because it had betrayed her, held her captive. She did the things she could, watched her diet, monitored her caffeine, and became serious about keeping herself in shape. The attacks abated for the most part, but whenever she began to wander over the line, they came back to haunt her, to remind her.

This attack had run its course. Lindsay, shaken, went to the alcove and lay down. She glanced at her watch. It was almost eleven. She hadn't eaten. She wasn't hungry. She would stay here for the night. She stared at the ceiling.

It wasn't an accident she was having these attacks again. They had broken ground on the Darlington Arts Pavilion that morning and it was the first she had seen of Sondra in three days. The morning after their weekend Lindsay had immersed herself in the neglected mounds of paperwork that had become her office. She was curt to Megan and Snag. "I said no calls, Megan." And no. Sondra still hadn't called when Lindsay reappeared hours later, right before Megan left for the day.

"Need anything?" Snag poked his head in an hour before he left. He was trying to be helpful. He knew how important the Darlington Pavilion was to Lindsay, and this was one project he absolutely supported. After all, he would be sitting in the audience on a regular basis.

"Darling, I'll do anything for opera," he nellied at her. They had shared a deep comrade-in-arms embrace, finally in concert with what this meant to them both in terms of personal sacrifice.

When Lindsay realized the cold war was official, she tried to reach Sondra at Earlsheart. Sooner or later she was going to have to call back. But there was still no response.

So it had been a mistake. And like the anxiety pulsing through her body, the questions barraged her mind. What did this do to their working relationship? Why had she been such a goddamn fool? What had the attraction been? Lindsay couldn't deny it had been building for weeks, but was that all it was? Transient lust was not her style. She knew Sondra's initial shyness, the compelling need to protect her, had drawn her in. But it was more. Her attraction to Sondra was unique in that it required her to be present and aware of Sondra's needs.

She heard the door open. It must be Megan . . . Snag. No one else knew the alarm code.

Joanne.

She walked in slowly. It was almost a staged entrance as she came from the darkened shadows into the pale cast of light, in evening attire, releasing her cape dramatically.

"God damn, schmoozing's hard work when your heart isn't in it." She sat at on the corner of the bed, slipped off her high heels.

"Joanne . . . what are you doing here?"

"I wanted to see you." Joanne made direct eye contact. "I've had an offer in New York to put together a sweetheart of a deal."

For a moment the old energy blazed between them. "I wanted to see if there might be any reason to turn it down."

But the moment had passed, and the silence gave Joanne her answer.

"So she's jumped into the pool." Joanne shook her head, her movement reflecting something between hurt and incredulity. Lindsay merely set her jaw. "She'll drown, Lindsay."

"Joanne—"

"Forget it." Joanne rubbed her feet. The silence became almost companionable. Then finally, "You know it won't last."

Lindsay was silent.

"Just . . . just tell me, Lindsay. You're not in love with her."

"No." Lindsay shut her tired eyes. "No. I'm not."

"What, then? Thrill of the chase? Straight conversion shit? I mean, what, what can you possibly find attractive in her? She's afraid of her own shadow. She's pulseless. Neurotic. A breakdown waiting to happen." Joanne's inquisition turned biting.

"Joanne. As I said before, she's not the point."

"I think she's precisely the point—"

"She had nothing to do with us—"

"Please. Spare me. I didn't come to argue about it." Joanne slipped her shoes back on. "I know when to bow out gracefully." Joanne's fighting spirit returned. She turned, and Lindsay's eyes met hers. They shared a moment that was peaceful and connected.

Lindsay put out a hand to her. Joanne grasped it in her own, then quickly dropped it and stood. She crossed the room and stopped before she walked out the door: "Here's to Snow White fucks."

◆ ◆ ◆

And the next morning, after a sleepless night, Lindsay prepared herself to run into Sondra at the Pavilion. Sondra had left a message with her service. Terse. Professional. She would be there, but a little late.

When she arrived Lindsay was deeply engaged in conversation with the excavator. They were installing a fully glassed four-story elevator. Sondra interrupted only briefly to let Lindsay know she was there and would be inside.

Sondra was just opening her briefcase when Lindsay entered, but Nathan appeared before Lindsay could approach her. "Well, ladies. Good morning on this glorious day." There was a bright shine of excitement to his face. "It was supposed to rain, but there's not a cloud in the sky. Do you suppose we can take that as an omen?" Nathan smiled.

"Yes, let's do," Lindsay remarked, for want of something better to say. Sondra greeted Nathan, nodded curtly in Lindsay's direction. She looked tired, Lindsay thought. Tired and ragged. Did Nathan notice?

But if he did, he did not show it. He was nothing but charming. "I've got to run to the bank. Sign the rest of these papers with Darlington. Is there anything either of you needs?"

No, all was well with the brilliant architect and lovely designer, Lindsay thought as she smiled through clenched teeth.

They were alone.

"Well. I've got to get back to Hank."

"The excavator?" Sondra inquired.

"Yes."

"Hmmm . . . fine. Well, I'm waiting for my assistant. We're going to do some measuring and then I'll be at my office."

"Sure. I'll call you."

"Uh . . . OK."

They were strangers.

Before the day had passed a lightning storm had appeared from nowhere. Hank called the office. "Goddamn transformer blew . . . traffic's piled up like cattle being slaughtered and the friggin' backhoe has a bleedin' cable. And this goddamn storm. I've never seen anything like it. Came outta goddamn nowhere."

Omen, indeed.

◆ ◆ ◆

It was the kind of storm when someone really important should be born, Snag decided, as the lights blinked on and off. Wind whistled outside, and if he weren't so concerned about the power going off, Snag would have enjoyed the so "very bleak and treacherous" cinematic effects of it all. But he was desperate to catch Depardieu in *The Woman Next Door*. Thank God for Bravo. Jared was having yet another business dinner and Megan was no longer available for these lonely evenings. So Snag had raided a convenience store, sat through rain pelting his car as he drove through Kentucky Fried, not for the chicken but for three orders of mashed potatoes and gravy, stopped at a liquor store for a six-pack of Heineken and beer nuts. When he laid his stockpile before him, spread out on the coffee table, he sputtered, "This is getting out of hand."

Listening to the storm, waiting for the movie to start, Snag thought back to last night, to being in bed with the man who gave meaning to his existence. Suddenly it seemed all wrong. They had had sex, but it was all very remote, detached, and, more to the point, safe. Jared had done something neither of them was willing to talk about. Condoms now sat on the night table, proclaiming their presence as loudly as a herd of white elephants bashing through their bedroom. But they had made love in silence. No questions asked. Sex was tentative, hurried, a release. Snag supposed he could take some solace in Jared's insistence on holding Snag in his arms, spooning him gently, shifting his wonderfully muscled thigh over the swell of Snag's hip, as he had every night for the last three years.

Oh, certainly their relationship had started out the same as so many others. At a bar. But they hadn't been cruising. They were both there with friends who happened to be mutual acquaintances. They gathered around a table, decided to go for dinner. Jared had asked for Snag's number.

When he hadn't called in three weeks, Snag allowed Jared's handsome visage to slip from the data bank of his fantasies and quit swooning to Megan. But then they had run into each other shopping for videos. It turned out Jared lived only blocks from the store in a fashionable loft in the fashionable Northwest.

"So . . . foreign?" Snag queried.

"Hey. It's . . . Snag, right?"

"Yes."

Jared didn't seem the least uncomfortable that he had run into him, or that he hadn't called. He made no reference to their earlier meeting. Maybe he was spoken for, Snag thought.

"No. I'm afraid I'm as lazy as the rest of this illiterate country. I love to read, don't get me wrong, but only books."

"Too bad. Because there's this really great Depardieu—"

"Oh, I can't stand him."

Snag sniffed disdainfully, but it made sense. Jared was the antithesis of Depardieu, classically handsome, leaner and more refined—and utterly void of animal magnetism. So there, Snag had thought as he smiled dismissively and made his way to the foreign film fare.

Moments later he heard a breath in his ear. "How do you feel about Rock and Doris?"

"Highly sophisticated," Snag snapped.

"Well, I've got a double feature here, *Pillow Talk* and *Lover Come Back*, and I make an exceptional bowl of popcorn."

Snag turned then. Jared's hazel-green eyes had been alive with excitement.

"How could I possibly turn down an invitation like that?"

They never did manage to watch Rock and Doris, not then or since. But they did manage to fall in love, quickly, magically and solidly. And for three years things had gone without a hitch. They had been devoted. They'd never had the monogamy conversation. It was as much a given they'd sleep with other partners as not. But now Snag wondered. Where had the fire gone? And, more important, once it was gone, did it come back? Or did people really fall in love all over again? He had no frame of reference. Once the magic was gone, so was he.

The distinction, he reminded himself wryly, was that he wasn't the one searching beyond this middle stage. Besides, they hadn't been a quick fuck. This relationship was big, for both of them. And now his beautiful paradigm had wandered from the fold. Did he let it pass, let whatever attraction Jared had found himself in fade? He remembered a conversation with Megan, who had observed, "See a good-looking guy, you can bet he's gay." And it was true. Their delicious enclave did seem to have more than its share of beauty. The problem was, for most of them the commitment was as fleeting as their good looks. Perhaps they should have an NA—Narcissists' Anonymous, their vanity a power greater than themselves. Of course, every meeting would end up one big cruise fest.

Snag sprawled against the couch. He didn't want to think about it anymore. Fiddle-dee-dee, he said in his best Scarlett imitation as he turned the channel to Bravo. He'd just mesmerize himself with Depardieu as he became obsessed with *The Woman Next Door*.

Lightning cantered wildly outside his window, thunder cracked like cannons, and then the unthinkable: the power was gone. Snag sat in the dark. With his thoughts.

◆ ◆ ◆

He had taken her home, led her into the bedroom, wouldn't let her touch any part of her clothing, undressed her slowly, very slowly, kissing her softly, caressing her flesh, tongue flicking her ear, his body covering hers, floating, sinking into her, entering her, gently, rhythmically as his thrusts got deeper, fuller, bringing her closer, his mouth upon her breasts, teasing her nipples, taking her, taking her, until she screamed, "I'm coming . . . I'm coming, oh Ryan . . . " And he came with her, shuddering over her body, whispering her name, insistently, his love for her, his worship of her.

A few hours earlier they had seen *Chain of Desire*, a courageous peek at sexual kink in the nineties, brave, intensely intimate and erotic. Ryan had leaned over. "I want you," he whispered hotly in her ear.

They had walked from the theater hand-in-hand, warmly aroused, when Megan overheard a woman behind her say to her companion, "I don't care. I don't want to see ugly or fat people doing it in a movie. When I see people falling in love on a big screen I want them to be beautiful."

Ryan had looked at the woman, a homely matron with bad designer clothes. "I just bet she does." Ryan took Megan's hand and kissed it so that the woman would have to see him wooing her.

She lay in the crook of his arm, after the storm of lovemaking, smiled as she thought of the lightning and thunder and now the gentle rhythm of his heart, in concert with the rain, soft and drizzly. She thought of the first time, how careful he had been with her, tentative for her sake, not his. He was very sure of what he wanted, so gently passionate, careful not to frighten her; and then as she became less inhibited, he opened her up to herself in a way she could never have divined. And in her were born raw, hungry, demanding, lustful, impatient desires. All the things she had read about. For skinny people, that is. Never had Megan read, or seen on television or film, love between flesh of any substance.

She had hungered for this windswept ardor never knowing it existed. Who ever heard of a size eighteen and a half being whisked off her feet? But Ryan made her feel as delicate as Cinderella, as light on her feet as Ginger, and whisk her off he did!

She devoured every moment of their lovemaking, but even more exquisite was that fragile intimacy afterward, the sacred secrets, vulnerable disclosures. The trusting. But even with this perfection, fear dug into her as nothing ever had before, not schoolground razzing, not her mother's taunts or her inability to see her own image without shuddering. And no matter how often Ryan insisted, "You are one of the most generous-hearted, gentle-spirited women I have ever known, I don't care if you ever lose an ounce of weight, and you have got to believe me," she still wanted to be for him the kind of woman the media had plastered on every billboard in town. He deserved that kind of beauty.

He sat up in the bed, gently took her by the shoulders to face him, then grabbed a small fleshy roll of pale skin at his waist. "This used to be the size of a semi tire. I spent my early twenties shopping out of sizes at Koppelstein's. I was fat, Megan. Obese."

Megan stared at him, saw an odd pain in his eyes. So he knew. Understood. That was why he could see beyond the layers that cloaked human flesh through to the spirit.

" 'Fat Albert.' That's what kids used to call me in school. 'Butterball.' 'He's my little butterball,' my grandma used to say. But you know, all the bullshit that comes with being large didn't bother me until the night my mother remarried." Ryan drew the covers up around him. "I was twenty-seven, had topped three hundred pounds and discovered, like ten moments before the event, that I couldn't get into the tux she had ordered for me three months earlier. I wanted to die, Megan. I was stuffed into these ripped tails, handing my mother to her new husband in front of her new family. Jesus . . . the pain and humiliation she tried to mask. God," he shuddered, "it was the worst moment of my life. It tore my guts out."

Megan moved into his arms, held him. "I knew who I was inside. Knew I was—you know—an OK guy, smart, reliable. And there's Mom . . . her eyes shining . . . shining with the pride and love she has always felt for me. She knew . . . but no one else would. For good or bad. It's just the way it was.

"I drank myself into a stupor during the reception and the next morning, hung over, I walked around the grounds, through the remains of the party. I think I sat on the ground for about four hours, just sat, and thought back, all the things I would never think about, what a life waged as a 'fat fuck,' 'garbage gut'—you name it, I've heard it—meant to me. I wanted it back. I wanted to do it over."

His voice calmed as he told her about his journey, joining Overeaters Anonymous, trying every diet on the market from Richard Simmons' Deal a Meal to outright starvation, how he bought every book on overeating in the self-help section of the corner bookstore and attacked the problem of his weight much as he would a complex program required for a new installation: with utter logic.

He put himself on a structured regime, lost the weight as quickly as possible, worked out slowly at first and then built up to an effective aerobics level. The rote discipline slowly became a way of life, and as his patterns changed, so he found his behavior around food and his need for it change. Three years later he had lost one hundred and thirty pounds.

Megan's eyes teared as he finished his story. She felt the familiar shame, guilt, regression. Even if he could see through to who she was, how could he be with someone who didn't have the will power and discipline to do what he did? She needed to understand. How did one do it? If she didn't she would lose him.

"Maybe I . . . could go to one of the meetings with you." Her voice trembled. She had always despised the idea of a bunch of fat people sitting around talking about not being able to eat. Powerlessness was not exactly something she found embraceable. But look what Ryan had done.

"If you'd like—"

"I need to know your secret. I need to understand how you've won. . . . "

"I'm not a warrior, Megan. I'm just like you. Fighting the same battle. A mere mortal."

No. *She* was a mere mortal. *He* was a god—anyone who had accomplished what he had surely was next to godliness. If only she could get nearer to it. She put her hand on his penis, already growing hard, guiding him on top of her, wanting him to plant in her the seed of his knowledge. It was only after he came, telling her over and over that he loved her, that she remembered the condoms.

◆ ◆ ◆

Samantha paced restlessly. Thunder crackled, then exploded through the house, rocking the windowpanes. This storm was making her crazy. As she listened to her mother's ranting on the other end of the phone, she wondered vaguely if there was some way she could be struck by her mother's lightning through her portable.

"Mom, I guess I don't understand what the problem is."

And her mother went into a furious explanation about the money, that Earlsheart had cost far more than she could ever have anticipated, that the architect had consistently pressed more expensive fixtures on her.

"But Mom, isn't this the same woman you're doing business with?"

"But that's it, don't you see? I have to work with her now. It's the only way I can even begin to get myself out of debt!"

"But I thought you wanted this job."

"I would never work under . . . under these circumstances if I didn't have to."

And then more tirade, and then the thickness in her voice gave her away.

"Jesus, Mom. You almost had me. You've been drinking."

"Sam! What are you talking about?"

"Mom!—"

"I'm not either drinking. And, quite frankly, I'm very dis—disappointed that simply because you don't want to deal with me you fob it off into this same old excuse. Why? Why do you insist on dredging up the past? Don't you know how painful it is for me to be reminded of all the mistakes I've ever made in my life? Do you enjoy it?"

"Of course I don't, Mother. I . . ." What—? Samantha felt suddenly guilty. Maybe it had been too easy to dump it all in a bucket called booze. Maybe she just didn't want to take the time. But it was difficult when her mother's voice sounded increasingly like flour added to gravy; pretty soon she would hear the lumps caking together.

"I need help, Sam, I'm telling you. I can't possibly handle this job alone and my assistant's usesul . . . useless to me. . . ."

She was drinking. Sam knew she was drinking.

". . . And Earlsheart is damn well useless to me if I can't pay for it. . . ." And on she rambled. Samantha held the phone away from her ear, stared at it. She gently placed it on the receiver.

Sondra talked another full minute before she realized Sam had hung up on her. She slumped to the couch. Damn her. Goddamn her self-righteous pious daughter. She gulped the remains of her cognac, poured another shot from the half-emptied bottle. That would be it for tonight. She had already gone a half inch past the line. She had to be at the Pavilion early tomorrow morning. She had to be together. She had to see Lindsay. Lindsay.

And as if the mere thinking of her willed her forward, Sondra heard the knock on her door. Knew it was her. Opened it. Tears on her face. She had been crying about Samantha, but Lindsay didn't know that. She could have been crying about them. Lindsay's eyes were dark. Like the storm. To Sondra she was handsome . . . no, beautiful. She was a knight on a horse, come to rescue her. That's what it was. Lindsay wasn't the enemy. Lindsay was her rescuer. Her strength would defy Sondra's demons and save her. Now that she understood, she could fall into her arms, be carried into the dark of night, and tomorrow be damned.

◆ ◆ ◆

The next three weeks Lindsay took the rollercoaster ride of her life. Because Sondra's involvement was secondary at the Pavilion in the initial stages of remodeling, they saw each other only on the increasingly late evenings Lindsay returned from there or the office. Those first few nights Sondra would open her door, cocktail in hand, flush of excitement on her cheeks, a sparkle in her eyes. Dinner would invariably get cold. They made love, they talked. They drank. Or at least Sondra drank.

"I don't know how you do it," Lindsay finally groaned one morning.

"Nothing to it." Sondra had laughed and rubbed Lindsay's temples. "You're just in training."

"Yeah . . . well, I don't think I'm going to make the cut."

"Some people just aren't made for water sports." Lindsay turned to her. The ghost of Joanne loomed about. She had never heard Sondra sound so jaded.

"I know I've already said it and God knows Megan won't let me forget it, but we really need to do the final walk-through at Earlsheart. And at some point take care of all the damn change orders." Lindsay got up, headed for the shower.

But that night Sondra wasn't in the mood. All she wanted to do was make love. Afterward, while they nibbled on a tepid beef Stroganoff, Lindsay told Sondra she would defray her entire bill until the end of the arts project. "After all, Nathan's hefty bonus will more than wipe it out."

"Deadlines make me nervous," Sondra fretted.

"I've never missed a deadline. Don't worry. I'll take care of it." And Sondra went to her, embraced her needily and told her she didn't know what she would do without her. Part of Lindsay flushed with maternal ego, the other part tried to swallow the cold lump of doubt and misgiving stuck in her throat.

Lindsay was late the next night and the night after. Sondra became angry and then furious, although finally what they were doing made sense, because this was home for Lindsay—being late, reprimanded, withdrawing. Sondra had dived headlong into the role of housewife, but Lindsay couldn't keep pace.

Arriving home, Lindsay never knew what to expect. Some nights she found Sondra exuberant and enthusiastic, making love to her aggressively, full of sexual play and uninhibited eagerness—so unlike Joanne's prediction—Sondra laughing, joking, humorous and undeniably at ease. Other nights Lindsay would enter the dark, smoke-filled apartment, Sondra "napping" on the couch, no dinner, no apparent movement in her day. Those nights she was uncommunicative, brooding and silent.

During those evenings, Lindsay would bring out the never-ending work from her briefcase, which gave her a secret pause of relief. She was aware Sondra was struggling, just as one is aware the weather has gotten cold. And just as one might delay putting on a sweater, so she postponed a dialogue that drifted at the edge of her mind. She would talk with Sondra, when and if she was willing. And she would help her. Guide her. But, for now, it was far easier not to wander into the depths of another's psyche, certainly not while Lindsay was this stretched. It was what Lindsay did best. This keeping clear of danger . . . the danger of being present and available.

◆ ◆ ◆

Sondra took another swallow from the heated snifter. The usual deliciousness eluded her. She refused to feel sorry for herself, but damn, it seemed that more and more Lindsay had just one more meeting, one more phone call, that she'd already caught dinner in town. Sondra needed to spend time with Lindsay. To continually relive their sexual exchange, to convince herself it was real. Lindsay was her lifeboat, and she was drowning in an unfamiliar whirlpool of emotions, and the deeper her cravings became, the more insidious the confusion.

She sat, tipping her snifter back and forth, watching the contents make mini waves. It reminded her of the beach. She needed Earlsheart. Long walks on the beach to clear her mind. She tossed off her cognac, decided what the hell, poured another. She had stopped nicking lines into the label weeks ago and Lindsay wasn't there to cast a disapproving eye.

Two nights later Lindsay surprised Sondra. She came home early with a bouquet of lavender roses. Sondra swooned at the romance of it all, fell into her arms, kissing her for long moments. She needed this revival to keep some semblance of reality. "I think this calls for a celebration."

"Doesn't everything?" Lindsay's comment startled both of them. It was the turning point in their young and brittle relationship.

Sondra told Lindsay to relax, she was preparing her famous spaghetti sauce. Lindsay fell asleep on the couch. When she woke an hour later, Sondra entered the living room with two heaping mounds of spaghetti swimming precariously upon their plates. Lindsay jumped up to rescue them.

"Ah, that's not the best part." Sondra returned victoriously with two frosted tulip glasses and a bottle of champagne.

"So. What are we celebrating?"

"Your being home at a decent hour," Sondra quipped, opening the champagne, pouring a glass for each of them. "To us." A hint of desperation gilded the toast. Sondra took a deep swallow. Lindsay mouthed a sip.

"What? Don't you like it?"

"I'm not wild about champagne."

"This isn't 'champagne,' sweetie, it's Mumm's. The best."

"I wouldn't know it from Kool-Aid."

"Well, let's not waste it then." Sondra poured the remains of Lindsay's glass into her own. "What can I get you?"

"I'd like a glass of milk, actually."

"One glass of milk for the faint-hearted." Sondra lifted the champagne glass defiantly and drained it before she returned to the kitchen.

They ate in silence. Sondra picked up the plates when they were done. Moments later when she returned from the kitchen, Lindsay was involved in paperwork she had pulled from her briefcase.

"What are you doing?" Accusation was in her voice as she glared at that damn briefcase, never far from Lindsay's side, an albatross about both of their necks.

"Just a few notes, then I'm yours for the evening," Lindsay promised. Sondra watched in anger the intense transformation upon Lindsay's face, the molding that had once fascinated her. She walked to the Mumm's and emptied the bottle into her glass.

"I hope you have an enthralling evening." Sondra raised the glass in mock toast, then walked to the bedroom and sat in the dark, entertained only by her stormy thoughts and the little bubbles she could hear bursting as they swam to the top of the glass.

The following morning, Lindsay sat, freshly showered, water dripping from her hair. She seemed so young, even childlike, pleading with her eyes for this to be different. Sondra's heart went out to her as she felt the familiar guilt that lived with her like an invalid relative, hanging on, wrapped in a shawl in the corner, stewing over a lifetime of regrets.

"I've been a little crazy lately. I'm restless, you know . . . waiting for my part to start." Sondra was indicating the project. "I'm stir-crazy I guess. Been letting my hair down a bit too much."

Lindsay's eyes lit up. Sondra saw hope shine brightly in them.

"Yeah . . . been thinking of getting back in shape, cutting down . . ." But she didn't finish her sentence. "Maybe even giving these damn cigarettes a break." Sondra bounced to the coffee maker, manically enthusiastic. "I'll get some veggies, make a great big salad. . . . We could drive down to the beach for the weekend, see what needs to be done, maybe take some long walks."

Sondra's mood became light and inviting. She was so heartened by the idea that Lindsay decided the change of scenery would do them good.

They drove to the beach, both anxious to repair what was already a rut in their union. Earlsheart was near completion and they jabbered excitedly about how far it had come.

"I'm sorry I've dragged my heels," Sondra said. "It's just that the sooner it's done, the sooner I need to make the move. And I can't bear for our separation yet."

Lindsay glanced at Sondra, smiled. This was the woman she had been drawn to. Yes, there were some problems. The depressions, the drinking. She knew she had been obtuse and preoccupied, but maybe if she could help steer Sondra in the right direction, be there for her in a more concrete way, maybe Sondra wouldn't lapse into this darkness that seemed to seduce her with increasing regularity. Maybe she wouldn't have to drink to drown the pain.

Sondra hadn't smoked a cigarette in four hours. When they were at the grocer's she didn't pick up a bottle of wine. Lindsay didn't say anything, but she noticed. And Sondra saw her notice. They smiled. They held hands when they got back in the car.

When they got to Earlsheart they made coffee, took a long walk on the beach, wandered through the entire house making notes for the final completion. Sondra made dinner, they chatted softly and companionably, almost politely. They lay in one another's arms near midnight.

Sondra was tense. Her skin was crawling. They didn't make love, and although Sondra thought they should, being there at the beach and all, the fireplace roaring, Sondra's physical drive was gone. Having spent the day with Lindsay, Sondra felt as though she was finally getting enough of her, that it was nice to have a normal day, be like normal people. She was going crazy without her cigarettes, but, she told herself, the suffering was worth it. She could see the approval in Lindsay's eyes.

Lindsay was seeing the woman she had first known. Perhaps a bit timid, and definitely more frenetic, but very engaging in her own way—and without doubt, less moody. The renewed closeness made what she had to say stick in her throat.

"Sondra?"

"Yes . . . isn't it nice? The quiet."

"Yes. Yes, it is." Lindsay waited another moment. "I guess there's no good time to tell you . . . but I've got to leave early in the morning." She felt Sondra's body stiffen. "There was no way to reschedule the Stantons—"

"Who are the Stantons?"

"An elderly couple building a small retirement home. They have to leave for Miami by noon."

Sondra tensed further, moved away. Then she stood and walked to the window.

"And it can't wait until they get back?"

"They'll be gone for ten weeks."

"But this is the only time we've had."

"I'm sorry."

"Don't be sorry. Do something about it."

"It's their lives, Sondra."

"What about our lives? What about our needs? I don't give a shit about their retirement home. Let them stay in friggin' Miami with the rest of the geriatrics." The malice in her words shocked them both. These were not the words of lovers. They were the sentiments of embittered partners trapped in a relationship they both resented. Their eyes locked. Stalemate. This wasn't working and they both knew it.

Sondra walked to the dresser and took out a pack of cigarettes. She lit one and inhaled as if it were her last breath; the relief she felt was instantaneous. The battles of sin were being balanced. She took another deep drag, calmed herself. "I guess it was too good to last."

She left the room. When it appeared she wasn't going to return,

Lindsay got up and went downstairs. She found her in the living room curled up on the couch, a snifter in her hand. She turned, lifted the glass. "Cheers."

◆ ◆ ◆

"Oh, how clever, 'mixing briefs and briefs—the number-one criterion for destruction in the office place.' Pu-leeese." Snag shook his head, rolled his eyes, pursed his lips. "Is this some sort of news flash?"

"What are you talking about?" Megan was typing at her desk.

"Oh, the *Oregonian* thinks its Life section is passing for urbane and witty—describing in revolting detail if you feel a need for extramarital flair why the last places you should pick are those you do business with."

"Annnnnd?" They both knew where this was going. Megan stopped suddenly. Her face blanched. She got up quickly and made a dash to the bathroom just as Lindsay walked into the office.

"Is something wrong with Megan?"

"No." Snag smiled. He had suspected, but now he knew. "I'd say everything is great."

Lindsay was confused.

"Meggers, preggers!!" Snag was delighted.

"No!" Lindsay's coloring brightened. "That's great. That's really great."

"Boss lady?"

"Yes?" she answered over her shoulder as she made her way into the office.

"Can we have an eensy weensy chat?"

"Only if it's eensy and the weensy isn't painful."

Snag closed the door behind him. "I'm not going to beat around the bush. I'm having a bit of distress here. No. Let's call it raging anxiety."

"About?"

"Ohhh . . . just what in the hell we're going to do about the fact that we're falling behind on everything, and that although you're

Superwoman, you've been dragging in here each morning like road-kill."

Lindsay smiled wryly. "Roadkill, eh . . . well . . . I guess I've heard worse."

"And I . . . well, fuck, Linds, I think a lot of this has to do with her."

"Her." The smile vanished.

"Come on, Linds. We both know."

"We?"

"Megs and I. We're not blind."

"OK. What do you want me to say?"

"Nothing. I guess there's nothing much you can say. It's just, if you don't mind my making a wee observation, with Princess Summer-Fall-Winter-Spring, you at least *seemed* relatively happy." He was, of course, referring to Joanne, and Lindsay thought about her briefly with a stab of regret.

Snag poured a cup of coffee for Lindsay, set it in front of her and put a gentle hand on her shoulder. "Just take care of yourself."

To Lindsay's relief, he left the room with a minimum of dramatics. He was right, of course. She wasn't sure if happy would describe her union with Joanne, but she suspected the outward appearance would substantiate the peppy adjective that meant nothing and everything. With Joanne she didn't have to think. Not that Joanne was predictable on the exterior. But her interior was consistent. She was only driven by one motive. Sondra leapt into the center of her mind, consuming hours of her time. Nagging. That's what it was. The sensation that she could never be free, the unseemly thoughts drilling her mind; that Sondra had never touched a sip of alcohol, before . . . before all this had begun, excusing her abstinence with losing weight, staying in shape.

Alcoholism brought to mind transient drunks in Old Town, shaking lunatics in hospitals, battering husbands, lushes on barstools who'd lost their looks, desperate for company. She knew her definitions were as clichéd and trite as they came, yet Sondra had shattered them triumphantly. It angered her that she hadn't seen it when it was so obvious, but at least it made some sort of sense, hellish sense, except now she was left with the tormenting question of what they were about, what drove Sondra's attraction to her, what had driven Lindsay to Sondra?

But there was no time to search for these answers, of course. She was to meet Sondra and Nathan in a few short hours for lunch at Delphina's.

Lindsay was first to arrive, then Nathan, apparently just off the golf course. While they waited for Sondra they went over change orders, addenda. Time passed. Nathan checked his watch every few minutes, impatiently. They exchanged polite smiles.

"Shall we order?"

Lindsay concurred. Perhaps it was best for Lindsay to simply conduct business without Sondra. They were halfway through lunch when she finally appeared, eyes bright and shiny, cheeks flushed, wearing a tank top that challenged the limits of good taste. Her hair was casually thrown back. She was half-crocked.

"Soooo sorry I'm late. Traffic was a bitch." Sondra sort of blobbed into the vacant chair.

Nathan glanced at Lindsay, eyebrows arched.

"Waiter." Sondra flagged a passing bus boy. "Can you bring me . . ." She noted Nathan's martini. "A martini. Two olives. Very dry." She then focused her wandering attention on Nathan. Every time she and Lindsay exchanged words it was self-consciously polite. Every time she spoke to Nathan she gushed.

Lindsay became increasingly embarrassed, while Nathan became more intrigued. When their drinks were finished he ordered another round for the table, including Lindsay.

"I don't care for anything." Lindsay glared pointedly at Nathan. Don't encourage this.

"That's right, Guy. Lindsay doesn't like to get fuzzy when she has work to do, which is practically all the goddamn time." Sondra realized she was slipping. "Well, I mean, it just seems like that's all you ever do. Very committed to her profession, Guy. Very committed."

"Very commendable." Nathan sipped his martini.

"Ohhh . . . I fully agree. But!" Sondra raised an admonishing finger. "Let's not forget ba—balance."

Lindsay excused herself. She walked into the bathroom, straight into a stall. Leaned over on bent knees. She breathed in. Out. Tried to assume a sense of calm as she strategized. She had to get Sondra out of there before she completely botched her reputation and damaged Nathan's faith in their partnership.

When she returned to the table, she stopped. Sondra was leaning over the table, armed with a deliberate pose of seduction, and as Lindsay drew closer she saw that she was not only gazing into Nathan's eyes but lazily flirting with the golden hairs on his forearm. Lindsay felt the impulse to retch. To scream. Unmitigated anger burned through her.

"I just called Megan. I've got to get back to the office." Lindsay heard herself utter the words, and watched herself as she packed her briefcase.

"Back to the office?" Sondra laughed. "Of course you have to get back to the office. Guy? Guy, are you a gambler? I heard somewhere you like to play the tables." Nathan clenched his jaws. "Put it all on Lindsay. She's going places. My partner. My partner, the brilliant architect." Sondra lifted her glass in a toast.

Before she could take a sip, Lindsay attempted to take the glass from her hand. "Sondra, you're drunk. Please let me take you home."

Sondra whipped the martini out of Lindsay's grasp, spilling most of the contents. *"I'm not drunk, dammit!"*

Silence. Turned heads. Admonishing stares.

As soon as conversation resumed, Lindsay grabbed her briefcase and left.

◆ ◆ ◆

She paced the length of Sondra's living room. Back and forth. Where in the hell was she? Running to the front door, crazy with apprehension, her stomach churning, waves of anxiety washing over her. How could she not have seen this coming? She should have stopped it. How? She just wanted Sondra home. Safe. Not dead in the streets somewhere, out in a bar with God knew who, or—the worst, of course—with him.

Lindsay drifted to the kitchen. She could no longer tolerate the inactivity. She had decided to make herself a cup of tea when she heard a motor running. A taxi. Lindsay ran to the door, opened it. There was Sondra, struggling to navigate up the front steps. She stopped at the bottom, dimly aware of Lindsay's presence.

"I shoulda known you'd be here." Sondra's voice was slurred and messy.

A monster swayed through the door, smelling foul, reeking of toxins and cigarettes, muscles twisted to limpness on one side of her face from the anesthetic effect.

"Sondra. I was worried to death. Where in the hell have you been?"

"Why inna hell you care"—Sondra stopped in the middle of the room as if she'd forgotten where she was—"where I been?" She stumbled forward, lurching toward the kitchen. Lindsay followed.

"We've got to talk, Sondra." Lindsay shook her head, as distressed with herself as the situation. "Now isn't the time. You're too loaded and I'm too angry." And then, more to herself, "Jesus, what in the hell is going on here?"

"Simple. Silly, fool girl. Very simple." Sondra giggled.

"Let me put you to bed." Lindsay reached for her.

"Goddamn let go a me." Sondra shrugged out of Lindsay's reach, barely maintaining her balance. "I don't need your help. Or your charity. Don't need you."

Sondra rummaged about in a cupboard, scattering boxes of rice, spaghetti, noodles, cans, more cans. "Where the fuck's my Hennessy's . . . where the fuck you put it?"

"You've had enough. Sondra, please, let me take you to bed."

"Too la—ate," Sondra belched, "too late, you're too fuckin' late. . . ."

Sondra clanked a kitchen chair to the refrigerator, climbed up. Lindsay watched with equal parts fascination and apprehension as Sondra unearthed a pint from underneath the toaster cover. Sondra kept singing a sordid madwoman's jingle about being too late and Lindsay felt the bile rise to her throat. She knew it was useless to talk to Sondra, but she couldn't help asking the question.

"What do you mean, too late?"

"Jus' what I said. Ya stupid or somethin'?"

"That's it." Lindsay's patience was at an end. "You're going to bed. You've had enough."

Sondra turned on Lindsay like an injured dog, teeth bared, all traces of silliness gone, all light vanquished from her eyes, dead, cold and direct, her voice as cutting as a machete, every stroke more fatal. "Don't you dare touch me. You think you're so fuckin' brilliant, but you want to know what you really are? You're a robot that has no life. Where do you think I've been tonight, Lindsay? You're so fuckin' smart you can't even figure that one out? God, you are lame." Sondra opened the pint, took a deep swallow. "I've been with Nathan. Nathan. A man. A man who knows how to be with a woman, knows how to fuck a woman, not some sicko per—perverted lesssbian. . . ." Sondra stopped.

She realized where she was for the first time. Her head twitched as she regained her bearings, a semblance of consciousness returning when she saw the eyes of the woman who was her lover staring back at her with incredulity and horror. She burst into tears, sobbing, stumbling with open arms to Lindsay, Lindsay the woman who had saved her and was now destroying her. Lindsay, whom she was now destroying. A pit. They were in a pit now, a dark bottomless pit they could never drag themselves out of.

Lindsay held Sondra in her arms as Sondra, draped senselessly about her, lamented over and over how much she loved her, adored her, needed her and promised, like a broken record, that she would never ever let it happen again. Lindsay led her to the couch, laid her upon it as Sondra passed out.

For a long moment she stared at her, remembering the many apparitions this woman had been the past few weeks. Stared in disbelief. She never could have imagined the depth of Sondra's pain. Loathing. Self-destruction. She removed her shoes, laid the comforter on the back of the couch over her.

Lindsay began to shake. With fear, confusion, pent-up anger and near hysteria, from the anxiety choking the reason out of her. And Nathan. She felt the desire to kill. She grabbed the pint of Hennessy's and knocked back a shot.

"What in the hell is going on here?"

The bottle fell and shattered. Lindsay turned in surprise.

A woman walked into the light. She stared at Sondra passed out on the couch, mascara bled across her face, her mouth a slack-jawed obscenity. The stranger glowered at Lindsay, who stood paralyzed by this woman's entrance, and by a memory so potent she found herself unable to concentrate.

"Who in the hell are you?" the woman demanded, poised for attack.

"Me . . . who are you?"

"I'm Samantha. Her daughter." Samantha gestured toward her unconscious mother, then turned and pierced Lindsay's eyes with icy accusation.

Book Two

ot, stale, she could smell the putrid sweetness of her sweat. Throat raw, dry. In the dream her head had been tilted back as she poured glass after glass of water down her throat, letting it spill cleansingly over her face; but the dryness never stopped. No matter how much she kept drinking, her thirst was never quenched.

But then she woke and the dryness could be assuaged. She poked an arm from under the sheet, fished around for the bottle she kept hidden beneath several old sweatshirts under the bed. She propped herself up on an elbow, eased her throbbing head into her pillow, then sat upright, opened the bottle with trembling fingers. As she drank, the first spasms of heat hit her throat, then her stomach, churning the acids, angry, swollen, irritated. But the liquor laced her nerves.

Her body began to relax, settling into numbing complacency. Took another belt for good measure. Only when the full effect settled in would she permit herself to revisit the previous night. How had she gotten home? Into bed? Then the sunkenness, the flashes of memory. Nathan. At the restaurant, they had still been at the restaurant, and then a suite at the Heathman—he must keep one there for unexpected pursuits—more champagne, the dizziness, his hot flesh on hers, grinding, the same rhythm all men had, remembering Lindsay's soft gentleness, how hard he was inside her, how good it felt to have him in her, filling her up, then crying as the motion became more primal. Finally sobbing. Nathan's confusion as he came, embarrassed by her hysteria, but she had, in that moment, figured it out.

She loved Lindsay, but couldn't be in love with her. No matter how much she drank, that wouldn't change, she thought, as she took another hit to soothe her ravaged mind. The memory of the evening became more intermittent, a strobelike disturbance as flashes came back to her. Nathan helping her into a cab: "Let's keep this between the two of us, shall we?" he had said. No gentle parting kiss, no soft pressure from a lover's hand at the small of her back; only the eyes of a man who had used and was finished. Coming home, she couldn't remember . . . any . . . no, wait. Lindsay! A lightning bolt shattered her vision, bursting in the back of her brain.

"Nooooo," she moaned quietly, "oh, God, noooo." Lindsay's face, her eyes, the pain, confusion, anger and disgust—the memory of it tangled together. She remembered her eyes, but the rest, the growing blackness distorted her vision, the pounding in her head, relentless. She closed her eyes. She was not willing to remember this. Not yet. She lifted the bottle, emptying the contents. Then she lay back, wondering if she dare venture out.

Lindsay would certainly be at the office. She struggled out of bed, made her way to the kitchen, heading for the backup bottle in the flour bin. She stopped abruptly when she saw the bin out on the counter, the bottle empty beside it. Lindsay was smarter than she thought.

She dashed to the bathroom and scrambled for the flask she kept taped to the upper side of the towel closet. Her breathing relaxed when she felt the smoothness of the bottle, tearing it from its bondage. She opened it and took a victorious swallow, almost choking, the overflow dribbling down her chin, running between her breasts bared by the loosened robe. She refused to stay conscious, so desperate was she to obliterate Lindsay from her thoughts. Another drink.

She felt the rapidly ascending intoxication. Tremendously wonderful to be going under again. She would sleep it off, deal with Lindsay later, when she could focus. Damn Lindsay. Damn all lesbians. Theirs was a place she didn't understand, a place about which she had no judgment. But she wasn't part of it. She wasn't one of them. This was only about Lindsay. And she couldn't hold on to it. A remarkable insight, she thought. That's why she drank. To get to these hidden truths. She raised the bottle to salute her profundity.

And as she did she saw the only presence that could erase Lindsay's image. Sam. How had Sam gotten here? What was she doing there, leaning against the door jamb, her jaw tight, the anger in her eyes irrevocable. No pity there, no softness, no give. This scene had played itself out a thousand times; Samantha staring at her mother, an oozing sore, the spirit sucked from her, the agony in her eyes married to guilt, avoiding contact.

"It's got to stop. Here."

"You don't know. You just don't know what I've been through. Sam . . . it's been awful." Sondra knew her voice was as pathetic as her appearance. "I didn't mean to start."

"You never do."

"It just sort of happened. Everything sort of slipped from my hands. But it really isn't as bad as it looks." Sondra sneaked a full-on glance at her daughter. Sam wasn't buying any of it. "Really. It's just that things have gotten so crazy . . . I'm so stressed about the money all the time. I just take a few drinks, to wind down . . . help me sleep better. Actually it's the only thing that lets me sleep. That's, uh . . . why I didn't hear you come in." But they both heard the question mark in her voice.

"The door was open. You were out cold. Your partner, or whatever she is, was having a shot of your cognac." Sam's voice was flat and firm. "So don't try and bullshit me, Mom."

"Sammy—"

"No, don't say another word. Just listen. This is the end of the line. I love you, but I can't stand this. I . . . I cannot do it anymore. Won't do it anymore. I'm either driving you to treatment—I've already made all the arrangements—or I'm getting in my car and that's it. That's it. It's over. You have fifteen minutes to decide." Samantha's eyes pierced through Sondra's. She meant it.

Sondra sat staring vacantly about her. Just like that. Ultimatums. That's all she ever got from her daughter. Ultimatums. Samantha didn't love her. She didn't care at all that her life was a wreck. All she wanted to do was wipe it under the carpet, just as she had done years ago when she left for Seattle to go to school. Her daughter didn't feel love for her . . . all she felt was irritation. She could see that in her cold, unwavering eyes. But she had loved her once. Yes, she must have. She had seen the love in her eyes . . . the music box. Hell. Did it matter now? Any of it? But then the cloying pity of drink took over and Sondra gulped down the remains of the bottle. Whether her daughter had ever felt the tender union Sondra was so desperate for, of one thing she was certain. Loathing had conquered love, at least for the moment.

◆ ◆ ◆

They drove in silence.

The treatment center was a good five hours away, which left plenty of time for tension to permeate and swirl about the car. Sondra could barely think, nausea overtaking her senses. Samantha thought too much. And they both thought back to the same moment.

To the day their separation began. Samantha's eighth birthday. It was a Saturday, and Sondra had been preparing for the party of twelve. *She had taken her first drink at ten A.M. The idea of twelve screaming, hyper little children running through the house was more than she could bear.*

By noon Samantha had cornered her mother and begged, "Please don't drink from the bottles anymore," with a force that was more demand than plea. *She peered into her daughter's eyes and saw a person instead of a child. It shook her.* "I think your mother knows how to handle herself, Sam, but thank you for the little party tip. Now, why don't you get dressed? We only have an hour." Samantha's eyes didn't waver. She was trying to extract a promise from her. Her mother softened. "Don't worry, sweetie. It's fine. Your mother's fine." *Samantha stood a mo-*

*ment longer and then, in apology and gratitude, grasped her thin little arms
about Sondra's waist.*

*"Damn," Sondra thought to herself as she poured another drink. Her little
girl was growing up. But it just wouldn't do—Samantha implying she couldn't
hold her liquor? No, it wouldn't do at all.*

One hour and several stiff shots later, Samantha's friends arrived
with their presents and party hats. Her mother and father had picked
out a new bicycle for Samantha. *But as a special present, from mother to
daughter, Sondra had found a beautiful walnut music box, with a porcelain
ballerina that twirled gracefully to the strains of Tchaikovsky's* Swan Lake. *It
had taken Sondra's breath away when she first saw it in the antique shop
window, and when Samantha opened the box she gazed at her with such love
and feeling, her bright eyes so honest in their appreciation, Sondra found herself
choking back tears. She escaped into the kitchen, delighted beyond words with
her success. She had never seen such beauty as Samantha's face at that very
moment. She always wished for a special mother/daughter union, unrealisti-
cally ideal perhaps, but something to surpass the numb link she had to her own
mother. She finished off her drink and treated herself to another for a job well
done.*

*By the time Samantha was ready for the cake, Sondra realized she'd
forgotten to finish frosting the salutation. She sloppily cut the increasingly
finicky children lopsided slices and spilled the orange juice several times while
filling puny Dixie cups. Why the hell did they make them so small? she
wondered with increasing irritation.*

Samantha's father had walked in at that moment, swooped her up
in his arms and played clown for everyone's amusement. *His voice grew
more boisterous and Sondra became confused. Had she poured the juice? One
of the boys started crying. Then a little girl. What was the fuss? Would Jerry
please be quiet!! She looked about her at the demented little faces, their needs
bigger than the room folding in about her, the kids screaming and yelling, Jerry
laughing at his own antics, and the music box, that damn music box, the
plinking notes getting larger and louder. A midget hand yanked on her skirt.
"What!" she snapped, scaring the little girl who wanted more juice, who then
began to wail as if someone had lashed her with whip. She poured it, knocking
over the cup, and saw the sticky liquid heading for the music box.*

Her mother had lurched to save the present, to protect it, but instead sent it flinging. The ballerina's left arm scattered across the floor. Her tutu whirled in the other direction. Samantha shrieked as she ran to pick up the pieces. The box continued to play, but the notes were mangled, all wrong. She had turned to her mother, the broken ballerina clutched in her little hands. Her voice was savage. *"I hate you," she screamed, and ran to her bedroom.*

The party was over.

Hours later Sondra tiptoed into Samantha's room. Her child lay sleeping peacefully on her bed, the limbless figurine clasped in her hand. The tears came then, and Sondra knew she had committed an irreparable act. But it had been an accident, a voice in her head whined.

And that's when their lives changed. Her father had quit drinking weeks earlier, urging Sondra to follow his lead, but she had refused. Samantha remembered her rationalization: "That's all very good for you. You're the one that keeps losing jobs," she'd remarked and left the room.

Samantha turned to her mother now and saw that she had fallen asleep. She could almost see her mother's skin prickle, watched her right eye twitch, knowing her sleep was filled with restless dreams.

She thought back to the mother's eyes of her childhood, lazy slits, pupils trying to adjust, then a hand flung in her direction. "Ohhhh, it's you. Mommy's tired. Napping. Go on . . . go on an' play." Not like her friends' mothers who brought you milk and home-baked cookies, wore aprons and easy smiles. This mom staggered between angry and tearful outbursts and soggy attempts at affection.

At first Samantha couldn't understand, thought her mother was hurt, something was terribly wrong with the unwashed creature before her, features distorted, drool seeping from her mashed lipstick. She would not leave her side, standing for hours beside the battered brown couch, legs shaking from fatigue, waiting for her to come back, tiny bladder threatening betrayal. *Please, Mommy, come back.*

Until later, once school started, when she simply tiptoed by, hoping she wouldn't. The red-bricked walls became Samantha's solace. When the bell rang at 2:30, a heavy sense of doom filled her small chest. She would dawdle along the sidewalks, made-up games keeping her company, or she would tag along with a friend, waiting until the very last moment to face the front door, the looming portal to a haunted house. She never knew what she would find inside, so would dash straight to her room. There she would envelop herself in the quiet safety of her mind, huddle on her bed, reading books progressively beyond her age, stretching her imagination, transporting herself to worlds where bacchanalian insanity did not exist.

She became her own best guardian angel, checking and double checking her mother's movements, gauging where the safety zone was. And even on those occasions when her mother quit drinking, Samantha kept rigid guard. Because just when Samantha would open herself up to the possibility that the world might be safe, she would smell the faint musk of rotted brandy on her mother's breath. There didn't seem to be a pattern, no logic to a morning after. Her mother's "condition" was a study in random chaos.

It wasn't until Samantha hit high school that she discovered that she had the power to affect the situation. She learned how to push her mother's buttons, how to manipulate and control the woman who was edgy and frenetic during the weeks she managed to stay dry, and completely pliant after a binge.

Samantha had two worlds. One that ebbed and flowed with her mother's level of intake, dependent on her mother's frame of reality; the other she presented to the outside world, controlled, slightly aloof, a little mysterious. She was cool without ever getting into trouble. Smart without being a geek. Popular without being easy. Nothing ever got out of hand until her senior year.

It was then that she first tried drinking for herself, joining her best friend at a drunken party. That night, before she threw up, before the spins took over, Samantha experienced utter ecstasy as her body and mind waltzed with newly discovered freedom.

This abandon, this ultimate uncensoring of thought and emotion finally allowed Samantha to feel an ease in life she had never known. It was a delirious sensation, one she embraced with abandon. For the first time in her life, she not only began to understand her mother, she could empathize with her.

She careened wildly out of control, on a crash course to catch up to her mother, a willed collision with fate. She began to miss school: there were calls from the principal, she fought incessantly with her mother, and even with her father, who attempted to help her understand the terrors of abuse.

And for a time she refused to listen, because the freedom she had tasted was the key to the person who lurked inside. But, ultimately, it meant losing control. And as seductive as that lazy emancipation had become, Samantha knew she could never really test the limits—because as much as she loved letting go, she was absolutely terrified of it. Control had long ago become her drug of choice.

Before the year was out, Samantha had made a complete reversal and returned to the rigid confines of her ordered life. Samantha knew her mother couldn't take care of herself, much less a delinquent daughter on the rampage. And since cleaning up all the messes in the household was Samantha's chosen calling, she pulled herself together just in time to graduate. She needed it. Graduation was her ticket out. To design school. To Seattle. Just far enough from her mother's life that she could pretend she wasn't there unless she needed to be.

And here she was again. To clean up the mess. She stared at her mother for a long moment, then gently put a hand to her shoulder.

"We're here." Samantha finally spoke as she parked the car. Sondra looked at the long gray building that stood in the long gray weather. She shivered. This would be where she counted the minutes for the next four months.

inds?" Megan tiptoed quietly into the room. "I know you said no interruptions, but there's a Samantha Pinchot on the line who said she must speak to you."

Lindsay continued to stare at the plan specifications spread before her on the desk. "Shit," she said just under her breath. Then, "OK. I'll take it."

Megan nodded and left the room. Lindsay sighed, braced herself to pick up the receiver.

"Lindsay Brennan."

"Yes. It's Samantha Pinchot." The voice was clipped.

"Yes. Hello." What could she say? What did this woman know? This woman whose eyes had seared everything they touched. Few words had passed between them that night, but it was clear that Samantha tied Lindsay to her mother's condition. That night she did not have the energy for explanations. Not after what she'd been through. She couldn't even remember what she had said, if anything. Her only image was that of the younger version of her mother, bending to the couch, a primal, strangled sound escaping from her mouth as she put a hand to her mother's face.

"I drove my mother to Eugene this morning to admit her to an in-patient program."

"I see." She was paralyzed into the defensive.

"I'm sure you're aware it's way overdue, and although she's not exactly zealous about the idea, she agreed"—the voice paused—"with the understanding she had unfinished business here."

"I . . . I hope she gets what she needs there."

"As I understand it, you were not only in the process of finishing the work at Earlsheart," Samantha breezed over Lindsay's concern, "but you and my mother are contractually bound on the Arts Pavilion."

"Yes. Is there some way I can communicate with her?"

"Through me." Final.

"That won't be feasible. There are things—"

"I'm sure there are. But the rules of the program only allow for immediate family members the first few weeks." Samantha dismissed any argument. "My mother and I discussed this at great length and we both agreed she is in absolutely no condition to handle any business. She needs to focus all the energy she has on getting well."

"Yes."

"May I come to your office to discuss the details?"

A gaping hole loomed in the conversation.

After a long pause, "Miss Brennan?"

"Yes?"

"I'd like to take care of this as soon as possible."

"Uh . . . sure."

"Will tomorrow afternoon be OK? Around three?"

"I'll be here."

Lindsay sat her desk. It was dark. She had turned out the lights an hour ago. She had tried to concentrate, but realized her focus was non-existent. She kept returning to the images, over and over again, the scenes replaying themselves endlessly. She thought of Julie Bracken, her father, mother . . . all the people who had left her. Work, her ancient friend, her solace, her soothing breast. It had always been enough. But no more. She studied the outlines of objects in her office, familiar, yet foreign in their shadows. Shadows. The only clear definition to anything was found on the pages of her drafting table. Beyond that her life was cast in darkness . . . and she had no idea where to look for the light.

◆ ◆ ◆

Snag chewed on a hangnail, intensely absorbed with the fine skin he struggled to remove without drawing blood.

"Fuck it." He stood.

He picked up another baby magazine as he waited in the doctor's office for Megan. Goddamn, he was as nervous as an expectant father. Well, he almost was. He would be the child's godfather, after all.

Last night he and Jared had spent several hours going through Hanna Andersson catalogues, picking out their favorite outfits. They were beyond delicious—pin-striped jumpsuits in grownup colors, none of this pale blue and boring pink crap which gave a child a bad start, defining a little soul, underestimating their ability for coordinates. It simply was too restricting.

Snag and Jared had played and laughed the way they hadn't in ages. There was an ease between them that hadn't existed in months. Snag had nabbed the catalogue, thrown it aside, and leaned forward to kiss Jared. He heard the catch in Jared's throat, knew he wanted him, and impatiently began to undo the tie on Jared's robe, eager, hungry, when Jared suddenly pushed him aside. "I'm tired" was all he would say.

What was happening? Was it just a casual fling or had Jared found someone else? And was now in that laborious process of figuring out how to tell him? Waiting for the Pavilion to be done because he knew how much stress Snag was under? It was amazing how their communication had been reduced to the banalities of laundry and garbage as soon as they stopped having sex, the richness gone from one plane, the other absent as well. Did it always work like this? And if so, what the fuck was the point?

Megan came out of the doctor's office, blanched, eyes wide. Snag jumped to her, took her by the hand. "Wellllll?!?"

Megan nodded numbly.

"Are we gonna be a mommy?"

She nodded again. Snag twirled her about, deliriously overjoyed.

"Snag."

"So have ye been sent a wee gift from the angels, Missy Megan?"

"You're making me dizzy."

"We've got to call Ryan."

Megan put a firm hand on Snag's. "No."

"But Megs . . ."

"I'm not ready. We're not ready for this. My God . . . a baby . . . a baby."

"Megs," Snag whispered urgently, "this is a gift."

Megan looked into Snag's eyes and saw the eyes of all the men who had seen and lived through so much death. Yes. Life was a precious gift. But not if it was going to destroy the one she had.

◆ ◆ ◆

They stood in the elevator together. Snag and Samantha. He kept glancing her way. She was clad in professional attire that instead of looking stiff and uncomfortable, actually appeared natural. She looked familiar. Maybe she worked in the building. An attorney or psychologist from the sixteenth floor. It bugged him, because he was good with faces.

"Excuse me?"

She glanced his way.

"No line, honey, but don't I know you from somewhere?"

"No. I don't think so." She was noncommittal.

"You work in the building?"

She shook her head. Damn. They stood in silence for the rest of the lift, and both got off at eighteen, stopped for a moment, then both headed for LINDSAY BRENNAN, ARCHITECT, pausing at the entrance.

"Allow me," Snag demurred as he opened the door. She let her cool demeanor drop and smiled at him.

Megan glanced up from her desk.

"Ahhhh, I knew your face was familiar. Related to Mrs. Pinchot, no?" Snag inquired.

"I'm her daughter." She extended her hand. "Samantha."

"Very nice to know you." Snag shook her hand heartily. Megan eyed her suspiciously. "Well, I didn't even know Sondra had a daughter. Are you from here?"

"No. Seattle."

"It's strange. . . . I mean, actually you look nothing like your mother, but I can see a very striking resemblance. Now how does that work?" Snag's brows furrowed.

"I'm not sure."

"Must be genetic flair."

Samantha turned to Megan, curt. "I have a meeting with Miss Brennan."

No. Megan didn't care for this at all. "I'll let her know you're here."

Snag's eyebrows rose as he walked to the corner of Megan's desk and perched upon it, full of curiosity. Megan hit the intercom button. "Miss Pinchot to see you."

"Send her in." Crisp. Well, Snag thought, if this wasn't the office of warmth and charm. Megan was about to stand, but Snag jumped to the fore.

"I'll show her in, Megan." He wasn't about to miss the fireworks.

He proffered a hand in the direction of Lindsay's office, walked behind her and then skipped in front to get the door. He opened it and followed as she entered.

Lindsay looked up from her drafting desk, then stood. Before anyone could say a word Snag felt a kick in his gut from the tension that flared between these two women. Amazonian warriors preparing for battle crossed his mind. He cleared his throat. "Lindsay, this is Samantha Pinchot."

Neither moved to make contact. They both simply nodded, acknowledged the existence of the other.

"You didn't tell me Sondra's daughter was in town?"

"Thank you, Snag. Can you ask Megan to bring in some . . . coffee?" Samantha declined with a raised hand. Snag glanced back and forth between the two of them.

"Snag," Lindsay snapped, "thank you."

A crackling silence followed Snag's departure. Lindsay moved behind her drafting table, a buffer.

"I've been thinking since we spoke. Maybe I can save us both time," Lindsay began, "and wrap this up very simply by releasing your mother from her contract. I will absorb any costs related to finding a new designer—"

"That won't be necessary. I plan to take over for her."

"What?" Lindsay choked.

"I don't know what my mother has told you about me, but I have my own interiors business in Seattle I've run for five years, have a well-established client base, which, of course, you're more than welcome to call for references." Before Lindsay could interject, Samantha proceeded. "Quite frankly, my mother's finances require that she complete this contract for a number of reasons."

There was a long silence.

"I'm perfectly qualified."

"I'm sure you are," although Lindsay's voice did not sound convinced, "but it's a bit more complicated than that."

"Yes. I realize that."

Another silence. At that moment Lindsay wanted nothing more than to erase the entire Pinchot lineage, retreat into her work, strike this increasingly difficult affair from her mind.

Samantha walked to the window, noted Portland's skyline, a town she both loved and hated. "May I tell you this was the last thing I had in mind when my mother phoned me—incoherently, I might add—three days ago. I was simply coming down to find out what in the hell was going on." Samantha turned and made direct contact. Lindsay's gaze did not falter. Samantha turned back to the window. "I don't understand why she signed on for this project in the face of what's been happening at Earlsheart—"

"What's been happening at Earlsheart?" Lindsay was confused.

"Yes." There was clear accusation in her voice, but Samantha did not turn. "In any event, the Darlington Pavilion is, ironically, the answer to my mother's problems. I understand about the stringent schedule and I can adhere to those conditions. I know you are not familiar with my work, but my portfolio is being sent down—"

"I . . . I cannot tell you how strongly I feel that this will not work."

Then Samantha turned, hostility seeping through her professional demeanor as she continued with her low, throaty and well-articulated speech. "I would not do this if my mother hadn't sunk all her funds into Earlsheart. It's the only way I can pay off her treatment *and* finish the place. She let her insurance . . . slip, and I really don't have the resources to cover it at present."

"Then perhaps we can make some sort of financial arrangement—"

"Look," Samantha snapped, beaming her angry eyes into Lindsay's, "I don't like this any better than you do. My mother has run her business, her life . . . pretty much everything . . . into the ground. From what I can tell of her sloppy books, Earlsheart has been her primary drain. I notice you had no compunction with change orders that doubled the cost of fixtures and appliances. I mean, what were you thinking? This place isn't exactly Trump Plaza."

Lindsay sat in stunned silence.

"I haven't seen her signature on one of those change orders, yet the bills reflecting that work are scattered all over her desk. In fact, the paperwork's nonexistent. Perhaps you can shed some light on that." The voice was losing its tight edge, the fury closer to the surface.

"Please . . . calm down—"

"Don't tell me to calm down. I want to know where in the hell the paperwork is for all the change orders."

"The fact is the paperwork did fall through the cracks." Lindsay couldn't explain that Sondra had been unwilling to complete her end of the paper trail, and Lindsay had let it slide as well, first because she felt so protective of Sondra, and secondly because they had become lovers.

"My mother's head has been in a cloud, and you, the architect she previously told me was the only one who could possibly do justice to Earlsheart, has been robbing her blind. Do I have this clear?"

Samantha turned to the window, her silhouette sparking a memory of her mother, who had stood just so weeks ago. And now Lindsay was in the middle of a nightmare. How could she tell this woman that during their brief interlude she and her mother had built mutual dreams for Earlsheart, that she had deferred her fees, that their relationship changed the face of everything they were involved in?

"I don't usually do business this way." Lindsay's defense was tepid at best.

Samantha merely cocked an eyebrow.

"I need to make something clear to you. I did not rob your mother. She and I became close friends, and it was more like a joint venture, a partnership in a way. There were so many things happening. . . . We changed almost every detail as we went along; the paperwork started slipping between the cracks and we let things get sloppy. Your mother knew I wouldn't take advantage of the situation, so it wasn't an issue. Besides"—Lindsay paused, not sure how to phrase the next part—"I was going to help her on the financial end."

"Lend her money?"

"Defer my fee."

"Why would you do that?"

"Because of our . . . friendship. Listen, I didn't know . . . wasn't aware of your mother's . . . uhm, situation. I trusted her. I knew she would honor whatever we set up between us."

"Honor doesn't exist with a drunk."

This conversation obviously wasn't going anywhere, and Lindsay wanted out. "As I said, I didn't know about your mother's condition. And for that I'm truly sorry. My only investment in all this now is that she gets well. I am more than willing to lend you the money for the treatment and we can dissolve the partnership."

Lindsay watched as Samantha paused to consider this option. The barriers fell momentarily, and there appeared to be a glimmer of hope at this suggestion. But then she seemed to jump through a complex hoop of interior roadblocks and the walls came back up, the anger flattened, but ever present. "I will take care of my mother's needs."

Samantha approached Lindsay's drafting table, centering herself just opposite on the other side. Her voice was calm, remote. "I don't want to make things more . . . difficult than they already are. My mother called me in desperation and you may well be the scapegoat. I don't know if you deserve that or not. This is the first time she's been willing to get professional help, so I want to remain here for her. I am very capable of keeping my professional and personal feelings separate."

Lindsay heard the mild insinuation as Samantha's eyes met and really locked into hers for the first time. Both deflected the contact. Lindsay got up and walked to a file on her desk, then turned.

"You're familiar with the specs?"

"Yes."

"Here are the addenda." Lindsay dropped the files on the corner of her desk. Samantha waited a moment, then moved slowly to retrieve them. "This is against my better judgment, but since there doesn't seem to be a helluva lot of options . . . Of course, this arrangement will have to be approved by Guy Nathan."

"I understand that." Samantha tapped the file against the desk. "And there's still the matter of Earlsheart."

"Yes." Lindsay sighed. "I know."

"Can we arrange a final walk-through to clear it up?"

"As soon as possible."

"Saturday morning?"

"I'll be there."

athan sipped an espresso, buttered his croissant. Lindsay had called the previous day to explain Sondra's condition, her admittance to treatment. He allowed himself a wry grimace of satisfaction. He had miscalculated that evening, had misinterpreted Sondra's lush drunkenness for mere tipsiness. It was only as she lay beneath him, her ungainly sloppiness killing his drive, that he was aware of how inebriated she had become. Since then he had been wondering how he would deal with her after the fact. Now that issue had been attended to. He would meet Sondra's daughter, who was ostensibly to pick up where her mother had left off. That decision, of course, would be entirely up to him. He held all the cards. His favorite way to play. Especially when he wanted to up the ante.

Lindsay arrived first to further explain the situation, to offer up Samantha Pinchot as a logical replacement, familiar with her mother's style. Nathan noticed that Lindsay did not seem eager in the least about the idea, but reasoned that it might be related to his entangle-

ment with Sondra. Lindsay sat, devoid of emotion. He picked up a
tenuous briskness.

"About the other day, Lindsay," Nathan began, "I hope you—"

"Nathan, I don't care to discuss Sondra with you." So she knew.

"Of course. I just don't want personal"—he paused, searching for
the right word—"involvements to get in the way of our work."

"They won't." Lindsay did what very few could—dismissed him.
At that moment, Samantha approached the table. Definitely her
mother's daughter physically, Nathan thought, but there the resemblance ended. She shook his hand briefly, nodded curtly to Lindsay,
and sat.

"You recognize we are under considerable burden, Miss Pinchot."

"Yes. I've studied the specs, Lindsay's drawings, your man Brock's
input and the addenda. I know what you're going for and I think my
mother was on the right track. However"—she glanced first at Lindsay, then settled on Nathan—"I don't think my mother was probably
the best choice to pull together the combination of Lindsay's design
and Brock's concepts."

"You don't, eh?" Nathan pursed his lips. "Go on."

"My mother is very talented, but she's a traditionalist. You have
two audiences. Both require that you maintain the elegance of tradi-
tion, while infusing it with an avant-garde allure. This will make your
target consumers, the successful baby boomers and their parents, shell
out good bucks for an evening of entertainment . . . to be seen in a
place that makes them look as good as their rented tuxes."

Lindsay put down her muffin and listened now. So, she was sharp.

"Yes." Nathan's eyes sparkled. "I agree. What do you have in
mind?"

Samantha launched into her description of a subtle union of the
upper-crust penchant for ostentation, toned down by minimalist mod-
ernism. "I'd like to have a softer line and color, not pastel, but a sleek,
dusky carmine to drape the walls by the circular stairwell. I'd echo that
in the theater, but offset it by using a deeper, more satiny two-tone for
the proscenium curtain. Keep it mellow enough for the archmatron
who will still turn herself out on a good evening, but needs to feel the
richness of days gone by."

"Very good." Nathan nodded enthusiastically. Lindsay saw his eyes and knew in that moment Samantha had sold herself. He was energized by Samantha's well-thought-out professionalism and enthusiasm as she became more animated describing her ideas. Lindsay found herself caught up in her pitch, impressed with the way she perceived the project and resolved the problems. For a moment, Samantha was a kindred spirit instead of the enemy.

"Splendid." Nathan flashed his winning smile at Samantha and then nodded to Lindsay. "I think we have found the perfect team."

Samantha waited for Lindsay. Lindsay sat forward then and smiled amicably. "Yes . . . I suppose we have."

"Good. Then we're all agreed, which makes it easier to present a proposition to you." Nathan paused, appraised them both. "As you know, this contract calls for one hundred fifty days, but I'd save quite a bundle if you can pull it off before the New Year . . . actually in time for the annual *Nutcracker* performance on Christmas Eve. The Darlingtons are very keen on hosting in their latest acquisition—"

"Can't imagine why that might be," Lindsay couldn't help interjecting acidly.

"Precisely." He turned to Samantha, unfamiliar with the intracity battle, to explain. "To prevent their staunch rivals the Spencers from having the performance at Spencer Hall. It's an ongoing battle for public supremacy between the two wealthiest families in town."

"That would cut twenty-eight days off delivery," Lindsay remarked.

"I know it's practically insane to even consider it—but they are willing to pay. Handsomely." Nathan watched with an amused eye as he saw Lindsay's spine stiffen, ready for the challenge. "If the two of you can figure a way to work your subs 'round the clock—whatever it takes—there will be an embarrassingly large bonus for both of you."

Samantha and Lindsay exchanged the briefest glance of consideration.

"Take some time to think about it, but let me know as soon as possible so I can do some restructuring on my end."

There was no question for Samantha. The extra money would help clear her mother financially and give her a little something as well. But more than that, it meant this project would be completed that much sooner, and she could return to her life. Whatever that meant. Samantha turned to Nathan.

"I can't speak for Miss Brennan, of course, but I'm in."

Nathan turned to Lindsay. It was perfect. She was addicted to the impossible and it always brought out the best in her. "It's crazy as hell. So, of course."

"Ahhh . . . too good to be true. Beauty, brains and type A personalities. My favorite combination." Nathan tipped his small espresso toward both of them in a toast.

Samantha pushed her chair abruptly from the table. "If that's it, then?" She rose, gathered her materials, shook Nathan's hand, nodded in Lindsay's direction and said good-bye.

Nathan watched Samantha as she made a stately and graceful exit. "Not a bit like her mother, eh?" He turned to Lindsay.

"I wouldn't know."

◆ ◆ ◆

Samantha sipped her cappuccino, stretched the tightened muscles in her neck and sighed. It was the first time she had spent alone in three weeks. This hour, right now, right here in the sun that streamed through the living room window of Earlsheart, melting her stiffened body—this was hers.

Torn in so many directions. Ever since the moment her mother had called from a pay phone, disjointed, incoherent. And then the phone had gone dead.

Samantha had jumped into her Saab, rain so heavy the wipers were cranked on overtime, each warped road sign to Portland bringing her closer to disaster. Two people drove that night: The one that ached for her mother, feared for her, wanted to take her life and stick it in her back pocket. And the other, the one that needed to blast herself free from her own life. Maybe propulsion was the only way to escape inertia.

She arrived to find her mother a sick, noxious creature whose body lay racked on the sofa, limbs unconnected, no musculature to its spine. Spent an endless night waiting for her to come to. Knowing she would have to put up with her defiance, the last remnants of self-esteem drained away with each passing moment of withdrawal. She stood so alone, now the child, her legs—always her best feature, she used to say—sticking out from the hospital sack, the whiteness enveloping the pale hollow-eyed waif.

And then the clinging, the crying, the lamentations, apologies, promises, until Samantha sat beside her on the narrow clinic bed, took her mother's face in her hands, gently turning it until their eyes met. "It's up to you now. I know we've said some hateful things the past twenty-four hours . . . but you have to know . . . I'm here . . . every step of the way." And then, softly, because it was as hard for Samantha to say as it was for her mother to hear, "I love you."

God, how she wanted to protect her. Wanted to take the pain away, but she had had a bellyful of Al-Anon, codependent psychobabble, and enough heartache to know better. Better than anyone, she knew the only way to reach bottom was to touch it yourself. And, she thought ruefully, walking from the doors her mother would not leave for fifteen weeks, someone was watching her twenty-four hours a day, cramming sobriety down her throat.

She had been afraid her mother's drinking would have corrupted Earlsheart into a wasteland of tasteless grandiloquence, but that was definitely not the case. She stood motionless in the large room, its heaviness no longer weighing upon her as it had when she was a child.

Now she could see why her mother had fallen hopelessly in love with this resplendent oasis. It had a grandness about it, filled with aesthetic treasures, some of which she recognized, others she presumed chosen with . . . *her*. Everything worked. Its design was elegantly sensuous. She could see why her mother had lapsed into indulgent consumption. This was heaven. Her mother could have retired here and quite beautifully drunk herself into a stupor, never needing to venture outside. Samantha shook her head. Stop! It was no longer her battle.

She wandered out onto the deck, then set her cup on the ledge and ran to the beach, the late autumn sun beating strongly upon her, taking the edge off the ocean chill. Her muscles strained; the sharp pain in her lungs felt delicious. She felt free . . . fleetfooted. A mile down the spongy sand she stopped, catching her breath, and walked along the tide line. She checked her watch. She still had time. She wound her way toward the sloping path that led back to Earlsheart. Perched behind a thick stump of beach grass, she stripped off her shirt and lay back, letting the sun beat down on her body. She laughed. Sometimes things could be so simple.

◆ ◆ ◆

The note arrived in the mail an hour before she was to leave for the beach. It was short and precise.

L . . .

I realize things have gotten murky, at best, but if I ever meant anything to you, even in the slightest, if only as a friend. She must never know. Please. She must never know.

S.

No words of remorse. The only hint they had even shared intimacy was Sondra's desire to bury it, the map locked in a dusty attic of self-denial.

"She must never know" resonated like the lyrics from a bad song, repetition driving her crazy as she sped through the last of the curves that met the final bend which led to Earlsheart. She jammed on the brakes, crunched onto the gravel road that meandered several hundred feet to the circular drive they had shoaled with crushed rock and pea gravel to drain the heavy winter rains. Yet another cost. Lindsay felt the *ka-ching* of a cash register, realizing every element and fixture she and Sondra had added would be viewed not for what it was, what it lent to the design, but as an additional expenditure. She had only just begun to understand Sondra's ability to leap into the extravagance of the moment. How could she explain that to her daughter?

Lindsay procrastinated as her car idled. She loathed the idea of entering this castoff tomb that had given her such joy, a creative wellspring that had held such promise. Now it was merely a joyless shell. The ghosts would confront her with every turn, every change, every item she and Sondra had so meticulously chosen together, discussions and arguments, laughter and joy at the merits of one style over another. And now she would do the walk-through with this adversary.

The self-confident one. The one with the edge. All the stateliness and self-assurance of a woman her mother's age. Somewhere they had shifted roles. And beyond the configuration of genetics—their long slender lines, the grace that propelled them both as if they walked on water—there was no similarity.

The eyes. Same color and shape, but the light that burned from Samantha's, bright and fierce, came from a different source. Their focus didn't waver. Her gaze was bold and direct, her mother's diffident and averted. Her stance to be unchallenged, while Sondra questioned her very existence. And where they both possessed anger, Samantha's was born of survival, Sondra's of self-loathing.

Lindsay juggled her keys nervously. She couldn't put this off forever. She strode forward, anxious to finish with the task before her as quickly as possible.

She knocked at the front door. There was no answer. She went around to the back, up the stairs to the deck and the French doors that led to the kitchen. They weren't quite closed. Either Samantha was out or she simply hadn't heard her. Lindsay poked her head in, called Samantha's name. There was no answer. She checked her watch. Still a bit early. She wondered if perhaps Samantha had gone to the store. She decided to take a quick stroll on the beach while she waited, trailed down the path she had hired a local handyman to clear.

It was the kind of day one prays for at the beach. Gorgeous. The sky was clear and the briny smell and the roaring quiet filtered Lindsay's senses. It was warm; unseasonably warm. She turned the corner where she and Sondra had planted a path of marigolds, a vibrant orange seam to the old steps. They had laughed easily with one another back then, before they had become lovers.

Lindsay rejected her memories as she removed her shoes and socks. She reveled in the warm sand mushing between her toes and continued to stroll, mesmerized by the stillness, captivated by the

sand dimpling beneath her toes as she dug her heels into the damp-
ness, tiny bubbles escaping with little pops. She bent to study the
texture of the sand and her deepening tracks. Suddenly she sensed
she wasn't alone.

They saw each other in the same moment.

Wind-swept, tanned and sandy blonde, lean, the flat muscles in her
stomach, the swell of her breasts, nipples taut from the chill. They
were stuck in this extraordinary moment, eyes locked into one another's. Shock. They both caught their breath, then Samantha's anger
rushed forward.

"Jesus Christ!" Samantha stood firm and resolute. "You scared the
shit out of me."

"I . . . I'm sorry. I thought maybe you had gone into town."

Samantha pulled on her shirt, started back up the trail, turned once
and glared at Lindsay, who wondered if anything else could possibly
go wrong between them. She followed silently up the path, then up
the stairs to the deck.

"What were you doing down there?"

"Waiting for you." It was done. They couldn't take it back. Samantha clenched her jaw, led the way into the kitchen. She turned,
less angry, but cool.

"There's coffee." Samantha indicated the coffee maker.

"No. Thanks." Lindsay checked her watch again. "Zusman should
be here any—"

"Hey babe?" A male voice interrupted from the stairwell.

"In the kitchen," Samantha responded.

"There you are." Robert entered the kitchen in a deep blue terry-
cloth robe, hair still wet from a shower. He stopped when he saw
Lindsay.

"Robert, this is Lindsay Brennan."

Robert extended a well-manicured hand to Lindsay. "Hi."

Polite but implicit understanding hovered in the air: Lindsay was
behind enemy lines. Still, they were well-bred, civilized grownups,
after all.

"I was going to head into town. Check out the bookstore, pick up some chicken for dinner. Need anything else?" He focused singularly on Samantha now.

"No. I don't think so."

"OK." He smiled at her, gently extracted a twig from her hair. And then Lindsay heard the muffled: "Sure you don't want me to stay?" But Samantha shook her head and turned to Lindsay. "I'm going to change. If you need anything . . . well, I guess you know where to find it." Her voice was laced with the ever-present edge of cultivated hostility.

Samantha reappeared just as the contractor knocked at the front door. Both women headed toward it and then Lindsay deferred to Samantha. After brief introductions they proceeded with the walk-through. Lindsay's professional mask fell into place instantly, obliterating any images of the past. She made few comments, merely jotted notes as they continued, and then stopped at a window ledge.

"John?" Both he and Samantha turned to Lindsay, who was fingering the trim.

"Yeah?"

"This isn't CVG."

"Come on, Lindsay, you know there isn't much difference if you're gonna paint—"

"Right. This fir's warping already."

"It's gonna cost ya."

"No. It's going to cost you. This was pointed out to you in the first addendum—"

"Yeah, but—"

"And John, you should know better than to try that on one of my projects." There was no room for negotiation.

John left the room, muttering under his breath.

"I think I caught 'goddamn women' somewhere in there," Samantha said. She grinned, only for a moment, but it transformed her face, erasing the hardness. They trailed into the kitchen and then, finally, to the living area.

"I want this gone." Samantha walked directly to the ornate built-in bar to the left of the fireplace.

"Now that's gonna cost—"

"I don't care what it costs. I want it out." The anger cloaked Samantha's face again.

"Lindsay!" John was confused. She turned to him. "This was her friggin' pride and joy!"

"John, just take it out. And put it at the top of the list."

Lindsay escorted him to the door. "I think that's it. Can you finish this up in two weeks' time?"

"Yeah . . . I'll pull some guys off another job." Shaking his head, John walked out the entrance.

"Thank you." Samantha's back was to Lindsay. She had moved to the window. "I guess we know what she was doing here. Her retirement home. A glorified drunk tank."

Lindsay had not allowed that thought to enter her mind. To hear it voiced sickened her. "I don't think you give your mother enough credit."

"Drunks don't get a lot of that, no." Samantha continued to stare out the window.

"There's more to your mother than her being . . . having an alcohol problem."

"It isn't a 'problem.' " Samantha whirled round to face her now. "She's a chronic alcoholic. Every facet of her mind and body is affected by it, so don't tell me that isn't all there is to her."

"What about when she's sober?"

"Sober? When's that? Those few idle moments while she dreams up new ways to keep it so unsuccessfully hidden from the world?" Samantha realized she was fighting with the wrong person. She dropped her combative tone. "Booze is all there is. Believe me. No matter what else she pays lip service to."

"It's none of my business. But I don't agree with you."

"I'm sure that's convenient for you. Denial makes for great bedfellows."

Lindsay's eyes darted to Samantha's, but immediately saw the term was a loosely thrown metaphor.

"I think it's best if we don't discuss my mother."

"That's fine by me." Lindsay checked her notes, closed the notebook, shoved it in her pocket and walked to the front door.

"Lindsay." Samantha's tone softened. "I meant to tell you earlier. This place is . . . exquisite. You did an excellent job." The praise was unsullied with anger, spoken begrudgingly but sincerely.

"Thank you. It mattered a great deal to me," Lindsay replied. Samantha's brow went up. She was about to ask something, then let it drop. An awkward silence fell between them until Lindsay turned and left.

he planes followed one another in rapid succession over the landing field. Samantha stared out the heavily blue-tinted window, lost in a dusky dreamland, while Robert waited in the line of weary travelers for a standby seat. Flights had been canceled into Seattle due to heavy fog, and they had been stuck in the crowded airport for over two hours. She glanced at him briefly; he held up his hands in a helpless gesture. She returned to watch the lofty birds fly in and away.

She wanted on one of those planes, and she didn't care where it was headed. Destination unknown. Cast her fate to the friendly skies. Buckle up for a new life. We are now landing anywhere but here. Join a kibbutz in Israel. Become a ski instructor in the Swiss Alps, break bread in Italy, feet dangling in the Trevi fountain, no plans, nothing to do. Wear a gauzy shift of white against a Mediterranean tan as she sauntered up the stone steps to a hidden Greek villa. Any adventure would do. Anything to jar the bedrock of stability.

She had to admit to herself what she wouldn't dare say to Robert: she adored this crisis. Despite her protestations to the contrary, being forced to take over her mother's project with this woman she wasn't sure whether to hate or merely distrust was exactly what the doctor had ordered. A challenge filled with a dangerous excitement she hadn't felt since she started her business. But how could she tell him that? It wasn't exactly a banner sign of mental health.

The need for tension had reared its ugly head; conflict, something to spark a pulse in her deadened life. And that need wasn't going away. That much had become clear over the past few months.

As she sat there, mesmerized by the flight of the elegant metallic birds, she thought back to her own migration, finally out of high school, flying north to Seattle for the rest of her life. Where she was able to conform her existence to an ordered regime of classes, part-time work, study and sporadic socializing. It helped that her father had relocated to Seattle with Stella, his receptionist-turned-wife, that he was close by, that they met for Sunday dinners at their house. It was calming to have a sense of steady familial influence, even fun in the beginning, but after a time, there seemed nothing worse than an evening with the two of them trying to solve her problems, stereophonic "shoulds" that peppered even the most harmless of conversations. She visited less, was busy with more, and began to lunch with her father alone as her life filled itself out and she made her own friends.

She dated very little. Her initial interest in boys had been fueled by an overworked imagination, first from her books in the most classical vein and now the matinees she could jam between classes. Lovers traipsing about the pages and edited images of celluloid romance were far easier than the awkward sparring, unintelligible dinner conversation and embarrassing make-out sessions that marked her sporadic love life.

She surprised herself by losing her virginity deep into a third date with Pierre, an exchange student from Paris, her arms wrapped about his thin neck, her mouth intricately involved with his lips, in quest of the ultimate mystery. Her mind drifted nearby, an objective viewer, in awe at the relentless drive her body showed in this endeavor.

Pierre's gentle passion and skill had persuaded Samantha to relax and enjoy the sensations that skimmed the surface before her mind even knew what was happening, burrowing their way to the burning sensation aching in her groin. Her body unabashedly relented to this sensation, meeting Pierre's insistence and hunger. Sweetly and utterly drenched, Samantha lay in Pierre's arms, letting his slender limbs caress her back to safety.

The affair had lasted three months when Samantha broke it off, Pierre confused by her abrupt decision. "We love well, no?" Too well, Samantha feared, since her body seemed to float further from her mind during their frequent meetings in his cramped studio apartment. Somehow it had become its own instrument and her mind had lost ownership. Its needs, demands and desires traveled into uncharted territory that her mind had no willingness or inclination to catch up to. There were moments during lovemaking she couldn't remember after long and enduring orgasms, where her body seemed determined to stay. Samantha became terrified she would never come out of them . . . the climaxes shattering her, separating her from her own will. Blackouts, she called them. It terrified her, for if her body left her, where would her mind descend?

An intelligent mind, drifting off in the universe in search of another body, she daydreamed. This time she would pick her circumstances better. Yes, Pierre's time had come. She was fond of him, but not as much as her body was. It was easy to make the break, and Samantha did not date for another year, until she met David, kind and gentle, his sense of humor his finest calling card; but, more importantly, he was charmingly inept in bed, and Samantha was able to develop a wonderful relationship with him without fear her body would leave her.

And now Robert turned to her and snapped her from her reverie, and she saw with perfect clarity why being in Portland was so potent, held so much more promise than this man, her partner; and why it was difficult to think of returning to Seattle. Her life there bordered on the exclusively mundane.

"Finally." Robert put his arm about her, edged her a few feet from another couple saying their good-byes. "I'm gonna miss you, babe."

Samantha smiled uncertainly. She wanted to ache at his departure. "Kiss me."

He leaned to her, gave her a quick kiss.

"No. Kiss me."

"Here?"

"Welllll," she whispered in his ear, "you could take me—"

"Sam!" He laughed. She had tickled his ear. "If you're so restless why didn't you take advantage of me at the beach?"

Good question.

The loudspeaker announced his flight information.

"I'll call you when I get in." Robert picked up his garment bag. "Take care of yourself, babe. And don't let *her* get to you."

"Oh. She won't. I don't think we'll have to spend too much time together. I'll do my job. She'll do hers."

"I was talking about your mother."

"Oh." Samantha cleared her throat, glanced up into Robert's limpid brown eyes. He bent to kiss her. Tenderly.

Drudge. Grind. Toil. Oppression. Samantha kept a running thesaurus on her feelings over the first few days. Long hours ran into each other, blending one moment of activity into another. Lindsay by her side. Silently. They worked. Day in and out.

Each morning Lindsay would meet Samantha at the Pavilion, where they would line the subs out for the day. While Samantha attended to the details of the interiors, Lindsay dealt with completing the exterior construction. They fell efficiently into a rhythm of coordinating supplies, ordering fixtures and materials, spotting delays, and troubleshooting. Lindsay would usually stop by toward the end of the day to pick up paperwork, go over addenda. They would track their scheduling, discuss any elements that might deviate from the projection. Their movements complemented one another's. They were both thankful for this *simpatico* as they felt the fatigue and anxiety increase.

The first few days had been filled with awkward tension, their meetings aloof, brief and impersonal. They would relax their guards only after a long day, too exhausted to carry the torch of anger or suspicion. Their interaction became casual, conversations retraced the details of the day, much like an old married couple who tolerated one another with grudging respect.

Samantha's consistency impressed Lindsay. She remained calm and steady regardless of the minute and inevitable crisis that threatened their schedule. Whether she only had four hours of sleep a night, or had painstakingly finished a shift of fine detail work, she maintained an even keel.

Samantha had decided early on she would do the actual trim work, in part because they couldn't find a qualified interiors person who could meet their scheduling, but also because it gave her a sense of unification with the project and kept her there to watch over the fleet. When things went wrong, they were handled immediately. It also gave Samantha a greater sense of purpose, and allowed her a creative outlet to ease the stress of the situation.

A week into the thick of it, Snag waltzed into Lindsay's office with an announcement: "You won't believe what 'the daughter' just did."

Snag always referred to her as "the daughter" with a sinister smile. He told Megan it added melodrama to the plot. Lindsay and Megan both turned to Snag, waiting.

" 'The daughter' has some sterling balls." He kept them waiting in suspense for an extra second. "Well, you know old man Kalsettes has been just having a fit and falling in it ever since those rockers from Ace Electric showed up to do the wiring and of course brought their boom box with them—"

"Oh shit." Lindsay rubbed the pinch at her brow.

"Yes, well, the old Greek put his foot down today. He goes storming over to the mohawk guy, the rather cretinous slimy one—as if there's a distinction between the two—and says 'You gotta turna de music down' in his best Anthony Quinn, he really is a darling you know, and the mohawk's equally cretinous sidekick yells back, 'Yeah, and whose gonna make us, old fart?' So they start screaming at each other, yelling at the top of their lungs, Kalsettes in Greek and these two schmoes in Tongues as far as Kalsettes is concerned, and I turn to Sam and I can't find her and all this ruckus has now stopped everybody in their tracks and . . ." Snag stopped to finish his cola.

"*Bammmmm!*" He crashed the empty can onto the desk. Both Lindsay and Megan jumped. "She demolishes it, the boom box. I mean completely obliterates the shit out of it." Snag laughed in utter joy. "Can you believe it? With one of those mini-sledges. Deathly silence fills the auditorium." Lindsay and Megan stare at Snag, then one another. "And then she pulls out fifty bucks from her pocket and hands it to them and says, 'You two go over to Radio Shack and buy two Walkmans, cram them on your ears and that's the end of this, right?' They just stare at her, kinda like you two are looking at me right now, and then she says, cool as a cucumber—very Kim Novak—'And I don't want to hear any more about it. Got it?' But they're still mute at this point, so Sam yanks this guy's chain, I mean literally yanks this retro macho chain with an ankh of all things at the end of it—'Got it!?' and he finally kind of nods, 'Unhuh.' She walks back to Kalsettes, turns him around and points to the plumbing, then picks up her paintbrush and goes back to work."

Snag laughs, "Isn't that wild?"

Lindsay shook her head. She had to hand it to her. Creative resolution. It wasn't until she sat at her desk and began to leaf through the papers piled before her that she found herself grinning.

She had watched Samantha those first days, her gifts similar to those of her mother, but her bias far more progressive and stylized. Oh, she was talented. But it was more than that. Her ability to stay grounded, to keep all the elements unified and even-tempered, kept Lindsay's respect growing as the days passed, especially when she was forced to admit that Samantha's professionalism and integrity in her work were equal to her own. Plus she had a sense of calm and balance that Lindsay lacked. There was a way about her as well. Maybe it was simply that she took the time, made a point of everyone taking their breaks, seemed genuinely interested and able to get outside of her own focus and to relate to others, that brought a sense of harmony to the crew. Crisis left her undaunted and the humor she reserved for the day laborers, painters and other subs rarely flagged. It was this ability, Lindsay realized, that finally would enable them to succeed.

When Lindsay went to the site next day, Samantha was leaning over her ladder reaching for a paintbrush. Lindsay watched her for a moment, then handed her the brush she had been stretching for.

"Thanks." She took the brush and continued her work, her back now turned to Lindsay. Then, after several moments, "I didn't think you were showing up."

"I got caught at the office." Lindsay moved to the other side of the ladder so she faced Samantha. "Nathan called."

Samantha glanced down. "Anything wrong?"

"No. Not really. He's just being a cheerleader."

"Yeah, well, he can keep his pompons to himself."

Lindsay grinned. "I heard about Kalsettes." Samantha continued painting. "Pretty gutsy crushing their God right in front of them!"

"Well, to tell you the truth, if I had to listen to 'Yo girl I want yo' baby,' " Samantha rapped, "one more time, I think I would have had to do something far more tragic. Besides, I felt somewhat conspicuous atop this ladder constantly hearing, 'Baby's got back.' "

Lindsay laughed. "Hey . . . you want to catch some lunch?"

Samantha paused, twisted her tight shoulders. "I guess I could use a break. Sure."

◆ ◆ ◆

Samantha peered over the menu. She studied the woman who sat across from her, handsome, with a gentle spirit. Not the Machiavellian villain she had made her out to be. Doubt was now creeping over the edges of Samantha's well-defined coolness toward this woman that she had been more than willing to blame for her mother's situation.

Lindsay glanced up from the menu, startled to run into Samantha's eyes. They held for a moment, then went back to the menus.

"I thought you were taking Sundays off," Lindsay said.

"Well, the way I see it, the only way we're going to pull this off is to work every conceivable moment between now and the end of the year. Besides, what's there to do in this rain, anyway?" Samantha put her menu down, stared out the window. "I hate this rain. I think people who live in the Northwest are masochists. . . ."

"Blue skies. Green trees."

"I know. I've heard all the ads. Anyway, my mother's business was basically at a standstill. It's not like I've got a lot of other things to attend to."

"And yours?"

"Mine . . ." Samantha wasn't certain anymore. "Let's just say I've been on hiatus. Actually you're the one I'm concerned about. My mother's pointed out more than once that you're terribly busy."

"I've got Snag and Megan. We always manage." Lindsay's voice was short, the walls rising.

"Relax. There was no implication. I just wondered how you were holding up."

"Fine." Lindsay's jaws tightened. Fine? No, she wasn't fine. This stress had added weight to her anxiety and panic, and she had been feeling the effects in sleepless nights, agitated days.

"One rule," Samantha interjected. "It's Sunday. No work talk on Sundays."

"Deal."

They ate their lunches in relative silence, both exhausted. A waitress placed a cappuccino before Lindsay and a latte before Samantha.

"Do you mind my asking how you got involved with Nathan?"

Lindsay flashed to Joanne, her exquisite body straddling her own as she had seduced her with the details of the Pavilion project. Perhaps that had been Joanne's point. To distract her. Lindsay cleared her throat. "Through sort of a mutual frie—acquaintance."

"He's the worst kind of asshole. The kind you almost have to like in spite of yourself."

"I hadn't really thought about it," she lied. She didn't have to like him in spite of anything.

"Well, my mother's taste in men defies explanation, anyway." Samantha's tone was light.

"Taste in men?"

"Yeah. She won't admit it, but I think there was something going on there. And Nathan—he's all over himself trying to be gracious." Samantha sipped her latte. "Guilty conscience. Asking himself, late at night, if he drove my mother into the tank. He'd give himself that kind of power."

Lindsay was finding it difficult to bring air into her chest.

"I talked to her today." Samantha nonchalantly played with her silverware, skirting dangerous territory. "She got her first phone call. No visiting for a few more weeks. She told me she wanted to do this on her own. Doesn't want me there. Or herself, for that matter." Lindsay sat mutely.

"She asked about you," Samantha remarked. "Said she had sent a letter?"

"I thought your mother was off limits." Lindsay shifted uncomfortably, damned if she was going to appear guilty.

"She didn't come right out and say it, but since I learned long ago to listen between the lines with my mother, she made it sound like you were manipulating her in some way." The tone was not an accusation. She was searching for information.

"If that's her perspective I can't change it." Her tone was neutral, but Lindsay's manner was defensive.

"Don't you think there's a reason people arrive at their perspectives?"

"Sure. But then perspective can be a very tricky thing. And as I can't change hers, neither can I change yours." Lindsay took control back, leaned over the table. "But I do think we should stick to our agreement."

"Look, I'm not attacking here." Samantha backed down, then came around another side. "I realize my mother is prone to melodrama, but there's no doubt in my mind that some of the torment she's suffering is somehow related to you and Earlsheart. I simply want to know what happened."

"I'm sorry. It's really none of your business. If your mother wants to discuss it with you, that's her prerogative." Lindsay shifted in her chair, eyes lit with anger. "Let's get this out of the way right now, OK? I did not rob your mother. I had no idea there were any financial problems or I would never have recommended the changes I came up with. If we are to continue working together, I don't want to discuss your mother. Not now, not ever."

Samantha stewed for a long moment, her exasperation renewed. "I think we should get back."

Lindsay pushed her plate to the side. They stood, paid the bill and drove back in silence. Lindsay left the car running, waiting for Samantha to get out.

"I just want you to know"—Samantha's voice was like ice—"I am not at all like my mother. Don't even think of trying to do to me whatever it was you did to her."

"Hi. My name's Jessie, alcoholic, addict."

"Hi, Jessie," the group said in unison. All except Sondra. She sat quietly smoking her cigarette. Whatever else she was forced to do in here, she refused to sound like a robotron. They were all alcoholics. Why did they insist on rubbing it in? Like they didn't know there was a damn good reason they were all sitting in jeans and sweatshirts, half of them looking like death warmed over, the other half chugging coffee and smoking cigarettes like they were on death row, speeding up, getting high on "appropriate" addictions, addictions that might ameliorate your lungs, cause test rats to eat one another after the equivalent of ten black cups a day, eating so much white sugar your mouth got dry and you ached for water just like any other morning after.

". . . And then I shot my boyfriend, but goddamn I was so drunk I only hit him in the shoulder. Guess that's one time booze worked in my favor." Some laughs over that one. And that was the other thing. This I've-looked-into-the-jaws-of-death-and-I'm-the-lucky-sucker-who-gets-to-tell-about-it humor wasn't funny in the least. Nothing about any of these people was the least bit humorous. At least not to Sondra. Nothing about drinking and losing everything you had could be the basis for a good joke. But they kept at it. And they all laughed. Loudly.

But not Sondra.

". . . Except I miss him. I loved him so much." Jessie was crying now, and Sondra looked around the group as their heads bowed in solemn compassion, and her jaws clenched at the tears that streamed down Jessie's acne-ridden face into a gap-toothed grin because this man she loved and missed so much had slugged her in the jaw. She was glad she had lied about visiting days to Samantha. There was no way she wanted her here, witness to these losers. None of this made sense. It was a joke, at that.

The meeting was coming to a close. The group stood, circled and grabbed one another's hands, said the Lord's Prayer and then cheered in unison, "Keep coming back, it works if you work it."

But not Sondra. She remained seated in the corner, smoking her cigarette.

*T*he next two days Lindsay showed up at the job site before Samantha arrived, and stayed only a few moments when she came to do her check in the evening. Words were sparse, economic.

The third day, Snag came in Lindsay's place. Snag found Samantha fascinating, so much more complex than her mother, a far more interesting set of dynamics with which to work. He guessed from Lindsay's tone and unwillingness to discuss the topic that Samantha had no idea about her and Sondra's affair.

Lindsay had kept it well guarded, but Snag was a keen observer, and when it came to the sparks flaring between them one morning when he had walked in unannounced, he knew they had slept together. When he had told Megan, she had gasped, mortified. "Oh, Snag. I thought Joanne was bad, but this is . . . is terrible. She's . . . she's—" Megan, ever delicate, searched for the right word.

"A fuckin' disaster," Snag finished for her.

"Disturbed. I don't know, but she's got problems. Please . . . you've got to do something."

"And what, pray tell, might that be?"

"I don't know. Talk to her."

"Oh, yes, and that's been so effective these past years."

"You've got to at least try. Lindsay doesn't realize what she's getting herself into and I think it's up to us to try and prevent it."

But he hadn't spoken to her. Snag simply shook his head. Just as Lindsay wasn't about to suddenly filter through everyone's hidden motives, neither was Megan going to be able to protect her from them. In the meantime, the workplace was beginning to unravel at the seams. Snag had hoped that Samantha would provide a breath of fresh air, but things were murkier than ever. Too bad, he thought, because Samantha and Lindsay made a great team. Incredible, actually. Their individual rhythms suited one another perfectly. There was just one minor problem: they didn't seem to like each other.

Snag watched as Samantha talked to several subs, getting ready to close shop for the day. Assertive, confident, together, striking in her beauty. Snag never much went for the femme fatale types. He found Joanne's patrician refinement boring, Sondra's suburban femininity the height of banality. But Samantha—she was, well, beautiful in an austere manner. She was also something of a conundrum; untouchable in one way, accessible in others.

"Hey!" he yelled as Samantha began to exit through a side stage door. "Wait up."

She turned. He could see the question in her eyes.

"She got caught up," Snag replied.

The shoulders edged up slightly—she didn't care one way or another. But Snag knew otherwise. "She wanted to make sure everything was OK here."

"Why didn't *she* just telephone?"

"Maybe she thought the personal touch would go over better."

Samantha flexed her lower jaw, preparing her hostile attitude, and then out of sheer weariness seemed unable to hold it. "Sure . . . whatever." She smiled dismissively and turned to go. Snag followed her.

"You know the Veritable Quandary is just down the street. Want to catch a drink? Maybe a bite?"

"You know . . . I think a drink is definitely in order," Samantha wryly agreed.

They locked up together.

◆ ◆ ◆

"How long have you known her?"

"Four years. She took me on as an intern my last year of school."

Samantha poked at the French fries sitting between them.

"You like working for her?"

"I adore working with Lindsay." Snag took a sip of his B&B. "But. There are many days I don't like working *for* her."

"Like her principles, hate her practice?"

"No, no, no. Love her practice. Love her principles. There isn't a more fuckin' honorable architect in this city. . . . She's right out of *The Fountainhead*. No. It's just that sometimes I want to make her stop."

"Stop?"

"Working!!" Snag winked at her. "It puts a dent in my social life. I love my work, but I try to put just as much into the little pleasures one must grasp on their way to the pearly gates."

"Lindsay isn't into pleasure?" Her voice was sly. Was she digging?

"Sure. Lindsay likes to savor as much as the next person, but you know, I just don't think she has as much need for it." Snag ordered another round. "I think she's just one of those who truly loves her work."

"Did you get to know my mother well?"

"No, I'm afraid I didn't."

"I . . . I just wondered . . . have you been to the beach house?"

"No. I saw the before and after pictures though. They did quite a job."

"At quite a price."

"I don't think Lindsay takes that much into consideration."

"Apparently not."

"Hey . . . don't get me wrong. She'd never steer a client off the path. . . . It's just not a part of her creative process."

Samantha's eyes glimmered with understanding, as though she had been searching for something, and perhaps just found it. "You like her, don't you?"

"As I said"—Snag popped another fry into his mouth—"I adore her."

◆ ◆ ◆

Samantha picked up her paintbrush and a wooden slat she used as a tray to hold her three tins of paint while hiking up the ladder. She was working on the intricate trim on the highest ledge, and didn't want to have to climb down again. On the next-to-the-last step, however, her makeshift tray jammed against a rung, and the colors went toppling down.

"*Shit!*"

Samantha tromped down the ladder, spouting a litany of self-deprecation with each descending step: "Jesus, fuck, shit!"

Laughter rang out behind her. She spun around, caught. "You know . . . I planned that," she quipped sardonically, then started laughing as well.

"Yeah. That's what I thought," Lindsay rejoined.

Samantha shook her head at the mess. "And what's your excuse?" she asked as she appraised Lindsay, drenched from the ceaseless rain and accompanying puddle splatter.

But Lindsay merely took a gallant bow.

"There is a device for this condition, you know. It's called an umbrella," Samantha informed her.

Lindsay grinned, far more interested in the paint splattered all over the floor. She started laughing. "You know . . . I'm sort of liking this."

"I don't believe it!" Samantha moaned, but joined the laughter, a slight hysteria ebbing toward release. "Jesus." Samantha stepped around the goopy run of colors. "We'll call it floor art. The patrons will eat it up."

"They won't know what it means, but they'll talk about it over brunch at the Benson."

"Ohhh, they'll love it, the ultimate power . . . stepping on art they don't understand."

At that moment Nathan walked in, shaking rain from his umbrella. As he approached, he took in Lindsay's soggy appearance and the mess on the floor with one disparaging glance.

"What have we here?" His voice was edged with impatience.

"We call it abstractum substratum . . . it's all the rage," Samantha supplied, then began cleaning up the mess. Lindsay bent to help her.

"When you're finished," Nathan sniffed with distaste, "can you meet me in the lounge? I need some signatures from the both of you."

"Sure. No problem." Samantha's voice was a polite fuck you. They mopped up in silence, then slopped the paper towels and dropcloths to the large dump can in the center of the stage.

"You sure don't like him," Lindsay said as she wiped her hands.

"What's to like?"

"Not a helluva lot."

"You think he's just as big a jerk as I do," Samantha baited her.

"Oh no. I think he's a much bigger jerk than you do." Lindsay smiled back, but Samantha caught the serious undertone.

"Yeah, why's that?"

But Lindsay didn't answer. She walked from the stage, down the stairs and back toward the ladder to retrieve her briefcase. Samantha followed, then noticed again how wet Lindsay's clothes were.

"You've got to get out of those clothes or you're going to catch the crud going around."

"As soon as we're done with Nathan I'm heading to the office. I've got some stuff there."

"In the cave."

"What?"

"You haven't fooled me. You're a cave dweller."

Samantha grinned at her. After a moment, Lindsay returned the smile, owning up, sweetly embarrassed. Samantha saw a new tenderness she found endearing. "I told you we were masochists."

They headed to the lounge, where they could see the downpour.

Samantha sighed. "I'm way over this rain. I cannot even tell you how way over this rain I am."

"All you need is little sunshine."

"Good luck."

◆ ◆ ◆

The next morning, on her first trip up the very same ladder, Samantha found a small bouquet of pansies, daffodils, roses and black-eyed susans, all hues of yellow gold, perched on one of the rungs, with a small note propped against the paint can vase: "Cymatium sunshine, by L.B."

he antagonism drifted, contention all but evaporated. Lindsay began a morning ritual of bringing lattes for Sam, cappuccinos for herself. Their meetings were no longer simple rundowns of the previous day's events, problems and solutions. Conversation had begun to wander into Lindsay's work, Samantha's business. They began to break outside of the Pavilion, meander two blocks down to Bean There, Done That, a small coffeehouse where the house brew was as rich and intoxicating as their dialogue; intent coffee-drenched talks, full-bodied conversations, shared connections, ideas and thoughts. They'd laugh, argue politics, dish movies and books. And then they discovered their pasts had a common theme, their youth created in the landscapes of their imaginations. They tentatively edged into childhood dreams, the muses who shaped the spine of their ideas and beliefs, and the realities that destroyed them in grownup nightmares. They relaxed, unburdened, as though they had the day to while away. Their easy conversations wound to digressive and tangential paths so that they never could retrace how they'd arrived here or there. Then they'd be off on another tangent. Everything was fair game. Except Sondra. They never spoke of Sondra.

They laughed often and well together. Lindsay realized this one day while driving to Nathan's office, catching Samantha's eyes bright from the light of the sun through the windshield, her smile broad and engaging.

Samantha, who was driving, turned to Lindsay, noting the stiff high-collared jacket, her appearance stark and militaristic. It brought out a masculine edge in her that Samantha found oddly appealing. Samantha touched the sleeve of Lindsay's jacket. "Are we dressed for the occasion?"

"What?"

"You seem prepared for battle," Samantha commented.

"I'm never prepared for Nathan."

Nathan's office was a study in bad taste. Nouveau art, new wave art, and a Picasso all adorned his walls, giving the waiting room the feeling of a secondhand gallery. All the cast-off pieces conveyed a covert sexual act of one type or another. Lindsay and Samantha stood in amazement. Janet Myers blasted into Samantha's mind.

"I have never—" Lindsay began.

"Oh. I have." Samantha stood close to her so Nathan's secretary couldn't overhear the conversation. "I think it's called being a 'player.' "

"What's the game?"

"It's better to have been nouveau than never riche at all?"

Lindsay began giggling and Samantha joined her.

"A good joke? Or simply overwork?" Nathan came up from behind them.

He ushered them into an equally ostentatious meeting room, darkly paneled with red plush highlights. He walked to the bar, poured himself a scotch. "Ladies?" Both declined.

"Down to business as usual, then." Nathan sat in a large wing chair, Lindsay and Samantha in smaller, less formidable ones.

They launched into a change that would resolve the greatest challenge to their schedule, explaining pros and cons of retaining the original plan with those of implementing a new one. Nathan listened carefully.

"What do you two want?"

They looked at one another. "We want to try this." Lindsay pointed at the schematic on the table. "We just wanted you to know there are considerations, a gamble involved, but we both believe that with the scaffolding delays this is the only possible way to deliver."

"Hmmmm." Nathan appeared to be thinking it over with some seriousness. Then he addressed Samantha as he looked directly at Lindsay. "Tell me, how is your dear mother?"

There was a jarring silence.

"She's fine," Samantha answered, watching Nathan's eyes shift from Lindsay's, taken by surprise, back to her own.

"Yes? That's good to hear. I do miss her. You two . . . ardent offspring of the feminist era are about work, work, work. Now, don't get me wrong. I wouldn't have it any other way. But your mother, much like myself, appreciates . . . the good things in life."

"Can we get back to it?" Lindsay interrupted abruptly.

"My dear. You are overworking. I wish I could say take some time." Nathan smiled with feigned concern.

Samantha watched them. The twisted thing. The thing that existed between Lindsay and her mother was linked to a kink in the chain called Nathan.

"I need to get back to the office." Lindsay stood, waiting for Samantha. "Let us know what you decide so we can proceed."

"Oh, I think you should go ahead. It makes perfect sense to me. Should have thought of it sooner. And I know your time is precious." He had now dismissed Lindsay, addressing Samantha directly. "However, I wondered if we might have dinner."

An awkward silence followed as Lindsay walked from the room. The silence persisted until they got back in the car.

"What the fuck is going on?"

Lindsay continued to stare, tight-lipped, out the window.

"So, they were doing it. It caused problems for you. My mother became a wedge between you and Nathan. You used to be lovers—"

Lindsay gasped. Samantha turned to see Lindsay's face, pale, blanched. Lindsay tried to breathe calmly. She was having one of her attacks. No! Please—not in front of Samantha. But she was, heart heaving wildly in her chest, her face crimson now, teeth clamped so tightly it shot waves of dark into her brain.

"Lindsay . . . are you all right?"

"I . . . will . . . be," she managed to get out. Breathing in. Out. Slowly. Deeply. Just regain her calm. Please regain her calm, so she could get it under control. Finally, her heart eased its rapid pace. She could think again. And then, embarrassed, she turned her face from Samantha. "I think it's just all piling up." And then softly, ". . . You know."

"Yeah. I know." Samantha's voice was gentle. She put a hand on Lindsay's shoulder. "I didn't mean to pry . . . I just . . . it's clear something happened between you and Nathan and my mother."

"Look. It's history." Lindsay turned to her. "And I think it should stay buried there."

◆ ◆ ◆

"Hi, I'm Bob and I'm a grateful alcoholic."

"Hi, Bob." Sondra mouthed the words with the rest of the group. She'd attempted a group therapy session once, even opened her mind to the possibility that the feedback from others could be good for you. But not in AA. Alcoholics seemed so narcissistic they could only rant about the good ol' bad days, like it was just another fix, a memory high, or an enough-about-you-let's-talk-about-me sort of round robin drunkalogue that she could frankly not see the point of.

Furthermore it was all the same lingo, over and over again. She was so sick of the steps she thought she'd scream. Especially since she was getting to the fourth step, a step that creaked and groaned as she gingerly put her weight upon it: making a searching and fearless moral inventory. What was the point in dredging up every single little thing she had done wrong under the influence of alcohol? She could understand it if she had killed someone, lost a job, destroyed a relationship. But then she thought of Samantha. Thought of Samantha's round, widened eyes, the breathtaking beauty in them, and how she'd move away from her as a child, fearful. A child afraid of its own mother. And she heard the speaker, and she listened.

". . . been in and outta treatment just about as many times as I been ta jail." His sardonic humor didn't bother Sondra so much. He was an aging old-time rodeo circuit cowboy, and they had absolutely nothing whatsoever in common, but whenever he spoke, she heard something he seemed to be able to find when sober: the truth. "An' I don't care what anyone says—I can handle myself with a cutthroat killer, ride bull so drunk I didn't feel my cracked hip bone, sleep in the gutter, vomit, and pee my pants, but there ain't been nothin' harder than seein' my kids last week in here. I know I can't do it for myself. I know this sure as shit, sure as I know the first step was written for me.

"But if I can't do it for myself I gotta do it for them. My eight-year-old daughter, she's cryin' in the night over me, tells me, 'Daddy, I love you, but you gotta stop bein' sick cuz it makes Mom so sad I don't know what to do and they told us in the family program that it isn't because you won't but that you can't, kinda like me in gymnastics, but I'm gonna keep trying. Will you please, Daddy?' she says and starts cryin' and I'm sittin' there listenin' to this kid, this kid that I had way too late in life, beggin' me with clear eyes and this bucktooth smile to get well." Bob broke down then and Sondra looked at her sneakers. "After they left, I went outside, I lay on the dirt, head down, and I just prayed, I prayed for surrender. Goddamn, I prayed like I ain't ever prayed to lift the curse."

Sondra saw a tear hit her shoe. She hated this damn place. One minute she wanted nothing more than to run screaming from its doors, and the next she felt like family to perfect strangers, wanted to hold them in their pain, because it belonged to all of them, sad, raw, exposed creatures who all needed one another and were the only ones that could help themselves get well.

The group session was coming to a close. She wouldn't say the Lord's Prayer and she wasn't about to do the little rebel yell, but she got up and held the hands of her cellmates and for the first time she felt like a member of the group. She belonged here.

◆ ◆ ◆

Megan paced outside the church on Pine, trying to stay warm. She had just gotten out of an OA meeting and was waiting for Ryan to pick her up from his last appointment.

She really liked this meeting. It had taken her a while to find the right group, and now that she had she attended a meeting almost every night.

"You know, Megs," Snag had pointed out the other day, "some people just don't have a problem with weight or body image."

"Well, I'm not one of them. Besides, I don't think it's healthy for the baby." Not to mention herself, she didn't add. She didn't want to argue with Snag about it. It was almost like he was taking the politically correct stance. But she hated being fat. She always had. She simply had no idea about how to not be fat and it was as simple as that. Now maybe there was hope.

Ryan shared his books with her, not just about diet, but those that explored the psyches of the damaged. Not that she knew anyone who wasn't damaged in one way or another. Some of them simply wore it on their sleeves more than others. But she and Ryan went to the darkest core, spent long evenings disclosing the embarrassing and often ugly depths of what food had been for both of them in various stages of their lives, what it meant to be fat, not only to themselves but in a culture that abhorred fleshiness. Megan began to slowly see behavior and patterns, fear and denial, phrases she'd listened to but never really heard.

Ryan drove up. She got in the car, leaned over to kiss him. He took her face in both his hands. "You are so beautiful."

"Really, Ryan, I can't get over you sometimes." Megan laughed. "I'm a mess. I've had a hellacious day at work, the wind's blown my hair into a rat's nest and my makeup's—"

"Yes, it's true. You're still a major babe."

"Hardly." Megan caught her breath.

"You sound exhausted." Ryan took her hand, inched his fingers beyond her gloves up to her wrist. Megan loved the way his smallest touch was gentle, delicious, penetratingly present. "Let's order in and you can tell me all about your day."

"Please. I thought Sondra was bad, but her daughter . . . aghhhhh!

She calls me today. Where's this, where's that. I've already told her I have to create everything from scratch because Lindsay—well, Lindsay just never gave me the paperwork. But it's like . . . I don't know . . . she's—I just don't trust her."

"Why?"

"There's something about her. I can tell she gets under Lindsay's skin—"

"But I thought you said things were going better."

"Well, they are. But it's just a way she has about her. Like she's hot and cold. Not like her mother was, poor woman, but dangerous in a way. And I don't know, I think I felt safer for Lindsay when they hated each other's guts."

"Oh, it's the getting-along stuff you don't like."

"Ryan. It's not like that." Megan squeezed his hand. She didn't know what it was like. But Megan's intuition was usually pretty good, and though the signs boded well for Lindsay and Samantha's newfound truce, the whole situation was too charged for there not to be trouble in the air.

he had been waiting impatiently for Lindsay to arrive with the purchase orders for the new paint. She was sitting at a window counter seat in Starbucks, sipping a latte, when she saw them: the paintings being hung in the gallery across the street. His work. David Richey Johnsen. The work she had seen four years ago when Robert had taken her to Carmel.

She had been wandering the streets, happy to have some time alone, playing tourist, window shopping, unmotivated to buy, just loving the cool sea breeze that wound its way through the streets, the smells of espresso from sidewalk cafés, and she thought this must be what Paris feels like.

Paris or New York, in the thirties. Her fantasy transported her there as much as the canvas hanging in the window of a gallery. Glittering, gold, alive and vibrant, the characters danced in an old hotel. Samantha felt herself being drawn up the steps of the gallery, beyond the four-by-five-foot canvas, directly to his other work, not as prominently displayed as she would have imagined, but in a darkened corner with triangular dividers so that she circled round and round falling deeper into the intense resonance of his colors until she came upon the canvas that stopped her in mid-motion. An involuntary sigh escaped her lips, a sound of awe.

"Evening's Debut." A creature of stunning and magical beauty stood in the center of a stairwell surrounded by the debs who paved the trail before and those who would follow in her footsteps, from below. Their dress material swirled flawlessly into one another's— they would always be linked by the face of their experience, their uniqueness unaddressed, countenances muted with the exception of the central character, her exquisite profile regal and commanding.

"Would you care to view this canvas, madam?" The art consultant approached her, a tight-lipped, pinch-nosed man with a vaguely British accent.

"Yes . . . yes I would." Samantha didn't look at the man until much later. She could not take her eyes from the heroine of the piece.

In the dimming room, as the light filtered upon the canvas, the artfully exposed shoulder blades softened to a cream-colored hue, her white evening gown cut low upon her back, Samantha could see the canvas come to life, even hear the laughter, giddy and hopeful, glasses clinking in the background, music swelling through the dimly lit stairwell where they had congregated in a metaphoric circle of life.

"Will madam excuse me for a moment?" Again Samantha could only continue to stare at the work before her. Then felt the tears flow softly down her face.

Witness to perfection.

That's what she tried to explain to Robert later, in their quaint bed-and-breakfast room, he lying on the quilted bed, playing around with a camera, only half-listening until she said, "I want to buy it."

"Well, sure, go ahead."

"You don't mind if I use the American Express?"

"No, babe." His fascination with the camera seemed endless.

"OK . . . I'm doing it." Samantha said, extracting the card from his wallet.

"How much?" As she was walking out the door.

"Eight."

"Whhooo . . . eight hundred for a painting. My, we've developed some very expensive tastes." Robert put the camera down, got up and came to her, good-naturedly put his arms about her neck. "But what the hell, sweetie, you deserve it." He kissed her forehead. There, there. Go ahead, little child.

"Thousand, Robert. Eight thousand." She loved wiping the patronizing smile from his lips.

He laughed. "No way."

"Way."

He put a hand to her arm as she tried to walk out the door. "Sam. We can't afford that."

She gently extricated herself, threw the card on the dresser—"I know"— then walked out.

The next day she went back to the gallery and sat alone in the viewing room with the painting. She cried, silently. She cried for the feeling it gave her. She had heard somewhere, in a movie, or a book perhaps, that there was a moment in every woman's life where they reached that perfect point, where they attained a peak physically, emotionally and psychically. This painting was about that threshold. It might have been more appropriately titled, "Life's Debut"; when one arrived at the place where they were completely confident after spending agonizing years searching to get to that threshold. And most importantly they were now ready to step over it and onto the path. She would do anything to know that much about herself. And for that she cried. But more she cried for what she saw in the canvas that she was not. That she knew herself so little.

And now, there across the street, was this artist's work being hung in a gallery in Portland. She was almost afraid to go see if the painting was among them. Certainly by now someone had bought it.

"Hey—" Lindsay breezed into her thoughts. "I know I'm late."

"No." Samantha was still caught in the torment of walking across the street to see if the painting was still there. "It's OK, really."

Then Lindsay rattled on about the paint specifications and Samantha didn't listen, but continued to stare out the window.

"I know this is scintillating information, but try to stay with me."

"Have you ever found something so perfect it made you cry?"

Lindsay saw the tears of Samantha's memory brimming at her eyes. "Hey . . . what's the matter?"

Samantha looked at her then for a long moment deciding whether she could trust her. "Across the street may or may not hang the most perfect canvas ever created." Samantha told her about her visit to Carmel and the moment she had taken with her from it.

"Well, there's only one way to find out." Leading the way out of the shop, Lindsay opened the door for Samantha.

They darted through the traffic, rushing, schoolgirls playing hooky. As soon as they entered the gallery, Samantha saw it. Her hand reached out for Lindsay's arm. Lindsay followed the direction of her gaze.

The painting was extraordinary. They both crept reverently toward it and stood several moments without being able to utter a word.

"What do you think?" Samantha finally whispered.

"I think . . . I think you should have it." She turned to her then. "It is, after all, where you are." Then looked back at the painting. "Isn't it?"

◆ ◆ ◆

Jerra flew down that weekend. Samantha took Sunday off, felt human for the first time in weeks. They brunched, shopped, went to a movie, and now sat in Sondra's apartment drinking a glass of wine, their shoes kicked off, settled comfortably on the couch. Samantha had finished her monologue, catching up, careful not to miss the important details Jerra thrived on.

"I don't know," Samantha sighed. Jerra had been grilling her with questions she couldn't answer. "What do you want? You're always the fucking drill sergeant of the heart."

"What you love about me, remember?" Jerra stretched her body, gathered herself into a new position. "Anyway, I don't want anything. It's you who's hunting for information."

"It's just that I used to want to hate . . . you know, blame her for Mom. But that's ridiculous. I can't."

"For one, she doesn't deserve it."

"I know." Her tone was reluctant, defeated.

"Sam . . . come on. I've watched you since last night. Something's up. You've been like a caged bird—all aflutter."

"Aflutter?" Samantha repeated. "Sounds so Scarlett O'Hara."

"I mean you're agitated, excitable, and quite frankly, my dear, a bit of a cranky-butt."

"Oh, God, I know. I'm sorry, Jerra. I have been kind of a shit, haven't I?"

"Yes, darling, you have. But don't worry, I know it's due to stress, insanity and hormones. Remember, I used to know you when you were sweet and wholesome." Jerra sipped her wine, then leaned over, put a hand on Samantha's. "What's goin' on?"

"I don't know. I really don't. I'm up to here with the Pavilion, I've had a bellyful of mind-fucking myself over my mother, I avoid Robert's phone calls, and then there's . . . Lindsay." Samantha launched into their history, how cold and hard it had started, the gradual meltdown, how much she enjoyed her company, their conversations, which reminded her of Jerra, "—and this sort of constant edge of danger that seems to hang in the balance." She told Jerra about the painting, how Lindsay immediately understood its significance, and then about the flowers. "I burst into tears. Guess I was PMS, but it was so unexpected—this woman I'd deemed the bitch from Calcutta. But she's not. She's actually quite gentle, and I wouldn't even say it's underneath the facade, because it isn't a facade . . . it's simply that she's so focused and concentrated so much of the time. . . . But when she's present . . ."

"So it was a kind gesture and you appreciated it," Jerra supplied.

"Yeah, but . . ."

"Something else?"

"Yeah, well, there's this sort of line that wavers between us. It's mutual respect, but more . . . you know I, I—"

"You like her."

"Yes. But there's—"

"Tension."

"Yes." It struck Samantha.

"And you find her attractive."

"Well, of course. I mean, you met her, don't you think she's attractive?"

"Very. But this isn't about me, Sam, and you're avoiding the question. You're attracted to her."

"Oh, don't be absurd."

"What?"

"I'm as straight as they come."

"You are aware—"

"What, that she's a lesbian? Of course," Samantha said loftily, but it was the first time she had said the word. And then she thought about having asked Lindsay if she and Nathan had been lovers. How obtuse.

"And you've never been curious."

"Have you?"

"Yes, actually. I mean how can you live in our culture, especially in our biz, and not be curious?"

"It just never comes up for me." Samantha was flip.

"I find that difficult to believe, Sam."

"So. Who were you curious about?" Samantha wanted nothing more than to have this particular conversation diverted from her.

"Well . . . if you must know, Vicky and her lover were very interesting, I thought." Jerra stopped, then turned honest eyes to Samantha. "I caught them once. I had walked into the back of the house, returning with carpet samples I think it was, and I didn't even know they were home. I was heading for the kitchen and there they were. Kissing. Vicky's hands were caressing Brenda in such a delicate sensual way. I have to admit I became slightly voyeuristic and found myself completely aroused by it all. I couldn't wait to get home and tell Jack. In intimate detail."

Samantha cleared her throat.

"Oh, I find women incredibly erotic to think about. But I'm in love with Jack, so it's not an issue. But if I weren't? I don't know. I might explore it."

"That's fine." Sam swallowed. "I don't have an issue with it. It's just not something I'm personally into. It's just not me."

But they both knew that wasn't true.

She never spoke of it.

She had met her at a dinner party. Her college roommate was throwing a "do" for a friend whose first novel was hitting it big. Samantha had tried to beg off, said she'd just slip out and catch a movie so they could use the apartment. Oh no, Randy insisted. Lest Samantha forget, Randy had endured the double-date-from-hell where forced clichés hung like thick cheese over tasteless pepperoni pizza, the banter as flat as the beer. Samantha was going to be there, and that was final.

A mixed bag of majors and minors; a couple of art students, a CPA, a marine biologist and her boyfriend, two law students who were already on their way to becoming hotshot producers. The only common denominator was the connection to the writer, Arianna, celebrating this first delicious success, a dark but humorous novel probing the depths of sexual obsession.

The minute Arianna entered the crowded apartment Samantha's world stopped. Wild hair the color of a burnished sunset, unruly, charismatic, with an electrical intensity Samantha found equally fascinating and disturbing. Having survived her mother, Samantha never courted reckless behavior. But Arianna was just that. Reckless abandon.

Samantha knew when Arianna's eyes were upon her, and she knew Arianna was aware of Samantha's casual aloofness. As they both receded into banal pleasantries their ions drifted closer toward one another, until they were almost on top of each other in the center of the room. Arianna turned to her.

"I'm afraid I have to catch a plane in an hour. I'm leaving for New York."

What was Samantha to say to that? How did she let this woman, this icon leave without even telling her . . . what? "Congratulations," she uttered dumbly.

"Thanks." Arianna's eyes narrowed as if she were going to say something more; instead, she shook her head as if perhaps she had misjudged the situation. Then her eyes bored into Samantha in a way no one's ever had, with such heated directness Samantha was forced to glance away, and by then it was too late. Arianna had disappeared.

Even when she thought of nothing else but Arianna's eyes, her hands, the way she moved, talked, gestured, the intensely exotic smell of her perfume, it wasn't until the third day of this ceaseless obsession that Samantha remembered Arianna was a woman. She believed her relentless fascination was nothing more than deep respect, for her accomplishment, her carriage; a beacon of light everyone gravitated toward.

Life returned to normal after several weeks of self-inflicted torment, the vision of Arianna settling into a lonely memory. It was then she had met David, his lanky childishness endearing, his sense of humor always his best feature.

After three months of deadly dull basketball games, groping date movies, bad school theater and pool at "Brewsers," Samantha found herself in David's dark and musty-smelling room. Artifacts of maleness lurked in every corner, lazy and wrinkled remains of gnarled house-keeping, ripped underwear, old beer bottles shoved behind books in makeshift shelves.

She cleaned the room thoroughly, washed the sheets, brought in fresh flowers, hung a picture or two on the wall. She easily fell into the pattern of meeting him there three or four a nights a week, usually after game night, and the other nights she was free.

She needed human contact, and it was easy to remain disengaged with David's kind and charmingly inept ardor. The less heated, the better. Even masturbation was uncomfortable. She continued to harbor the fantasy she might be stuck in its exquisite yet terrifying ecstasy forever. So her body met David's with gentle pleasure but without the disturbing ramifications or side effects of falling in love.

It was on the afternoon of one of her free nights that she saw it in a shop window . . . *Linger*. By Arianna DuPres, her photo prominently displayed next to an article from the *Seattle Times*, "Hometown Writer Wows New York." Her eyes were as intense and resolute through the dot matrix as they were that night five months ago.

Samantha ran into the store, purchased the book, cut her last class of the day and burrowed herself on her twin bed. She read, taut with suspense, as page after page the heroine painfully excised all the relevant parts of her life to be with this man, her professor, until she was no more than a bird in a cage. The words leapt off the page, Samantha's throat tightening as it built to its humorous but horrifying climax. After the last page, Samantha sighed with intense feeling. Intuition, empathic reasoning—she didn't know. But she knew this woman—not the woman on the page, but Arianna—in a way she had never known anyone.

Three weeks later, they met quite by accident. Samantha was sipping a double espresso at a coffee shop, finishing a take-home final before Christmas break, when she felt compelled to glance up from her work. There was Arianna ordering at the counter, a newspaper tucked beneath her arm.

All motion stops. Surreal, she is in a movie, the sound tracks mix the world out; rack-focus to the actor, larger than life, as all else fades in the background. Sweeping, epic, more important than reason, Arianna, as she takes her cappuccino and walks in graceful slow motion to the table in the corner. And who knows how many minutes, hours or eons pass until Arianna's eyes lift slowly to meet her own, blink, then narrow in recognition, a smile, a nod of salutation, and then she hears the beating of her heart, louder and faster, as Arianna gets up, walks in that beautiful gliding manner until she is right before her. Slow motion jars back to present time. Pandemonium of the real world comes crashing in and the heartbeat muffles in her ears because now Arianna is asking if she can join her and she is responding with a calm she doesn't possess, "Yes, that would be nice."

"You're Samantha. From the party."

"Yes." So nervous she ached from it.

"Arianna DuPres."

"Yes. I know." As if it weren't evident this exotic creature wasn't *the* Arianna DuPres. "You sure put a new spin on the affair with the professor."

And then they talked. About everything. Backgrounds. Family. School. About Arianna's degree in journalism, which she doubted she would ever use. "I can never be remote on any topic," Arianna stated simply. "I'd make a very poor reporter." Samantha agreed. Arianna's writing came from the heart.

They shared laughter. Smiles. Gentle grins that left their mouths but not their eyes. Somehow hours had skipped by, and all Samantha knew was that she never wanted the afternoon to end, but it had; and Arianna said she had a dinner date and Samantha hated whoever her dining companion might be. Arianna, returning from the phone at the counter, telling her she'd canceled; it was a second date that never should have been made in the first place.

They walked for hours and then happened upon a small Italian restaurant, as if it were in the script, played with their wine glasses and menus to scratchy violin music. They ordered a pizza that sat before them, finally cold. Arianna told her about her new book, which was loosely based on her last lover, and no, she had never had the relationship with the professor. It was actually a friend of her father's who spent a lot of time with the family. "It was all very *The Graduate* and such a mess I left home, holed myself up in a friend's cabin in Colorado and wrote *Linger* in four weeks. It was a purge . . . and extremely lucrative." Arianna had winked at her then. "See? Therapy pays after all."

"Is this one therapy as well?"

"No. Just rewriting history."

"That must be sweet revenge. Rearranging it all in your head."

"It can be . . ." As Arianna searched for a word, she stopped suddenly, her eyes burning an emerald glitter. "Soothing." In that moment Samantha thought this woman was beautiful, in a way she had never thought of a woman as being beautiful . . . powerful, sensual, with a wiry magnetism that made her wonder if she would feel an electrical pulse if she were to touch Arianna's skin.

"I want to touch you," Samantha heard herself say, thinking it was the wine. Knowing it wasn't.

"Oh, God, so do I." Arianna's eyes swept over her, drawing her in, capturing her from that moment on. She became the victim of *Linger*, lost forever in that second. Arianna's hand found hers. Hot, textured, smooth. Samantha was desperate for Arianna's hands on her, the hands that wrote the words she would live, wresting the control from her, firmly commanding her every movement.

"Please." Samantha could barely utter the word. Arianna paid the bill and they left the restaurant. Several feet from the entrance, Arianna drew her into a darkened alleyway, grasped Samantha to her, her hands swiftly under her shirt, firmly clutching the small of her back, bringing her mouth to Arianna's own, hungry, incurable aching.

The swimming dizziness, the disarray of desire, confusion—all melted into a black hole that made Samantha tremble from the disorientation. As much as she wanted this, could not walk away from it, she could not bear the intensity. And as they made it through the front door of her apartment, stumbled their way to Arianna's bed, stopping every few feet, revitalizing transfusions that intensified with every connection, Samantha knew she would faint if they did not stop.

Coming together with this force of will, so much stronger than her own, gave Samantha only one choice: to subvert herself to this veritable stranger . . . begging her, pleading with her as they made love deep into the night, into early the next morning, never sated, only desiring more. Every fiber of control she had sewn into the fabric of her life unraveled. By morning Samantha was stripped raw, tender and bleeding, exposed to the entire world. And she relished it.

Until she was safely back in her apartment several hours later, her head aching from lack of sleep, pretending she was prepared for the final; her life, as she knew it, over. Hazy and uncertain she wandered into the classroom. Did she even care? How could anything matter next to this . . . next to Arianna?

And what was this thing called Arianna? As the moments of her day passed and took hold of her, Samantha's anxiety heightened. There were only two things she knew with utter clarity: she was in a twilight zone of impassioned combustion—and she would never be able to stay away from it.

A fraught push-pull would characterize the next three blissfully tormented months of Samantha's life. After she unceremoniously dumped David over the phone, she entered into life with Arianna: playing, talking, being, but mostly making love, each time the black hole growing larger and darker, the explosiveness of their union more intense, until Samantha gave up trying to define or to understand it. It was not a matter of comprehension. It was primal. Perhaps cosmic. Both or neither.

No explanations. Only a pattern of terror as their exchange became more potent. The loss of control overwhelmed Samantha into physical panic and she was desperate to pull back inside herself and retreat to a place called sanity.

But there was no such place.

◆ ◆ ◆

Arianna left for two weeks in the spring to promote her book in the U.K. An interminable span of time fired the transatlantic cables, passion laced with anguished torture. They became disconnected first by time differences, then by technical problems and, finally, frustration at their separation. It became fearful and misread. Their investment crumbled as fear crackled over the lines, static accusations.

The mottled information became clear when Arianna returned. Her ex-lover wanted her back. By then, Samantha had so recoiled into her own fear at losing this thing, this thing she had no words for, she was terrorized into calm. She could not respond to Arianna's relentless question, "Do you want to make a go of this?"

A go of what? The insane coming together that rendered her functionless in a world she had once perched upon, in control, in complete harmony with the movements she now had lost all interest in? What had they to offer one another? They were so different. Samantha defined her existence by constant grounding, stability; by the removal of chaos two hundred and eighty miles south of her. Arianna thrived on explosion. Samantha was driven by containment, Arianna by passionate extremes. Samantha wanted a life that was filled with the dailiness of moments strung together, Arianna a life of moments come where they may. Samantha felt like a survivor in a mid-air collision, lost in the rubble and debris of the fallout; and, in the end, even after

Arianna came to her, begged her with eyes burning jade, Samantha could not look into them.

Samantha's body backed out of her skin, and the person who had responded to Arianna became aloof and remote in her calm good-bye.

Detached and safe, Samantha returned to her life, and when she did, she lost what she thought she was saving. Her soul.

indsay finished the details of the final changes she had prepared for Nathan. She twirled her chair around; she was jazzed. They were good. This project was good. And working with Samantha on it—well, ironically, it had become the best part.

No two predators had ever been more wary, more distrusting, she thought as she smiled at the sketches before her. It made her hopeful for world peace. They had sixty-three days under their belts and another five weeks ahead of them. Lindsay felt it in her gut. They were going to make it.

Samantha was a dream when it came to work. Lindsay had never before met anyone so dedicated or disciplined as herself, and yet . . . it was more, she had to admit. She respected Samantha as a person. She was drawn to her. Once the dust had settled she quickly developed a great admiration for her, found herself attracted with ungrudging envy and a desire to wrap herself in Samantha's balance.

She was giddily energetic as she waited for her at Bean There, Done That, anxious to get Samantha's input on the final sketches before she submitted them for Nathan's approval. She ordered their standard fare; latte for Samantha, cappuccino for herself, and added a cranberry muffin for Samantha.

Samantha blew in, excitable, eager, a flush on her cheeks from the damp November cold. But there was more reason for her color than the cold.

"Yes?" Lindsay could tell she was ready to burst.

"I did it."

"Yes?"

"I put half down." Samantha shut her eyes as if she couldn't believe what she had done.

"Oh, God!" Lindsay laughed from shared joy. "That's great!"

"Is it? Am I crazy? I don't have that kind of money."

"Samantha." Lindsay's eyes and tone were serious now. "You deserve it."

"Do I? What makes me deserve it?"

"That you want it."

"That's an interesting correlation. Everything I want, I deserve."

"Yes."

Samantha laughed, diffusing some of her anxiety. "OK. I'll buy that. Now . . . I guess we should get to work so I can afford this wonderful philosophy of yours."

Lindsay showed her the sketches. Samantha sat still for a long moment.

"Have a pencil?" Samantha asked. Lindsay handed her one. She etched several lines, shoved the top sketch back beneath Lindsay's nose. Lindsay then made several passes, returned the pages.

Samantha made three short marks. "Keep the techy arches," she said, then swirled small circles at intermediate spots, "and hide a few modern gargoyles in the border. Makes the gentry happy. Voilà!" She shaded in several monsterish creatures. "God, why do they love ugly things?"

Samantha turned the final drawings around for Lindsay's approval.

"I'm impressed."

"So am I." Samantha smiled back.

Their minds had met. A delicate tension passed between them.

"You've thought of everything."

She had been stuck in one of the endless days. Lindsay had stopped by with lunch. Samantha had watched her as she laid out the deli sandwiches, gingerly placing the paper towels by their sides, preparing the plastic silver as if it were a sit-down dinner, and then after standing a moment, opening the bag of chips and propping it to the side. Just right. Samantha smiled. Lindsay was charming. Guilelessly so.

They sat down. Lindsay spotted an abandoned boom box. "What's this? I thought they were banned."

"Oh, this belongs to one of the painters. We listen to it when everyone else is gone."

Lindsay grabbed it, set it before them, rummaged in her briefcase and retrieved a cassette tape.

"Evidence of culture." She slipped it in, pushed PLAY. The first strains of Khachaturian's adagio from *Spartacus* filled the theater.

"Very nice." Samantha smiled. "Is this an attempt to live in the moment—especially when they're so few and far between?"

"Something like that." Lindsay held out both sandwiches. "Turkey or turkey? Which would you like?"

"How about the turkey?"

"I wasn't sure about the red meat thing."

"You can't be these days."

They ate in silence, listening to the swell, the ever-increasing intensity of the music. Samantha watched Lindsay stop eating, entranced by the music, eyes closed, inside the journey. Violins teased the melancholy sweetness of the melody while the drums echoed its strength, and as it hit its crescendo, a victorious smile crept at the corner of Lindsay's mouth. "Yessssss."

She opened her eyes then, as an afterthought. "I love that part."

Yes, Lindsay was charming.

◆ ◆ ◆

They had made another lunch date for two days later. Samantha brought turkey meatloaf, made from a favorite recipe of Robert's. Generously sliced portions on rye, with a smattering of mayonnaise. . . .

". . . and very liberal on the Dijon. It's a variation on a theme." She handed Lindsay a sandwich, set hers on a storage box. "And"—she presented a cassette and stuck it into the boom box—"for your dining pleasure, a little Bach."

They ate listening to the music. Then Lindsay held up her sandwich. "Great meatloaf."

"It's all in the spices."

"But what I love is there's no soggy bread. Hate soggy bread."

"You will never find soggy bread in my meatloaf."

◆ ◆ ◆

". . . and it's just one of the nicest gifts anyone's ever given me." Sara Winters, the colorist for the drapes, was showing Samantha a mug inscribed with the names of her favorite movie stars.

Lindsay joined them and Sara shoved it under her nose. "Don't you think it's great? Custom and all that? I love that kind of personal touch." Sara nabbed it back before Lindsay actually had a chance to form an opinion. "Anyway, I've got to get back to the store. If you don't like the carmine, and personally I think the dye lot has changed from the swatch we all agreed on, I won't mind taking it back. But with this time limit, well, you know, it's gonna be extra."

Lindsay and Samantha exchanged resigned looks. "What's new?"

"Well, you let me know."

"Go ahead. We've got to have the drapes in by the fifteenth." Lindsay rummaged in her briefcase, dismissing Sara. She rubbed her temples. "Doesn't that woman have anything to say other than 'it's gonna be extra'?"

"Well, she did share her very lovely gift with us," Samantha grinned.

"Unhuh."

Samantha returned to her paint chips. "I think it was kind of neat."

"What?"

"The mug."

"Oh."

"Only I'd have mine with my favorite heroes on it. You know, to get me started in the morning."

"Yeah?" Lindsay glanced up from her paperwork. "So who y'all starting your day with?"

"Well, Judge Ruth Bader Ginsburg, for one."

"OK."

"Gloria Steinem."

"Goes without saying."

"Hillary, of course."

"Of course."

"Vivien Leigh."

"Vivien Leigh?"

"Absolutely," Samantha insisted. "I mean, where would feminism be without Scarlett O'Hara?"

"Well . . . maybe."

"Your turn."

"Hmmm." Lindsay dropped the paperwork. "OK. Margaret Atwood. Marilyn French. Carolyn See."

"Very good."

"Martina."

"Ah, yes."

"Ayn Rand."

"Of course. You would have to be a Randy."

"Would any adolescence be complete without it?" Lindsay asked. They laughed. Samantha dropped her paint chips, moved closer to Lindsay. "I bet *The Fountainhead* did a number on you."

"Are you kidding? It changed my life. I read it in two days. And then devoured *Atlas Shrugged* the following week, lying about feeling sick. I kept it under the covers, and as soon as Mrs. Gardner, our housekeeper, left, out it would come, and I'd race through it, and then I actually did get the flu from lack of sleep."

"Oh, that's great." Samantha shared a smile of camaraderie with Lindsay. "Ayn Rand's a very serious thing, you know."

"Very serious," Lindsay mocked. "But I don't think it has the same impact unless you read it at an extremely impressionable age."

"Yeah, adolescence and black and white have a lot in common. Gray doesn't exactly fit into the Ayn Rand color wheel."

"That's just it. You sit on one side of the fence or the other. No middle ground."

"Exactly my point. I know very few people who don't straddle the middle on most issues in their life."

"Like?"

"Truth. Reality. Justice. The American Way."

"But what about the really important stuff"—Lindsay's eyes turned serious—"like meatloaf?"

"Well, that's another matter." Samantha's voice was purposeful. "Very black and white."

"Absolutely no soggy bread," they completed in unison.

◆ ◆ ◆

Samantha turned off the last of the lights when Lindsay entered.

"I didn't expect to see you tonight."

"I was on my way to a meeting, actually." They both stood half-in, half-out of the doorway, awkward. "Megan called. It was canceled."

With the opportunity of a new direction for the evening suspended between them, neither was sure in the wisdom of pursuing it.

"Probably good it was canceled. You look . . . well, exhausted." Samantha began to move outside the doorway toward the stairwell. Lindsay followed. They walked in silence through the unfinished halls to the back entrance and parking lot. Samantha locked the stage door. They turned, simultaneously.

"Well," each said at the same time.

"See you tomorrow." Lindsay decided not to push it. She had been feeling anxious all day, skirting one attack after another. Tonight she needed a safe place.

"Yeah. Get some rest." Samantha watched Lindsay walk to her car. "Hey!" she called after her, then began running toward her. "I completely forgot. I don't have my car. They won't be done with it until tomorrow." They laughed.

"Well . . . have you had dinner?"

"No."

"Hungry?"

"Not really."

"Neither am I."

They drove in silence for some time. Lindsay monitored her breathing. She had become adept at suffering the low-grade anxiety in the presence of others. It was the big attacks she couldn't control. But just as she was beginning to feel a shred of inner calm, her stomach convulsed, throat constricted . . . *I can't breathe. I can't breathe. Heart, too fast. It's happening. God, no. Please don't let this happen in front of her. Breathe in. 4-6. Breathe in 4. Breathe out 6.* But nothing was working. Nothing. *Bigger now . . . bigger inside me. Will swallow me. Have to stop. I can't let her see me.*

But she had. "Lindsay, are you all right?"

She pulled over, parked the car, got out. Samantha followed her, but Lindsay put her hand out: "No." Bent over, heart raging, pin prickles shot through her body, nausea, stomach heaving, *think . . . get calm . . . I'm dying . . .* vertigo as she leaned against the car . . . *it's passing . . . please . . . it's passing.*

"Lindsay, what is it?" Helpless.

"I'm . . . it's OK. It's OK." Lindsay's breathing was returning to normal. And in seconds she could feel another wave come and go, and then her body, cold, her teeth clamped together so hard her jaw hurt, freezing. She was frozen. "Let's get in the car."

"I'll drive." Samantha stood by the open passenger door waiting for Lindsay to get in, then got in the driver's seat. Before she took off, she glanced at Lindsay. "OK?" Her voice was gentle, soft, concerned.

"Yeah." Helpless.

Samantha edged out onto the highway, drove slowly.

"Shit." It was spoken under her breath. She felt mortified. Exposed.

"Are you sick . . . the flu?" Samantha asked.

"No." They drove in silence for a bit. "That's never happened before."

"What."

"In front of anyone, I mean." But it was all that Lindsay would say. Samantha pulled up before an apartment complex, let the engine run while their thoughts idled.

"I was lucky to find a friend's apartment . . . where I could house-sit." Samantha shifted uncomfortably. "It didn't feel right at my mother's. Look, I don't think you should drive yet. Why don't you come up?"

"These apartments have great views." Inanity was all she had the concentration for. Disorientation. *Skin feels like rubber.*

"I'll make you a cup of tea. Get some food in you. You look so tired, Lindsay." Samantha turned then and looked at Lindsay. A companionable silence passed between them, and then Lindsay was about to say something, but Samantha killed the engine. "Don't argue with me, OK?"

Lindsay nodded.

Sam switched on the light to the apartment: simple lines, clean, streamlined. Lindsay didn't care for it. She found it cold. She walked to the encompassing view of the city with its lights and bridges.

"It's not the warmest place, but her view makes up for it." Samantha had read her mind. "A gal I went to school with keeps it for the rare moments she gets home. She's in the film business and travels all the time."

"What does she do?"

"Set decorator."

Lindsay turned. A meager smile cracked her pale countenance and they both laughed, appraising the minimalist decor.

"Ahhh, the shoemaker's shoe strikes again."

"Tea. Wine?"

"Some wine would be great." Lindsay hoped it would combat the anxiety.

Samantha returned with two glasses of wine. They sat. Silence. Not awkward. A weaving of two energies, trying to find their rhythm. Neither felt forced to make conversation. They listened to the silence they created.

"I'm sorry . . . about in the car."

"What happened?"

Lindsay took a sip of her wine. "Panic attack."

"Ouch," Samantha sympathized. "Ohhh, they're terrible."

"You know about them?"

"Yes. Robert worked in one of the few panic disorder clinics in school. He told me about them. God, they're awful. Painful." Samantha's voice was so engaging Lindsay began to feel safe.

"It's hard, you know, I feel like they're this aberration of my psyche. And they tend to get worse—"

"—the more stress you're under, which you would know nothing about, of course." Samantha smiled, and then her eyes got serious. "It's not unlike being an alcoholic . . . what you do. Your drive, your need for it, its all-consuming nature."

Lindsay turned to her then. "What do you mean?"

"I've sort of made an amateur analysis of it—having a mother devoted to one, a father to the other. Come to think of it, everyone I know seems addicted to something. Except Robert." She stopped a second. "The muse of moderation . . . . Anyway, I have a pet theory about it all."

"Do tell." Lindsay was relaxed now, enjoying this new side of Samantha.

"No. Don't get me started. Besides, I don't want to barrage you . . . not while you're feeling this way."

"Come on . . . I'd really like to hear."

"OK. But remember—you asked for it." Samantha sipped her wine, took a moment to reflect, then smiled kindly. "As with everything . . . it starts out slowly. Subtly. Especially in the beginning."

Samantha tugged gently at her bottom lip, chose her words carefully. "Like a faint breeze. Hardly noticeable. Work a weekend or two. Nobody says anything. In fact, like the person who can hold their liquor, you're patted on the back. You," Samantha emphasized, "are a good American. You are a producer in a society that measures success in terms of quantity, not quality. Product, not process. Elementary.

"Beginning stages tend to last a long time—years, usually—which is unfortunate because it's during this tenure that one learns to work it into every corner of life." Samantha got up, not pacing exactly, but moving with the rhythm of her words. "The drinker has her first blackout. The worker almost has a nervous breakdown getting that final project in to the big guys up in executive suites. Scares the shit out of them. The drinker lays off for a while, the worker takes a ski trip, maybe gets a tan by the pool in Palm Springs. But both plod along, reasonably well adjusted. They now know how to rejuvenate until the drinker masters a new level of tolerance, and the worker gets a bigger project under her belt.

"They become intoxicated. Absolutely relish the inspirational flight of the mind, in complete ecstasy. They still have some semblance of control, but now they're becoming consumed with the very thing that will make their lives miserable. So they ask themselves, is it really the booze or the work that makes them uncomfortable, or is it the rest of the world's perception of their relationship to it?

"The drinker becomes invincible, mistakes inebriation for indestructibility. Orders another drink. The worker gets more money, praise, realizes power and seeks another project. They're caught. Neither can walk away. Neither can do without, and both will do anything to maintain their habit; tell small tales to get what they want, lie to their families, spouses . . . they'll cut down, get it under control. Neither has the remotest desire to do so, of course. Nor the ability.

"And now for the depressing part. At this point the drinker usually begins to lose things of material value: her family, her job, her money; and then the more intangible: self-respect, physical health, sanity. It all goes down the drain. Then the drinker is faced with two options. Quit, or die.

"The worker, on the other hand, will have acquired many material possessions, and for all intents and purposes has achieved success. But she's usually promoted poor familial relations and for all the glory she's achieved, it borders on meaningless because she never has any time to enjoy it, anyway. She too may suffer poor physical health, much more subtle than the drinker's bloated liver. Maybe an insidious stress-related cancer. Unfortunately she's just as driven by her workouts as her workload . . . which leads to a seemingly fantastic all 'round good gal Sal. And that's why it's so difficult to pinpoint. So what if she's suffering from lack of balance and quality of life?" Samantha stopped pacing, sat back on the couch.

"Anyway . . . you get the picture."

Lindsay had sat still during Samantha's soliloquy, listening. Actually hearing. She sipped her wine, then closed her eyes for a long moment.

"Unpredictable."

"Unpredictable?"

"Yes. Your mother rarely spoke of you and now I spend every day with you."

"I don't think there's a thing connected to my mother's tentacles that is predictable."

Lindsay didn't know why she had brought Sondra up. She didn't want to talk about her. She didn't want to talk about anything.

"I'm sorry about mounting my soapbox. Should I put on some music?" Samantha asked.

"Yes. That would be nice . . . and thank you. For your soapbox."

They listened for the next hour to a medley of classical meditations, speaking very little, each very much immersed in her own thoughts. Samantha was going to ask Lindsay if she wanted more wine, but when she turned, Lindsay had fallen asleep.

Samantha gazed at her for a long time. The similarities between Lindsay and Arianna were not lost on her. Their darkness. Strength. Mystery. Passion for their work, to the exclusion of all else. But Lindsay was different in one important way. She was remote. Arianna wore every single emotion like a bright new outfit. Lindsay cloaked hers beneath a heavy woolen cape. But their eyes were the same. Fierce intensity. Utterly focused.

She thought back to when she had returned to Portland, their first, then subsequent meetings. She couldn't see Lindsay then. All she had seen was anger. Red. Primordial. Protection for her sick mother. Lindsay had been the enemy. And then, when she admitted what she had known to be true all along, that her mother had been and always would be her own worst enemy, she allowed herself to finally take Lindsay in. On her own terms.

Samantha got up, retrieved a blanket from the closet. When she put it over her, Lindsay woke, but only enough for Samantha to help her off with her shoes. She adjusted a pillow beneath Lindsay's head.

She was about to turn off the light, but caught the highlights in

Lindsay's wonderful hair, thick, black and sensuously silky, caressing the high cheekbones; and her lips, tensed a bit even now with the first surrender to unconsciousness. A handsome woman. Terribly handsome, Jerra might say.

Samantha bent to touch the hair, then immediately pulled back her hand as a tendril brushed her finger. She turned off the light and went to bed.

The next morning Lindsay was gone, reappearing at the theater at ten with coffee.

"Got something new for you." Lindsay handed Samantha her coffee as she came down the ladder. " 'Bout last night . . . Guess I sort of crashed."

"Guess you sort of needed to."

"I'm sorry—"

"No problem. I just wondered how in the hell you could sleep on that thing."

"I could have slept on a concrete slab."

"Oh . . . this is divine." Samantha's eyes sparkled delightedly over the coffee. "What is it?"

"Eggnog latte."

"Ohhhh . . . this is really not good." Samantha took another sip. "I'm going to be a maniac now."

They smiled at one another. Samantha put her coffee down. "Speaking of eggnog, I thought while the drywallers were finishing up here Wednesday I'd head down to the beach and make a little Thanksgiving turkey. What do you say?"

Lindsay could not think of a good excuse to say no. In fact, didn't want to. "Sure."

"Good. How 'bout three?"

◆ ◆ ◆

Lindsay, Snag and Megan all bustled through the office on a singular mission: to finish so they could begin Thanksgiving festivities. Snag and Jared were flying to San Francisco to spend Turkey Day with their best friends. Megan was meeting Ryan's parents at what he termed an "unearthly large gathering of relatives, near and far. The problem being that none of us have left Portland." Megan could barely stand the idea of meeting his parents, but to have to endure every uncle, aunt and cousin was simply too much. Frozen Stouffer's had its merits.

"And what are you doing, doll?" Snag asked Lindsay as they were finishing off the last of their notes with each other.

"Oh . . . I've got plans."

"Let me guess."

"So, Megan," Lindsay changed the subject, "have you told Ryan?"

"Or do you plan to make a family press release out of it?" Snag winked at her. But Megan didn't answer. "Megs? You have told him, haven't you?"

"Well . . . actually, I was sort of waiting for the right time?"

"And when might that be? When the water breaks?"

"It's just got to be the right time, that's all." Megan handed several files to Lindsay. "These need to be signed. And these. So, where is it you're going, Lindsay?"

"I'm . . . I'm, uh, heading to the beach." Lindsay signed the papers before her. "Is that all?"

"Where?"

"Snag, does it really matter?"

"We just don't want you to be alone, Lindsay. You're more than welcome to come with Ryan and me. He already asked me if you had plans."

"Well, I do, but thanks. I hope you both have a great weekend." And before either could respond, Lindsay disappeared into her office.

"Snag?" Megan questioned, but he just shrugged his shoulders.

Lindsay sat at her desk late Wednesday night. She had tried to get to sleep, but was overtired, and ended up staring at the ceiling in the alcove. Sondra's image flashed through her mind. A vague sense of loss twisted about her insides. But did she really feel any pain at Sondra's absence? Or only the idea of it? Did that mean she hadn't loved? That she was heartless? Not given to romantic scenarios? And then she thought of Heather and her detachment from their relationship. Heather's involvement with her Ouija board, her worship of tarot, *I Ching*, and Lindsay's rejection of the "woo-wooness" of it all. Her rejection of conventional belief systems. Where did she find a spiritual base? The only true reverence she had ever felt was for her work.

She wondered. Well, didn't everyone? What it all meant and what a cliché it was to wonder. Trying to cap all those clichés about "it" under an umbrella that made some sort of sense to her, but never did. And even now as she sat in her dimly lit office, she only knew what she didn't believe in: organized religion or the new-ageism that capped its doctrine in an "abundant universe," but still leaned heavily on "shoulds" and "should nots" and a system dedicated to either guilt or taking no responsibility whatsoever. Metaphysics was as close as she could get to putting a label on her beliefs, but it still wasn't pragmatic enough to accommodate her need for control. How could she possibly dictate the path of an alternate reality when she couldn't control the one she was in? So what did she hold on to?

She rested her head on her desk, eyes closed, thought about the sameness of her days and moments, and knew what it was supposed to be all about. The Process. Being in the Now. Moments. All strung together, moments of life you breathed, loved, mourned, felt deeply, numbly; sorrow, terror and great joys. And still, she could not give meaning to it.

The medium of their culture, television, had responded to her vague malaise on a grand scale, sweeping through a rash of prime time dedicated to "shows about nothing." Maybe that was it. Maybe it was all nothing. So why? What was the point? Even if you were, say, Oskar Schindler or Hitler, and made either a heroic difference or challenged humanity to the core with evil, if there was no proof this wasn't a finite planet whirling about on its axis, its inhabitants grounded by a thing called gravity, what did it mean?

She was sinking into an abyss. Samantha briefly floated through her thoughts. Her image startled her. On the ladder, a startlingly bright light swung above her on the ceiling, blowing out her image as it swayed back and forth. Samantha as she floated from the ladder, down to her, her face drawing closer, her eyes alight with laughter, the

gentle smile, and then her lips parting and maggots and worms crawling from the face that was no longer Samantha's, but something
grotesque: Sondra, eyes of red, the devil boring into her own, de-
monic laughter ringing, ringing shrill in her ears.

She woke. And it was then the hole within Lindsay almost swallowed her up. She wished. She craved. She desired as never before.
But she didn't know what it was she yearned for. And since the
answers didn't come, she would return to what she knew: work. It
was the one thing that grounded her, that enabled escape—from the
questions that frightened her, the doubts that plagued her and the
sameness of a quest she had no direction for.

◆ ◆ ◆

"It's me."
"Hi."
"Just wanted to call and wish you a happy Thanksgiving."
"Thanks." Then after a moment, "How are things going?"
"Better."
A long pause.
"So what are you doing for Turkey Day?"
"I'm heading to Earlsheart."
"Oh." Sigh of envy? Consternation? "Robert coming down?"
"Not until next weekend."
"So you're going to be all alone?"
"Um . . . yes."
"That's too bad. I wish we could have been together. Don't you?"
"Yes." She lied again.

◆ ◆ ◆

The turkey was almost finished. Samantha sang and whistled, a flush
of domesticity in the kitchen, lighthearted, expectant. It was so
good to get away from the Pavilion, if only until the following
morning. She had taken an early-morning trek along the beach, ex-
hilarated by the cold, the ocean wild, a stormy gray. When she had
returned to Earlsheart she was warmed by the smell of the turkey
baking.

She traipsed giddily about the house, making sure everything was just so. She didn't know why it was so important, but she wanted Lindsay to have a perfect day. Hell, they both deserved it. She heard Lindsay's car, ran excitedly to the door.

"There would have been nothing but a few pathetic bones if you'd gotten here any later." Samantha stood in the doorway.

"I made it, didn't I?"

"Hurry up. It's freezing out there."

"Go on in. I've got to get my briefcase."

"If you bring one shred of paperwork in here you'll be dining at Bill's Lagoon. And you know what happens to people who go there, don't you?"

"Sam! Just get inside." Lindsay had never abbreviated her name before. Samantha turned, leaning the door ajar, renewed warmth spreading over her. She dashed to the kitchen to check the turkey. A beautiful bird. She felt like Martha Stewart tending the home fires, and had to laugh at herself.

"God, finally—" Samantha reentered the living room as Lindsay was setting down an extremely large brown-paper-wrapped object. Lindsay backed away from it. "This is for . . . you."

Samantha approached it slowly—"What have you done?"—then stood before it, not certain where to begin but knowing, knowing what it was before she began unwrapping it.

"Please say you didn't." But she tore the brown paper away and there before them both stood "Evening's Debut." Samantha couldn't say anything for moments, struck once more by the beauty of the painting, and then as potently by Lindsay's gesture.

"Before you get embarrassed, I want you to know I chose several of his paintings to hang on the Pavilion's west wall and bargained this in—along with the money we saved on the marble. It would have come to us anyway, indirectly—"

"Lindsay, that's your profit."

"It's our profit. It was your idea to change the marble."

Samantha stood in awe for several minutes, then moved toward Lindsay. "She's so beautiful."

"Yes . . ." Lindsay found herself suddenly shy. "She is."

"God, I love it." Samantha was filled with genuine emotion. She put out a hand to Lindsay's arm. "Thank you." And then mocking her own awkwardness, Samantha leaned to hug Lindsay.

They both sensed it. Samantha conscious of the smell of Lindsay's hair, her perfume. Lindsay embracing the length of Samantha's body against her own. They broke away. Simultaneously.

"Well"—Samantha stepped back—"ready for the best damn turkey this side of Earlscove?"

"I think that leaves three houses?"

"I didn't say I was a master chef. But I do have my moments." Samantha began to retreat into the kitchen. "We're going to eat out here. Turkey picnic, as it were. By the fireplace."

"Let me help."

"No. You just build up the fire and make yourself comfortable."

Lindsay turned to the hearth. Within the fire's warmth a picnic tablecloth had been set with china, wine glasses, silver. Lindsay threw several logs on the fire to build up the smoldering embers. Samantha returned with broccoli, potatoes and gravy, stuffing and then a platter of sliced turkey.

They sat, and Samantha began serving. Lindsay gazed at the ocean, mesmerized, easing the tenseness of the previous moment, watching the simplicity of the waves, never ending, never beginning. It reminded her of her thoughts the night before, contemplating the quality of her life, and then the nightmare. She quickly glanced at Samantha. Yes. She was real. Exquisitely real.

And here they sat, in a house she had built with her mother; created, but never shared. Samantha handed Lindsay a plate, her eyes brimming with life.

"I think that's what Thanksgiving is about," Lindsay heard herself say, meaning Samantha's eyes, which she was really seeing for the first time, their depth, their clear intelligence, their fire.

"What?" Samantha sat down across from her with her plate.

But Lindsay couldn't share her thoughts. Instead she said, "The sunset. See it? God's colors light up the sky."

"My, you're sounding spiritual this afternoon," Samantha remarked, then joined her gaze out the large picture window. "Look.

It happens so fast. Like a giant ball of mercury oozing its way into the water, inch by inch, and poof . . . it's gone."

"Gone." Lindsay's voice was low.

The darkness fell over them, leaving them lit only by firelight and a couple of candles Samantha had set up for the picnic. They ate in easy silence. Then, as Samantha put her plate to the side, she began recounting the history of Earlsheart, a softness in her voice. She told of the war-torn town, the large domicile used as a beacon for the widows and children of men who'd given their lives, how old Mrs. Hunziker had been a friend first, an organizer second in her efforts to keep the community together.

Samantha cleared the plates, wouldn't let Lindsay help. She returned with espresso. She handed a couple of pillows to Lindsay, who stretched out, leaning against the hearth while Samantha lounged a few feet from her.

"Actually I guess she wasn't old then, although she seemed ancient back then when Mom and Dad would drag me to visit. Anyway, she singlehandedly made the war effort in this burg." Samantha paused with her thoughts, caught somewhere in the flames of the fire. "There used to be a raggy piece of driftwood her husband carved. It hung above the door and read 'Earlsheart is where the home is.' " She paused. "It's still up in the attic, I bet. The next time I come down I'll search for it. Wait till you see it. It is the most incredible labor of love."

Samantha saw the firelight reflected in Lindsay's eyes, turned back to the dancing fire. "They were great people. Mrs. Hunziker died the summer I was twenty-three. The house was stuck in probate for years when Mom finally snagged it." Samantha sighed. "I think it always represented pure good to her, and if she could just get her hands on it, it would cure her of all her problems."

They sat for a while, both lost in their own thoughts.

"Is it hard for you to be here?"

"The first time I came down— Now that was . . . difficult."

"Yes, and I made it so easy for you."

They glanced at one another. The natural fading light was gone now, and Lindsay noticed the shimmer of the fire in Samantha's hair.

"I . . . I was sad about your mother."

"Lindsay." Samantha's voice was soft. "I'm sorry. I'm sorry for being such a . . . a bitch. I went into a tailspin of protection. For my mother. For me. You know, I stopped blaming you a long time ago." Samantha took a sip of her coffee, set it aside. "Shit. How well do I have to know my mother before it all sinks in? You know . . . wanting to blame anyone but her."

"Because you love her. Don't want to see the dark side. Do any of us? Really?"

"No. Denial is our culture's favorite hobby."

Another silence passed. They were treading on dangerous ground. "So . . . what happened? To my mother. Was it Nathan?"

"Oh, Sam . . ." Again, the familiar endearment. "I . . . I really don't think we should talk about your mother. It's over. Can't we just keep it that way?"

"Well, maybe." Samantha paused. "She'll be out of treatment after the new year. I hope this time it takes."

Lindsay's laconism closed the discussion.

And then after a bit, "Tell me a Lindsay story."

"A story." Lindsay considered. "What do you want to know?"

"Tell me your favorite childhood memory."

Lindsay briefly flitted over her mother's leaving her, her father's misery and absence, and Mrs. Gardner taking her away to the farm. "There was a summer that was as near to perfect as it can get. I think . . ." Lindsay removed her sweater, the heat from the fire filling the room. "I think everyone has a point in their lives where they have a moment . . . a slice of pureness . . . that's about living at its simple best. Sights, sounds, smells—they're perfect. Colors, scenes . . . the hay in the barn, the fields after a thunderstorm, mist rising off the ground, mystical and mysterious. I remember early one morning I saw Star, this bone-old German shepherd, barely any teeth left, with a possum in his jaws—had broken its neck in one snap—but there was such a beauty to this old guard dog with his last prey . . . he could barely keep up with me and my best friend Billy when we ran and jumped bales. The game was to see how many we could make it over without stopping—whoever got the most won. We never got tired. Never." Lindsay smiled wryly. "Now it seems like that's all I ever

feel. . . . Anyway, the best part, the thing I remember, is the smells. . . .
If I get anywhere near an apple pie I go back there . . . or bacon frying
in the mornings . . . or just the way the air smelled. Clean. Clean and
sky blue. That summer I came to a primal understanding of hard
work, hard play, simple pleasures. I don't think people are conscious
they have these moments . . . but I think it's then"—Lindsay's voice
got low—"we find a clarity . . . an understanding of life that we spend
the rest of our lives searching to get back to. . . ."

Samantha watched her.

"Jesus, this fire is hot!" Lindsay took off her shirt now. Underneath
she was clad in a contoured body-T.

Samantha studied Lindsay's body, her exposed arms, beautifully
sculpted, strong but soft, so characteristic of Lindsay. She imagined her
legs under the jeans, smooth-muscled, lean, long. And her eyes traced
their way back to Lindsay's breasts, clearly defined through the thread-
bare fabric, full, not large, a gentle swell to her nipples, erect from the
prickling heat of the fire.

Even from five feet away she could feel Lindsay. The power of her
body, its energy vibrating outward. Remembering the feel of it against
her own when they had embraced earlier seared her stomach.

Samantha swallowed, her jaw clenched tightly in self-defense. She
had known since Arianna that she adored the female body. But it
didn't mean she wanted to sleep with one. She had always justified her
encounter with Arianna as something that defied logic and conven-
tion. Genderless. A force beyond physicality. She hadn't been attracted to another woman since. She found them beautiful to look at,
to appreciate, but she hadn't been drawn to them, to touch them, to
fondle or feel.

Until now.

have no idea where the Merrick file went and his secretary's on the phone again . . . and I swear if I get on the line with him, Linds, I'm going to bust his sweet homophobic ass—"

"OK . . . just try and calm down, Snag. Where's Megan?"

"She's on her way from the doctor's."

"She's OK?"

"Well . . . yes, we hope."

"OK, let me call Merrick. Also, I need Stanton's prelims and I know Megan was copying those. Do you know?" But she stopped. Snag had begun shaking his head.

"I haven't a clue."

"Well, do you at least know where the Rand file is?"

But Snag didn't have to answer. The door opened and Megan walked in. Snag ran to her, took her purse and led her to the desk. "Our Queen Savior," he said, holding her chair for her.

"We're glad you're back." Lindsay approached the desk. They studied her expectantly, seeing her rosy cheeks, her eyes shining with a glint of heightened disbelief. "So?"

"You're not going to believe this."

"What, honey buns?"

"Twins?"

"Get out of here." Snag embraced her. Lindsay's grin exploded as she put her arms around Megan, held her close.

"I know. Isn't it too ridiculous? What am I going to do with twins?" Megan's voice trembled.

"Have double the fun, babe." Snag kissed her cheek. "Have you told the doting father that it isn't one, but two little Meggsteroonies who'll be keeping him up nights?"

"Well . . ."

"Megan, you get on the phone right now," Lindsay said. "Better yet, take an early lunch, get reservations at Abernathy's and tell him eye-to-eye."

"My, haven't we gotten romantic," Snag interjected.

"I have my moments," Lindsay declared with savoir faire. She turned to go, then stopped. "But before you leave, Megan, please, oh please, get Snag and me organized."

"Of course." Megan snapped back to reality, began bustling efficiently at her desk. "Get back into your office and stop staring at me," she ordered Snag.

"I'm just taking you in. It's true. Pregnant women are divine." Snag blew her a kiss, then left.

Megan began to shuffle through the papers on her desk, but once she was alone, she let the tension she'd been carrying ever since she left the doctor's office snap her professional facade and she collapsed into tears. Tears of delirium and joy. Everything had happened so fast. Ryan . . . now this. She had to tell him. She couldn't keep up this pretense any longer; the pretense that OA and the changes she had made in her diet weren't working for her. She had to tell him that her weight loss had been replaced by the phenomenon of life attaching itself to her womb. Not that he monitored or even cared about her weight. If anything, he didn't see her girth. Or perhaps he reveled in it. What if he was just a sicko who got off on flesh?

"Megan, stop it." She knew she was driving herself insane. She couldn't go on like this. Every waking hour was consumed with how and when she was going to tell him, and then how she was going to deal with his leaving her. Ryan was everything she could have ever dreamed about in a man. A mate. He was Snag, Lindsay, her father and her best friend all rolled into one. Yet the longer she waited to confide in him, the more threatening the risk of losing him became. For the first and only time in her life this part of her was complete, absolute, and now she had to risk losing it? If she had told him straightaway, she believed she might have been able to survive the aftermath. Now she was sure she wouldn't.

"I made you resos at Abernathy's." Snag had returned to Megan's desk. He took one look at her. "No. Oh, no way! You haven't even told him about the first one yet?!"

But the tears that continued to roll down her cheeks made it very clear that she hadn't.

◆ ◆ ◆

Things had grown increasingly awkward between them, a sense of displacement that began the moment Samantha opened the door and saw Robert standing before her, big Cheshire cat grin spread over his face as he presented roses with his surprise arrival. "It's me!" He had missed her so much, he said, and decided "What the hell, I'll live dangerously for once," and was there for the weekend.

Now they were in her car on their way to dinner, an invitation from Snag she had accepted before Robert had decided at the last minute to surprise her. They sat in silence.

"I can't believe you couldn't have just canceled."

"You've sure changed your tone."

"Yeah . . . well." He had. At first he was amenable to dinner plans, wanted to be a good sport. After all, he had shown up unannounced. Besides it could be a good slow build. For later. He often enjoyed watching Samantha around people, thinking about her, knowing he would be inside her later, filling her up, seeing her face when she came. But as Samantha kept her distance, increasingly remote and aloof, it began to matter to him a great deal that they were going to be spending what little time they had with people he didn't even know.

"Look, Robert. How 'bout we go to Earlsheart tomorrow? Spend the day and back your flight up to Monday?" She put a hand on his arm. She was trying to be solicitous of his feelings. He had gone to great lengths to put some romance into their weekend. At least he was making a real effort. It wouldn't kill her to do the same.

"That would be great." He turned to her, smiled. His green eyes turned a soft, tender hazel. She almost couldn't look into them. "Just the two of us. Hope it's stormy. We can spend the day in bed."

That's exactly what she didn't want. If she fell into the quiet space between Robert's arms she would go crazy. There was too much inside her. Too much aching to get out.

Snag opened the door. He kissed Samantha, shook Robert's hand, then behind his back gave Samantha a "not bad" sign as he led them into the living room.

"My God, Snag. This place is . . . beautiful." And it was. A mish-mash of antiques, tasteful staging of musical one-sheets, props and paraphernalia tied together by an oriental motif all snuggled in a spacious loft apartment overlooking the Willamette River.

"We call it Eclectic Fag."

Samantha laughed. "I don't know how, but it works."

Jared walked into the room from the kitchen. "Ahhhh, and the pièce de résistance," Snag declared proudly, displaying his lover for them both. Jared clasped Snag's hand, raised the other with a serving spoon.

The doorbell rang again. It was Megan and Ryan. Megan's face fell when she saw Samantha. "You didn't tell me *she* was going to be here," she said through clenched teeth that formed a painful grimace as Snag took her coat.

"Give her a chance, Megs. She's not like her mother."

But Samantha hadn't been prepared for Megan either, and felt the cold judgment slice through her every time their eyes met. Megan had never made any pretense at warmth the few times she had been in the office. So she was protecting Lindsay as Samantha had been protecting her mother. Maybe it was time they made amends.

"Megan, I'm so glad to see you." Great. She sounded like an uptight spinster out of a wooden PBS period piece.

Megan merely smiled. Weakly.

Jared felt the discomfort. "Drinks, anyone?"

◆ ◆ ◆

"OK. So it's the dinner party from hell." Snag nuzzled Jared's neck in the kitchen as Jared pulled fresh-baked bread from the oven. "Let's eat fast and get rid of all of them. You know what it does to me to see you in an apron."

"So . . . who actually likes one another in there?" Jared responded.

"Well, I'm not altogether sure, but I can tell you Meg hasn't spilled the beans to Ryan yet. She, of course, isn't exactly in love with Samantha, and Samantha's beau is either the most handsome boring person on the planet, or would simply rather be anywhere but here, and I couldn't be positive but Samantha doesn't seem overly thrilled with her surprise weekend guest." Snag stopped to consider. "But other than that . . . I think everyone's destined to be soulmates."

"You're supposed to be making drinks." Jared reminded him.

"Make them doubles."

◆ ◆ ◆

". . . and there really is nothing as exquisite as French cinema," Snag announced as he helped himself to the last of a raspberry zabaglione.

"Please God, don't get him started." Jared sniffed distastefully. "He'll go off on that pig Depardieu."

"What do you think, Sam?" Snag had eaten too much.

"I adore both French film and the pig." Samantha had drunk too much. She wanted to blur the lines between Robert and Megan, who sat next to one another. They actually knew a distant friend in common from early school days and chatted, eager to make connection in their misery, and Samantha had become their scapegoat.

"And there you have it! Coming from a woman of charm and good taste. And you, Robert?" Snag pronounced his name in French.

"I agree with Jared." Brusque.

"Yes, Snag, how many times do we all have to tell you we find him repulsive?" Megan snapped uncharactistically.

Snag and Samantha glanced from Megan to their partners to one another. Of course Robert agreed with Jared. They shared a moment of wistful resignation.

"Oh, you men." Snag tried to make light of the moment, but Samantha could tell Robert did not appreciate being lumped with Jared, or the implication. Snag turned to Samantha, effectively blocking the others out. "So . . . what are your favorites?"

"Anything with Isabelle Huppert—"

"Exactement!"

"*Jean de Florette* and *Manon of the Spring*."

"Oh, I love those films." Ryan directed his comment toward Megan, trying to soften the gentle hostility that had seeped from her the moment they entered the apartment.

"Oh my God, yes!" Snag swooned. "How can anyone find themselves sobbing over a water well, much less for four hours?" Snag sipped his espresso excitedly. He usually never got to talk about all this with anyone but Megan. And she knew nothing about French film. "Louis Malle's *Au Revoir, les Enfants*."

"Yes, but"—Samantha had given up trying to involve Robert—"what in the hell happened to *Damage?*"

"I'll tell you what happened to it—Jeremy Irons."

"No, no no. The book was divine. Obsession from a man's point of view—"

"As seen through a woman's eyes—"

"And then a male filmmaker's perspective of that female interpretation."

"Yes. Can we get any more convoluted?" Jared sallied.

"Oh, and what about the one, I can't remember the name, but the sort of horsey-faced actress with Depardieu—" Ryan made an effort.

"*The Woman Next Door.* Total obsession," Samantha supplied. Maybe she could weasel her way into Megan's affections through her boyfriend. The question remained: why was it so important that Megan like her? For Lindsay, of course, her tipsy brain clarified.

"Yes, I suppose that would have to take the prize for obsession." Ryan smiled back at Samantha.

"So . . . what would our main obsessions be?" Snag looked at each of them expectantly. "Ryan?"

"That's easy." He took Megan's hand and beamed at her.

"You two don't count. You're beyond all goonie-pie redemption. I suppose mine would have to be, besides you, of course, darling"—he winked at Jared—"living with as much joie de vivre as one can pack into any given moment."

"Yes. We know." Jared squeezed his hand.

"And you, my sweet?" Snag directed at Jared.

"Well, it would probably have to be stage props from musical numbers."

"That's a hobby, dearest. I think we often confuse hobbies with obsession. Obsession is maniacal desire, codependent frothing of the mouth, not the need to needlepoint!"

"Sort of like Lindsay is about her work," Megan stated.

"We can always hope she'll find something a bit more, shall we say 'well rounded' to become obsessed about," Snag said, smiling.

"No. I don't think so." Megan directed the conversation to them all, but for the first time in an hour made eye contact with Samantha. "Some people are happy with their work. And what they give to the world is their reward."

"You're sounding a little puritan, honey," Ryan pointed out.

"I'm just saying some people are better left alone. To do what they want with their gifts."

"Are you trying to say Lindsay's professional talents preclude personal happiness?" Samantha asked.

"Of course not. But Lindsay needs the right kind of person. Someone who will take care of her. Attend to *her* needs, not take, take, take." Megan stood. "Excuse me. I have to use the ladies' room."

Awkward silence.

"Robert, would you care for more espresso?" Jared broke the tension.

"No. Thanks." He put his napkin upon the table, cleared his throat. He was ready to leave.

"Yesssss????" Snag twirled to him. "What is your deep dark obsession, Robert?"

"I don't believe in obsession," Robert stated calmly.

"Oh." Snag leaned on his elbow and gazed at Robert with utter sincerity. "That's too bad."

◆ ◆ ◆

"So you've made some new friends." Robert was undressing with even more calculated movements than usual, taking great time and care in removing each article of clothing and folding it in its precise place. "I prefer Jerra."

"You don't even like Jerra."

"Exactly."

"Well, I adore Snag."

"And he clearly adores you."

"Oh, come on. Get serious."

"I know he's a fag."

"Gay. Gay, Robert. He's brilliant. Witty. And he's a hell of a great guy. Let's just leave it at that."

Robert continued to disrobe. Samantha put on a pair of grungy washed-out sweats, T-shirt, and started searching the bookshelves for something to read.

She sensed Robert behind her. His nakedness. His heat. It did not beckon her, although she hadn't had sex in weeks. Lips on her neck. She didn't move. He stopped.

"Sam."

She turned to face him. His magnificent body stood before her, his penis half-erect, his eyes dim with hunger.

"I'm . . . I'm not . . ."

"Yeah . . . that's pretty clear from your wardrobe."

"I wanted to get comfortable."

"Since when do you sleep in sweats?"

"I wasn't actually going to sleep yet. I'm—" Samantha didn't know what she was. "Wound up, I guess."

"I haven't seen you in four weeks." His voice had become soft, somewhere between hurt and husky. Samantha's heart went out to him. Whatever changes she was going through, whatever insanity from the bizarre situation with her mother, the Pavilion and working with Lindsay—they were about her, not him.

She put a hand to his cheek. "I'm sorry. I've just had so much on my mind. I wasn't expecting you."

"Well, you keep harping on spontaneity. I was trying to be fuckin' spontaneous. I know we're in trouble, Samantha. I know something's wrong."

"Come here." Guilt spasmed through her being as she was repulsed by his need. She caressed him gently in her arms. She felt his muscles tense, his breathing quicken, felt him hardening.

"Sam . . ." his voice ragged, pleading.

"Yes."

◆ ◆ ◆

Sunday morning. She had pulled an all-nighter. Bid for the latest high-rise. It was the largest project she had ever considered undertaking. She could feel the energy emanating from her body as she gradually emerged from her trance state. There was nothing—no high in the world—that matched taking a concept from visual imagery and making it physical reality.

Heart. Skipping. Palpitations. They kept tap dancing in her chest. She had to move from the alcove. She felt too hemmed in, a hermit in her cave.

She got up. *Dizzy.* She didn't dare approach the window. She walked back to the desk. *Concentrate. On the drawings. Won't feel it.* She had successfully kept the irregular rhythm in the background for hours. Lindsay removed the untouched Chinese take-out Megan had brought in before she had left, admonishing her to eat.

She sat at her table. Drawing, sketching, restructuring and revising, until she had gotten it just where she wanted it. But now it was done. An awful stillness crept into the office, circling the chair, filling the room until it was all around her, up the back of her spine until she had to move, trying to escape it. But where?

She walked to the window. Her heart caught against itself at the open expanse of the city. She stood, immobilized, spinning between vertigo and the desire to crash through the thick-paned glass.

All the words traveled through her head: "The more you have the more you need . . . you're only really alive when you have a new job . . . stop eating for days . . . gorge yourself on your projects . . ."

And Samantha. All the things she said that night. True. But what could feel more alive than the current that pummeled through her veins, like a pure cocaine, pervading her body and mind even with the warning bells clambering madly in her brain. *Block them out,* trembling in exhilaration, experiencing the rush, especially sweet when she had far more than she could handle. So she would never run out. Never.

Her heart beat faster now. Straining. A wave of disorientation engulfed her momentarily. She looked at her hand. *Is this my hand? Foreign. Frightens me.* Its dull fleshiness was cold to the touch. *Am I dead? Am I dying? I can't feel my skin . . . life flowing out of me. Sinking.* Terror consumed her.

She grabbed her keys, ran from the office. She couldn't take the elevator. She could not be confined. Inhaling like a distance runner. *Not enough oxygen. Keep breathing.* Was this the moment she would die?

Somehow she made it outside the building. She pressed her body against the granite, swallowing the air in great gulps. She tried to focus on breathing. *In. Out. In. Out. Deeper now. Yes.* Finally. Breathing normally. Her heart, although trepidant, calmed itself.

Unsteadily she crossed the street and walked to the park. It was barely light, an early Sunday morning. She was a character out of a postapocalyptic scene; surreal, alone—for what is reality if not the mirrored image of humanity—and felt she must be insane.

She sat on a park bench. The cool, crisp air braced her, revived her. She breathed it in gratefully. She buried her head in her hands. It wasn't as though she didn't know or have all the information. She understood all the head stuff. It was a cliché in a culture dedicated to progress and product. But it was more. It was about Samantha. *The truth. Say it. Say it to yourself.* But she wouldn't.

A movement. She tipped her head so she could just see through her fingers. An indigent, years on the streets, lay on the ground several yards from her, just regaining consciousness. She hadn't even noticed the figure before. Lindsay kept still. She didn't want him approaching for a cigarette or money. But as he stretched and went to the far side of a tree to relieve himself, Lindsay realized it was a woman.

She was ageless, pain-lined, her skin ravaged by the elements and abuse. She returned to her makeshift burrow: a torn carpet remnant and large tattered coat. She pulled a half-finished bottle of Thunderbird from a soggy paper bag and swilled a long gulp, then semi-crawled, making epileptic jerks as her body rejected the contents. Lindsay was caught in horrified fascination as the woman, her face mottled with blemishes, bruises and sores, lifted the bottle to her face in pure anticipation, easily downed the remaining purple-black liquid and belched loudly. The smile of a slow child crept grandly about her face, as she tipped her head to Lindsay in a comradely salute, then sank slowly back into her oblivion.

"Hi. I'm Sondra and I'm an alcoholic."

"Hi, Sondra." She heard the uni-voice.

"When I first came here . . . I didn't think I belonged here. I suppose most of us don't. I guess I've had a problem for a long time. . . ." As she spoke, she looked at the bars on the windows. They were always the first thing she saw when they sat in this room. And that was a problem. Bars didn't work for her.

While she continued to talk, in the back of her mind she carried on another dialogue about how the bars infuriated her. They had from the moment she had arrived. They weren't prisoners here. So why the bars? This was supposed to be about adult choices. They kept harping about it in the damn group meetings. "Choices. The choice to drink and die . . . or the choice to live." Concurrent discussions had become natural for her, one real, one imagined. Like the one she had in her head with Samantha, explaining the "click"—that moment, that fraction of a second, unrecordable time when she would fall off the wagon, where her mind sped forward to the moment she would take that first sip in weeks or months, and her body simply followed as if on command.

And then there was the real conversation she would have with Samantha on the phone, where she told her she wasn't ready for her to visit.

"I'm sharing tonight because I think it's important to get to this place . . . acceptance . . ." Damn right she was sharing. She had learned after the first week, not sharing meant that you weren't getting well. And she didn't care what the hell their prognosis was about getting well. She wasn't drinking and that was the only thing that mattered. So she shared. Kept to her basic history, but every so often, out of sheer boredom and a competitive edge she thought she had long ago buried, she'd make up something really harrowing so the group could "ooooh" and "awwww" over the horror of it all.

Well, they were so melodramatic about the whole thing they deserved it. Besides, they fed off it. They were as addicted to the drama as they were to the drink. She hated the trauma. The tears. Family day where spouses dribbled all over each other in agony. She had lied about family day to Samantha for as long as she could get away with it, and then, finally, told her she simply needed to do this alone. Her counselors wouldn't force the issue, and her case worker actually thought it might be in her best interest, since she had always run to Samantha, unable to sort messes out on her own.

Only three and a half weeks more. Then she would get her walking papers, and she would have three and a half months of sobriety under her belt. She had to admit, she was proud of it. Whatever the hell it all meant, the hospital, the Big Book, all of Bill W.'s lingo that was recited with the mantra of holy tongues, whatever it was, it worked. So here she was, sober. And now she wanted the hell out.

◆ ◆ ◆

Lindsay had tried to go back to the office. But at the last moment, the tremors began again. After the attack she had gone home and slept for several hours. Woke. Reheated dead pasta from dinner several nights earlier with Samantha. She had wanted to call her. Needed to talk to her. But she couldn't begin to formulate what she would tell her. Or how. And had then fallen into another deep slumber. Comatose.

Sunday morning. A lost weekend. She felt as if she had lost a great span of time. And she had. To dreams. Her line dream. Variations on it and other macabre images that teased her waking mind as she stumbled about in a gray path, memory tenuous from oversleep.

She wanted to be pragmatic about her attack. She wanted her body not to betray her. But it was.

Her life was breaking down, and she didn't know how to put it back together again. She had no desire to analyze it. She just knew that it was. Wait it out. Like she always did. This thing—stress, anxiety, terror—was not going to win. She was.

But what about the other? The other thing that wouldn't go away. Wouldn't leave her mind even as she made her way back to the office, as if, now that her body was spent of its attacks, her mind had settled on the obsession of telling Samantha.

For three hours she wandered between working and pretending to work, her mind floating between the papers at her desk and the fact that she had to tell her. She had to. It didn't matter what Sondra wanted anymore. She should have told her sooner, but it would have caused too much damage. And still might. And that's where her mind stayed, in a track of timing. She obsessed over the what-ifs?, questions and projections over which she had no control but pretended she did as the groove wore deeper and deeper. No matter what she did to refocus her concentration, she couldn't retain it. It was one thing to control her body, but quite another if she couldn't exercise a sense of will over her mind. She continued to stare at the unfinished work before her.

◆ ◆ ◆

Samantha stared at the red roses. Blood-red, marble-carved petals. It was close to the most perfect image she had ever seen. Robert had brought her a half dozen with baby's breath. Her favorite. He was trying. So hard.

She bent to take in their cloying fragrance. What were they doing here? Pretending at romance. Make-believe passion. Illusions drunk like honeyed tea, the pleading message behind the hungry eyes. Soothe me. Make it better. Make it go away.

They had been in this thing for so long now. Of course they were going to hit lows. It was natural for the supply and demand of any relationship to dip the scales. You gave and you got. You tallied up the equation at the end of each day, week, month and year, and if the bottom line was not a deficit, you counted yourself happy. There were a lot of positives about her relationship with Robert. She knew there were. She was just being a nudge.

Before, after Arianna had left, Samantha had made a solemn oath. Grand sweeping passion was over for her. Heathcliff and Catherine on the moors were wonderful to watch, but she never again wanted to find herself on the windswept trail, heather filling her senses with toxic illusions that only led to the dark abyss of chaos and pain.

So Samantha had remained with Robert, secure in the conviction that the extreme passion she had felt with Arianna was an isolated event, could only have happened with her, and her alone. It set her free from the haunting of the wild red-headed ghost. But as the years had trickled by, Samantha had come to realize that Arianna had been a gift, a catalyst for what she could feel inside. The secret was not to fear it, but to find someone with whom to share it.

It wasn't just about losing control. It went far deeper. It was about being met. David, Pierre, even Robert all had one thing in common: they followed. If someone else was leading, she would have to find in herself something to offer up that matched the pace. Did she still possess it? Maybe it was easier—maybe? hell, she knew it was eas-ier—to live in gentle harmony, content with companionship and comfort, than to risk exposure of the soul.

Samantha stared out to the vague line of movement, the ocean's pulse beating steadily. It was raining, heavy to the north, drizzling to the south, and almost directly in the middle was a Godspot—a brilliant ray of sun, shining through the clouds, its reflection shimmering an oval over the water. Robert was out there somewhere. He had gone for a walk and was probably getting drenched. They had fought. It had been over the dream. She had brought it up to him because she hoped it would lay the groundwork for the discussion they were going to have to have. Sooner or later.

In her dream, inside a vaporous netherworld, she had been designing a house, a bizarre and creepy setting with empty rooms on one side and on the other, cluttered, dusty and confusing, something out of Miss Havisham's attic. Suddenly, a baby appeared from nowhere. She picked it up and placed it in her palm. It wore its afterbirth like a shield, but its features were fully defined and Samantha was not so much in shock as she was in awe when the baby uttered, with perfect articulation, "Actually if you examine the depths of possibility you could make this place quite wonderful."

Samantha had put the baby down, although it had already indicated to her it couldn't walk. But walk it did. Wobbly and uncertain, shaking with pride as it uncurled from its fetal bearing to a full upright position. Samantha was amazed with its accomplishment.

Suddenly they were outside, and the baby was on the beach. Her mother appeared from nowhere and she realized the baby was lost. Robert came up from behind her and told her he wanted to show her the film they were shooting down the way . . . they had all this dynamite for these explosions they had rigged. She numbly followed. Where was the baby? But he was calm and methodical and kept saying, "Don't worry, I'll take care of it." And then she saw the barrage of light against the sky, terrifying, bright red-orange ballasts of combustion filling the landscape. She stood in wonder and fear at the majesty of it all and then glanced at Robert and saw the reflection of the thunderous detonations on his face. But not in his eyes. There she saw no reflection.

Now, remembering the dream, she shivered. Putting on a sweater, she wandered up to the attic. She had decided to hunt for the old Earlsheart carving she had described to Lindsay.

Lindsay. Samantha didn't want to think about her, either. If she did, she might end up near a dark cave she felt compelled to venture into.

The attic smelled faintly like the house before the remodel: old and beach-musty. She stood for a moment breathing it in, then navigated through dilapidated boxes, dodging the corner of the old rolled-up carpet, hunting doggedly. She was certain her mother would have kept the carving. She continued to rummage about, throwing boxes this way and that, and finally spied the tip of the sign, far in the corner.

She went to retrieve it when she saw, in her mother's handwriting, "Remodel—Earlsheart." She stopped. Intuition met suspicion as she opened the box. A spasm rippled through her stomach. Why the suspense, she wondered. She flipped over the edges of the carton and found scattered papers, change orders that had never been found, receipts, ledgers, scribbled notes. Her mother's life, in short, in constant disarray. Then a photo. Her mother and Lindsay.

Lindsay's smile, full, fun. Samantha recognized the glow in the eyes. From the moment she had first seen Lindsay at her mother's house, bottle in hand, she had been drawn to the intense light from those eyes, the electric tension piercing her. Samantha swallowed. OK. Was she going to admit it to herself, in the dark safety of this attic . . . and leave the information where it belonged? That the anger she had held on to, the delicious anger she could bite into whenever she had been around Lindsay, had merely been a ruse for the real feelings that were floating to the surface? That this woman, whom she had held as an enemy, had raked the dormant feelings buried so long now . . . this woman had opened Samantha up again, evoking a giddy, dizzying awareness she hadn't known since Arianna.

Her hands trembled as she stared at the photo, as if by gazing into the polarized eyes before her she could will a communication to Lindsay. She laughed at herself and continued to sort through the papers, trying to come to terms with the feelings flooding through her as she found the original proposal Lindsay had drawn up. She skimmed through it. She saw the correspondence, dates. Everything legitimate and valid.

There was nothing in here. She began to close the box, and then saw the corner of her mother's personal stationery in the bottom of the box. She pulled it out. It was sealed, with Lindsay's name scrawled across it. She hesitated a moment, her heart pounding wildly. Then she opened it.

It was clear her mother had been drinking when she wrote this, merely by its illegibility. She held it apart from her, contemplated trespassing her mother's privacy for an agonizing moment, then began reading:

Lindsay,

What happened between us will never happen again. I will make sure of it, if only by replacing you on this project. I am more than happy to pay for your services but can never see you again.

The script was more difficult to read after that . . .

I only let it happen because I was swept up into a sick need . . . I don't agree with what you are and could never be fully involved in such a life.

The next paragraph was splotched and stained as if her mother had been crying.

But I need you. I need you, don't you see? Why oh why did I think I could write this to you and send you away. Am I sick because I want you? Am I twisted . . . ugly . . . a deviant because I want you to never stop making love to me? I need you Lindsay . . . need

The words trailed off.

Samantha could not breathe. Her hand was clenched so tightly about the letter she felt the pricks of numbing anger. She put the letter into the light again, reread it. The breath she let out was long and deliberate. She had never known such pure and primal rage. She sat for an hour without moving.

Finally Samantha made her way back down from the attic, slowly, moving into the kitchen with delicate precision, as if by making the wrong turn something would crash to the floor. Suddenly she wanted Robert to return. She didn't know why. Everything seemed so outside of her, but she needed him to take this away.

She knew what he would say in his dry, clinical and calming terms: that her mother was sick and her disease had made sick choices for her. And he would continue until his voice became a lull and she would nod mutely as he further detailed the extent of her impaired judgment under the influence of alcohol.

But none of that really mattered, because her mother was not on trial here. Lindsay was. How could she? How dare she do this to her mother? To them . . . their friendship? When she had so many opportunities to tell her . . . but of course she wouldn't tell her she had taken advantage of such a pathetic situation, that under the smooth facade of integrity lay the instincts of a predator. Friendship. The word made her sick. She would have her investigated. She would go to the Architectural Review Board. She would threaten the one thing that held any meaning for Lindsay: her work.

Revenge lay on her tongue in a quiet and powerful way. Yes, to take away Lindsay's work . . . to banish her in her chosen field, to smear her reputation would be to cut her supply, extinguish her light. She allowed the taste of it to fill her up, but the flavor turned sour, the bloated anger rising to her throat.

A half hour later Robert walked through the door. She listened to his footsteps. He wandered through the hallway and then upstairs, heading toward the bedroom. He was probably looking for her. Samantha followed him.

When she entered the room he was changing his shirt. He turned, taken by surprise.

"Oh . . . I thought you were downstairs."

"I was." Propelled forward by a fury she could not release she walked directly to him, touched his chest.

"I want you." But there was no desire attached to the words. "Now."

"Saman—"

"Don't talk. Just make love to me."

Robert hesitated briefly, then allowed her to remove his shirt. He bent to kiss her in his predictable manner, sensitive in his approach, gentle, unhurried. Samantha pushed him onto the bed and kissed him back savagely, thrusting her tongue into his mouth. Robert was taken aback by her aggression, moving her gently to the side, trying to accommodate her in a less savage way.

"Don't be gentle. Jesus, Robert! . . . just fuck me. Now." Samantha yanked the drawstring of his sweats, her movements frenetic.

"What the hell is going on, Sam?"

"Will you please just not talk. Later. Just please . . . do this for me." She found his penis, stroked it roughly, hurriedly, frustrated with his softness. She knew he hated to rush lovemaking, knew also her need had nothing to do with making love as she tumbled forward with careless disregard.

He grew hard. She guided him into her, dry, unyielding. As he thrust into her, she winced in pain.

"You're not ready—"

"Robert—" Exasperation now as her body begged him into her. He tried to slow down the pace but she urged him forward. He knew she wasn't enjoying it, but she pressed him, faster, harder, the larger he became inside her the more she leaned into it, while at the same time she was clearly in agony. When he came she pushed him from her, choking on racking sobs, crying, full, hard.

Robert tried to hold her, but she wouldn't let him touch her. After all the tears were shed, she lay numb and lifeless, Lindsay's dark eyes taunting her . . . forever. She fell asleep curled into a tight circle at the edge of the bed.

indsay walked through the darkened alley behind the stage looking for Samantha. She had been through the front and back end of the Pavilion and couldn't find her anywhere. As she turned, she heard a sound from a utility room. She walked toward it and saw Samantha cleaning paintbrushes.

"There you are." But Samantha did not acknowledge her presence, instead continued working turpentine through the bristles.

"Sam?"

"When were you planning on telling me, Lindsay . . ." Controlled and low, voice laced with anger. Like before.

"What?" Lindsay moved forward but stopped when she saw Samantha's eyes, narrowed, dark and injured. She knew.

". . . You were lovers." The statement sounded like a death sentence. Lindsay tried to breathe as Samantha stood, hair scraped back so tightly it pulled at the corners of her eyes. Lips compressed, everything about her pinched. Closed off.

"I never understood why you were so emphatic about not talking about my mother. You must have thought I was such a fool." Samantha brushed beyond her. Lindsay felt the faintest sense of relief. She no longer had to lie.

"I . . . Samantha, for what it's worth . . . I was going to tell you. Actually, I realized this weekend I needed—"

"Who the hell do you think you are?" Samantha turned at her now. "What were you doing to her?"

"Saman—"

"Why? Why didn't you tell me?"

"Sam. Please." Lindsay tried to remain calm as Samantha's fury fed itself. "There's a lot to this you don't understand. It was—"

"What? You knew my mother was strapped for money—was that the hold you had on her, Lindsay? Couldn't get it anywhere else? Because you're so wrapped up in your little world—your little world that's only about you and your work and the hell with everyone else!"

"Samantha—"

"Don't. Don't talk. Please."

Samantha walked past her again, finished wrapping her brushes in cellophane, then stood, shook her head, frustrated, defeated. "And my mother, so low and pathetic. So easy. Is that what it is, Lindsay? Easy so you don't have to think, be there, just do it?"

"If you'll just let me tell you—"

Samantha stopped. Swallowed. Cleared the tears that were threatening her strength. "OK. Tell me, Lindsay. Tell me something that's going to make sense."

"Samantha. Your mother . . . I didn't know she was sick. I certainly had no idea she was broke. It's like you said before. She made her own decisions. All along. The beach house, her moving there—all the changes she couldn't afford. And me. They were all *her* decisions."

"And you had nothing whatsoever to do with it? I find that hard to believe."

"What I'm saying is the decision to be with me was hers as well as the decision not to tell you—"

"How can you expect me to believe that, when she was so drunk most of the time she didn't know what the hell was going on?"

"That's not how things started between us. She wasn't drinking." Lindsay's voice was low. "Not at first."

"Maybe not. But that's what got her there." Samantha took the letter from her back pocket and threw it on the supplies table. "It doesn't take a lot of reading between the lines to see she hated it."

Lindsay slowly opened the drunken missive, glanced at it, but did not read. She looked at Samantha.

"She was drunk when she wrote this."

"Obviously your favorite position."

Lindsay flinched.

"I . . . I didn't know." Lindsay's voice was broken.

Samantha stood before her. What could they say? The anger drained, her eyes bewildered and weary. "What have you done to us?"

◆ ◆ ◆

It changed after that. Everything. The drudgery of the previous two months returned for both of them. They distanced themselves from one another as much as possible, communicating only when necessary. And when they were forced to speak they could barely discuss the business at hand, never mind any attempts to resolve the chasm that continued to grow deeper, darker, more impenetrable.

Samantha worked with resolve. She stopped taking her breaks, as if she could will away the hours by simply shoving as much activity into them as possible. For Lindsay, overwork was the natural course of action, but when she saw it in Samantha, it was as if she were seeing the fine details of her life reflected in a mirror before her. Every nuance of avoidance, every objection to rest, the wear of exhaustion, the gasp for renewed energy—they were all there.

Lindsay was torn. She knew trying to explain the situation to Samantha would only further their impasse. And it was difficult for her to accept her lack of awareness, the tunnel vision of her own little world that had brought them to this place. All the strides they had made, all the hurdles they had overcome, obstacles that would have made bitter enemies of most people. Gone. All they shared now was the estranged void that connected them and the inability to escape one another.

At the Pavilion they were coldly professional. On the phone, terse conversations. Where was the plumber? What happened to the paint supply? Lindsay deferred most of the calls to Snag and employed him as emissary as often as possible.

The project was scheduled for completion the twenty-third of December; only a few days to go. Both women were of a single vision: finish this job and resume their separate lives, never to touch again.

"Hmmm, don't you look absolutely dreadful," Snag remarked when he dropped by with the paint Samantha needed to finish the trim. Samantha's energy had been flagging for the past couple of weeks. She looked pale and drawn; dark circles contoured her eyes.

"So I've heard." Samantha forced a grin.

"I'm taking you to lunch."

"No. I just want to get this damn thing done."

"Yeah . . . well, you're going." Snag reached over, removed the fine paintbrush from her hand, thrust it into her water pail, took her hand and led her from the Pavilion.

They sat across from each other. Samantha rubbed her forehead, twisted and cracked her neck.

"Ohhhh, that sounds lovely."

Samantha played with her coffee cup. "I should probably see a chiropractor."

"Yes. I think that's in order." Snag flagged a waitress, ordered food for both of them. "Look, Samantha, I don't know you that well, but I'm no fool, and I'm thinking major shit has hit the fan, and I can guess what it was, and I know none of this is any of my business, but here goes anyway. I like you, and I love Lindsay, and I just think you should know, Lindsay . . . well, Lindsay's a strange one." Samantha glanced at Snag. "She's kind of obtuse, you know? Doesn't see a lot in front of her nose . . . friggin' out to lunch sometimes . . . but there's one thing about Lindsay you have got to remember. She's real. She's honest and she is, beyond a shadow of a doubt, the most decent person I have ever known."

"You're right, Snag." Samantha pushed her coffee away, stood up, "It's none of your business."

She walked from the café back to work, retrieved her paintbrush and picked up as if she had never gone. She focused on the task at hand, but she could not rid herself of the images that betrayed her, a constant battalion of memories, so many of them, all Lindsay; striking, bold, passionate, tearing feelings from her she had never before experienced. Even with this ugly pain, she somehow wanted to remain accessible to Lindsay.

No. She wouldn't show it. She would not allow a trace of her need to be seen. But she knew the feelings were there, in direct conflict with her anger, and she battled with it every hour. She wanted Lindsay to have a knowingness of her. She wanted to continue what had begun between them. She wanted to show Lindsay her strength, her independence, the passion that Lindsay evoked in her, wildly irrepressible. But then the anger flooded over these images in a black wave of despair and she simply could not fathom which was stronger: the passion guided by her anger, or that provoked by her desire.

◆ ◆ ◆

"Where have you been?"

"I stopped by the river."

"I've been waiting here for twenty-five minutes."

"I'm sorry. At that moment, looking at the river took precedence."

"You know Nathan doesn't like to be kept—"

"Since when do you give a shit about what Nathan likes?"

They both stopped. Sullen. This was ridiculous.

"Samantha. We have to talk."

"There's nothing to talk about."

"Yes. There is."

"As far as I'm concerned, after tomorrow I will never have to talk to you again. Can we get this damn meeting over with?"

"Look—"

"No. Let's just go."

They turned to the door simultaneously, their shoulders touching. They stopped. Lindsay caught Samantha's eyes, flat and cold.

"I'm sorry."

"That doesn't change it."

"I didn't put your mother where she is today, and you know it."

"I only know that you . . . you used her and you lied to me."

"I was honoring your mother's privacy."

"Your loyalty is touching."

Lindsay's shoulders slumped in resignation. Samantha wasn't going to budge.

"Can we go now?"

ecember 23 fell on a Thursday. Snow misted about, inspiring holiday cheer, excitement and anticipation. Samantha walked from her car to the crowd gathering at the Darlington Arts Pavilion. Banners were flying. Huge and elaborately lettered signs heralding The Family Darlington's Premiere Event: *The Nutcracker Suite* spiraled about the exterior in colorful ostentation.

Samantha stopped before entering. Studied the building as an impartial observer might. Yes. It was good. It had elegance and style. They had achieved the impossible. She allowed the spirit of pride to slowly take over the wild emotions that bound her like a strapped corset, so tight about her middle that she had felt breathless from the moment she woke that morning. As she walked up the stairs and to the entrance, she paused at the placard bearing both her name and Lindsay's, graceful fonts with their titles side by side.

Samantha faltered. Through the milling crowds she saw Lindsay, immaculately dressed in sheer black pants and tunic. She knew she would be here, but was not prepared for the sight of her. She exhaled carefully. Even weary and exhausted, Lindsay was riveting. Undaunted by the fanfare, she was playing the good architect, answering questions professionally while standing next to Nathan and several of the upper-crust board members of the Arts Pavilion.

Lindsay turned her head slowly. She knew Samantha had come into the room, could feel her; and then sensed her eyes upon her. Samantha was wearing a cream knit dress, impeccably tailored, outlining the long slender lines of her body. Lindsay felt her throat tighten. They appraised each other for a long moment, then Samantha severed the contact.

Nathan, regally adorned in a silver-gray suit, spouted accolades about his "girls," pulling them tightly beneath his wings, praising their efforts and his own ingenuity. He never missed on a sure thing. Paparazzi and champagne, the cutting of the burgundy ribbon, a toast, people crowding in, congratulations, beefy handshakes, the two women thrown together, commandeered this way and that . . . the prizes of the party. Bombarded and maneuvered until Samantha felt a headiness she could no longer endure. She had to get out.

When her name was announced and she was called to the podium to accept her tribute, a perplexed Nathan and confused audience waited. She did not appear. She was nowhere to be found.

Lindsay put down her drink, swallowed with difficulty and tried to hold back the tears.

◆ ◆ ◆

Cold wind. So cold her face was alarmingly numb. She was crying. Samantha's tears froze on her cheeks. She couldn't remember how she had escaped through the endless throng of people, but now she walked the streets of the city, covering miles. Miles of heartache, wind whipping her legs, particles swept up from the stormy gales cutting into her face. Raw. Everything outside and in was raw.

She finally made her way back to the hotel, exhausted. But not exhausted enough. All she wanted was to fall into slumber, to drive away any conscious thought of the previous hours, days, weeks and months.

She lit the fire that had been laid in the grate of the hotel fireplace. Arlene, her friend with the apartment, had returned for the weekend, chattered hospitably—endlessly—offered Samantha the couch; she was more than welcome to stay, they could catch up. Samantha declined. She couldn't be with anyone. Not now. And she wouldn't go to her mother's apartment.

She moved a large overstuffed chair to the fireplace, slipped out of her dress, removed her shoes and sank into the chair, her satin slip cozy, luxurious; her body finally warming. She stared into the fire. A vision of them flashed through her head. She could blot out her mother, but not Lindsay. She could not erase the images of Lindsay from her mind: Lindsay at work behind her desk, Lindsay at the Pavilion, below her on the ladder, at dinner, across from her drinking her cappuccino, Lindsay's hands, the hands of an artist . . . builder, creator. Such familiar hands. She wondered then: What had her mother thought of those hands? What had her mother felt as they caressed her as a lover?

The intensity. The turbulence. How had her mother reconciled that? By drinking? Could she feel it even through her anesthesia? Could she see the shine in Lindsay's agate eyes, the dark hair her hands recklessly swept through, the carriage of her body as she was that afternoon, graceful, classical, utterly entrancing? Samantha removed all the barriers to what her mother might feel, her sexuality dormant so long, her excursions with Carl meaningless. How her mother must have ached lying beneath that dark wildness, staring into Lindsay's eyes full of want and longing. And as she fell into the first trance of sleep, it was no longer her mother whom she saw with Lindsay. It was herself.

She had dozed off. It took her a moment to get her bearings. A thick depression smothered her. The irony of celebration for a project that had cost her so much emotional turmoil and sacrifice. She knew everything was compounded by the completion of the project, the giving up of her baby. It was over. All of it.

She was startled by a knock at the door. She froze. No one even knew she was at this hotel. Maybe it was Arlene. She snapped on the table lamp, checked her watch. It was near eleven. Dark. She decided to sit very still, try to ignore it, but the knock came again. She got up, walked to the door.

"Yes?"

"It's me."

Samantha didn't want to, but she opened the door, leaning around it to shield her slip-clad body. Lindsay stood there, envelope in hand. When their eyes met they simply looked at one another, then away.

"May I?" Her voice was hostile.

Samantha was certain she was not going to let her in, but did.

Lindsay entered, still decked in her finery. Samantha closed the door. Lindsay walked to the window, hesitated as she looked out at the city. Her office was several buildings east. She stared at the cubicles of light, and it struck her how empty and foreign they appeared, and how often the single light at her drafting table had cast a speck of existence into the night. She turned around.

Samantha moved to the bed, pulled a fleecy hotel robe about her. Their eyes caught again. Averted.

"Why did you leave?"

"Why not? Pomp and circumstance hold little appeal for me." Samantha tightened the sash of the robe. "It was over. So I left."

"You could have at least stayed to get your bonus."

"Why? I know where to find you." Dry. Acerbic.

"Here it is. Cash." Lindsay unceremoniously dumped the envelope on the bed. "Well . . ." Lindsay glanced up at her.

"Well."

Lindsay turned back to the window. Sighed. So much inside her needed to get out, but no words were going to be spoken. She had hoped, now that it was over, that Samantha would at least hear what she had to say. She glanced at the carpet, decided she was wasting her time. She began to move toward the door, but as she was about to pass, Samantha moved from the bed.

"Wait."

They stood motionless, unwavering, the line of tension drawn between them. Samantha walked very slowly, her eyes now lasered into Lindsay's. Hate, passion, desire—all the feelings that had crowded inside her for as long as she'd known this woman. Now at her side, shaking her head, softly. What was she doing? And watching her hand as it just barely brushed Lindsay's, trailed the length of her arm to the side of her neck, and drew Lindsay close until Lindsay could feel her sweet breath.

"I want to hate you."

And then her hand grasping the back of Lindsay's neck, drawing her mouth to her own, kissing her savagely. The silk of Lindsay's mouth, her lips full and soft, urgent and caressing, tongue swiftly brushing her upper lip as they parted.

Eyes, liquid, clear and full of need. Lindsay gazed into them, desire blocked by confusion, but Samantha quelled any hesitancy, never once losing contact. She caressed the nape of Lindsay's neck and again drew her close.

She kissed her now, with intent, lips pressing lips, tongues exploring, wet and sweetly devouring, gentle then firm, insistent, greedy, falling inside the kiss like a deep well. Coming up for air. This was what it had been all along. This rage was want. Dizzying, heady, exquisite desire every time this woman entered the room, the searing agony of her body, unclaimed, until this woman's presence owned her. This was, simply, what she had been waiting for: passion.

Lindsay tore at the sash of the hotel robe, Samantha tremblingly unbuttoned Lindsay's shirt, tunic discarded, shirt untucked, robe dropped to ankles. Lindsay's nails grazing the upper side of her arms as she wrapped the sash through Samantha's wrists, chills pulsing through parts of her body she didn't know existed, leading her to the bed, her captor, sweeping them both upon it, Samantha's arms gently bonded above her, captive. Lindsay's body lay the length of her own, hands locked to Samantha's. She bent, lips grazing Samantha's, tender bite at her chin, to her neck, eagerly devouring the length of the dip at her throat, owning her, tongue at the edge of her slip, wet, grazing the nipple through the satin, circling the shiny fabric until Samantha gasped, freed herself and brought Lindsay's face to hers.

She needed her skin. Tore at Lindsay's shirt, fumbled with her bra, until Lindsay sat above her, breasts freed, so beautiful, this woman so incredibly beautiful before her. Her hands aching to touch, palms and fingertips alive to the fluid skin, traveling to Lindsay's sides as she shivered, gently cupping her breasts, then sweeping behind Lindsay's back to draw her close.

Lindsay resisted. She pushed Samantha back, her fingers now at Samantha's thighs, circling, teasing, as she lifted the slip and slowly, painfully slowly, drew it up the length of her form, over her head, removing her own pants, shoes thrown off, fingers delicately tracing the boundaries of the lace panties, tugging them down, unclasping her bra. Their bodies now shimmered with naked longing.

Samantha's moan was low and primal as Lindsay laid her body fully upon her own, Lindsay's skin melting into every fiber of her being, their bodies moving into a rhythm beyond their control, roughly caressing, driven, heedless of sensation, overexposed, their minds racing to catch up.

Samantha's nails raked Lindsay's arched back, gliding to hardened thighs, buttocks, the pressing need to have Lindsay's body closer, pushing the swelling mons into her own. Samantha had never been captured by the insanity of desire as she was this moment. Not even with Arianna.

"Ohhh, God, go inside me." At this moment she could die for want, the intense hunger for Lindsay rocking her foundation of control. But she had given up control, knew that in the dizzying blackness of her mind.

Her legs curled about Lindsay's, felt the sharp jab of pleasure as Lindsay's fingers lightly pinched her hardened nipples, guiding Lindsay's mouth to the tautly exposed flesh, the pleasure achingly sweet as Lindsay nibbled gently, provoking the tips with tender bites, Lindsay running the edge of her teeth in a circular motion, until the stab of desire increased with each pass, over and over, the pleasure ever tighter, until she could not tell whether it was Lindsay's mouth or the rhythmic motion grinding into her body, bringing her to orgasm. She came, hard, so hard it hurt, and then felt the pressure of Lindsay's thigh press into her, came again, quickly, more intensely as Lindsay's mouth bent to kiss her own.

Samantha threw Lindsay to her side, kissing her ardently, fervent drive to explore this gift back to herself, gratitude for this release, tears on her face, fire in her soul, kissing Lindsay's eyes, her forehead, nibbling on her brows, circling her ears and devouring the sensual arc of her neck. She labored artfully at the muscles, sending exquisite chills through Lindsay's body. Lindsay felt the wet lips suckle her breasts, a starving babe, her arched body aching for more as Samantha's tongue met a desire that had no name, begging for release as she traveled languorously, now teasing, taunting the contours of muscled flesh, along the curves and angles of Lindsay's flattened stomach, pelvis, shaking her hair over the wanting skin, brushing it lightly over Lindsay's clitoris, the fineness sending slivers of arousal through every part of her body.

And then Samantha's tongue. On her. In her. Gentle strokes, lengthening strokes of her tongue, hardened peak a breath away, but the tongue kept urging her to a new plateau, until Lindsay did not know where her body would take her, the tongue dissolving into the pulsating folds, provoking, alluring Lindsay into a spiral of ecstasy until she screamed in orgasm as Samantha's fingers thrust inside her. She came and felt herself around Samantha's fingers, as if their skin had melded, then drew Samantha up to her, needing the swell of her stomach, the soft clinging pressure, as she lay wrapped in Samantha's flesh and hair.

And then Samantha made her way to Lindsay's eyes. But Lindsay could not look into them yet, pulled her close. Samantha wrapped her legs through Lindsay's, her arms clasping the heated skin to her. There they remained until the chill of the outside cold prickled their skin. Samantha disengaged halfheartedly.

"Maybe we should get under the covers." And then they allowed their eyes to bear witness to each other, the windows of the soul exposed before them both, raw, unedited. Anger gone. Passion-inspired lids at half-mast, love entering the space between them.

Samantha pushed Lindsay back against the pillows, moved on top of her, kissing her, their lips opened to one another, tongues playing lightly, then probing with rekindled urgency. Lindsay gruffly turning Samantha over, straddling the long slender body, her wetness meeting the mount of Samantha's hips, bending, the tip of her tongue dancing almost imperceptibly along the crevasse of Samantha's spine, following the ridge to the swirl of hair dressing the nape of her neck. She smoothed the curls and grazed the tingly hairs, sending electric quivers through Samantha's body. Lindsay led her tongue back down the length of Samantha's back, kissing the moundy flesh, kneading her buttocks, Samantha moaning lightly, a catch in her breath as Lindsay's fingers caressed her, gently rubbing the swelling vortex, seducing her ever nearer, only to hold back until Samantha wondered, vaguely, about the limitlessness of pleasure, and then the fingers at her anus, probing gently until Samantha was racked with orgasm so immediate and resonant her body cried out, tormented at its own pleasure, until she wept, fully, freely, completely.

"You own me," she whispered in Lindsay's ear, Lindsay still inside her.

Lindsay grasped Samantha to her. Owning her. Possessing her in a way she had never understood before this. They were in a brave new world that had no words, only raw feelings and rebirthed sexuality. They lay lovingly in one another's arms until Samantha's tears had dried, their breathing synchronized. They slept as one breath.

◆ ◆ ◆

She woke early. Excited. There wasn't much time for her to pack her things and get ready to board the train. She stretched, yawned with anxious excitement and realized her body felt good. Well, it should. She had worked out with the others every day. There was something to be said about natural endorphins.

She lit a cigarette. Yes. That was one habit she wouldn't give up. She couldn't have survived the last few months without them. But as they said, what's a little vice like the slow rotting of your lungs next to certain death? She supposed everything, besides time, brought you a little closer to the end. And she had wasted enough of that.

Not a waste, she reminded herself. If she hadn't gone through this ordeal, she wouldn't be where she was today. And that was sober. Clean and sober. What determined clean? She wasn't an addict and she didn't pop pills, and compared to most everyone in this place she was a saint. Saint Lush, they nicknamed her. Well, her life was more manageable than most and she was infused with a new ambition to get out into the world and make her life work. But most importantly, she intended to mend things with Samantha.

Samantha who tormented her dreams. Samantha, a child, crying, eyes swollen and lost, like those children Sally Struthers was always trying to get you to adopt on paper, their broken hearts on their sunken faces, imploring her to make it OK. Well, now she could finally do that. Would do it for Sam, and for herself. It had become her oath. Would become her deed. Her action. Instead of all the "talk" that spewed from these old-timers like beaded parables in Rosary reverence, so familiar, so trite that she simply smiled and turned the other ear.

But now she would not have to listen any longer. Her life would be her own. She was on her way home. She couldn't wait to see Sam.

◆ ◆ ◆

Samantha held Lindsay in her arms. Christmas Eve morning and not a creature stirring. Samantha admired the angle of Lindsay's face, the fine slant of her brow. Never had she felt so right in herself, holding this woman to her, the missing piece of her existence, the full cycle of her experience. She knew she couldn't have gotten here without all the other steps, and now finally it all made sense. This must be peace, she thought, the quiet stillness and certainty of truth.

Her mother's image jolted that serenity for a moment. Had she simply gotten all the steps mixed up? If one fell through the rotten planks early on, was there no hope for repair? But then the peace returned, an absolute absence of guilt over her mother. It no longer mattered that Lindsay and her mother had been lovers. Partners in misery? Linked by needs that had nothing to do with the connection she and Lindsay had just shared. It had become so clear.

After she had found out about the relationship, her attraction to Lindsay had become incestuous in her mind. But now she was as certain, as sure as she had ever been about anything, that she and Lindsay shared not simply the loving of two women, but the loving of two people, clearly destined for one another. She did not want to become sweepingly romantic about the whole thing or reach into a cosmic clutter of explanation. She felt a bit pragmatic, actually. Because now she understood what had been nagging at her for months. She was in love with Lindsay.

She blew lightly at the dark brows above closed eyes. They twitched and Lindsay's forehead furrowed. Samantha leaned over and soothed it with a kiss. Lindsay's eyes opened. She smiled. Samantha smiled back.

"God. I want you all over again."

"Again and again and again," Samantha purred in agreement. Their eyes held each other's for a brief moment, just long enough to see the commitment and affirmation that last night had not been a dream. Lindsay stroked Samantha's arm, down her side and to her leg. Samantha pushed Lindsay on her back.

"I have never wanted anything like I want you."

◆ ◆ ◆

"It's Christmas Eve."

"I know."

They lay in one another's arms, not quite sated, but exhausted, raw.

"What do you want to do about it?" Samantha asked.

"Ohhhh . . . I don't know. How 'bout get a tree—"

"—put really cheesy Newberry ornaments on it?"

"Yeah . . . and strings of popcorn, and really hokey Christmas carols . . . Bing Crosby—"

"—Julie Andrews' Firestone Album!"

"Hey, that's one of my favorites."

"Mine too," Samantha conceded. They laughed.

They couldn't stop. Laughed through the morning, finally getting dressed. Samantha jumped into the jeans she had thrown into her overnight bag.

"How did you know where I was?"

"I went to the apartment."

"But I told Arlene—"

"Yeah. I know. Let's just say I got resourceful."

"I bet you did." Samantha strolled up to her, still topless. She kissed her, long and deep, then stood back. "What do you say . . . we take a tree and stuff to the beach?"

Lindsay glanced around the hotel room. It certainly was no place to spend Christmas. "I think that's a great idea."

Samantha turned Lindsay's face to hers. "Will it be OK?"

"Yes."

"Thank you." Samantha lips curled in gratitude and then she kissed her tenderly on the eyebrow.

They found a tree at a deserted lot where an old-timer had stuck solidly by his remaining spruces and evergreens, certain there would be just one more couple, one last family picking up the tree that would make their Christmas complete. Samantha and Lindsay passed the nice full trees and zeroed in on a scraggly Charlie Brown Douglas fir. They would plant it on the north side of the house and give it a fresh start, after they were done decorating it, of course.

Tinsel, small blue balls, tacky ornaments of every size, shape and color, a fake popcorn string and slow alternating lights adorned the tree, until there was very little tree left to see. Johnny Mathis crooned "I'll Be Home for Christmas" in the background, while shadows blipped on naked bodies moving in an unhurried rhythm. Lying by the tree, covered in quilts, loving, gentle, finding a new path called intimacy, their eyes, holding one another, drawn to respect the power of their languid and lasting moments.

Later Samantha lay in the crook of Lindsay's arm, half covered by a quilt, the firelight dancing on their skin, the room still now, but for their shallow breathing and the wind whisking stormily outside.

"It's exquisite. Our lovemaking." Samantha's dreamy voice broke the silence.

"It's never been like this for me before," Lindsay whispered throatily.

"Nor me."

"You've been with women before."

"Yes. One." Samantha touched the top of Lindsay's hand with her own. "How did you know?"

"Intuition . . . the way you knew my body . . ."

"I would have known it anyway."

Their silence was gentle. Everything about them felt sweet and tender.

"You crept inside me the first moment I saw you, you know. With that damn bottle."

"That was the worst night of my life," Lindsay said.

"I can imagine."

"You know"—Lindsay shifted—"I didn't understand, Sam. I was so unaware. You were right about that. I tend to simply skim through every part of my life that isn't about work. And with Sond—your mother, I felt a protectiveness, acted on it, without thinking about the ramifications . . . on any level."

"I understand floating. Robert and I have been floating for years."

"What about him?"

"What do you mean?"

"I mean, what are you going to tell him?"

"That I've fallen off the edge of a high cliff and landed in the arms of a dashing pirate, and I have to follow my fate." Amused romanticism colored her tone, but then Samantha's voice turned soft and serious. "That he and I are over, that we've been over for a long time. That I've fallen irrevocably in love."

Lindsay's breath took a long time to release. She turned Samantha's face gently with her hand, gazed into her eyes, then embraced her, deeply, madly, lovingly.

"There's only one other thing then," Lindsay said quietly.

Samantha didn't respond for a long moment.

"Not yet." She knew what it was and she didn't want to talk about it. Not yet. Dreamland was too young to be spoiled. "Please."

"Samantha. I love you." Lindsay had never before said those words and meant them. They sounded so different. So powerful. So right.

"Jesus, I need you, Lindsay." Their lips met. The lights blinked. On. Then off again.

◆ ◆ ◆

Thighs. Arms. Warm hand resting gently on a flattened stomach, breathing lightly, leg thrown over leg, all swimming together. Makeshift bed of quilt, pillows, discarded blankets, their bodies became each other's through the night.

Her daughter's hair lay possessively about Lindsay's throat. Murder filled her heart as she let the presents in her hands crash to the floor.

Samantha jumped. Lindsay woke, startled. They both turned to see Sondra, fury and betrayal blazing from her.

"How dare you!" Clenched teeth, narrowed eyes, her target was Lindsay. "How dare you! Get out!" Hysteria mounting. *"Get out!"*

"Mom!" Samantha scrambled to her feet, drew a discarded shirt over her. "Mom . . . Oh, God, I don't believe this. . . ."

"She's done it to you!" Sondra screamed.

"Mom. Please. Try to calm down." Samantha rushed to her as Lindsay began assimilating the situation.

"No. Get her out of this house. *Now!*" Sondra's entire body trembled. "Get her out. She doesn't belong here."

Lindsay gathered her clothes. "It's OK. I'll go."

"No. We've got to talk this out," Samantha interjected.

"Sam . . ." Lindsay picked her clothes up. She indicated for her to attend to her mother while she left for the bathroom.

Samantha closed her eyes, turned to her mother, who seemed frozen in the same position.

"Mom." Sondra did not respond. Samantha drew her by the arm. "Mom. Come on. Let's go into the kitchen. I'll make some tea. We'll talk."

"Talk?" Sondra was enraged. "Talk? What's to talk about? She's done it to you. She did it to me, now she's done it to you. You think I'm sick? No. She's the one who's sick and she spreads her sickness wherever she goes. She's the disease. Not me."

"Stop it!" The glare in her mother's eyes frightened her.

"I've been working so hard. To get well. To come home. To you, Samantha. And *she's* here? What is she doing here? Samantha, what is happening?" Sondra began to cry.

Lindsay reentered the room, dressed. She stood hesitantly by the hall.

"Make her leave." Sondra was sobbing now. "Make her leave, make her leave."

"Mom, please." Samantha tried to hold her, infuse understanding through her by touch, but the sobs were getting bigger. "Please. We have to talk this through."

"I will not. I will not talk with her here."

"Samantha. I'm going to go," Lindsay offered. "You and your mother spend some time together. Alone. And when you get back to town, call me."

Samantha glanced from Lindsay's face, shut down, overly calm, retreating, to her mother's insanity—torn between who first to salvage. She clasped her mother's hand, then walked to Lindsay. Her eyes questioned, but Lindsay's were void of answer or emotion.

"Call me when you get into town," Lindsay repeated numbly.

"OK. Maybe you're right. Let me deal with her. Lindsay"— Samantha's voice was tight—"it's OK. Isn't it?"

"Yes." But she was remote. "This is . . . shit, Sam. I . . ." Lindsay was lost.

"I know. Don't worry. We'll get through it. She needs to calm down, get her bearings." Samantha's eyes pleaded. "I love you."

"Me too." But it was unconvincing as Lindsay turned and walked out the door.

Sondra stood behind Samantha, calmer now. "I wanted to surprise you. That's all." Anger faded in the face of her tenuous reality. "I just wanted to make a good Christmas for you. After you told me you and Robert were having problems, I didn't want you to be alone. They told me I left you alone too much when you were a child. . . . I didn't mean to. . . ." Sondra's tone had become dangerously singsong.

Samantha went to her mother, momentarily conscious of the heady smell of Lindsay that remained all over her body, took her hand, stroked the hair that had fallen out of place. "Mother, you have to listen to me now. I need you to understand what this is all about. But first things first. Let's just try and focus. I'm going to make some tea."

Samantha continued to talk in calm soothing tones while she put the water on to boil, wondering why people's first instinct in any crisis was to put something in their mouths, while Sondra listened mutely, like a small child too vulnerable to digest the information.

But there was a thread of thought that made itself known to Sondra, a thread of reality she could hold on to in the midst of this nightmare. It had nothing to do with her daughter or Lindsay, but it made all the difference in her world. After three months, two weeks and three days, she was free. And freedom could see her through anything.

◆ ◆ ◆

Blueberry blintzes, almond croissants, strawberries and cream, the most divine Portuguese sausages, eggs Benedict on crumpets, and flutes of fresh squeezed orange juice covered the tray Jared placed over Snag's legs. Plus a mocha the likes of which he had never seen, piled high with whipped cream, sprinkled liberally with cinnamon, shaved chocolate and nutmeg.

"I'm in heaven, right?" Snag questioned groggily as his eyes adjusted to the light.

"Merry Christmas, my love," Jared said with such intensity that Snag's eyes darted to his, startled.

"Sweetie, what have you done?" Snag asked, almost afraid. Wasn't this rule number 407—leave with such utter magnificence that you destroy their very existence?

"It's Christmas, silly." Jared leaned over the tray, kissed him, then took a napkin, spread it over his lap, his hand lovingly patting the softened mound that rested between his legs.

"Careful. Wouldn't want to disturb the family jewels, now would you?" Snag teased. But there was a hesitant tone. The lovemaking—rather the lack of it—was no longer an issue they talked about. Silence, anger, humiliation—they were all too big, and Snag's heart couldn't handle it, much less his ego. But Jared's hand just now. Had that been a pass? He had stopped trying to read signs. But he wondered. What the hell was going on? Jared was never this spontaneously festive.

Jared grabbed a strawberry, dipped it in cream, popped it in his mouth, then sighed as he stretched out next to Snag. "I adore strawberries. Did you know that, Snag?"

"I've always known you were fond of them."

"No, Snag. I *adore* them. I absolutely adore them." Jared leaned up on an elbow. Snag's breath was taken away by Jared's glistening eyes, his tousled hair, the handsome granite features, softened now into the face of a boy.

"You're lovely, Jared. Right this moment, I think you are the most lovely thing I have ever seen."

Jared picked up his marvelous body, removed Snag's tray, set it on the floor beside the bed, leaned over and retrieved a small scroll wrapped with streaming red, green and gold ribbons.

"Open it."

Snag fumbled with it a moment. Everything was so un-Jared-like that he was suspicious. He delicately removed the ribbons and then flattened the missive on his lap. An involuntary sound came from his chest.

"Why didn't you tell me?" Snag was bewildered, hurt and relieved in the same moment.

"I . . . I couldn't. Not until now." Jared brushed the hair from Snag's face. "Oh, please don't be angry. Oh, baby, please, celebrate with me."

Snag lunged into Jared's arms, grasping him tightly. He would never let him go. Their mouths found one another's, their bodies joined in joy, desperation and reverence for the earthly gifts of being primal.

Snag's foot knocked the scroll to the floor. He would pick it up later, tears would fall from his cheeks as he reread the results from Burrough Hills Hospital, the results of the test, and his eyes would focus on the that universal hieroglyphic that indicated life: HIV−.

◆ ◆ ◆

It was late in the evening when they finally got home from the last of the family festivities. Ryan had uncles, cousins, sisters and brothers in every part of the city.

Megan sat wearily on the couch. She was exhausted. Needed to sleep, badly. Ryan came up from behind her, rubbed her shoulders, and then shyly brought his hands together in front of her, bearing a small beautifully wrapped box.

"Open it."

"Oh, Ryan . . ." Megan had tears in her eyes. She was always so emotional these days, she barely knew what she was doing. Between the rigors of the pregnancy and hiding it from Ryan, and fighting with herself to tell him, she was dropping with fatigue. She had to tell him; as Snag said, it was "the height of nincompoopery" that she hadn't. It wasn't going to go away.

She lifted the small, delicate box into her hands. Ryan came around from behind her and leaned at the edge of the couch. She gently unwhirled the ribbons, took pains with the paper. Inside a jeweler's box. She hesitated a moment, then opened it.

Elaborately detailed porcelain baby booties stared back at her. A pair of booties for each earring. Megan's hand flew to her face.

"Oh . . . oh . . ." Megan began sobbing, choking back her tears, caught between panic and joy. "How. . . . how did you know?"

"I'm not exactly unobservant, Megs. Especially when it comes to you. And"—he took her hand—"even if I were an obtuse idiot, Snag spilled the beans a few weeks ago—"

"Snag!"

"It's OK. I knew. I think I knew before you did."

"But how?"

"Call it . . . a man's intuition." He smiled at her, easily the most gorgeous smile she had ever seen.

He fell to his knees before her, burrowed his head into her lap. Megan stroked his hair, feeling the fullness of maternity, the power of her ability to give life . . . give life to the man she loved. Ryan's eyes, when he lifted them to hers, showered her with intense love.

"Will you marry me and be the mother of my children?" He was crying now, pulling another jeweler's box from his suit jacket, fumbling with it as he opened it before her, displaying the glittering gold band.

"Yes." Megan's heart bubbled to her throat. "Yes, Ryan. I think that . . . that would be good."

◆ ◆ ◆

One foot in front of the other. She kept focus on her feet, dulled by the repetition, one foot moving in front of the other.

She had walked for miles. Hours. It was cold. Damp. Every so often a flurry of snowflakes would dance about her, teasing her with their lightness. She kept her head down, continued her movement.

She had tried to go to the office, but couldn't. There was nothing there. Nothing. For the first time in her life she felt absolutely nothing for her work. No drive. No inspiration. She was empty. She could chuck all of it tomorrow.

So she walked. Eventually her clothes were soaked through, her body as unfeeling as her mind. Thoughts of Samantha warmed her, images of their being together, her love for her, the absoluteness of their union; and then Sondra wiping it all away into darkness. And then words . . . words. Joanne, Megan, Snag, Sondra—everyone's words, a lifetime's worth, cluttered her mind, jumbled like the lines in her dream: "workaholic . . . never seen anyone so driven. Obsession."

The phrase "quality of life" kept churning in rhythm with her feet. In all the years of complaints, accusations and hurled venom, she had never been able to hear those words as she had heard them from Samantha. From her they resonated with truth. Lindsay was sick; had been stuck in this compulsive mode for so many years. She had no way to distinguish the normal from the obsessive. It was made all the more difficult because of the passion she felt for her work. How did one distinguish one from the other when her work was like taking in breath? How did you control or monitor that?

But she had no answers. So she walked. One foot in front of the other.

◆ ◆ ◆

Samantha and her mother sat by the fire. A quiet filled the room. After all the talking. Three days of endless tirade falling from both their lips. Rage and fury stormed into defensive accusations, and then, finally, the gauntlet would be dropped and real words could take the stage between them, and they communicated. It was a pattern endlessly repeated.

At first they had simply tried to get past the initial shock: that Samantha knew of Sondra's affair with Lindsay, had been told about the ugly night of Sondra's demise, her association with Nathan. Of

Sondra discovering them together, with only the best intentions, and then seeing Samantha swept up in the same hysteria she had known. It was more than she could handle.

"But you have to handle this, Mom," Samantha gently insisted. "This isn't exactly what I would have recommended for your first crisis back on the streets, but since it is, don't you see how important it is that we get through it? Without either of us retreating into our corners. Without me running back to Seattle. Without you . . ."

"Drinking?" Sondra finished for her. "Don't you think I've heard the word just about as many times as a person can in the last few months?"

"I'm sorry, Mom. I just didn't want you to get defensive."

"Who's defensive? And if I am, don't you think I have a right to be? Why didn't you tell me what was going on when you called?"

"Why didn't any of us say anything, ever?" Samantha stopped, realized they were on their way to another spiral. "Look, Mom, it's done. We've got to deal with what's here, now. You two were lovers, you didn't want to be. You're not a lesbian."

"And I suppose you are? What about Robert? What about this man who helped you with your business, that you've built your life with, that you promised someday you'd have children? What about betrayal?"

"I have not betrayed anyone except myself!" Samantha screamed. They stood apart from each other staring into the booming silence. Samantha got her coat. She would go for a walk. When she returned, she would make tea, they would resume.

For two and a half days Samantha didn't think they would find resolution, that they would ever overcome the damage. Her mother seemed stuck in a sort of fanatical logic without room for compromise, her head turned, eyes averted, lips sealed tightly. Then suddenly, as swiftly as thunderclouds rolling in, her mother pelted her with anger, berating Samantha with shame and humiliation one final time. And again Samantha defended herself with the conviction of her feelings, trying to make her mother understand that her love for Lindsay was the purest thing, the most honest thing she had ever known. For anyone. And then, just as unpredictably, the sky cleared and her mother, like a final gust of wind, sighed resignation. Sudden surrender. Something had broken through. Or merely broken.

"Is it really what you want?" Sondra's thin voice had finally asked.

"More than anything in the world," Samantha had answered.

"Then I hope you have it, Sam, I really do." Comprehension appeared to shine in her eyes. "I hope you find a measure of happiness in this unhappy world."

"What about you, Mom? What's going to make you happy?"

"Getting rid of Earlsheart."

"What? But Earlsheart is—"

"Is filled with too many bad memories." Sondra lit a cigarette, calm now. "I guess I was always holding onto some ideal here, something that never existed. What would I do anyway? Isolate, become an eccentric hermit?" Sondra smiled for the first time in days. "No. I need to go back. Get myself out of debt. Clean up the unsettled, unraveled ends of my life. That's the only way. According to the program." And then she laughed.

"You hated it, didn't you?"

"Every blessed minute." But Sondra's eyes were kind and accepting. The anger was gone. "Anyway, it's time to get on with it. I've wasted too many days and hours."

Samantha went to her mother, took her hand. Their eyes met in peaceful agreement as she sat next to her, and they watched the fire until the embers were the faintest of glows and the room grew cold.

They drove back to the city in comfortable silence. Samantha could not shake the irony of making their way back in Lindsay's car. They had agreed to exchange cars so Lindsay could return Samantha's rental, several days overdue. Her mother's jaws had tightened, but she had made no comment.

Samantha dropped her mother at her apartment. They stood, silently facing one another, both aware their relationship was changed forever.

"Well . . ." Sondra did not want to cry in front of Samantha. She wished she could serve as a totem of strength and confidence for her daughter. Wellness, as it were. But as Samantha turned to walk away, Sondra reached out to her, pulled her close.

"I love you, Sam." The tears fell freely. "I love you." The words soft and sincere.

Samantha could not swallow.

"Oh, Mom, I love you too." Samantha held onto her for a long time.

"OK . . . you better go now." Sondra broke their embrace.

"Sure."

"Sam—?" Sondra's voice trailed off.

"What?"

"Always believe in your strength. You have more of it than anyone I know."

"Getting philosophical on me, Mom?" Samantha needed to lighten this somber exchange or her tears would cascade into something unstoppable.

"No." Sondra shielded her eyes from the sun. "It's just . . . I always wished I could be strong like you."

Samantha smiled, then turned again to wave as she walked to the car.

◆ ◆ ◆

"Did she say when she would be back?" Samantha stood at Megan's desk. Imperious Megan, close-mouthed, defending the castle walls.

"No."

Samantha was frustrated. Crazy. There'd been no communication. A couple of phone-tag messages, void of any emotion from Lindsay's end. Creating apprehension. Anxiety. And now here was Megan, with her barely disguised hostility, who had information but would not give it to her.

"Well, she must have left some word."

"No. She didn't. She hasn't been feeling well, though." Accusation now.

"Is Snag in?"

"Yes. But he's in a meeting."

"Listen, Megan, I know you don't like me—"

"No. I don't dislike *you*, Miss Pinchot. I don't know you. But I just have to say this. Since you and your mother have been involved in Lindsay's life, she's been miserable."

"I'm not going to defend myself to you, Megan. All I can say is I care for Lindsay deeply. You're going to have to believe me. I need to see her."

But Megan would not be moved.

"Just tell me . . . is she OK?"

"I told you. She's not very well. She's exhausted. She needs rest." Megan was clearly finished with the inquisition.

"Will you have her call me the moment she gets in?"

Samantha watched Megan write the message in duplicate on the spiral notebook, crisply tear it off and put it in Lindsay's in-box, then look up, wordlessly waiting for Samantha's departure.

Samantha wandered to the elevator. She drove back to her hotel room, sat on the corner of the bed. In limbo. Listless. Where was she going? Back to Seattle? Robert? She had to talk to Robert. Soon. Talking. She was sick of talking.

Eleven o'clock: still no word from Lindsay. Samantha paced the hotel room. She picked up the phone, then dropped the receiver. She picked up again, dialed.

"Yeah?" Raspy, breathless on the other end.

"Did I wake you?"

"Uh, not exactly," Snag's tone intimated she was interrupting.

"Jesus, I'm sorry, Snag. I'm looking for Lindsay."

"Oh, she's had the worst flu, sugar."

"So she *is* sick."

"Yeah. It's pretty tragic . . . fever, the whole bit. She's been working out of her apartment the last couple of days. Didn't Megan tell you?"

"No." Damn that Megan. "Thanks, Snag. Sorry my timing was so bad."

"No worry. I love suspense." Then he hung up.

◆ ◆ ◆

She felt a little foolish, perhaps mother hen-ish, standing at the threshold of Lindsay's apartment clutching her bag of vegetarian minestrone, juice, oranges and tea. She hesitated on the last step. Was this trespassing on sacred ground? But hadn't they done that already? Was it too late to turn back? Did she want to?

Samantha knocked. Lindsay opened the door, clad in a short blue and black flannel robe with matching boxer shorts, rumpled thick black socks, one up, one down. She looked five years old, little-girl flushed cheeks, tousled hair, snuffly eyes.

"Jesus. You look like shit." Samantha heard her voice shaking.

Lindsay nodded, perturbed, confused, and then held out a hand, inviting her in. "Uh . . . enter at your own risk."

Samantha walked in, aware she was in Lindsay's environment now, took in the comfortably furnished apartment: antiques, easy chairs, a sense of a warmth, not what she would have thought Lindsay's place would be like at all. It was encouraging. She strolled past the makeshift bed/desk/couch where plans, specifications, files and papers commingled with head cold medicine, aspirin and empty glasses of juice and tea, at the center of which was a small heap of blankets and pillows littered with Kleenex.

Samantha turned to her. "Lovely." She resorted to sarcasm. She hadn't known what to expect, but it certainly hadn't been this. "I'm going to take this into the kitchen."

Samantha turned in the general direction of where she assumed the kitchen was. When she returned she went directly to Lindsay, threw her arms around her neck, her body melting with memory. Lindsay's arms wrapped themselves about Samantha, assuming a will of their own. She moaned deeply, involuntarily, but then stepped out of the embrace, distancing herself.

"I feel like . . . well, you get the picture."

"That's OK. We'll get you better in no time." Samantha realized her words sounded presumptuous. "Have you taken your temperature?"

"No."

"Do you have a thermometer?"

"Uh . . . yeah, I think in the bathroom . . . or the hall closet." Lindsay coughed, then hobbled to the couch, sat down, clearly weak and exhausted. "Uhm . . . Samantha?"

Samantha walked to the couch and turned to sit next to her, then realized there was not a square inch of clear space left.

"This is ridiculous, Lindsay." Samantha began picking up the papers. "I won't get them out of order . . . just let me move some of this stuff."

Samantha cleared a space. Sat. She touched Lindsay's forehead. She was burning up. "Come on. You've got to get some aspirin in you." Samantha picked up the bottle, dumped two into her hand, gave them to Lindsay with her juice.

Lindsay swallowed them, then set the glass down with a certain finality. "Sam. I'm really feeling lousy. I . . . I hate people being around me when I'm sick, and I'm busy trying to get this damn bid finished."

"I don't believe this."

"I have to get it done before the new year."

"Lindsay . . . look at yourself! You're falling apart." Samantha got up from the couch, paced away from her, then returned. "What's happened? Second thoughts? No thoughts? What?"

"No . . . no . . . it's not that. Really, I'm just miserable . . . and this damn bid is due."

"Bullshit! Something's happened."

"Can't it just be that I've got this deadline?" Lindsay's voice was so strained and tired it made Samantha flinch.

"No. It can't be. Don't you think I know this is the ultimate test? You're waiting for me to start harping on you like everyone else? Well, I won't do it. I won't do it, Lindsay." Samantha's anger, the anger Lindsay first knew, had returned. "You're scared. I'm scared. It's big and we're sitting here thinking, how can I ever give this what it needs. Deserves. Can I do this . . . can I make it work?"

"Well"—Lindsay's tone was soft but defensive—"maybe that's it, Sam . . . maybe I can't give it what it needs. Maybe I don't want to give all this up." Lindsay indicated the work scattered before her.

"I'm not asking you to give up what's you. I'm just asking you to give us a chance. Find out who you are beyond your work."

While Lindsay sat stoically, Samantha continued to pace. Then she stopped. She'd been here before. The anger ebbed out of her as an incredible sadness floated inside and around her heart. "I won't do this. I've been through it too many times and I simply won't watch someone I love destroy themselves again."

"Then maybe you ought to stick to what's safe, like Robert." Lindsay didn't know what she was saying. She didn't want to be this way. Samantha was everything she had been waiting for, and then to see her at the doorway, like a dream, an angel; and here she was pushing her away, provoking her to leave. But she couldn't stop. "I'm so sick of people telling me about my work. All I want is to be left alone when I'm working. Is that too goddamn much to ask?"

"No," Samantha said dryly. "Not at all."

"Sam—" Lindsay started, but didn't know what else to say. She didn't have the energy. She didn't have the compromise in her. Not yet. She didn't have the courage.

And Samantha saw that. Saw it as plainly as seeing her mother on the couch, in drunken oblivion, unable to face the challenge of living with her pain. Or the real world. Lindsay's eyes said the same thing. She was seeing her mother all over again.

"Good-bye, Lindsay." Samantha grabbed her purse.

"Sam—?"

"Good-bye." Samantha cocked her head, pursed her lips as if there was one last question she wanted to ask, a "maybe" floating through her mind. But she decided against it. And now it was too late. In that moment, they both knew it was over.

◆ ◆ ◆

Sondra hung up the phone. She still had on her face the same serene smile she had the night she and Samantha had finally come to terms. She peered calmly out the window. Samantha had thought they'd finally arrived at an understanding. But Samantha had never and would never understand her mother.

"God grant me the serenity to accept the things I cannot change. The courage to change the things I can. And the wisdom to know the difference." Sondra would have liked to say she was uttering those words at an AA meeting. She was supposed to attend at least five a week. But it was like the prayer said. Things were as they were. The serenity prayer was probably the only useful sentiment she had gotten from the damn treatment center. It might as well have been invented for her. Because she couldn't quit drinking. She would never quit drinking unless someone was controlling her life twenty-four hours a day, and the moment Sondra had realized that, a calm had settled over her unlike any she had known before. It breathed in her every movement. It made her walk with grace and dignity. She held her head high. She finally knew who and what she was. A drunk.

When she thought of Samantha, a painful frown momentarily knit her brow. God, she loved her daughter. More than anything. Anything. But bless her heart, Samantha could never really grasp this part of her. And she knew she would eventually get over it. She had the iron will to get over anything. And Lindsay? She couldn't think about Lindsay without the thread of pain that twisted through her insides, threatening to choke her. But Samantha. She would live forever. She was a survivor. No one would get in her way.

And, after all, you either were a survivor or you weren't. The peace really was in knowing which side of the line you climbed up over or fell down into. Sondra raised her snifter in salute to her daughter and that particularly hard-earned knowledge, and gulped the first Hennessy's she'd had in precisely three months, two weeks and six days.

◆ ◆ ◆

Lindsay's heart pounded her body, jarring, irregular—terrorizing. She jumped from the alcove bed. *Different. This is different.* But it wasn't. The sameness of the attacks were that they always felt different. Each one was always the first time.

But this time the erratic movement of her heart was heightened by a pain that shot through her chest, tight and constricting. She couldn't breathe. *This time I really can't breathe. God. Help. Help me.* She glanced about frantically. She had to get downstairs, get to the car—a hospital. She got her keys. It shot through her chest again. *Sit. Just sit a minute. Think.* But sitting made her panic more. She felt her pulse. Timed it. *130. Please . . . please.* She breathed in and out. She bent over. She tried to loosen her diaphragm as her doctor had taught her. *Dizzy. Going to be sick.* She dashed to the bathroom.

Vomited. And then some more. *Please, God, just let me get through this* . . . but she didn't really know how to pray. She'd never sat quiet long enough to learn how and now she felt too foolish. *You are a fool, Lindsay. That you never paid attention.* And then another spasm ripped through her chest.

Remain calm. Calm? And then a calm finally did wash over her, full, pervasive and peaceful. For at that moment she *knew* without a shred of doubt, this time she was going to die.

She couldn't bear the mirror. She couldn't stare any longer at the puffy-eyed, tear-swollen face, the remnants of self-castigation. How could she have been so wrong? How can one meet one's soul and walk away from it? How did one let go and surrender to that?

She needed to heal. Seek refuge, lick her wounds, until the visions of this hellish incubus left her. So many mistakes: her mother, Lindsay, Robert. She would go to Earlsheart. Maybe facing the potent, provoking memories that existed there side by side would set her heart free. Besides, she could think of no other place to escape.

She packed her bags and checked out of the room. She was going to jump onto the freeway directly in front of the hotel, but decided she would make one last pass by the Darlington Arts Pavilion. She had to see it. Yes. She would just take the Morrison Bridge, and then cut over to the beach highway on the other side of town.

Epilogue

he slept. Her face was cemented against the vinyl hospital chair. Bodies in blue silhouette, in the first light of dawn, feeling the warmth and memory of her skin, desire reawakened. Then eyes . . . crystalline into midnight blue like the sea turned stormy, a clouded gray . . . and the lines . . . drawn over it all, more lines, more lines, eyes . . . different eyes now . . . Sondra's eyes.

Snag woke her. "You OK?"

Lindsay jarred herself back to reality, cleared her throat. "Yes."

"Here." Snag handed her a cup of coffee. "It's crap, but it's better than nothing."

"Thanks." Lindsay took it, set it down beside her.

"Can't stand the waiting," Snag said. But Lindsay was numb.

"Waiting?"

"Yes . . ." But Snag sensed that she was in another place.

The morning stayed gray. Hours of gray. Snag smoked more cigarettes. Megan had come and gone.

They saw her at the same time. Stepping from the elevator. She saw them, but did not acknowledge their presence. She walked directly to the information desk.

"Yes?" The nurse asked.

"I'm here for Pinchot."

As the nurse checked her charts, her face dropped.

"Yes . . . um . . . well, and are you related?" She hadn't yet learned how to deal with telling people.

"Yes," she said quietly. "I am her daughter."

He took her hand. She glanced up at him. He smiled at her with reassurance. But then he always had. Robert stood beside her, the same strong handsome figure, resolute and caring, as they lowered her mother's coffin into the ground. Her father on her other side.

Snag was there. He had embraced her in front of the church, tears in his eyes. So sweet of him. She had spotted Carl at the back of the church pews, but he hadn't shown up at the cemetery. Well, he'd always been only sort of there. And then scattered at the gravesite were several colleagues from the community, but other than that, her mother's private life held few personal attachments. So it was predictable.

As in retrospect so had been her mother's death. Suicide, actually. The only thing that Samantha still couldn't figure out was why she took Lindsay's car instead of her own. Was it a metaphor? Was she taking Lindsay down with her? Or was it no more complicated than a dead car battery? Samantha would never know. Did she care? She couldn't even tell if she was sad or not. Or simply relieved. And then hated herself for the thought. Was it so difficult to love someone who was sick? Weak? Hopeless? Or was it that she was so close to those failings herself at that moment, and hated herself for it?

The service was over. Robert and her father guided her along the path of other graves, new markers with fresh-cut flowers. They escorted her as they had the last two days, with love and caring, as they led her back to the parking lot. She glanced at her henchmen, respected them for their grace and nobility.

Funerals were such a paradox . . . the worst of times, the best of people . . . the stark reality, yet numbing complacency . . . the letting down and erecting of barriers.

She felt Robert's hand tense at her arm. Lindsay walked to her. The awkwardness fell over them like a blanket of doom.

"May . . . may I have a moment with you?" Lindsay asked.

Samantha glanced at Robert, reassured him it would be all right. She disengaged herself from his grasp and walked several paces away from Robert and her father.

Their closeness felt good for both of them. They didn't know what to do with it, other than simply allow it to soothe them.

"Are you . . . all right?"

"I think so." They walked a few more paces away from the others. "You know, I've grieved for my mother so many times. . . ." Samantha's voice trailed and then she peered at Lindsay, dry-eyed, but with a catch to her voice. "I'm used to it."

"Samantha." Lindsay ached for her. "I'm so sorry."

"It killed her. She didn't have the strength. That's all. I mean, it was all she ever really had." Samantha stopped to consider, an ironic smile curled at her mouth. "I'm glad she was blitzed. At least she didn't know what hit her."

They stood silently.

"Are you going back?" Lindsay asked.

Samantha sighed, glanced about her, as if she were deciding.

"Sam . . ." Lindsay knew this wasn't the time; went ahead anyway. "Can we . . . fix this?"

"Fix it?"

"Yes. Samantha, I . . . when I had to face the possibility that it might have been you in the car, I . . . I went crazy. . . ." Lindsay tried to come up with words to convey how tortured she had been all the hours they didn't know who was behind the emergency doors, all the hours of the past few days. "I love you. I don't want to live without you."

"It's funny, isn't it, how tragedy does that to a person. Puts things in perspective. Like myself. My mother's death drove home what I already know to be true about you." Samantha's voice was not sarcastic. Just flat. "Your work. It's your everything. It's all you really have. You and my mother are so much alike. Maybe that's why I was drawn to you. Classic bullshit, you know. Only I'm so in love with you I don't know how not to hurt every goddamn minute—" Her voice broke.

"Sam—"

"But I won't do it again, Lindsay. I won't let it happen."

"Please. We love each other. Let's not let go of the one good thing in our lives."

"The one good thing in *your* life. I . . . I have plenty to sustain me." Samantha smiled kindly at Lindsay. "Don't you see? This will only last until things get too intimate. You'll go so far and then get frightened, make a mad dash to your office—shut yourself in."

"Saman—"

"Lindsay. We need time." Samantha was gentle, as if she were talking to a child. "Time. Time to heal. Right now we're . . ." She paused, searching for the right term, then said calmly, without cynicism, "Damaged goods. The only chance we stand in hell, with all we've been through—all that's happened—is to come back when we're both more than hollow shells."

Samantha moved to go, then stopped and touched Lindsay's face, so gently it would remind Lindsay forever of a shadow. "I do love you."

"Sam . . ."

But Samantha would not look at her. She simply touched Lindsay's hand and returned to Robert.

◆ ◆ ◆

"You have two incredibly beautiful girls, Ryan!" the doctor pronounced joyfully.

"Oh, Lord. Oh, Lord." Ryan held Megan's hand as he stared with elated disbelief at his two new daughters. "Oh, sweet Megan, I love you so. Look at them. Can you see them, darling? Can you see the beautiful babies you made?"

"We made," Megan croaked. Credit where credit was due, after all. She was happy, she thought. She must be. All she wanted was for everyone to go away and let her sleep. For seventeen hours. That's what she needed. Sleep. But then Ryan's face got close to hers and she saw him crying, tears streaming down his face.

"Megan, you are . . . you are . . . oh, sweetheart, our daughters. Our daughters."

Yes, she thought, I am happy. I am ecstatic. Divinely euphoric. Now let me get some sleep.

◆ ◆ ◆

Lindsay, Jared and Snag cooed at the twins in the nursery.

"Birth. A miracle." Snag was crying.

"Oh, sweetie. You're such a little weeper." Jared put his arm around him.

"I want one." Snag crooked his head into Jared's shoulder. "Please. Please?"

"Sure, sweetie, we'll just take a couple of these to go on our way home."

"Well, then how 'bout a monkey? They can't be too much trouble."

"Snag. Really. You couldn't even keep our damn parakeet alive."

"Jared . . . that was the birdy flu it got. I loved Tweety-Bird. Come on. Let's have a baby. A real one. Play house like Megs and Rye—"

"We'll discuss it later, Snag."

Lindsay felt the calming influence of their prattle as she stared at the pink-ripened faces, the delicate perfection, so vulnerable before the world. Her throat tightened.

She turned to Snag and Jared. "I've got to get back to the office. Wrap some things up."

"Need any help?"

"No. You stick around here. You'll have plenty to do when you get in tomorrow." Lindsay put a hand to Snag's shoulder, said good-bye to both of them and walked from the hospital.

◆ ◆ ◆

Lindsay sat at her desk. Cleared. Organized. She stacked the last of the files before her. They were alphabetized. The final projects that Snag would take over during her absence. She put her hand on the day calendar. May 15. She would not return for six months. She took a deep breath, let it out slowly. Leaving wasn't nearly as hard as she thought it would be. Going forward, on the other hand, was terrifying.

She went directly to her car and took the Morrison Bridge out of town. She stopped the car right in the middle of the bridge, leaving a stream of cars honking furiously in her wake. She ran to the bridge railing, grasped it with one hand, leaned back, and then flung with all her might.

It arched through the air. It could have been a large bird flying gracefully until it plummeted to the water with a resounding thwack. Lindsay watched just long enough to see her briefcase disappear into the depths of the unknown.

◆ ◆ ◆

She selected a combination of beans with care, ground them to a very, very fine powder, fitted the cup in the espresso maker. She filled the pitcher with half milk, half cream. It would be very rich. The steam billowed about as the milk frothed to a delightful cloud. She poured half the contents of the dark murky liquid in one cup, the other half in another. She spooned the whipped foam into one cup, poured the remainder of the cream into her own. Sprinkles of cinnamon and chocolate. She carried the two cups into the living room, sat one down on the end table, and eased herself into her favorite overstuffed chair.

Samantha took a sip. Smiled.

Soon she would no longer be alone.